Saucy Jacky

Saucy Jacky

A novel by

Doug Lamoreux

Copyright (C) 2018 Doug Lamoreux
Layout design and Copyright (C) 2018 Creativia
Published 2018 by Creativia (www.creativia.org)
Cover art by Cover Mint

This book is a work of fiction. Names, characters, places, and incidents are the product of the author's imagination or are used fictitiously. Any resemblance to actual events, locales, or persons, living or dead, is purely coincidental.

All rights reserved. No part of this book may be reproduced or transmitted in any form or by any means, electronic or mechanical, including photocopying, recording, or by any information storage and retrieval system, without the author's permission.

*Dedicated to
Lila and David*

For the inspiration, the ideas, – and the light!

Acknowledgments

To Jenny, always to Jenny, thank you.

To the Ripperologists, all of them (right or wrong), from the first reporter for the Star – to the latest Final Solution.

To the dedicated, resourceful and brave journalists of 1888 London and their papers. The writers are long gone, most of the papers have ceased to publish. Their contributions to the history of these fiendish events (many mentioned or quoted in part here) were invaluable to me as, surely, they must have been to Jack the Ripper.

To Robert Bloch, who was right, Jack the Ripper belongs to the world as surely as Shakespeare.

Contents

One – How to Begin?	1
Two – Poor Emma Smith	5
Three – George Yard	11
Four – Soldier's Whore	18
Five – The East End	23
Six – Murder in Whitechapel!	30
Seven – Mrs Griggs, Dress Reformist	38
Eight – Miss Adler, Archie, and the Cock-up	42
Nine – My Victim Identified	49
Ten – Ye Olde Shoe Shoppe	53
Eleven – Hellfire and Whitechapel Road	60
Twelve – Queen of Tarts	65
Fourteen – Buck's Row Outrage	71
Fifteen – Heroic Inspector Abberline	76
Sixteen – Leather Apron Fear	81

Seventeen – Stockings	90
Eighteen – Flower and Dean Street Riot	99
Nineteen – Morning in Hanbury Street	105
Twenty – Drunk with Blood	111
Twenty-One – Leather Apron Farce	119
Twenty-Two – Mile End Vigilance	127
Twenty-Three – Inquests, Inquests, Inquests	131
Twenty-Four – The Hospital Chat	140
Twenty-Five – Dear Boss	146
Twenty-Six – Gone to Gateshead	151
Twenty-Seven – The Squealer	156
Twenty-Eight – Escape From Berner Street	164
Twenty-Nine – Coppers Converge	170
Thirty – Singing Whore	176
Thirty-One – 'Call me, Kate, deary'	182
Thirty-Two – I am Invisible	187
Thirty-Three – Coppers in the Square	194
Thirty-Four – Goulston Street	201
Thirty-Five – Busy Morning	208
Thirty-Six – Who Saw Yours Truly?	215

Thirty-Seven – Kidney and Onions	223
Thirty-Eight – Jack the Ripper!	229
Thirty-Nine – The Search	236
Forty – Murder Is Good Business	245
Forty-One – Bloodhounds and Vigilantes	251
Forty-Two – A Fitting Verdict	256
Forty-Three – From Hell Mr Lusk	262
Forty-Four – Waiting... Waiting	266
Forty-Five – Grapes of Wrath	272
Forty-Six – London Fog	280
Forty-Seven – Toff for a Tart	286
Forty-Eight – The Irish Lass	291
Forty-Nine – 13 Miller's Court	296
Fifty – Masterpiece of Horror	303
Fifty-One – It's Only Me... Saucy Jacky	309
About the Author	313

One
How to Begin?

The first time I stabbed her, I think it surprised me as much as it surprised the whore.

Surprised, perhaps, isn't strong enough. I'll use *startled* instead. We were, both of us, startled when out of the blue I grabbed her throat from the front, with both hands, and pressed with my thumbs and squeezed with my fingers. The whore gasped. That was all she had time for. All she had air for.

I gasped too. The experience was as new for me as it was for her. Though, I admit, I was probably getting more pleasure from it than she. I'd halted the release of her stinking beery breath, at least, and that was certainly a plus.

Her eyes grew wide, I could see that even in the dark. I released her with my right hand. *Oh*, fear not, I still clutched her fat throat with my left. I...

Quite an amusing debate would arise in near future as to whether I was left or right-handed, or possibly ambidextrous. But, there I go, off on a tangent. It's a bad habit of mine. Allow me to end the argument before it begins. I'm right-handed... as I was about to demonstrate on the gasping whore.

I reached in and drew from my coat the long blade, the shiny surgical knife I'd, let's say *borrowed*, from hospital. I turned it in my hand as I lifted it above both our heads then, blade down, brought it down hard into her left breast.

She tried to scream.

But, of course, she couldn't. I still had her throat. But her wide open mouth, and her even wider open eyes, showed she wanted to scream. Mouth and eyes together gave me all the joy an audible scream might without the accompanying risks. As quickly as the entire affair had come upon me, as little thought as I'd put into the details of the deed, I did consider the noise. The small medical knowledge I'd picked up along my way told me the voice box was a wind instrument, like any other. Without the passage of air, there could be no music.

I say 'little thought'. Allow me to explain... if I can.

I'd conceived the notion of murder on a whim, a quick solution to a nagging problem. From then on, I didn't concern myself with the murder; I worried about the problem. I grew angry, then furious, at the problem. (At those at the heart of the problem.) I never plotted murder. On the contrary, for the longest time, I fought the urges to... Eventually the urges won.

But I hadn't organized any plan. I was nervous when I nicked the knife. I was hesitant but, at the same time, thrilled when the drunk whore presented me with the opportunity. I caught myself off guard when I grabbed her and began to throttle her. And I was startled when I stabbed her.

But, if I'd given little thought to murder, I'd given none at all to the moment when the whore would go unconscious. It took me by complete surprise when she suddenly became dead weight.

That first stab had done the trick. She might have been dead, I didn't know and didn't really care. But she was certainly unconscious and I had all of her weight, only by the throat, by one hand. That was no good. There was no way to work, not like that, and I had a job to do.

I had no choice but to let her fall to the stone landing. Then, as I was puffing hard from the labour, and from my own fear and, I confess, from a stirring of excitement as well, I paused to catch my breath. To look around and make sure the two of us remained alone.

I heard a dog barking distantly, and a horse-drawn cart a long way off, but we were alone.

I pushed the long blade back into my coat. Truth be told, I wasn't sure about the long one. Like I said, I'd only nicked it from hospital; had used it for the first time. I wasn't sure how I felt about it and didn't feel like going on with it. Instead I pulled the other blade, the penknife, I'd bought in a junk shop in the Whitechapel High and had had in my possession for a good while. It was shorter, with a sturdier blade; the tool I'd always imagined taking on the job, when the job was merely the spark of an idea. Now I was there, and about it, the shorter blade felt better in my hand, as if it belonged. More at home.

With a tight grip on the more comfortable tool, I kneeled beside the woman who, by her indecency, had chosen through her own free will to take up boozing and whoring and thereby forced me to stab her to death – and I got on with the job.

But I'm getting ahead of myself in the telling. I see that now. Another bad habit. I go off on tangents and I get ahead of myself. Let me back up a bit.

Allow me to introduce myself. I can't announce my true name, of course, that would give the game away before it's started. For the present, I'll refer to myself as Mr __.

ha ha. That's appropriate. In the beginning I really was nothing after all, a blank space, a place holder, until I found myself and my reason. Later, I became something indeed; something to be reckoned with. In the course of the telling of this tale, I'll let the cat out of the bag, I'll name myself. Because the world ought to meet its legends. But for now, I'm Mr __.

It may surprise that I'm not a feeble-minded cockney dropping the 'aitches from the 'eads, or the gee's from the bleedin' tails, o' my sentences like a costermonger losing apples into the gutter through a hole in the bottom of his barrow. Sorry to disappoint, but I'm an educated man. No, I have not been to university. I am not a gentleman. But I can read. I devour books and retain that which I've read. That's one of my secrets.

I can describe myself, and will, for all the good that might do. I'm in my thirties or thereabouts, five and a half feet tall give or take an inch or two. I've a fair complexion with darkish brown hair and a well-groomed brown moustache on a charming full face. I have extremely dark brown eyes, all but black. I have broad shoulders, strong hands and, when necessary, the ability to run like the wind. But, again, none of that matters.

As this tale unwinds, I will be described – by so-called witnesses – as short and tall, as old and young, as dark and as ginger, as thin and as stout. I will be clean shaven. Or have a reddish moustache. I will have a black moustache that curls at the ends. Or a full beard. I'll appear to be a labourer. I'll seem to be a clerk. I will pass as *shabby* genteel. I'll clearly show myself to be a slumming toff. I will wear an opera cloak (although I do not own one). I will tap the wet pavement with a walking stick (though I've never used one). And of course, (though I walk empty-handed) I will be seen to skulk the dark streets carrying an ominous black bag.

Allow me to offer this warning in advance of the eyewitness reports of my appearances: It'll all be a load of tosh. I can look like anyone I choose. That's another of my secrets.

Here's a third: When it suits me, I walk unseen. No, this isn't a bogey story. It won't be owing to a trick of the light. I walk the teeming, poorly lit streets of Queen Victoria's London like any other man. I am there to be seen, but nobody bothers. In the slums of the East End no one dares to ask who it is that stands beside them. Or looks to see who walks behind them.

I occupy space like any other man, but I am unseen. For I am not any other man. I am a societal necessity. I am a legend in the making.

Two
Poor Emma Smith

The moment with which I started this tale, the moment when I initially stabbed the first dirty whore, that was early in the morning of 7 August, 1888. I'll return to that, and tell it proper, soon. But first... As I think of it, and if I want to tell the full story true, it really began four months earlier in the spring of that year. Yes, of course!

And, yes, I could go back further still. If you do crime, or commit murder, or what have you, it all probably started earlier. I could blame my drunk mother, or my filthy auntie, or the upbringing the pair of them afforded me, or the monarchy, or my finances, or what have you. But chuck that. I don't give a damn about that and won't waste time telling it. I am what I am, however it was that I came to be. But the story I'm telling here, the story of my summer and autumn of glory, actually began in April of 1888, the morning following Easter Sunday.

I hadn't been feeling *right* for some while. It's difficult to explain exactly what I mean by that. I wasn't potty, don't think that. I wasn't hearing voices or anything of the sort. But I was plagued by my strong sense of responsibility. A fellow ought not come into this world and thereafter simply take. He needs to give as well. My eyes could see, my mind could consider that which I saw, my conscience spoke to me of duties owed my fellow human beings, my city, and my world. I didn't care about them, don't get me wrong. I'm not some compassionate bleeding heart. I'm not talking about feelings at all. I'm talking about duty and responsibility. Things were not right and, owing to that, there were steps needed taking. It was my duty to make the world a better place.

The first of those steps was to find work which allowed me to do right, to help mankind. I was already well-down that road. For several years I'd been volunteering my time at London Hospital, a charity concern towering over Whitechapel Road in the East End. Know this, the posh, the well-off, the titled upper classes did not go to hospitals; when ill or injured, they summoned their private doctors, who went to them. Hospitals were for the working classes. And the lowest classes. The poorest of the poor came to hospital for treatment when in the midst of an emergency or when the work house casualty wards couldn't or wouldn't deal with them.

Some might look upon volunteer work as lowly, but I never saw it that way. In fact, I was proud of my position for the opportunities it provided. I needed no medical knowledge at all to accomplish my tasks; moving patients, tending to their physical needs, bringing them food, taking away their waste, answering the commands of doctor and nurse alike. And, as I imagined might happen, when the tasks got nastier, and the willing volunteers thinned out, the work became real employment for those loyal few of us. The doctors were paid, most of the nurses were paid and, from that time on, as an official orderly, I was paid.

Carrying bed pans was no longer one of my routine activities. Instead, I was preparing the surgical theatres, shunting patients to and from their operations, cremating diseased and amputated organs and limbs, and shunting corpses to and from the pathology annex, *eh*, the mortuary. I was not only more important than the meager volunteers on the floors above. I was necessary. Without me, there would have been no order. The filth would have, quite literally, overrun the place.

They counted on me to eliminate the filth.

There were benefits far beyond the contents of my weekly pay packet. Each assignment provided an avenue to knowledge; offering a man with a keen eye, and a keener mind, the opportunity to learn and to gain much. The sights I saw at hospital, the diverse education I received, and the pay put me above those around me and freed me, financially and spiritually, for other pursuits.

The seed of my purpose had been planted.

I was in my exalted position that morning, attending to patients in the *foul ward*, beds dedicated to the women the government called the *Unfortunates*. Those who, not appreciating their alternatives, took to a life of prostitution. Unfortunates; I found that generous and forgiving. The police called them bang-tails. I thought that frivolous, a fun reference to a filthy work. They were whores, why decorate it? Entire streets in the slums of London were inhabited by whores, guzzling cheap alcohol between bouts of spreading disease. Every working night I passed among the dirty bitches. The worst cases were shipped off to separate 'Lock Hospitals' to be caged like animals. But the law wouldn't allow their eternal confinement. When their acute phases passed, the whores were discharged back to the streets to infect new customers. There was no cure for syphilis; no end to the suffering for their unsuspecting prey but insanity and death.

Forgive me... I go off on tangents.

I was hauling waste from the foul ward early that Monday morning, 3 April, when a middle-aged woman of the street was helped into hospital by friends of hers. I was summoned to the Emergency Room to give them a hand with her. She was called Emma Smith. She'd been attacked that morning, assaulted and robbed in the dark, she claimed, by a gang of three men. They'd grabbed her, beat her, and stole whatever items of value she carried. Then, if what she claimed was true, in what amounted to a *grand finale*, the trio had knocked her to the ground, pulled her legs apart, and savagely inserted some blunt object – a stick or like instrument – up inside of her.

She survived the attack, 'by some miracle' her friends claimed, and made it back to her lodgings. There she informed them of all the juicy sordid details. Soon thereafter, they hurried her to hospital. As I said, I was summoned to assist upon her arrival. I did not recognize it as such at the time but, with the registration of Emma Smith, destiny had altered my life.

The seed of my purpose took root.

Being the acute care orderly on duty, I personally had a hand in undressing her. Her laboured breath stank of beer, made the air heavy and turned my stomach. I would have abandoned the room and left my work undone had it not been for her groans. The girl was in incredible pain. I cannot explain why, but I found her cries to be a balm to my irritated spirit. Her pain soothed me. The sickness in my stomach left. I found my mood lightening as I washed her filthy bits. I was positively cheery as I wheeled her into the surgery theatre and readied her for the knife.

The nurses and Dr Haslip, the house surgeon, took over. No longer needed, I slipped quietly out of theatre. And, even more quietly, I slipped in and stood to the side in the otherwise empty surgical students' gallery above... to see what I could see.

What I saw was the nurses peeling back the sheets to expose her injured nether region. They bent her knees and spread her pale white legs. As I suspected, washing her had been a waste. The filth could not be washed clean. The whole of her... lower area was thick and red with fresh blood.

They covered her mouth and nose with cotton and dripped laudanum onto it. The girl selfishly disappeared into a dreamy oblivion, depriving me of the pleasure of her cries.

I saw the doctor climb between her splayed legs and go to work. While she *cooed* and lolled her head, he inserted clean white bandages, touched and tamped away, then removed blood-covered rags. He examined and probed the depths of her injuries, he stitched and packed as best he was able; all to the tune of her drifting moans. It was altogether thrilling. And revolting beyond description. And saddening – without being sad. And engaging. And enraging.

When the surgery ended, I caught my breath. I drew a handkerchief and wiped a considerable sweat from my brow. Then I got myself back together. I hurried below, returned to the theatre, and made short work of transporting the woman to her bed in the post-operative ward.

But, as I had determined early on, the effort of everybody involved had been wasted. Emma Smith fell into a coma and died from her injuries the next morning. It was a horrible shame.

I admit, I held it against her. Had she died immediately, it would have been my duty to remove her to the hospital mortuary. There, in the cold solitude, I might have had a few minutes with her. As it was, some other orderly had the pleasure. A horrible shame indeed.

Let me state up front, categorically, I had nothing whatever to do with the attack upon Emma Smith or the death that resulted. Again, I was working. But, I confess, the event affected me more than I ever imagined it might. Further, I honestly believe and therefore state, her accidental murder altered forever the course of my thoughts. Not my feelings, perhaps, but most assuredly my thoughts. I cannot express the disturbance that welled within my being upon my discovery, by way of the morning papers, she had died; the violent thoughts that sprang to life and had, since that day, more and more frequently occurred to me. Not only thoughts but violent stirrings I had never known.

All because of that woman of the streets. That whore.

Emma Smith troubled me, visited me in my dreams, tormented me. More so the knowledge the streets were full of the likes of her; boozing, whoring Emma Smiths, drunk as a lord, drunk as my mother, filthy as my auntie, ruining good men all around them. They were bringing down the whole of society. Something, my conscience told me, something had to be done. I saw it then, my responsibility to the community.

For months I agonized over those concerns. Yet, as troubled as I was, I continued to do my bit for the people of the East End. I continued my important work in hospital. As I stated earlier, I had much to gain from my profession, a sense of worth, an understanding of right, the medical knowledge necessary to take on the new job my conscience insisted upon. All gain.

Now, four months later, early morning of 7 August, as I left the hospital, I quietly and unobtrusively gained a surgical knife with a fine and shining steel blade. It had been inappropriately left out and I covertly picked it up and slipped it into my coat as I headed for the door.

Three
George Yard

My lodging was south of, but relatively near to, London Hospital. I only mention it to make it plain that, with Emma Smith four months dead yet unaccountably again on my mind, though I lived close by, I did not feel like going home. When I left work, I needed air. I needed to walk and to think.

In order to truly understand this tale, it must be understood that upon stepping outside... I did not step into a romantic Victorian London, with Big Ben glowing magisterially above Parliament down river from a fog-shrouded Tower Bridge. Those did exist, in their own form, but west of there. West of there. I did not hail a satin covered hansom or a polished black hardwood coach with a thick-coated, thick-tongued cockney at the whip steering a snorting team of beautifully coiffed horses across rain-swept cobblestone streets. Those did exist, in their own way, but west of there. Well west of there. I did not enter beside high-hatted toffs into gay music halls, or arm-in-arm with respectable ladies into legitimate theatres or fine restaurants. I didn't go there. I didn't make faces at the rigid guards standing tall before Buck-place. I didn't tip my cap at the crisp, round-helmeted bobbies standing in the bright halos of gaslight on every street corner. Any of that might have taken place in London of 1888 but, if it did, it would happen in the City and in the West End. Well west of there.

This was the East End. I left London Hospital, walking west – through the East End.

Gay laughter was in short supply even in the entertaining streets of the East End. Hoots of derision and the cheers that followed the act of having put one over on someone, those were the sounds likely to be heard. There were few music halls (and those by the docks), no tapping feet, no cheering crowds. Joy, rarely expressed, came in the form of too-loud drunken bleats. There was no champagne, only cheap wine. There was no best bitter, only cheap gin and cheaper beer. Instead of the sounds of wafting West End gaiety, the streets here were filled with the plonks and plinks of tinny pianos, one after another, escaping the doors and windows of one drab public house after another. The sounds of carousing, arguing, and fighting were the music of the crowded pubs in the East End.

There, square-jawed constables who'd missed a button on their uniform coat, or skipped a day in shining their boots, traveled the thin poorly lit streets (one lamp for every four in the West End) and the unlit back alleys in patrols of two (or in some streets of Spitalfields, four), jamming their lanterns in gin-clouded eyes demanding, "Here now, who do you think you're talking to?" or "Get out of it!" as they slammed a boot up an arse or a hand against the back of a head.

There were plenty of cabmen (or carmen as they're truly called) in the streets of the East End. But most were on foot, walking from their lodgings to work, or from their work back home again. Their cabs, hansoms, and coaches were owned by someone else and stabled elsewhere, mostly in the city. There were wagons and carts in the streets, plenty of them, pulled by tired work horses and over-tired nags; filled, not with toffs in evening dress, but with the fruits of labour, the products of the wharfs, the fields, the furriers. There were barrows, barrows by the hundreds, pushed by hand by the fishmongers, the costermongers, the greengrocers and fruiterers, the butchers, the bakers, and the trinket peddlers.

By day the streets were filled with labourers, salesmen, customers, and children; dirty rag-wearing children everywhere. By night the streets of the East End emptied until only the criminals, the coppers, the drunks without doss money, and the whores remained. And the streets were dark.

So, needing to think, I headed west – through the East End. I followed the Whitechapel Road south and further west. I passed the workhouse, then the County Court, on my right. As I said, I'd been feeling out of sorts for some time and that night was no exception. The sights and sounds of dirty Whitechapel hit me like never before, adding to my confusion.

London was the largest and wealthiest city on earth, the heart of the British empire; a fact incomprehensible to anyone walking the streets of the East End in those early morning hours. There before me on the curb, barely touched by the amber nimbus of a gas lamp above, sat a grand example; an emaciated Jew by his looks, dark and swarthy, dirty and unkempt, muttering to himself (talking to voices?) in the foreign language of the Russian or the Pole. It was impossible to tell which as it was under his breath. Clearly he suffered as the result of years of indulgence in solitary vices. While he carried on his insane conversation, he picked wet bits of bread from the gutter and devoured them ravenously. I walked on, wordlessly, leaving him to his madness. But I couldn't forget him. He was a symbol of life around him in that filthy slum. Violence, drunken brawls, robberies, deprivation, poverty, and hardship were everywhere.

The driving forces behind all? Obviously... I was certain. Emma Smith had made it clear. They were the combination of cheap alcohol and women of low character.

Headed west on the Whitechapel High, I paused again at the corner of a northbound side street and stared up through the gloom at the sign overhead. I looked again and, this time, really took it in. Osborn Street. Another crashing wave of thoughts overtook me. Osborn Street.

The attack on Emma Smith had taken place on Osborn Street, there in Whitechapel. One block up, past the County Court, at the corner of Osborn and Wentworth. Four months had passed yet, suddenly, more fiercely even than it had earlier in the night, it all came back. Easter. Osborn Street. Emma Smith, a drunken whore bringing down the whole East End.

That's what must be understood! The affect her kind had on society, the city, the people. *Cor*, my landlady, had gone on about it endlessly! True, she could never get enough of colourful or infamous street gossip, with tragedy and violence being particular favorites of hers, but she wasn't wrong. And Emma Smith had already been heavy on my mind. Now again, four months on, I stood at the foot of Osborn Street – where it began.

I reached into my coat; felt the long bladed knife I'd borrowed from hospital. Still there. I slipped my hand into my pocket (ignoring the string, chalk, and matches I always carried) and touched my short, sturdy penknife. Where it belonged. I had everything a boy could need. Isn't that how my vicious mother would have said it, breathing beer all over me? You have everything a boy could need!

Forgive me. I'm having trouble keeping my focus as I tell it.

I was having the same difficulty that night as well. Standing there on Osborn Street, it had suddenly all become too much. Overwhelmed! Yes, I was overwhelmed. I needed to get away; to go somewhere quiet. Some place I could be alone with my thoughts. Someplace where I might put my thoughts in order. I had to get away from Osborn Street. I hurried on another short block down the Whitechapel High. Then I slipped through a covered archway, into a dark and narrow, seemingly out of the way place... I paused, backtracked several steps to find and read the sign. George Yard.

I found myself suddenly entering a quiet dark little thoroughfare called George Yard. I needed to sit down. I wanted to have a think by myself.

I hadn't been there long, hadn't begun to do the thinking I'd intended, when I was startled by the *click-click-clicking* footsteps of someone approaching quickly from the north; the Wentworth Street entrance. I leaned back into the shadows but continued to stare in the direction of the sound as the approaching figure took shape. It was a woman, all alone.

As she drew nearer, I made her out... to be young, pretty, carrying a bag of what I guessed to be groceries in her arms. She stopped before the entrance to the residential George Yard Buildings and slipped a hand inside her pocket. Searching for a latch key? This she did in the dark for neither of the two gas lamps at the top of the stairs, above the building entrance, were alight. She seemed indifferent to the dark, at home; suggesting a tenant, well-used to the conditions. She also seemed ignorant of my presence; completely unaware how near to her I was. I could have reached out and touched her. I could have... done anything to her. But... she was respectable-looking.

She didn't require cleaning. Why would I touch her?

It didn't matter. Key in hand, she climbed the wide staircase and disappeared inside. I took a needed breath. But I felt nothing. My hands shook, my heart was trotting, I admit that. But I felt nothing. I had to think.

But it wasn't my night to think. It was destined to be my night to act. For, in no time at all, came another interruption. It was a couple this time, a man and a woman headed my way, also from the north entrance. She was short, plump, middle-aged. (She might well have been my mother.) He, of all things, was a soldier of the Grenadier Guards. No sooner did I make them out in the gloom than I was angry with both. He ought to have been resplendent in his bright red uniform, but he wasn't at all. No! He was staggering drunk; an embarrassment to Queen and country. The woman seemed to have all she could do to hold him upright as they came deeper into the Yard. She was an obvious women of the streets, drunk and immoral, nothing at all respectable about her. He should not have been with her. She should not have lured a man in his cups away from duty and decency.

They stopped in roughly the same spot as the respectable woman moments before; near me. I leaned further back into the shadows not to be found out. I slowed my breathing not to be heard. Still, I remained near enough I could have touched either one – and neither knew I was there.

"C'mon, love," the woman said, pushing her arm through his and assisting him up the wide stone staircase, the same used by the good woman, to the dark entrance to George Yard Buildings. But they did not enter. I watched from below in rapt attention.

I heard a church bell sometime round then, I'm not sure which church or from which direction, St Mary Matfelon or Christ Church maybe? I don't know my churches as I should. I'm not sure when, either. It's a bit confused in my head. Two gongs it was, whenever I heard it. It had to have been, or only just gone, 2:00 am.

What I knew was what was happening a few steps above my dark hiding place. The drink sodden soldier and the woman of the street struck their bargain. They agreed upon a price, then moved to carry out their evil compact. He struggled to open his belt and drop his trousers. She fell back, standing, against the cold bricks of the entrance wall and hoisted up her skirt and petticoats. She burbled something at him, encouraging him to get the deed started. He teetered, with his trousers round his ankles, complaining he wasn't ready. She huffed impatiently and reached out to help him.

That's when something went wrong.

It might have been a sudden attack of conscience on the part of the soldier, but I doubt it. Most likely it was on account of his severe inebriation. Whatever the cause, the fellow was not able to... He could not perform the vile act of coupling which he'd commissioned.

That difficulty, in turn, caused the woman to giggle. A sickening drunken giggle. Then she dropped her skirts and she laughed in his face. The soldier ought not to have been there, involved in such a ridiculous transaction. Still part of me stood with him. To be unable to function was enraging; to be ridiculed for it was devastating. It must have been. Then, as if she hadn't done injury enough, the woman demanded her money; the amount they'd negotiated.

The soldier refused payment, of course. When she objected he threatened her with violence. I can't say I blamed him. It wasn't fair. It wasn't right, the way she'd treated him; laughing in his face, demanding payment without fulfilling her wretched service. It was no way to treat a member of Her Majesty's Grenadier Guards. It was no way to treat a man. Wasn't bad enough she spread her muck about the city.

I found myself joining the soldier in his rage. In my mind, at that moment, the woman stopped being a woman. She became nothing but a common street whore. She was the problem with those filthy city streets. She was Emma Smith all over again. The more I thought of her, the more furious I grew.

Four
Soldier's Whore

As to the pair on the stairs above me... Unpleasantness might well have followed had either been sober enough. But they were not. The unsatisfied soldier picked up his trousers along with his wounded pride, stumbled down the stairs and, righting himself, abandoned the Yard by way of Wentworth Street.

The unpaid whore descended to the foot of the stairs. There she stood, sniffling and weakly calling curses after him until he was out of sight.

That was when I stepped from the shadows. I silently approached the soldier's whore from behind. I reached for her shoulder but stopped my hand short. I didn't want to touch her – yet. I wasn't ready to touch her – yet. Instead, in a voice that shattered the night silence (a voice I barely recognized), I asked her, "Have you been cheated?"

"Lord," the woman exclaimed, turning quickly to face me. She fluttered a hand over her breast. "You scared the life out of me!" Her crocodile tears instantly dried. She took a breath, then another for good measure, calming herself. Back in control, she asked, "What did you say?"

"I asked if you'd been cheated."

"What's it to you? Who are you anyways?"

"It's nothing to me, really. I'm someone who wouldn't want to see a lady cheated."

Even in the gloom, I saw her eyebrow go up. "A lady, huh?"

"I'd be willing to make it right," I told her.

Her second brow joined the first on high. "Yeah?' she asked. Then, with a muted laugh, added, "If I'm willing, eh?"

"But not here, of course; not in the street."

"There are plenty of places, love." She chucked a dirty thumb over her shoulder. "Nice dark little nest right up here." She beckoned me, then started back up the dark stone staircase, back to the spot she'd abandoned, where moments before she'd failed and insulted the soldier.

Neither originality nor superficial social formalities appeared to be of import to her. That was fine. While I enjoyed the first, I could live without it. I was entirely indifferent to the second. I followed her up the steps.

She reached the flagstone landing, and stopped as before, not twelve feet from a resident's door. (Its position suggested it belonged to none other than the building superintendent.) I joined her there. As she turned around to face me, I think she smiled. Lamentably that spot was even darker than the street; too dark to clearly see the expression on her face. That was a shame.

I'd imagined this moment for a long time – and had always envisioned the rise of terror on the face of. . . whoever the lucky whore happened to be. Now, with that moment finally at hand, to find it too dark to really see. Yes, that was a shame. But don't think I allowed that to put me off. More light would have been desirable, but wasn't necessary. The job ahead would hold excitements that couldn't be seen, I was certain; joys that stimulated all of the senses. Don't think I was dithering. I was looking forward to it. Not merely for what I hoped to receive from the act. Don't think me selfish.

Don't think I was putting it off, either. I was not afraid to proceed. Nor was I embarrassed or unsure. The job needed doing. The East End teemed with the barking mad, who believed, and existed by their belief, that filth, disease, illicit sex, drink and gluttony were meant to be the ways of this world. They would not admit their wrongs and therefore would not correct them. Someone else, someone wiser, was needed to issue those corrections.

To exact the cure for the Emma Smith's all around us. Yes, I was needed. On with the job.

That brings me back to where I started this story.

Don't think I immediately stabbed her.

I wasn't a fool. I didn't need her squealing her head off and bringing the neighbourhood out and the coppers down on us. No. I was wise and knew I had to go about my work quiet-like. As I said before, I grabbed the whore by her fat throat, clutched her voice box with all the strength in my hands, allowed not a wisp of air to pass and thereby prevented anything like a squeal. Then I switched to a one-handed grip and, with my free hand, reached into my coat and took hold of the long knife I'd nicked from the hospital's surgical theatre.

That was when I startled the both of us. For the first time, I pulled the knife – with measured and full intent. I raised the blade on high. Then, without sign of nerves or so much as a 'by your leave', I stabbed down and into the whore's left breast.

No questions remained. Her actions with the soldier had cemented my thoughts, my will. That was how I felt about her. She wasn't a girl; girls were innocent and she clearly had not been that for ages. She wasn't a woman either; not anymore. Women were respectable. She was a whore; nothing less than filth. Removing filth from the streets was the job needed doing. A job made easier, made exciting, by the fury I felt for her – for being what she was. It was nothing to throttle her where she stood and even less to stab her. She'd got what she had earned.

Once she'd gone unconscious, or dead, if dead she was, I let her fall to the flagstones. In so doing, she made virtually no noise at all; she was a plump thing after all (standing little over five feet) and was soft all around. She hit her head good and hard on landing but even that produced only a dull *thump* of no consequence. She lay on her back with her tightly clenched hands at her sides. But how she lay, I suppose, was neither here nor there. I had no compassion for her. All I felt for her was a strangely muted fury, the dirty whore.

I switched knives. I tucked away my new but unfamiliar long blade and, instead, pulled out the trusty penknife I'd carried for ages. I opened that blade.

Then I opened her long black jacket. I saw she really was a plump little thing, past middle-aged, but still with – now that her black bonnet had been shaken from its place – mostly dark hair. She had a matching dark complexion. I wanted to hate her!

With a heat rivaling hate, I stabbed her left chest. I stabbed her again. And again, again, again. I stabbed her right chest, and again. Back to her left and a good hard stab into her treacherous whore's heart. I moved down, below the heart; stab, stab, stab, four, five, six, seven. Then on to her round gut; six more stabs there, each as vicious as I could deliver. Dozens of times, I stabbed her. I lost count, of course. I was too busy, and far too agitated, to keep a proper count.

Then as quickly as it had started it all came to an end – or I thought it had.

I was panting for breath... fighting to keep my balance for a strange dizziness had suddenly come over me. But, even as I steadied myself, I realized the job was not done. She was a filthy whore, wasn't she? Though I had put her in her place, I had yet to address that specific fact at all. To make amends, I grabbed the hem of her green (slightly besmirched) skirt, lifted it, and tossed it up above her stomach. I repeated the motion with her brown petticoat. This helped to clear my head as the fabric, on falling, covered her bloody upper form and gave me a respite from having to look directly down into the results of the work already completed. Likewise, the act exposed her stockings, the old and worn pair of side-spring boots with which she was shod, and...

My mouth went dry. I had to lick my lips.

And... her lower region.

Regarding that area... I hadn't seen... that... since Emma Smith. I had no other choice now, I had to look at it. The look, by necessity owing to the gloom, became a prolonged stare. I couldn't see clearly, yet I couldn't turn away. I thought of Emma Smith's bleeding... region. She'd deserved it. This whore deserved it as well.

Time was getting on. Others would inevitably come. I wanted them to come. Whatever else would have been the point? Others had to see. But, needing to be away by then, I had first to finish the job. Resolved, I tore my eyes from the centre of her evil and went back to work.

Nervously, I admit, I took the whore by both knees and spread her legs. Then I took up my penknife again and slashed her evil spot one hard time; a gash three inches long by a good inch deep, above her own dirty gash. With her already dead, there was no spurt of blood, more's the shame, but there was an oozing and pooling as the blood and juices drained into the natural crevices between her separated legs.

Didn't that show her for the whore she was! Wouldn't all who saw it, or eventually learned of it, then know? Gasping for breath, I stood and turned, heading quickly back down the steps to the dark George Yard byway. My job was done.

I got the hell out of there, leaving the soldier's whore to rot where I'd killed her.

Five
The East End

It was an interesting walk back to my lodgings – to say the least. Not on account of any particular event that took place. Merely for all that was happening inside of me. Forgive me, if I fail utterly in reporting it clearly. I shall try.

First, I must say, I struggled physically all the way home.

I wanted to run. Charged with energy, exhilarated, I wanted to run and shout. But, of course, that was out of the question. The last thing I should or would have done at that moment would have been to draw attention to myself. Still, despite the insanity of it, my whole inner being was thrilled and wanted to shout it to the world. So I concentrated, like a child learning how to walk, like a cripple regaining his legs, like an accident victim wobbling to his feet from the depths of unconsciousness, I concentrated mind and soul on walking *normally*.

I wanted to stay in the shadows. The cold cruel darkness of the East End was suddenly my friend. But I knew it wise to fight that friendship as best I could. Flitting from shadow to shadow would, too, give me away. I needed to stay true to a course, a fellow out for a stroll following a long night at work. Out for a think and a breath of air.

People passing... nothing there. Always people in the streets of Whitechapel, day or night. Ignore them. Hands in pockets. Head down. Watch the pace. Walk. Don't let your good work show on your face. Much better. I felt so much better now, on my way back to my lodgings.

So much less confused.

After all the turmoil, Emma Smith – and her ilk – finally made sense in my world. I had found purpose. I'd discovered my place. Don't misunderstand, I make no claim to having moved comfortably into my future with that single event in George Yard. But I knew I had found my niche. I was at home with myself – and would make a special home for myself in this East End.

I already said, I'm a reader. And so, as I take that walk again in my mind, I offer a short but necessary history lesson:

The East End is the urban area of the Tower Hamlets (and was *before* it was the East End), its earliest residents owed military service to the Tower of London and the crown for their existence. While the term East End did not appear until recently, the first written reference to the area as an entity (I said I am an obsessive and attentive reader) appeared in John Strype's 1720 'Survey...', where he described London as being comprised of four parts: the City, Westminster, Southwark, and 'That Part beyond the Tower'. The bulk of my story concerns only 'That Part beyond the Tower'; specifically, the parishes of Whitechapel, Spitalfields, St George-in-the-East, and Mile End Old Town as they existed in 1888.

While there are no universally accepted boundaries to the East End, and probably never will be, it is generally thought to commence outside the eastern (ancient Roman) city walls, running with the old roads leading from Bishopsgate and Aldgate, and along and north of the River Thames; in other words, part of Central London, East London, the London Docklands, and the East End (once all marshland). The Aldgate Pump, on the edge of the city, was the symbolic start of the East End. On the river, according to some, Tower Bridge served that function. To close the loop it should be mentioned, I suppose, the various channels of the River Lea are considered to be the eastern boundary. That debate rages and, for my tale, doesn't matter a jot.

The East End has always been a no man's land.

In medieval times most trades in London-town were carried out in workshops in or around the owners' homes. By the time of the Great Fire (in 1666), many of those trades were growing to become industries. And, as many were unpleasant or noxious (they offended the posh noses), they needed to be removed from society. Examples? Certainly. Processing urine for tanning stank like hell and London's prevailing winds traveled west to east. The East End put those occupations downwind of the high and the mighty. Huge amounts of space, vast tentergrounds, were required for cloth dying and rope making. The wide open moorfields to the east were the perfect answer. The manufacture of gunpowder, and the proving of weapons, were decidedly dangerous and had to be conducted away from the masses. Lead making, soap making, china making, gilding, slaughtering and butchering; one by one, all of the unpleasant but necessary activities of city life were moved east. Likewise, the marshes along the Thames to the east and south called for the docks and their industries, the transportation, warehousing, and distribution of... Well, of everything.

Everything the toffs would deem necessary – but outside of polite society. With all this awful industry, and the awful peoples supporting it, it had always been the most productive of London-town, also the least, the lowest, the poorest, and the worst. That was the East End.

Now an even more brief history of the rabble who inhabited her. As barbarism was driven east from the city, so too went the barbarians.

The hardest work often brought the least pay. Many East Enders worked in lowly but respectable occupations; slaughterers, porters, costermongers, labourers in every dirty trade. Sadly, with the low pay also came the shiftless, the untrustworthy, and those who thrived in and contributed to their own continued poverty. Then, of course, there lived and worked the criminal class.

When the filthy southeast slums and rookeries, made famous by Charles Dickens, were demolished in 1827, for the construction of St Katharine Docks, over 11,000 port workers and their families were displaced (without compensation). What choice did they have but to create new slums in Whitechapel and Spitalfields. More overcrowding, more disease, more criminality, with a healthy dose of bitterness.

A major theme of the East End has always been migration (from within) and immigration (from without). The rural poor flooded in from all over England, while foreigners slammed the shore from Europe. The Huguenot refugees swamped Spitalfields in the 17th century. Then came the Irish weavers. Then the Ashkenazi Jews. Now the Russian and Polish Jews. In the past twenty years so many Jews arrived that over 150 synagogues had been built.

The population of the East End greatly increased during the 19th century. House building could not keep pace. This influx of peoples only added to the notorious deep poverty and the overall misery; and helped to contribute to the social upheaval. The immigrant inspired socialist riots of Bloody Sunday the previous years. The strike of the Bryant and May matchgirls over working conditions. The constant strikes by the dock labourers. The trade union uprisings. Any wonder Londoners viewed the residents of the East End with fascination and fright?

Do-gooders moved in with feigned concern – to steal the farthings from dead men's eyes. With organisations like Oxford House and Tonybee Hall masquerading at helping, encouraging university students to experience the slums, to live there, to work to alleviate the misery, while pushing their social and political agendas on a half-million people willing to sing for their suppers. Poverty made for a receptive audience.

True civility reached periodically into the darkness. A committee to promote 'Cleanliness among the Poor' (in 1844) built a laundry and bathhouse in Glasshouse Yard, East Smithfield. In three years, at a penny a wash or a penny a bath, the facilities were serving over 4,000 people per annum. That great success led to an Act of Parliament encouraging other East End districts to construct like-centres. But the fingers of those helping hands were often bitten and, while many slum residents desired cleanliness, many more were happy to stay filthy.

William Booth organized his 'Christian Revival Society' (in 1865), preaching in a tent erected in Thomas Street. His mission to help the poor grew and, in August of 1878, Booth's *Salvation Army*' came into being at a meeting in Whitechapel Road. Occasionally a barbarian or two were rescued, but it was always a battle. God was in the East End, but so was his adversary.

Dubliner Thomas Barnardo came to London Hospital in 1866 to train as a medical missionary to China. Soon after, a cholera epidemic swept the East End. Three thousand died. Families fell destitute. Thousands of orphans were enslaved in factories or forced to beg for bread in the streets. Many slept there as well. China would wait. Barnardo stayed in England and, in 1867, started a '*Ragged School*' to help educate the little bastards. He opened a home for boys three years later. When one died after being turned away (no room at the inn), the policy became 'No Destitute Child Ever Refused Admission'.

It wasn't all gloom. The do-gooders had made some progress. Novelist Besant's dream of a concert hall for the downtrodden to hold fêtes and dances, his 'Palace of Delight', had in one form or another met and married philanthropist Currie's notion of an East End 'People's Palace'. Subscriptions were sold, trusts robbed, and acreage secured on the Mile End Road. Victoria herself had come down from her thrown to christen the resulting 'Queen's Hall' last year. But that's what it was, a hall. The 'palace' didn't appear, the 'people' were left out of the name, and the 'delights', like the proposed winter garden, library, swimming pool, and gymnasium failed to materialize. That's the rabble.

Now for the coppers who protect them.

There were no police in London before the 1750s. Crime was punished, and social order kept, by local magistrates and volunteer parish constables backed by government militias. Paid constables were introduced by 1792; they were few and their authority yet derived from magistrates. These organized crime fighters had nothing to do with the protection of the citizenry or their personal property. They existed solely to protect the docks.

England was an island, London its capital. From earliest times, the welfare of the city and country depended upon the importation and exportation of goods via the docks. The only labour that mattered to authority was that which supported those cargo shipments. The only crime that mattered was that which threatened same. It made sense the first coppers in England, formed in 1798, were the Marine Police Force (based in Wapping High Street) to prevent the looting of ships anchored in the Pool of London and the lower reaches of the River Thames. Beyond the river, and particularly in the slums, crime was a personal problem.

The regular coppers, as we know them today, didn't come about until 1829 when the Metropolitan Police Force was formed under the direction of Sir Robert Peel. Hence the terms used throughout the eastern districts to refer to the constables on foot patrol; bobbies and peelers.

The Met was now a force of a thousand men; seventeen divisions, each with its own superintendent ordering about four plod inspectors, sixteen sergeants and, obviously, one-seventeenth of the total bobbies (or peelers) to pound the pavement. Each and every one, at the time of their recruitment, under thirty-five years of age, at least five foot seven, well built, literate (if not well-read), and of good character. All organized to keep watch of the streets within eleven kilometers of Charing Cross.

Financed as they were by a levy on ratepayers, the coppers were always widely disliked. And, it goes without saying, it took the force another twenty-plus years for their patrols to reach the dark and scary streets of the East End.

The Metropolitan Police formed a 'Dockyard Division' for Thames River shore patrols in 1841, a Department of Detectives in 1842 (later the Criminal Investigations Department), and 'J' Division in Bethnal Green in 1865. That's law and order.

Now for the real problem.

One of the greatest (by which I mean *largest*) industries in the East End, servicing the downtrodden workers of the district and, especially, the seamen moored off the Pool of London, was prostitution. For over two hundred years that abomination was tolerated. But in this modern 19th century, attitudes needed to change. I was not alone. William Acton described whores as a 'horde of human tigresses who swarm the pestilent dens by the riverside'. The Society for the Suppression of Vice estimated over 1800 prostitutes between Houndsditch, Whitechapel, and Ratcliffe; and nearly a thousand more between Mile End, Shadwell and Blackwall. (Who could count the whores in the Spitalfields rookeries?)

The social reformers called them victims; blamed their circumstances, lack of a welfare state, high death rates of men in dangerous low-class jobs leaving destitute wives and daughters. Some of which was true. But when the women choose, of their own free will, to bathe their struggles in alcohol – they forfeited all rights to consideration.

Society had attempted to *repair* the whore problem. Religious reformers introduced '*Seamen's Missions*' to the docks to see to seafarer's needs while helping to save them from the temptations of women and drink. The passage of the Contagious Diseases Prevention Act (in 1864) allowed the coppers to pull the whores off the street and hold them in hospital. But the formation of a Ladies National Association (by agitating feminists) led to the repeal of the act two years ago, once more setting the drunk and diseased women free upon unsuspecting males.

That's where I come in. The East End was the machine that made the City of London live. The East End did not live itself. It got by, it survived, by hook or by crook, by sweat, by tears. For some... by blood. Like everybody else in London's East End, I'd been forced to find my niche. Now that I had made a start, I had no choice but to carry on.

Six
Murder in Whitechapel!

I slept late that Tuesday. There was nothing unusual in that. In fact, that's the point.

I had begun my new work in Whitechapel, returned to my lodgings afterward, quietly retired, and slept the sleep of the just. I woke refreshed. I rose from bed, conducted my ablutions with a light heart, dressed myself happily – with a growing curiosity – and waited to hear... whatever there would be to hear concerning my initial effort in George Yard.

To my surprise and, I confess, my disappointment, that amounted to nothing. The street outside my window was quiet. All appeared normal to the eye. There was neither sound or sign of alarm visible anywhere. I don't know exactly what it was I'd been expecting. But I had expected... something.

Of course, my work had taken place a good ways away, more than half-a-mile. The thought occurred that, if I wanted to see and hear what was happening in and around the neighbourhood in which I'd done the job, I should... But that would be reckless, at best, and probably insane. A thinking man did not return to the scene of his...

I was about to say *crime*. ha ha. That was foolish. I had eliminated crime. I had made my first bold attempt at cleaning up those awful streets.

Still it wouldn't do to go showing my face about. Not until I knew the situation. Not until I knew whether or not anybody had seen that face. No. What I needed to do was to sit, to dive into a book, and make certain all I did and said at home appeared completely normal. I had to allow things to take shape as they would.

In early evening – very early indeed, as it was a Tuesday – Mrs Griggs brought me my supper.

It may help if I explain.

I was a lodger in a small but tidy and well-kept house, above a now permanently closed shoe shop, on... Well, it wouldn't be prudent really to say where I lived. Would it? Let me say, in the East End of London, but on a decent street south of Commercial Road and east of Backchurch Lane in the parish known as St George-in-the-East. My landlady was a respectable widow called Mrs Griggs.

And, yes, Mrs Griggs is also a manufactured name. If I don't protect myself, who will?

I liked Mrs Griggs very much. And do not make the mistake of thinking it was because she mothered me. Precisely the opposite was true. She didn't say or do anything to remind me of my mother. She didn't remind me of any woman, thank god, and that is what I truly appreciated about her. Mrs Griggs was quite unlike most women. She was a respectable and logical human being, who saw the world as it was and understood what it was meant to be. She deplored emotional, irrational thought. She valued intelligence. She was a reader of books. She had a firm understanding of moral foundation.

Many women, most women, do not. Women, by their natures, are unmoored and immoral.

Owing to her unique understanding of right and wrong, Mrs Griggs quite rightly despised drink and the many evils alcohol brought to society. She had no kind words for layabouts. She hated the idea of prostitution. She respected the monarchy, but distrusted the government. She was, in every regard, a fine example of an up-right woman.

As I said, Mrs Griggs knocked on my door and entered, moving efficiently with the tray holding my evening meal, as was her habit on her *meeting* nights. She carried the usual two evening papers to which she subscribed tucked under her arm. (The *Times* and *Daily Telegraph*, of course; she was a Tory after all.) "Forgive the meager chop," she said, depositing the tray on my table and the papers on the top edge of the tray. "It is..."

"Tuesday," I said, finishing her sentence, and accepting her apology, with the same smile. "No chop, prepared by you, Mrs Griggs, could possibly be meager." Then, as if I didn't care a wit, I nodded in the direction of the papers and asked, "Any news?"

She breathed an unexpected sigh, then said an unexpected sentence. "Nothing really worth mentioning."

I paused, trying to think, and could only hope the disappointment which struck my heart that instant had not, in its progression, registered on my face. Nothing worth mentioning?

Evidently Mrs Griggs saw nothing unusual in my expression as she had moved on, vocalizing the substance of the headlines she'd found appealing. "A Select Committee of the House of Lords continues to examine the so-called Sweating systems of these local factories. Deplorable. If you ask me, they should hand the matter over to Baroness Burdett-Coutts and be done with it."

I hummed my agreement and my landlady went on.

"Thousands, they say, stood in the drizzle at Alexandra Palace over the Bank Holiday, to watch that young American acrobat, Professor Baldwin. We read of him last week. Extraordinary. He ascended 1000 feet in his hot air balloon, then jumped to the ground using only a parachute."

Without meaning to, I hummed my disinterest (a different sound entirely). "Nothing else?"

"More trouble with the dock workers' union. More trouble, as always, with the socialists. More rain. What Mr __, in particular, were you expecting to hear?"

"Nothing at all, in particular. It's merely that, in the capital city of the modern world, one would think something of note had taken place." I began perusing the Times.

"Yes. Well, what is it they say? No news is..."

"There was a murder!" I said, turning the newspaper and tapping the page with my finger to bring the matter to her attention.

"Oh, yes," Mrs Griggs relented without undue alarm. "I saw that."

I'm not surprised she didn't mention it, even having seen it. It was the shortest blip of an article, with the rather small and uninteresting headline: 'SUPPOSED MURDER'. The poorly informed piece related little more than the fact that an unknown woman had been found early in the morning, dead of an apparent stab wound, in George Yard. Witnesses had seen the victim carousing with soldiers in a public house shortly before her death. That was the lot. "Little to be had in this report," I said, with perhaps a tad too much dismay.

"What ought they have said?" My landlady asked, with a sideways glance. "Violence in Whitechapel is hardly front page news."

"No. I'm certain you're correct. I thought perhaps... Well, it was a murder, after all. A word with the investigating officers. Something to calm the residents."

Mrs Griggs had ceased all motion and was staring at me. I shut my mouth. I smiled. She shook her head wonderingly. "Calm the residents of Whitechapel? Really, Mr __. It has always been my opinion that *they* thrive on turmoil."

"Yes. But what about us; the remainder of the East End residents? Doesn't murder so nearby give you a feeling of insecurity, Mrs Griggs?"

She seemed taken aback. "Certainly not. We're nowhere near George Yard. It's blocks and blocks away. The poor woman's killer is probably further away still. Surely he's a foreigner and surely he comes from the slums."

"Yes," I agreed. "You're probably right."

In one way, Mrs Griggs was like every other woman; she liked being right. And, having achieved as much, my landlady chose that moment to wish me a good evening and end our meeting, in order that she might hurry off to hers. She left me.

She left me... If not on pins and needles, certainly disheartened and disgruntled.

One small article, in the combined two newspapers, written with literally no information and no investigation. No thrill. No fear. No message for the community. That was not what I had expected. It most certainly would not do.

I had to go out. Don't misunderstand; I did not want to go out. In a way, I confess, I was afraid to go out so near to, so soon after... my work. But, risk or no, I had to see if the hoped-for ripple was any larger in any other parts of the East End pool.

Have no fear. I had no intention of venturing anywhere near George Yard. I would head straight north and, quickly and quietly, visit a newsstand with which I was familiar midway in the Whitechapel Road between St Mary's and London Hospital. I would see what the other papers (there were more, after all, than one would care to count) had to report. I would hear what the word on the street (if word there was) had to say. Then, regardless of my discoveries, would hastened back to my lodgings.

Possessed of my plan, I took the only little precaution available on the spur of the moment. I bundled up, though it wasn't particularly cold, with collar up and soft hat pulled down, to show as little of me as possible. And set out.

I walked with purpose, and happily without diversion, north up Backchurch Lane, up again on the back side of St Mary's (that's St Mary Matfelon, the brightly whitewashed white chapel from which that parish drew its name), and turned east off of Adler onto the Whitechapel Road. I diverted around the professional peddlers (and the multitude of sad women, and their filthy broods) selling their wares from barrows and baskets all up and down the way, walking in the street when necessary, around the unending piles of straw and horse shit, I quickly reached my sought after newsstand and, in the same instant, found my inner peace.

There, beside the young boy hawking fresh copies of the *Star*, stood a whiteboard on the curb with the brilliantly lurid headline 'MURDER IN WHITECHAPEL' scrawled excitedly across its face.

Damn the Tories. Thank god for the radical press!

"Murder!" the news boy called out. "Murder in Whitechapel! Horrible Murder in Whitechapel!"

"Good evening, Mr __." It took an instant to realize my name had been said, and that the speaker was still going on, to me. "What brings you at this hour?"

It was the news dealer, Mr Frogg, who I normally saw late in the evening on my way to hospital. While I'm on introductions, the boy at the curb loudly proclaiming my work was his son, Tad. I'd always wondered, but had never asked, if that was the child's actual name or a corruption based upon the family surname; had Mr Frogg begot a Tadpole? No matter, certainly not then.

Mr Frogg handled all of the newspapers, local and national, morning and evening, Tory, Liberal and, thank god, those of the radical press. As it turned out, it was only the radicals – always eager to stick a pin in the government or the police – who'd bothered to give the murder story any coverage of note.

I made an excuse for my presence at the odd hour, bought a copy of the *Star* (which Mrs Griggs wouldn't allow in the house on a bet), relished their headline, and took in what little story they were able to provide:

"*A Whitechapel Horror.*
A woman, now lying unidentified at the mortuary, Whitechapel, was ferociously stabbed to death this morning, between two and four o'clock, on the landing of a stone staircase in George's-buildings, Whitechapel.

George's-buildings are tenements occupied by the poor laboring class. A lodger going early to his work found the body. Another lodger says the murder was not committed when he returned home about two o'clock. The woman was stabbed in 20 places. No weapons were found near her, and her murderer has left no trace. She is of middle age and height, had black hair and a large, round face, and apparently belonged to the lowest class."

"The murder?" Mr Frogg asked. "That is sad."

"Yes," I agreed, taking special care to govern the features of my face. Of course, a look of sadness was out of the question; I'd have never pulled it off. But I did manage neutrality, I think, and something suggesting concern. "Very alarming indeed."

"They say," Mr Frogg said, "Inspector Reid's in charge of the investigation."

"Inspector Reid?" I asked.

"Head of CID in 'aitch Division."

"CID?"

"Criminal Investigations Department."

I nodded gratefully, then sheepishly asked, "Aitch Division?"

"Mr __!" Mr Frogg groaned in exasperation. He repeated it slowly as if speaking to an idiot. "The letter 'H'. 'aitch Division. Whitechapel. Ain't you evah seen the little 'aitches on the coppers' collars?" He shook his head at my abominable ignorance. "They say," he went on, "though I can't say I recall, this murder occurred only a coupla' blocks from an earlier murder, one what happened last Christmas."

I held my tongue, resisting the urge to correct the foggy Frogg. It had been one block distant. And Emma Smith had been killed at Easter, not Christmas. It would be my secret.

Mr Frogg didn't notice my heroic restraint. He'd gone back to sorting his stacks and shuffling his papers. A moment more and he lifted another paper, one of the locals (the *East London Observer*), and read aloud... an opinion piece he'd obviously read before and with which he clearly agreed:

"It is inconceivable that in a great city like London, the streets of which are continually patrolled by police, a woman can be foully and horribly killed almost next to the citizens peacefully sleeping in their beds, without a trace or clue being left of the villain who did the deed."

Mr Frogg looked to me for a reaction. I nodded quietly. Who was I to argue?

He moved on to another local (the *East London Advertiser*), and again read to me, for free, a story he ought to have been trying to sell me. The murder, it was clear, had gotten under the skin of the news dealer. Perhaps he wasn't alone? Frogg spent the next ten minutes regaling me with news and opinion from the left-leaning press (the conservatives had taken little interest) concerning the morning outrage committed upon the unidentified woman.

The newspaper editors complained, Mr Frogg complained, that *'virulent savagery'* had been employed by the killer. That the poor woman had been *'literally butchered'*. Each of his wood pulp rags went out of their way to stress the *'feeling of insecurity'* that had arisen in the neighbourhoods surrounding George Yard Buildings.

Again he paused and examined me for my response. I provided it, in the form of a question. "Tell me, Mr Frogg, do you feel insecure?"

"*Bah*," he said, replacing the papers in their stacks. "What d' you expect? It's Whitechapel."

Seven

Mrs Griggs, Dress Reformist

I walked home feeling somewhat vindicated. My work had made headlines, if only in the radical press. As to the meagerness of the news they'd had to print, it was hardly their fault, I'd left them with precious few facts; the victim unidentified, no suspects, Inspector Reid, Head of CID in H Division was in charge of the investigation. And, again, only in the radical press.

The other papers and, presumably and sadly, the citizens of London who had heard of the murder at all, considered it merely an activity of *those people* in the slums.

Ultimately, the message I'd delivered and the fear I'd hoped to generate had reached regrettably few. My first outing could not be considered an unparalleled success. I would need to work harder.

With that in mind, I contemplated my immediate future. I felt it too risky to spend much time on the streets without knowing the status of the police investigations. But that presented problems. I had not taken into account how seriously political bias affected the way news was disseminated. The Tories didn't like sensationalism. The Liberals didn't like facts. The Radicals didn't like the government and used their papers as sharp sticks, weapons of war. If I was to know, what I needed to know for my safety, I would need to bide my time, to seek out varied sources of news and to sift that news carefully.

I arrived safely home at the same time I arrived at a conclusion. I would need to collect information without being nicked in the streets or drawing undue attention to myself at work or at home. Luckily for me, my landlady was a busy woman.

This would, perhaps, be the correct moment to provide a few details regarding my landlady. As I've made it plain, Mrs Griggs was a respectable widow. She was a church goer, yes, of course, but not to excess. Religion was not her passion. What fueled her was *social justice* for women. She'd chosen one aspect in particular as her fight; Mrs Griggs was a Dress Reformist.

To my landlady, and her followers, stays (or *corsets* as the posh would have it) were a dangerous moral evil. Stays, they believed, promoted promiscuous views of the female body and a harmful preoccupation with fashion. In particular she, and those she gathered round her, railed against the practice of *tightlacing*. The health risks, Mrs Griggs insisted, were many; damage to internal organs and compromised fertility being the two most obvious. The poor health of women could, in their vociferous opinions, be directly blamed on excessive corsetry and tightlacing.

Supporters of stays... ha ha. Forgive me.

Corset advocates... insisted they helped women maintain upright postures, figures to please the eye, and the necessary elements for a moral and well-ordered society; fashion, beauty, and health.

Dress Reformists could not have disagreed more, and they were not alone. Many in church authority spoke against tightlacing owing to the risk to the female soul, some doctors counseled against health risks to the female body, and not a few journalists used the subject to condemn the vanity and frivolity of women in general. Mrs Griggs, and her Dress Reformists, utilized all of those arguments, declaring stays and the practice of tightlacing to be morally indecent, physically detrimental, and the result of a male conspiracy to make women subservient.

Energized, apparently, by news reports of the public orations and political agitations of American women active in various movements in the United States, Mrs Griggs believed a change in fashion would not only ease physical movement and add needed comfort, but might alter the female place in society; allow opportunity for mobility, decent wages, and independence *from* men and marriage.

The weekly meetings of the Dress Reformists occasionally rotated from one member's residence to the next, but mostly the burden (or the honor) visited our residence. Often, on the nights Mrs Griggs acted as host, I heard my landlady's authoritative voice through the floorboards of my room, speaking to the gathered like-minded ladies of the community. "Burn up the corsets!" she would shout.

Then would come the excited replies:

"We will never need whalebones again!"

"Make a bonfire of the cruel steels!"

"Free our abdomens!"

"Heave a sigh of relief for our emancipation!"

Following this breathless climax, they'd all bask in their afterglow, clinking tea cups and devouring cakes, their digestion unfettered by nasty old stays.

Why this long recital about the political and social activities of my landlady? Not merely to be frivolous. Indeed, there was a point. It's important to understand what the Dress Reformists' meetings were usually like, in order to fully grasp how different those same gatherings would (over the next several months) become. More, how vitally important those gathering would become to me.

I heard a lot of rumors, probably some truths, and what must have been a great many whoppers over the next three weeks, mostly from Mrs Griggs. She told me of the stories in the streets, increasing daily, regarding the horrible murder in George Yard. I tried to stay off the streets myself, not knowing what anyone – particularly the police – knew (I mean, really knew) about the murder or the murderer. I went to work, because I had no choice. Otherwise I kept to myself in my rooms... with one exception.

I will relate that exception in time. Until then, know, I kept to myself and let Mrs Griggs and her Dress Reformists bring me the world.

Eight
Miss Adler, Archie, and the Cock-up

Mrs Griggs' home, my lodging house, stood well south and east of the low-class slums. Though both were in the East End, there was no comparison at all. Our streets were made up of respectable working class individuals, much cleaner and far safer than the murder neighbourhood. Still, gossip and loose talk crossed all financial and moral boundaries and street talk and rumors did find their way to the parish of St George-in-the-East.

I heard the talk as I walked to work. And rejected the majority of it. Aware of human nature as I was, I had little doubt what I heard was more interesting (but probably less reliable), than the talk in the murder neighbourhood. There were plenty of liars there, don't misunderstand, but there was no telling how tall that tales had grown in the retelling as they made their way east to our streets. I heard much to consider on my walks to work.

At work... I should tell something of my life at London Hospital.

To understand the events taking place around me, to understand me, it is vital to understand something of medicine at the time of the... of my work; in particular to understand the nurses of the time. Yes, I said *nurses*.

In my lifetime, nursing had changed dramatically as a profession and as a part of society. Before Florence Nightingale's valiant efforts in the Crimean War, no part of nursing was thought to demand skill or training, and nothing about nursing commanded respect. As that icon of healing, the maiden of the deathwatch, so correctly put it, nursing was left to "those who were too old, too weak, too drunken, too dirty, too stupid, or too bad to do anything else." Modern nineteenth century or not, to intimately touch an unrelated stranger, let alone hospital wards full of them, was thought immodest and unseemly for unmarried or well-bred females. Feeding, and especially cleaning, another person were regarded as domestic tasks for lowly servants.

Before 1880, hospital treatment of illness was rare. The wealthy were treated at home by family doctors and nursed by female family members and servants. The working classes treated themselves. The indigent were treated in workhouse casualty wards by other indigent residents. But with the birth and application of anesthetics and antiseptic surgery hospital treatment came into its own, for all classes of people. Training schools opened and women with educations, with developing specialized skills, created a profession – and an art of its own – called nursing.

I relate that history only as preamble to this:

There were four nurses at London Hospital, working many of the shifts that I worked, whom I regarded as *the coterie*. I was forced to conduct my business beside them, to work among them, but was in no way a part of them. They worked together. I watched them from a distance and, sometimes, from very nearby. They took breaks together. I often took breaks at the same time. Two of the four were of no importance and I shant mention their names. A third, Miss Lister, is important as a comparison to the fourth. I shall introduce and describe Miss Lister for that reason, then she too can be forgotten. It will be Miss Adler alone, the fourth nurse, the mouthpiece of the group, who ultimately matters.

For the record, neither Lister nor Adler were their genuine names. I have changed both; not for their protection, but for mine.

Miss Lister was impeccable in her soft blue uniform, with its wide white cuffs and collar, her frilled white *mob* cap, and stark white bib apron always expertly donned and spotless; her scissors, keys, thermometer holder, and pocket watch dangled beautifully from the ornate, yet delicate, chatelaine on her wide belt. As she went about her work, her hand drifted instinctively to hold the chains and prevent the instruments' *clacking*. When she took a seat, she lifted and laid them noiselessly on the table beside her. She was compassionate in her care-giving, ladylike and moral in her manner, careful in her diction, and demure in her composure. With those remarks, I finish with the fine Miss Lister.

Miss Adler, in comparison, was an always late, always rumpled, always yakking, brass band of a female who treated her patients because that was the work, lived for her breaks, and spread rumor and gossip as if doling out manna. She shook her chatelaine bag as if it were a tambourine. She took no notice whatever of her faulty diction, her haphazard method, or her slovenly manner. She was as immoral as a whore on the street. Yet she had one saving grace; she did not imbibe alcohol.

I fully expected immorality from women, save for the rare estimable creatures I have chanced upon (Mrs Griggs and Miss Lister, in example). What I could not abide was dousing immorality in booze then selling the results as a mattress for fornication. No, Miss Adler, as difficult as it was to remain long in her company, was saved by her sobriety.

Soon after the George Yard affair, I discovered Miss Adler had a genuine and, ultimately, important use to me. The addled young nurse steadily courted a constable from the Metropolitan police.

Mind, that was fairly routine. Around London Hospital, one needed only open one's eyes to discover that many coppers copulated with many nurses in and out of sanctified relationships. It came with the work, apparently. Miss Adler's bobbie boyfriend was called Archie; that was all I knew of him. Beyond that, it was none of my business and, more to the point, of absolutely no interest until...

That first evening, Thursday, it was, 9 August, when my interest in Miss Adler's relationship was forever altered. That night, while taking tea and minding my business in the break room, whether by accident or providence, I overheard a block of tittle-tattle that not only amused me greatly but forever changed my perspective on the trysts between caregivers and law enforcement.

Stuffing their faces (with the exception of Miss Lister, obviously) and gossiping as usual, one of the coterie began by repeating as fact a newspaper's claim that the police suspected a soldier of having committed the George Yard murder. The women tittered and bandied that about. Then Miss Adler quieted the lot by assuring them, "You don't know the story by half."

The other nurses were all ears after that. I confess, so was I.

Miss Adler, being a peeler's girl, had heard all about it from Archie and had inside knowledge that few, certainly not the newspapers, possessed. As Archie told it...

The George Yard victim spent the Bank Holiday, Monday, 6 August, doing whatever street women did, in the company of another of her ilk. Following their day of debauchery (I'm paraphrasing both Archie and Miss Adler, I'm sure), the women wound up drunk, in a public house, swapping gin-inspired witticisms with a couple of red-coated soldiers of the Grenadier Guard. The women left the pub with their pickups at a quarter of midnight.

Soon thereafter, the second whore vanished from the story. Miss Adler may have said why, how or when; I don't recall or care. Both soldiers wound up alone with the soon-to-be-murdered woman outside of George Yard. An illicit deal was, no doubt, soon struck. The woman and one of the soldiers went into the Yard, leaving the other standing alone in Wentworth Street.

Yes, I thought, sipping my tea at a nearby break room table. I remembered it in detail; the moment when the pair arrived in George Yard, the woman and the soldier, with no idea in the world I was there in the shadows of the staircase only a few feet away. While I (I'd just learned) was equally ignorant of the presence of a second soldier, their comrade, waiting in the street only a few yards away.

But there was more, much more, to come.

"Well," Miss Adler went on, "one of the constables patrolling nearby on the night of the murder was a fellow named Tom Barrett; my Archie knows him. About two o'clock that morning, Tom sees this soldier, a private of the Grenadier Guards, loitering in Wentworth Street. So Tom stops and asks what he's doing there. Archie says, the soldier says, he's waiting for his chum who's gone with a girl, and he points into George's Yard."

Eavesdropping as I was, I didn't dare show my surprise (or alarm), but can admit it now. Suddenly a bit breathless, I listened as Miss Adler told it the way her fellow had told her. On that night, outside of my dark little hiding spot, outside of my hearing, a few steps outside of George Yard, a police constable on his rounds had accosted the second soldier loitering (after his mate under my watchful eye). A crowd was forming! I slowed my eating and pricked my ears.

Well, Miss Adler's Archie said, this PC Barrett was either unconvinced or unimpressed with the loitering soldier's explanation, and rousted him; ordered him to take himself down the street and away. The soldier did, abandoning his mate.

"Then what happened?" one of Miss Adler's table mates asked.

"That's the sorrow," the gossiping nurse replied. "Archie says, Tom thought no more of it. Drunk and loitering soldiers could be found at that hour on any street in Whitechapel. He went on about his patrol up Wentworth Street. If he'd gone into the Yard, he might well have caught that second soldier..."

"Murdering her?" demanded one of the coterie.

"If it was the second soldier," cautioned Miss Lister. "If there was a second soldier."

"Course. If there was a second soldier," agreed Miss Adler. "Archie says, he thinks there was. And he thinks Tom might have caught him in the act of killing the girl."

I realized I'd been holding my breath. I took in air, quietly, as I considered all I'd heard. A copper, only yards away, minutes before I killed the girl. It was frightening. It was thrilling. As I was safe at work and picking at my meal, it was damned amusing. I thought I might burst out laughing. But I held it in check as I realized Miss Adler had more to tell; funnier yet. I had more listening to do.

The investigator on the case, Inspector Reid (so Mr Frogg had said), following up the possibility of a murdering soldier, took Barrett to the Tower of London the day of the murder to be shown several prisoners confined in the guardroom. The constable failed to identify his man among them.

Owing to that failure, an *identity parade* was arranged for the following morning. Returning to the Tower, Barrett was sequestered by the sergeant's mess while the garrison's sergeant-major mustered every Grenadier Guard absent or on leave at the time of the murder. Once the soldiers were standing rank, Inspector Reid warned Barrett, "Be careful. Many eyes are watching you and a great deal depends on your picking out the right man."

Barrett walked the line staring down each soldier. Near the centre of the rank the constable stopped and touched the shoulder of a private; the man he believed he'd seen in Wentworth Street. Barrett started back, but Reid met him halfway. "I've picked the fellow," the constable said.

"I want you to be certain," the inspector insisted. "Go back and have another look."

Barrett passed down the line and picked again; a different man than he'd first selected.

"How did you come to pick out two men?" Reid asked.

"The man I saw in George Yard had no medals," Barrett sheepishly replied. "The first man I picked out had."

The garrison was dismissed and the selected soldiers escorted to the orderly-room. There, Barrett insisted he'd made a mistake in picking the first; the soldier with medals. That fellow was dismissed. The second soldier (Archie called him 'Leary') denied being anywhere near George Yard and gave a detailed account of his movements the night of the murder. He'd gone on leave, he said, with a private named Law that Bank Holiday night. I could repeat the details of their drinking and pissing, but why would I? Point was Private Law corroborated Leary's account through 6:00 am. Reid's case against the soldiers collapsed and the identity parade was filed at Scotland Yard under *C* for *cock-up*.

It had been a delight to learn I'd caused such excitement amongst the police and, *bless me*, the Guard. It had been one of the more interesting breaks I'd ever taken at hospital.

As it ended and we went back to work, it occurred to me that knowing what the police knew and learning what they were doing, and how their investigations were progressing, might be nice indeed. It might even ease my mind over worries of the unknown, as if were. A pipeline to, dare I hope, inside the Metropolitan Police? Though I kept it to myself, I'll confess now the nurse's relationship with her bobbie suddenly became of the greatest interest to me.

From that night on, I made every effort to be kind and helpful to Nurse Adler.

Nine
My Victim Identified

Late the following morning, after carrying up my coffee, Mrs Griggs read to me from her papers (from the previous evening) of the Coroner's Inquest into the death of the George Yard murder victim. George Collier, Deputy Coroner for the South-Eastern Division of Middlesex, presiding (in place of the vacationing coroner, Wynne Baxter; on holiday in Scandinavia), convened the meeting at the Working Lads' Institute in Whitechapel Road. Detective Inspector Reid, 'aitch Division, appeared on behalf of the CID. A lot of *blah, blah, blah* followed, through which I tried to look interested for the sake of my good landlady. I'll mention a few bits.

Of the witnesses, Elizabeth Mahoney, who lived with her husband at No 47 George Yard (the respectable woman I spied unawares), assisted the jury in establishing *Time of death* by what she had not seen; neither body nor murderer at 1:50 am when she returned with provisions from a chandler's shop in Thrawl Street. Alfred Crow, a cab-driver lodged in No 35, confessed to stepping around a body (he should have said *the* body) on the stoop at 3:30. Vagrants on the doorstep, he explained, were nothing new. John Reeves, a waterside labourer living in No 37, rediscovered the corpse at 4:45 and, rather than ignore it, notified the authorities. Peeler Barrett, of the soldier cock-up, also testified (probably with a red face).

Mrs Griggs, in reading, mentioned something about an off-handed comparison having been made to Emma Smith. By whom (acting coroner, jurist, witness, or reporter?), I didn't know. I didn't want to know. I didn't like thinking about Emma Smith.

Dr Killeen, who'd examined the corpse, saw no evidence of a struggle or sexual intercourse. He confirmed death occurred due to hemorrhage and loss of blood. My landlady was breathless, appalled. Poor thing. "They don't even know the victim's name!"

Funny, until that instant, the question of the woman's name had never even occurred to me. I had comfortably fallen into thinking of her as 'the soldier's whore'.

Unfortunates, it seemed, had a habit of using aliases on the streets. The corpse had, so far, been identified by three separate witnesses (all of the lower or working classes), each by a different name. One called her Emma. Another, Martha Turner. Another, Martha Tabram. Her true identity, the paper reported, remained a mystery. Collier adjourned the inquiry until Thursday, 23 August, to allow the police time to make a positive identification and to gather further evidence.

If the men of the Metropolitan Police found any further evidence, I had yet to hear of it. Nearly a week passed without any news at all. Nothing in the papers. Nothing from the streets. Outside of several abysmal recipes and a report on the most recent medical problems of her hypochondriac mother, nothing from the talkative Miss Adler in regards to police activities. Nothing until the afternoon of 14 August, when...

"They'll get him now!"

That was the shout that issued from my excited landlady. Of course, it brought me from my room. Anything to make that upright woman act so undignified would have brought me out. I looked down the second floor stairs, to see Mrs Griggs looking up from below. Yes, she was holding a newspaper. "I'm sorry, Mrs Griggs?"

"I said, They'll get him now. The murderer! It says here..."

She opened her newspaper and, from below, projecting in her most serious Dress Reformist's voice, proclaimed the details.

"Seventy locals, working men and students, recently met at Tonybee Hall. They appointed a committee of twelve, the St Jude's

Vigilance Committee, to organize patrols. They will, between the hours of eleven at night and one in the morning, take turns to assist the police in watching certain *at risk* streets throughout Whitechapel. They will meet once a week to report their activities and reassess their security measures." She lowered the paper, staring up for my reaction.

"That's... interesting news," was the best I could manage. A rant, I imagined, concerning Nosy Parker vigilantes getting in my way might have been met with suspicion. As it turned out, my response was of no consequence.

Mrs Griggs had turned the page and moved on. "She's been identified!"

"I'm sorry?"

"The poor murder victim. She's been identified." With that, Mrs Griggs was reading again. "After reading of the victim, referred to in a 13 August news report by three names, Emma, Martha Tabram, and Martha Turner, Henry Tabram, a foreman packer at a furniture warehouse, visited the mortuary on 14 August..." *Blah, blah, blah.* She read on.

The point, which both the article and Mrs Griggs took too long to reach, was that this furniture packer packed himself down to the shed that passed for a morgue in Whitechapel. There, he formally identified the corpse of the George Yard victim as having once contained the essence of his wife, Martha Tabram, age 39 (from whom he'd been separated for thirteen years).

"Sad," Mrs Griggs editorialized.

"Oh, eh, yes," I agreed.

"You know," Mrs Griggs went on, "the East London Observer, I believe it was, featured a full two columns. They called George Yard a murder as unique and mysterious as any in memory."

"Did they?" I allowed my wonder to show, while doing my best to suppress my pride.

Mrs Griggs folded her paper and returned to her sitting room.

I returned to my rooms, beaming. That's why I liked my landlady; one of the very few women in whose wake I was able to experience a feeling of calm. Despite having delivered bad news regarding the busybody street vigilantes, she'd found a way to cheer me by complimenting my work.

Ten
Ye Olde Shoe Shoppe

As I said, outside of work, I stayed in my rooms. The only exceptions were trips to the backyard (to the well hand pump) for water for Mrs Griggs. Hauling water for my landlady, I had to pass through the late Mr Griggs' shoe shop; abandoned at his death, but relatively untouched by time, on the ground floor of my lodging house.

I should say protected rather than abandoned. Mrs Griggs would allow nothing of her late husband's to be disturbed. More, she frequently added to it. The lady was a compulsive pack rat. As the woman trusted me, over the years I had become – for want of a better title – the curator of the old shoe shoppe. I swept and dusted. I watched over her cherished relics and stored and tended the new junk the woman brought in. I carried requested items upstairs and, following a tearful reminiscence, dried the items off and returned them to the pile. In time, as dear as the old shop was to her, Mrs Griggs no longer visited. With me toting her memories up and down for her, she no longer needed to. Owing to my calculated enabling, the shop had become nothing more than the *vaults* Mrs Griggs passed in trips between the street and her living space. In the same time, it became my own personal playground.

The late Mr Griggs was a shoemaker, obviously. He'd practiced his profession, as I understood it, all of his life; long before the industry had become an industry and gone from little shops on East End side streets to large automated factories. Mr Griggs had been a shoemaker in his own shoe shop.

In the glass-fronted (but shuttered), show room of the former store, upon the three interior walls still hung a fine selection of men's work boots and men's and women's shoes, in as many styles and colours as the mind could conceive, all unclaimed or unsold at the time of his passing. Row upon row, to the west, north, and east, surrounding his antique low-to-the-floor shoemaker's table and bench, where he did the fine finishing work that impressed the customers who once wandered in off the street to the south. Sorry, it would be imprudent to say which street.

In the back room were the other pieces of equipment, less artistically impressive, but vital to the work (and the saving of work); the stitching machines, the stretching machine, the polishers and grinders. And more shoes and boots, an uncounted collection, stacked, hanging, and in boxes. Shelves of boxes of materials; leather, wood, cork, nails, glue, threads of all sizes and colours. A closet bursting with close and the gathering's of Mrs Griggs. Another work bench, more old than antique, for serious late night work as opposed to show, several mobile floor length mirrors, a normal height work table, and a well-worn writing desk with chair.

Against the back side wall, stood a massive cabinet housing a world of assorted accoutrement, including a fine selection of shoemaker's tools, and a collection of sturdy knives; several of which, outside of Mrs Griggs' knowledge, I'd ground down, keenly sharpened, oiled and made ready to be put to use – in the event I could think of a good use. Perhaps I could.

I got to the break room late on 15 August, a busy Wednesday night. I quietly and unobtrusively got my tea (the cakes looked awful) and took a seat at table alone. I went unnoticed, as usual, by Miss Adler and her coterie of nurses at their tea and gossip nearby.

I was tired and did not feel like eavesdropping. Particularly as they appeared to, again, be going on about the identity parade fiasco involving the Grenadier Guards. I did hear a word or two. Enough to discover they were not talking about the confused PC who'd picked two soldiers to match the one he'd seen and spoken with the morning of the George Yard murder.

They were talking of a new identity parade, conducted for a witness of whom I was unaware. It goes without saying I slowed my tea sipping, secured two (suddenly appetizing) cakes, and returned to my chair with a determination to chew slowly and listen intently. Thus situated, I bent my ear.

The witness appeared out of the blue at Commercial Street Police Station, nearly a week gone now, claiming to be the woman in company of the George Yard whore on Bank Holiday night. Mary Ann Connelly was her name but, as none of those sluts used their names, the street denizens knew her as 'Pearly Poll'. Poll knew the victim as Emma; they'd been *friends* for several months.

According to her, on that fateful night, she and Emma had pub crawled (with two soldiers; a corporal and a private) through Whitechapel from ten until nearly midnight. The foursome broke up at 11:45, when Poll veered off to Angel Alley with her corporal. Emma and her private went up George Yard. I had to bite my tongue, of course. I should not have been eavesdropping, let alone reacting to what I heard, but Poll's story (as leaked by Archie, and retold by chatty Miss Adler) was rubbish. She'd either been too drunk to remember the details, was making it up, or simply wasn't half-a-liar. Whichever, it was rubbish. Who, other than Yours Truly, knew the drunk whore had come up George Yard with her soldier at just after two in the morning? I'd heard the church bells. The soldier ran out on her and it was damned near 2:30 when I killed his stranded date.

But that was merely what had happened.

What Miss Adler said, that Poll the whore said, happened was, "About forty minutes later, once she'd finished her business in Angel Alley, Poll and her corporal bid each other adieu at the corner of George Yard. Poll set off toward Whitechapel while her soldier walked Aldgate way."

Again, crap. Where she went, nobody knew. But the soldier stayed at Wentworth and George Yard, as that's where peeler Barrett accosted him and chased him off – while I was busy. Point was, Scotland Yard had finally interviewed a woman for whom they'd been searching for a week; a possible key to a murdering soldier.

It was then Miss Adler's chatter truly sparked my interest (and struck a note of humor). On Monday past, at 11:00 in the morning, Inspector Reid – with Pearly Poll in tow – returned to the Tower of London where the previous identity parade cock-up had occurred.

Behind the Tower, unseen by the plentiful tourists, every non-commissioned officer and private on leave at the time of the outrage was paraded out for Poll to ogle. "Can you see either of the men you saw with the woman now dead?" Inspector Reid asked.

Hands on hips, Poll looked the men over, then shook her head.

Hardly satisfied, Reid asked again, "Can you identify anyone?"

With all the class inherent of her class, Poll replied, "He ain't here."

The guards were dismissed. "Then, Archie says," Miss Adler said, "Poll told Reid and the Guards' officers the soldiers she and the murdered woman picked up Bank Holiday night had similar uniforms but had white bands round their caps. The Commander of the Grenadier Guards replied those were not his men at all. That it sounded like the uniform of the Coldstream Guards."

"They had the wrong soldiers all along?"

"Archie says Tom Barrett says, No. But Pearly Poll..."

"She said..."

"Yes. They were from a different regiment. So this morning, Archie says, at Wellington Barracks, in Birdcage Walk, they held another parade of the corporals and privates there who were absent at time of the murder."

"And?"

"And, Archie says, Poll identified two men, one as the corporal she took to Angel Alley and the other as a private that her friend took to George Yard."

"And?"

"And, Archie says, the corporal she picked was really a private called George. He had three badges for *good conduct* and an alibi for the night of the murder. The second man, the private that went with her friend, really was a private. Archie says his name was Skipper." The nurses groaned in unison. "Yes!" Miss Adler agreed. "And Skipper had an alibi too."

"How could she have been so wrong?"

"Inspector Reid doesn't think she was. He thinks she deliberately identified the wrong soldiers. Out of pique, Archie says, because of earlier troubles she'd had with the police."

I owed a debt to Miss Adler and her gossiping Archie. For myself, I enjoyed that break immensely. Two garrisons of guards, three identity parades, three cock-ups. And the men of the Met were still in search of a murdering soldier.

Three days later, Saturday, 18 August, Mrs Griggs rapped three times with excitement and entered my room waving the *Illustrated Police News* as if it were a flag and she leading a charge into battle. It was unlike her to show such heightened emotion; and fantastic that particular lurid newspaper should even be in the house. Times were changing! But I could see the editors had done their best to stimulate that excitement in their unsuspecting readers. Even the upright Mrs Griggs had fallen prey.

Oh! To have my work so recognized!

The front page of the rag featured six graphic drawings of what the artists imagined both victim and murderer looked like. It had to be imagination, the plod inspectors did not allow reporters into their crime scenes. As much fun as the drawings were, they were inaccurate. Who knew that besides me? I'd seen the victim in her own blood (and the murderer in the mirror). ha ha. While I took in the images, my landlady read aloud to me the new gory update.

"The wound over the heart was alone sufficient to kill and death must have occurred as soon as that was inflicted. Unless the perpetrator was a madman, or suffering to an unusual extent from drink delirium, no tangible explanation can be given of the reason for inflicting the other thirty-eight injuries, some of which almost seem as if they were due to thrusts and cuts from a penknife."

"My heavens, Mr __," the blushing Mrs Griggs exclaimed. "He stabbed the poor woman thirty-nine times. My heavens!"

I nodded in silent understanding. But I confess, deep in my dark place, I smiled. Thirty-nine delicious stabs. The soldier's whore had earned each and every one.

Five days later, I visited Mr Frogg's newsstand again. I hadn't intended it; eager to get off the streets, I was merely headed home from work. But I admit to an ego and Tad's new cries of "Foul murder in Whitechapel!" drew me in. And confused me.

Was another killer about? It turned out, such was not the case, the boy was still championing my work from George Yard.

The story he and his dear old dad were selling was an update on that day's reopening of the Coroner's Inquest into my stabbing of the soldier's whore, now officially identified as Martha Tabram. Among the witnesses were Henry Turner, the carpenter with whom the slag had lived for twelve years. And her real husband, Henry Tabram, from whom she'd been separated but never divorced. Others, including the infamous Pearly Poll, testified but who gave a damn? It had all been said before.

One piece of fresh meat was tossed to the public – but it was old news to me. Deputy Coroner Collier, still sitting for the vacationing Baxter, let it out that two different weapons had been used on the victim. Why, yes, they had... indeed. And skillfully I might add.

The *Daily Telegraph* printed the Deputy Coroner's summation in its entirety, including his breathless opinion the murder was 'one of the most brutal crimes that had occurred for years... almost beyond belief'. Then, done and dusted, Collier charged his jury. They, in turn, returned his requested verdict: 'Wilful murder against some person or persons unknown'.

Nearly three weeks had elapsed since I'd cleaned that whore up. The verdict, rather than closing the book, merely made me wistful. I finished my walk home on edge. I wanted to go back to work again. Not at hospital; my real work, my life's calling.

I arrived back at my lodgings to find Mrs Griggs out of the house (no doubt attending to her duties as the leader of the Dress Reformists). Rather than go upstairs to my rooms (and this was the exception I mentioned earlier), I took that quiet opportunity to visit the back room of Mr Griggs' shop. I took down a carefully stored box from a shelf of many shoe boxes. I carried it to the old desk, set it down gently, and slowly opened the lid – as if lifting the mercy seat to unseal the Ark of the Covenant. Wordlessly, reverently, I stared at the Holy of Holies within. Despite being unworthy, I reached in and, one at a time, lifted them out into the gaslight – my knives. The shining eight inch amputation blade (that had done the soldier's whore). The penknife (that had decorated her up). And a sturdy shoemaker's knife I'd selected and specially fashioned for the vital work ahead.

I sat. I held the three cold blades to my chest. I closed my eyes and dreamed of future. It was delicious – and just for me.

Yes. I longed to return to work.

Eleven
Hellfire and Whitechapel Road

If history were to repeat itself, and I knew it would, the newspapers would soon be screaming of another 'Horrible murder!' That I could guarantee. Humorously, I imagined, following that eventual outrage, the idiotic reporters would wonder aloud in print 'How did the Whitechapel murderer come to target this poor girl?'

"Fools," I could reply before it happened, "I spied her out the window."

Let me tell the whole of it.

It started simply enough. At just gone 10:00 pm, Thursday, 30 August, as I toiled away in a south ward of London Hospital, I chanced to look outside and saw the night sky aglow in a strange shifting orange light. As I was alone and had the time, I ceased my activities and went to the window. It was then I saw it plainly, to the south and the east, where the River Thames did its massive meander round the Isle of Dogs... the world was on fire! Brilliant reds. Brilliant oranges. Massive tongues of blue (yes, blue) and yellow flames!

I would learn later it was the London docks, the warehouses of the South Quay ablaze, but that night it didn't matter. I didn't see what it was, I saw what it meant. I saw a city in flames and well understood its meaning... for me. Hell had opened its portals wide. The infernal regions hungered for a new arrival. I was being called upon to provide her.

I leaned heavily on the window frame, needing the full structure of the great hospital to support me against the overwhelming swoon. I closed my eyes against the dizziness, swallowed by the magnitude of the job I was again being called to perform. In my first outing, I had been the least of amateurs, timid and frightened. I had accomplished my ordained task but had failed to experience all that came with it; failed to relish its pleasures, to understand its importance, failed to understand *my* new importance in the scheme of things. I was being given a second chance. I was being called… by the fire.

What occurred an hour later was inevitable. Back at work (and biding my time) in a ward on the hospital's north side, I was led again to a window and, looking out, saw a prostitute walking south along Whitechapel Road. No, not a prostitute; *the* prostitute. The dirty drunken whore for which the fire was calling.

Don't think I jumped to conclusions. I did not. Getting it right was all that mattered to me. I took my time; it was a slow night and I had the time. I made sure. It was easy to distinguish a whore *on the game*. Like all criminals they left clues. One needed only to observe, the teetering strut, the repeated passes over the same ground, the bleary eye on every male passerby.

I watched for some time. I've mentioned my ability to go unseen in the streets. I had the same powers at work and, when I wished, was good at not being found out. So, unmolested by empty duties or the random dictates of Mrs Price (our Commander-like matron nurse), for some little time I watched unseen from above.

The whore strolled up and down the thoroughfare shamelessly strutting and displaying her dubious wares. She repeatedly poked and patted at her covering, a flash black bonnet atop her bean that, by the way she carried on, you'd swear she thought was a crown and she Victoria Regina. Horrible! Horrible! Bad enough the streets teemed with whores filled with evil, but to be filled with pride as well went beyond the pale. I had always been a supporter of the monarchy, but I felt nothing but a bubbling hate for this 'Queen of Tarts'.

I've wandered again...

Point was, by her long and steady parading, she showed herself for the drunken slag she was. Not merely lost, confused, or aimless, the teetering Queen of Tarts walked her beat, tapping her crown, looking to sell her sex and her soul to the first king, prince, or ponce willing to part with his pennies. I couldn't wait for my day's employment to reach its end – that I might go to work and oblige her.

I'm sad to say that, round one-ish on that Friday morning, 31 August, when I caught up the trifles, finished my duties, and returned to my overlook window, I found the street empty of the one thing I wanted to see there. The Queen of Tarts had gone. She might easily have dropped into one of the endless pubs in the district, of course. Or slipped off into the shadows with some... To do the other. I didn't know. All I knew was, she no longer walked the road.

I felt a flash of panic, an accusation heard only in my head that I'd missed my opportunity. But my sanity soon returned; I quickly got hold of those ridiculous thoughts. I'd had my heart set on her for a reason. She'd been ordained. The fires of hell had named her and god had led me to her. I could not, would not, go back to my lodgings without fulfilling – our destinies.

She was a whore, wasn't she? That was her beat, wasn't it? She'd be back. She would be back. All I needed to do was to wait and, upon her return, claim her.

There was no question as to where to wait. I had my very own infinitely quiet chamber of solitude within the walls of the hospital. There I could wait without fear of being found out. For who went there in the middle of the night? Even if I was found, I would not be found out. A well-respected orderly, I needed only keep something in my hands, a basin, a cleaning rag, anything really, to be anywhere in the building without so much as an odd eye cast my direction. There was always something I could appear to be doing, always something needed sorting, in my quiet place. So I slipped quietly downstairs into the mortuary.

Three others were there, in the cold morgue, when I lit an oil lamp; an old bloke, a crone, and a young thing (I didn't know which sex). The old ones had been left uncovered. The young thing, covered over with a sheet, I made out by its size. I didn't investigate further, I didn't care what lay beneath it. Fact was I took the time to cover the old ones myself. I said, I wanted solitude.

Finally alone, undisturbed, I could contemplate what had been and what soon (I had to trust) would be. I sat in the corner and waited. Several times during my vigil, I checked the lower hall, found it empty, and slipped outside to gaze up and down the road. Each time I dealt with the disappointment, fought off thoughts of hopelessness, and returned to hiding. She would return.

Providence was kind to the faithful. My perseverance paid off. Just after 2:30 in the morning, I slipped quietly out to check again and... glory! The Queen of Tarts had reappeared; stupid with drink, and still patting her posh bonnet crown, she was wobbling her way back up the road.

Mrs Griggs had taken great pains to keep me up to date on the news of the George Yard murder investigation, such as it was; needles of fact hidden in a haystack of rumor. One fact stood out to me at the moment I spied the return of the whore in Whitechapel Road. It was this... The Coroner's Inquest into the death of Martha Tabram had concluded on 23 August with the jury proclaiming: 'Murder by Person or Persons Unknown'.

I thought of that verdict now. And considered it a challenge.

I would meet that challenge. Soon, I determined, the authorities, the people of the East End, all of London, were going to know Yours Truly!

The fire burning in the south had tempered me even as it devoured the London docks. I'd accepted my place in, my importance to, society. Keenly aware of my power, I moved away from the hospital and toward the filthy street with a light heart and a determined steady hand.

Before me walked the proof. I didn't need to hunt. The Queen of Tarts, a royal prize, had been sent to me. She paraded, twirling her skirts, touching her bonnet, begging me (though she couldn't see me and didn't know I was there) to set her right. The previous day's drudgery, the do-gooding, had ended. A new day was at hand. The time had come to get on with the important and delightful real work for which I had been destined. I started across the Whitechapel Road.

I reached the north side of the wide street and made myself visible.

She saw me and her face lit up. In her head, I could see her already counting her doss money. I could see too, as she passed beneath a gas lamp, I'd been correct; her bonnet was new, black straw trimmed in black velvet. She touched her topper, coming my way.

I took her in as best I could in the light. She wore a reddish-brown ulster, loose and worn, with seven large brass buttons. The heavy coat looked especially tired in comparison to the brown linsey frock beneath (looking as new as her bonnet). Her shape and the cool morning air suggested other layers of clothing at which I might only guess. All funneled down to a clomping pair of men's side-spring boots. She stood no more than five feet two, with dark-brown hair that, even in the poor light (peeking from beneath her crown), could be seen to be turning grey. She had a dark complexion and, I saw then, brown eyes as well. The whore reached me, raised a hand to touch my chest and, without pretense, asked, "Want the business?"

The last came out a slurred 'bish-ness' and, though she was not staggering drunk, I could smell alcohol on her breath. She had a small scar on her forehead and was missing an upper front tooth, yet she could not be described as haggard. She was probably middle aged but, preserved well-enough and adorned in that stupid bonnet, managed to look younger. I nodded in agreement to her question.

Yes, I did indeed want the bish-ness. In return, I thought, I would give her the business as well.

Twelve
Queen of Tarts

Chirping and chattering, leaning occasionally on my arm and, more than once, needing to be steadied herself, the Queen of Tarts led me from Whitechapel Road, through Woods' building, a thin underpass and lane the locals called Piss Alley. Wasn't that appropriate? Didn't that prove the excellence of my selection? Drunk on her feet, leading me through Piss Alley to a paid-for coupling; the filthy whore. We emerged into Winthrop Street, then circled slightly west and around the board school building into a street called Buck's Row.

Buck's Row ran from Baker's Row on the west to Brady Street on the east. As I said, running parallel on the south, and meeting it half-way along its length, was Winthrop. Going east down Buck's Row from the junction of Winthrop, on the south side of the street, was the board school, Brown's Stable Yard, and a long row of tenement houses. On the north side, across the street from the stable were the Essex Wharves. East of the wharves was Browne & Eagle's Wool Warehouse and Schnieder's Cap Factory. Beyond the factory stood a low brick wall that continued east to Brady Street. Buck's Row, down its length, featured only three lamps; one on the north side (west end of the wharves); a second hung from the first floor of the residential cottages about a third of the way up; and a third lamp stood at the far east end, on the northwest corner of Buck's Row and Brady. Three isolated pools of amber light in the otherwise bleak darkness.

Two fun facts; one, Buck's Row was frequented by prostitutes; two, the street sat about one-half mile from George Yard, where just over three weeks before I'd had a date with, and done a job on, a beer besotted member of that ancient profession.

It was in places like these, settings of pitch black night and long shadows thrown by grossly limited gas-light, these women plied their trade. They were, all of them, too filthy to be embarrassed in public, too drunk and oblivious to care about the risks in private. I had to wonder if, for some of them, that risk made it all more interesting? What I had planned carried risk as well; and I can absolutely guarantee that made my endeavor more interesting. Besides, as I've mentioned, as I've confessed, I had an urge I needed to fulfill.

We strolled for a moment up Buck's Row like a couple of lovers taking the night air. (How sickening was that?) But I didn't let it go on long. I stopped her before we reached the row of residential cottages on our side of the street, outside the closed gates of the stable yard entrance, across the street and only a few steps past the first street light. There may well have been plenty of people about, sipping tea behind the many doors or snoring behind the darkened windows that faced us, but the street was empty – save for me and my date. There was risk, no doubt. But, like I said, that made it all more interesting.

I raised a hand to cup her chin, my fingers both sides of her jaw, and I smiled; the charming client, lover for a few pennies. She giggled. I smelled the booze on her breath. Disgusting! I hated her for it!

Quickly, and without warning, I pinched my fingers, scissoring her face. She screwed up her lips as if to yowl. But that wasn't going to happen. With my free hand, I grabbed her by the throat before she had a chance to make a sound. I clamped on with the other. My hands are strong, my grip powered by fierce intention. She didn't get out a gasp. The Queen's appointed hour had arrived. She grabbed at my arms, scratched at my wrists and hands. She struck me uselessly and tried to kick me, to no avail. Small, soft, and weak, she hadn't the least chance in the world.

I shook her as I choked her. Her brand new bonnet came loose, flipped off, and landed on the filthy street. *Awww!* No more crown!

The Queen is dead, long live the whore!

Her mouth fell open as she fought for breath. I saw then she was missing several more teeth in the lower jaw of her left side, and I hated her for that too. Now, there, she looked the mirror image of my drunken whoring mother and I hated everything about her. Her eyes, already wide with fright, soon bulged with terror – and the realization she was going to die. Several minutes I held her, thus clamped, until she slipped into unconsciousness.

I lowered her onto her back on the ground, lengthwise along the footway, with her head to my left, her arms at her sides, and the fingers of her left hand just touching the stable gate. The muscles of my own arms were shaking now from the pressure I'd had to apply.

I couldn't see clearly in the gloom, but I saw enough to get to work. Her eyes were wide open, staring sightlessly at the sky, but I didn't let that bother me or slow me down. I drew my shoemaker's knife. I slashed her throat from left to right, twice; the first a short one to get the feel, the second a ferociously deep and long swipe, ear to ear, through the left artery, the windpipe, and all the way down to her spine. As she was already dead there was no delicious spurt, but don't think there wasn't some fun all the same. The jagged gash in her throat opened and there came a nice red gush.

This time there was no hesitation. I moved down the length of the disease-ridden bitch and raised her skirts to her chest, baring her stomach. Her legs lay stretched out, a little apart, and I couldn't help but laugh at her cloddish boots. I reached across to her left side, dug into the meat and fat with my knife, and cut a long jagged wound through the gut. That went so well, I gave her a second slash with relish. Then I added another three or four like-cuts, on the near side running down, so she opened up wide. I saw the snakes of her intestines in their slimy red nest. I'd seen others, before, at hospital obviously, but these were mine. This was my message. The world, when they saw this, would know without question the rubbish had been taken to the bin.

Then something came over me. I couldn't resist. I didn't want to resist. Slowly, tremulously, I reached out and inserted one outstretched finger into her open abdomen. I touched her intestines. Then I pulled hurriedly away. I took a breath, steadied myself (my breathing was starting to race). I reached in again. I touched the intestines, allowing my finger to linger this time. I applied the slightest pressure, panting now despite my desire for self-control. It felt better than I'd hoped it might. Soft. Warm. Giving. Just as I had always imagined the wet sex of a respectable woman might feel.

Ohhhh.

But by then 3:30 must have come and gone. I had to be gone as well. The people of the streets would soon be up and about. Not to mention the coppers, on foot patrol, would eventually make their way past regardless of where their beats took them. I forced myself to remove my finger from the slag's warm and steaming insides.

Something, I don't know what, made me look up the street. It was well I did. Someone was coming!

Though I could not make him out in the poor light, I could see a man's silhouette... No, two men, one well in front of the other, both backlit by the lamp at the corner. They were nearer to Brady Street than to me, and nearly the full block away, but both were headed this way.

I left the whore where I'd killed her, along the footway outside the stable gate, and retreated into the shadows. Hugging the wall of the board school, staying as far from the north light at the corner of the wharf as I was able, I slipped down the wall to the west (where Buck's Row opened out wide) and around the corner of the school.

Then the jolly night got, *oh,* that much jollier.

"Come and look over here!" I heard one fellow excitedly shout to the other.

What a delight! Despite the darkness, I saw it in my head. On his way down Buck's Row, on the way to his daily toil and despair, the first bloke had missed seeing me but had spotted my leavings.

He thought he knew what it was but, in the dark, couldn't be sure. He was even less sure he wanted to step up and take a closer look. Not alone. So he called out his find to the man behind him (thank god for the man behind), further up the street, deeper in the dark, coming his way.

I stood pressed against the wall on the west end of the school, listening and keeping my presence to myself. I held my breath and, difficult as it was, held in my delighted laughter. For wasn't it a lark that I was close enough to step out, shout, and scare the living hell out of the finder of my fun? And, like the couple in George Yard, he had no idea I was there.

But now I had a conundrum. Listening was fun, listening was delightful, but I wanted to see. I couldn't help myself. Despite the terrible, ridiculous, risks involved, the nearness of the discoverers who outnumbered me, the nearness of the flickering street light with the chance it offered to show me off, still I had to look. I slipped one eye beyond the edge of the school building and took a peek.

There he was, the first on the scene to see my work. He was an old bloke, a laborer it appeared, standing in the street looking nervously back and forth between the fast-approaching second fellow and the pile of diseased remains before him. He'd already called out once. Now, with a notable rise in the pitch of his voice, he added to it. "There's a woman lying on the pavement!"

Indeed there was, my good fellow. Indeed there was. Shout it out. Tell the world.

The other joined him. The pair stood together in the middle of Buck's Row gawping like a couple of simpletons. I hadn't imagined this development. Me, still there at the time of the finding? Nothing like it. I stayed a while longer, having a glorious time of it, listening and peeking; for they and the dead whore made for an entertaining trio. I would have loved to stay all morning and watch.

But it wasn't right, was it? Listening in and spying on folks? What would people think of me?

Saucy Jacky

Fighting a new urge to laugh, I slipped quietly down the school wall, crossed briskly to the far south side of wide open Buck's Row, and headed west on cat's feet. I turned the corner onto Court Street then slowed my pace to a gentleman's stroll and became unseen again.

Whitechapel Road lay straight ahead.

Fourteen
Buck's Row Outrage

'*A REVOLTING MURDER*'

I cannot express the shock to my system!

No, not from the banner headline. I'd worked hard for that. It was expected, and deserved.

I cannot express the shock I experienced when Mrs Griggs entered my room, set down the tray supporting my evening meal, and unfurled a copy, her copy, of the 31 August edition of the *Star* newspaper. The *Star*! Of course, I had my earlier edition, covering the George Yard killing, well-hidden away. But a radical newspaper willingly brought into the house by my conservative landlady's own hand; stunning! My work was opening minds. She held the newsprint aloft and, with meaning and the slightest noticeable shake in her rarely shaken voice, said, "Mr __, have you heard?"

I shook off my shock, without comment, and read the splash headline a second time, aloud, "A revolting murder." I pinched my lips, doing my best to look concerned, trying not to laugh, as I considered her question. All I'd heard had been a shrill police whistle or two, distantly (behind me), as I walked home from Buck's Row early that morning. But that, of course, was none of Mrs Griggs' business. Once I'd arrived home, no, I'd slept like a dream. In all honesty, I hadn't heard a thing – and I said so. Then I asked, "There's been another murder?"

"Eat your supper," my good landlady said. "I'll fill you in."

So we proceeded. I devoured her lovely Shepherd's Pie while she disseminated the street rag's version of this newest unimaginable crime. "Another woman found horribly mutilated in Whitechapel," she read with feeling. "Ghastly crimes by a maniac."

Then she regaled me with an unending litany of the comings and goings of all of those involved in any way, shape, or form with the so-far-unidentified whore's life, her movements in the hours preceding her untimely (but well earned) demise, and the discovering and disposition of her worthless carcass. Being the upstanding lodger I was, I listened with a feigned interest that would have convinced the esteemed body of the House of Lords I cared.

It took some sorting in my mind but, if I got her facts in order, the morning unfolded thusly:

The body of the newest victim had been discovered in Buck's Row, at 3:40 that morning by Charles Cross, a carman (for Pickford's for more than twenty years), walking to work down the north side of what he believed to be a deserted street. Nearing the west end of the narrow portion of the street, before it widened beyond the board school, he saw an object lying across the gated entrance to Brown's Stable Yard on the opposite side of the street. In the dark, he thought it a tarpaulin at first but, upon drawing nearer, realized his mistake. It was a woman.

Startled by footsteps, Cross turned to see a figure passing the coal depot on approach from Brady Street; the same path Cross had used. He called to the man, Robert Paul, another carman. Together the two approached the body.

The woman lay on her back, her skirts raised to her stomach. Cross felt her cold and limp hand, thought her dead, and said as much. Paul was unsure. He listened for breath and heard nothing. But, when he touched her breast, thought he felt movement. "I think she's breathing," Paul said. "But very little if she is." He wanted to sit her up, but Cross refused.

Mrs Griggs' newspaper account was sketchy regarding the actions of the two carmen. It merely jumped to them heroically running for a copper. Bollocks! I knew, didn't I? I saw and heard them both. Once Cross refused to move her, and both realized she was merely an unfortunate, Paul excused himself from not fetching an officer, saying, "I am behind time for work." Cross confessed he too was late for work. He pulled the woman's disarrayed skirt down to cover her then, together, the pair set off for their jobs, agreeing to report their find if they saw a constable. They hurried down Buck's Row without looking back – and without seeing me disappear down Court Street.

The remainder of the details I got from Mrs Griggs and later street gossip.

The pair of carmen reached Baker's Row and headed north. At the junction (with Old Montague and Hanbury Streets), they happened upon a patrolling peeler named Mizen (Badge 55 of H Division) and were relieved to report their find. "She looks to me to be either dead or drunk," Cross said, "but for my part I think she is dead." Mizen took off running.

Meanwhile, back in Buck's Row, no sooner had the carmen – and Yours Truly – vacated street than a different policeman, PC John Neil (97 J), patrolling eastward on his regular rounds, discovered the body all over again. Just as the carmen had, Neil walked up on the object in the dark. But the constable had a lantern. He turned it on his find; a woman laying on her back, lengthways along the footway, outside the gate to an old stables. Her eyes were wide open, staring but seeing nothing whatever. Her throat had been cut completely across; the wound was oozing blood.

I was amused to hear that on the ground near her cold left hand, Neil noted a new (if slightly soiled) black bonnet. Instead of understanding the *royal tragedy* upon which he'd stumbled, the peeler was using his brains to juggle the oddest thought; that the woman had killed herself.

From the corner of his eye, the constable saw distant movement. He turned to see another member of his blue club passing by Buck's Row, patrolling Brady Street from the Whitechapel Road. Neil flashed his lantern and shouted. The other officer, PC

John Thain (96 J), barely reached him when Neil shouted, "Here's a woman has cut her throat. Run at once for Dr. Llewellyn."

Thain took off without question for the police surgeon's home in Whitechapel Road.

Neil watched him disappear into the dark, then turned to see a breathless PC Mizen (the carmen's copper) arriving from the opposite direction, on the run from Baker's Row. "Sorry," Neil said, rising to his feet, "but you've more running to do. Get on to Bethnal Green Police Station (the home of J Division). Tell them we need an ambulance and more assistance here."

Mizen peeled his eyes off the woman, nodded to Neil, took a deep breath, then took off like a shot for the end of Buck's Row. The clomp of his running shoes echoed in the dark. Then, a moment later, he reappeared in the amber nimbus of the corner light, turned north and disappeared.

Neil, with time to pass until help arrived, scouted with his lantern. The nine foot gate to the stable yard was closed. As was the board school to the west. To the east stood a line of two-story houses that, though shabby, were in this neighbourhood (as opposed to the Spitalfields slums more than a half-mile away), inhabited mostly by respectable working people. The Essex Wharf stood on the north side of Buck's Row, opposite the body. All seemed quiet. Neil examined the street around the body. He saw no trace of wheel marks, shoe marks, or horse shit; no sign, save the victim, of another human. If a clue to the identity or whereabouts of the killer was there, it was not showing itself.

Neil's sergeant, Kirby, arrived and ordered an immediate canvas of the near residences. The sergeant took the cottages on the south side of the street. He gave Neil the wharf on the north. Both began to knock up the neighbours in search of witnesses.

The manager of the wharf poked his head from an upper window in answer, then came down in his nightshirt. "Did anyone hear a disturbance in the street in the last hour?" Neil inquired. Neither the manager nor his wife had heard a thing.

Opposite, Sergeant Kirby's knock at New Cottage, the first door east of the gateway, awoke the ground floor residents (a Mrs

Emma Green and her daughter). I'd killed the whore with the pair asleep in their bed a few feet away. Neither had been disturbed in the least; neither knew a thing.

One delusional harridan, Harriet Lily of No 7 Buck's Row, denied knowledge of the murder, but insisted she had heard the murderer and his victim. She'd been awakened at 3:00 by the sound of a good's train passing through the block. (The tracks bifurcated Buck's Row.) As the noise abated, she heard gasps in the street, followed by a whispering. The old biddy may have heard what she described but, as that was a full half-hour before I'd done my work, it had nothing to do with me or the whore. There were no trains, cries, or screams while I was in Buck's Row. The only gasp had been mine, I admit, when I'd fingered the whore's innards. Otherwise, no sounds. Only me and my knives quickly and quietly doing our job.

According to Mrs Griggs' papers, PC Thain returned from Whitechapel Road at 4:00 with the police surgeon. Dr Rees Llewellyn examined my work; I mean, the body. He observed the throat injuries and officially pronounced her worthless life extinct. The woman's hands were cold, but her still warm trunk suggested she'd been dead for no more than half an hour. Not a bad guess.

Unaware that, upon first discovering her, Carman Cross had moved the woman's skirts back down to her knees, neither the doctor nor any of the coppers flitting about thought further than the whore's slit throat. They did not look for other injuries at that time.

In Llewellyn's opinion, in fact, they were running out of time. The neighbourhood of Buck's Row was coming awake. Sightseers were already beginning to gather. (One paper mentioned 'three horse slaughterers from Barber's slaughterhouse in nearby Winthrop Street' who, owing to their blood-stained aprons were detained for questioning.) Llewellyn ordered the body be removed to the mortuary to prevent the crime becoming a public horror show.

Fifteen
Heroic Inspector Abberline

At 10:00 am, the morning of the murder, the police surgeon conducted his post-mortem of the Buck's Row Queen. Among his findings, to be reported to the Coroner's Inquest: The victim was missing five teeth (not my doing, blame her slag lifestyle). She had a laceration on her tongue, a bruise on her lower right jaw, and a circular bruise to left side of her face, possibly from thumb and finger pressure (those were mine). She had a four inch incision on the left side of the neck, one inch below the jaw under the left ear. A second throat incision *blah, blah, blah...* ran eight inches in a circle around the throat, *blah, blah...* severing all tissues down to the spine, including the large vessels of the neck on both sides. No blood was found on the breast of clothes or body (I'd taken care). There was a small pool of blood on the footway; not more than would fill two wine glasses. (Wouldn't that disappoint the drunk bitches?)

Dr Llewellyn did get a surprise when he lifted her dirty skirts. Her stomach was cut up. There were three deep, jagged wounds on the left side of the lower abdomen, dissecting the tissues, and four similar cuts on the right. What would the gossipers say to learn he'd missed those at the scene?

Speaking of gossipers...

Saturday evening, 1 September, Mrs Griggs hosted the first meeting of her Dress Reformists after the event the people of the streets had christened the 'Buck's Row Outrage'. My good landlady's followers, Mrs Knight, Mrs Barrett, Mrs Stewart-McCormick, and the rest, came in off the streets chattering like magpies and, it's fair to say, began a meeting unlike any before. Instead of ranting on the subject of evil stays and raving regarding sinful tightlacing, the latest news and rumors of the second Whitechapel murder were the only items on the agenda.

Don't think I stooped to eavesdrop on the old girls. I did not. It wasn't necessary. Their voices, the lot of them, carried up the stairs, through the ventilators and, when their excitement rose, even penetrated the floorboards to my rooms. The thrills were palpable. The air around them was electric with terror.

Mrs Griggs got the evening started by relaying the news that the Queen of Tarts... Yes, of course, I mean *the victim*. The Buck's Row victim had been identified. An Edward Walker, the unfortunate father of the dead unfortunate, and a William Nichols, her estranged husband (with their son in tow), had gone to the shed that passed for a morgue at Old Montague Street and identified the cut up corpse as all that remained of Mary Ann 'Polly' Nichols. According to my landlady's newspaper account, when morgue attendant unveiled the body, Nichols told his cold dead wife, "I forgive you as you are for what you have been to me."

The Dress Reformists '*Awwed*' at that. I was touched myself. ha ha.

There followed a rattling of news print as one paper after another was consulted, by one Dress Reformist after another, in an effort to suss the story, and find the clues. The community-minded women were most affected by the event.

One of the ladies, Mrs S-M, I believe, reported a good number of citizens and businesses had begun demanding a reward be offered by the government for the capture of the fiend. They debated the pros and cons for some time. The official stance of the Home Office, one insisted, was that they did not pay rewards for information on crime or criminals. It was the duty of the citizen to help law enforcement as they were able.

"How can the people help?" Mrs Knight ventured, "when the killer comes and goes in the night?"

The ladies moved on, other questions awaited. What was the killer's motive? Was it common robbery? Jealousy? Revenge? They confessed, in league, to being baffled. What had the murderer of those poor creatures had to gain?

The possibility the Whitechapel murders were *gang* related was discussed. This, according to several articles, appeared to be a favorite among the police. The theory was these gangs promised to protect the women on the streets, for a weekly fee. When the victims refused, or failed to pay, their protectors responded violently. Of course, it wasn't protection at all. It was simple blackmail, dressed up in a lie.

Mrs Griggs read a piece from the *Star*. I remained flabbergasted; the *Star* in our lodging house! My sturdy conservative landlady was in jeopardy of becoming a radical! The article concerned all three recent murders. (Yes, three; the paper and the Dress Reformists were taking it for granted Emma Smith had been a victim of the Whitechapel killer.) It read:

'In each case the victim has been a woman of abandoned character, each crime has been committed in the dark hours of the morning, and more important still as pointing to one man, and that man a maniac, being the culprit, each murder has been accompanied by hideous mutilations... All these crimes have been committed within a very small radius. Each of the ill-lighted thoroughfares to which the women were decoyed to be foully butchered are off turnings from Whitechapel Road, and all are within half a mile. The fact that these three tragedies have been committed within such a limited area, and are so strangely alike in details, is forcing on all minds the conviction that they are the work of some cool, cunning man with a mania for murder.'

The women loved the recital. One might have heard a pin drop as it was being read; and couldn't hear oneself think for the shrieks when the reading was finished.

For my part, I had all I could do not to blow a raspberry from the top of the second floor steps. *'To which the women were decoyed...'* ha ha. I had decoyed nobody, and had to fight an urge to descend and tell the lot of them so! I had no association with the Smith tart on Osborn Street. Tabram had interrupted my attempt at meditation in George Yard. The scofflaw Nichols had led me to Buck's Row herself. So much for my decoying them. So much for competent reporting or informed opinion.

Another of the gathered Dress Reformists (Mrs Robertson?) confessed to being shocked that the Coroner's Inquest into the death of Polly Nichols had already been convened that day. Mrs Griggs, on the other hand, reported her lack of surprise. She opined that clearly the authorities had no intention of letting the grass grow beneath their feet in regards to the murders. "Scotland Yard," my landlady intoned, "has assigned Inspector Frederick Abberline to head the search for the Whitechapel killer."

There followed a succession of *oohhs* and *aahhs* of delighted approval from the gathered ladies.

"Who better?" one of them demanded. "Who better?"

Of course, overhearing that... Well, it was too much to resist. Despite the fact I was not in the least hungry, I devised a trip downstairs (in the direction of the kitchen) to better hear the goings on in Mrs Griggs' sitting room. The ladies were gushing over the news of the police inspector.

Abberline, I would learn, had served twenty-five years with the Metropolitan Police; fourteen in the Whitechapel slums, nine as H Division's 'Local Inspector'. There was no denying his expertise in the crimes and criminals of the East End. As a 'faithful, conscientious, upright officer' he'd been promoted to Scotland Yard, the Metropolitan Police headquarters, last year and given a dinner and a gold watch by the inhabitants of the district and his colleagues upon his departure. Now, owing to his knowledge of the district, he'd been sent back to co-ordinate the work of the divisional plods in the hunt for the killer. The hunt, that was, for me.

I'd seen Abberline's fresh-complexioned face in the papers many times. Over the years, I'd even seen him in person in London Hospital on occasion. Nothing about him, at the time, had particularly stood out to me. He was an average looking man with hazel eyes, dark-brown hair (with a balding crown), a thick moustache and bushy side-whiskers. In his mid-forties, he was five feet nine and a half inches tall, and stoutly built. By all accounts he was soft-spoken and modest.

Yet, by the way the women in Mrs Griggs' sitting room were cooing and carrying-on, you'd have thought the man to be a star of the West End stage rather than a copper. It gave me an uneasy feeling. I suddenly found myself hoping Abberline's reputation had grown as a result of hot air as opposed to hard work and that he had much to be modest about. Inspector Abberline indeed.

The heroic Abberline began his new duty by attending the first day of the Nichols Inquest on behalf of CID. Another plod and two Detective Sergeants kept him company. The jury was conducted to view the body at the morgue. After which, they returned to the Working Lad's Institute, Whitechapel Road, where the Coroner for South-east Middlesex, Wynne Baxter (back from holiday, sated on pickled herring and cloudberries), opened the show.

The witnesses included, Walker, the father; John Neil, the peeler who'd tripped over her in Buck's Row; and Dr Llewellyn, who read the results of that excellent post-mortem (mentioned earlier). Once they'd established identity, the scene of murder, and doctor's opinion as to *Cause of death*, the inquiry was adjourned until Monday, 3 September, to give the coppers time to sniff out evidence – time enough, perhaps, to catch the killer.

The Dress Reformists' meeting had been the strangest in their history. What none of the good ladies knew when they adjourned that particular gathering, with faces flushed and pulses racing, was that the agenda for their future meetings had been established for months to come.

Sixteen
Leather Apron Fear

On Thursday, 6 September, unable to control my jitters, and needing to be rid of them for my own safety, I left my lodgings early. I headed west for several blocks, before circling back north and east to Whitechapel Road. In that way, I gave myself a long walk to my scheduled shift at hospital through the busier sections of the East End and along the edge of what the local residents had begun to call the *'Murder District'*.

I confess, I did not do so boldly. I wore my collar up. I tugged the brim of my soft cloth cap down. I kept my eyes moving, my mouth shut, and my ears open. I'd spent too long indoors, hiding. I needed to be out and about. I needed to hear what the East End had to say.

What tales I heard!

Tales told with such pride one would have thought the gossipers spreading them to be a part of the investigations themselves. Startling stuff. For instance, imagine my surprise to discover the police had identified the miscreant. They knew exactly who the Whitechapel murderer was and, if what I heard was true, they were on his trail!

Immediate panic turned to high hilarity as I listened further and learned the truth. The truth, that is, as brought to light by the London papers; meaning total rubbish.

My first brush with the written version of the story (proving me a day behind the times) came when I found a scrap newspaper blowing along the pavement through an alley just off Backchurch Lane. I scooped it up, flattened away the wrinkles, and read the *Star* headline from the previous day. I couldn't believe what the bold print trumpeted:

'LEATHER APRON.'
THE ONLY NAME LINKED WITH THE
WHITECHAPEL MURDERS.
A NOISELESS MIDNIGHT TERROR.

That's correct. Police inquiries following the Nichols killing had put them onto the murderer. If the *Star* reporter was right, the Whitechapel prostitutes walked in fear of a local man known to them only as Leather Apron!

I re-read that incredible headline, then moved on with an interest that, even now, is difficult to put into words, to the sinister line that followed after:

*The Strange Character who Prowls About
Whitechapel After Midnight – Universal
Fear Among the Women – Slippered Feet
and a Sharp Leather-knife.*

Even as I devoured the article, I'd turned and headed toward the High street to buy that day's edition. I had to know. Who? What was Leather Apron? Why had he been pegged? Why was he currently being hunted as the ghastly Whitechapel killer?

The initial article was long and lurid. I was totally engrossed as I took it in. So much so that, on crossing the street I was nearly struck by a hansom cab and two pony-drawn carts and, reaching the other curb, was nearly done in by a labourer pushing a barrow. Such language! A police constable standing stationary duty on the corner cried out to me, warning me rather sternly, I was a goner if I didn't pay more attention.

"I'm reading about your Leather Apron!" I informed him.

He nodded his understanding but insisted, "All the same, sir. No need your becoming one of his victims as well!"

He smiled and I laughed outright, both of us amused, likely for different reasons.

In the High, I found Mr Frogg and his boy dealing death in the form of that day's latest editions. I was not disappointed by the updated (6 September) story. I bought the paper, swapped pleasantries with young Tad, then hungrily started reading the newest, equally long, exponentially more lurid, follow-up article on the same subject. . . the hunt for the lead suspect in the Whitechapel murders.

Leather Apron was a slipper maker, a Jew of course, who had abandoned his profession in favor of nighttime prowls wherein he tormented and blackmailed prostitutes throughout the East End. Like the earlier suspected gangs, he demanded the whores pay protection monies and, so the complaints went, beat and terrified those who refused. Though victims claimed not to know his real name, their descriptions tallied: A villainous character, five feet four inches in height, about 38 years. He was thickset with a stump of a neck. His wore his black hair close and sported a thin moustache. His beady eyes glittered with menace, his lips were parted in a repellent grin. His sinister expression, said the reporter, held nothing but terror for women. He wore work clothing and a dark close-fitting cap. But his distinguishing feature was the ever-present leather apron from which he got his mysterious name.

The CID were anxious to discover Leather Apron's true identity and track him down (if only to eliminate him from their inquiries). An intensive search of the common lodging houses he'd been reported to frequent was begun. The coppers, the reporters complained, were not pleased the press had gotten word of their interest in Leather Apron and were not forthcoming with additional information. That didn't stop them asking.

A George Yard grocer, who'd known Leather Apron for years, called him "unquestionably mad," adding, "His eyes are never still, but are always shifting." He concluded his accusation (if that's what it was) with the damning comment, "He never looks anybody in the eye."

"He's an absolute villain!" another resident declared. "For several years he's subjected the prostitutes of Whitechapel to a reign of terror."

Leather Apron's method, according to the article, supported by street gossip, was to peep into public houses (after midnight) to select his victim. He then waited in the shadows and, when they emerged, followed them. He had apparently created his own special *skulking* footwear, a form of slipper, which allowed him to tread silently in an unfortunate's wake. The hapless whores were ignorant of his presence... until it was too late.

Leather Apron menaced them with a keen knife (a shoemaker's tool?) he always carried. He terrified his victims, kicked, bruised, and injured them. Not more than a fortnight since a victim (referred to in one article as 'Widow Annie') was accosted by the villain as she crossed the square south of London Hospital. Leather Apron reportedly pulled his knife and, with hate-filled eyes and a sinister grin, threatened to "rip her up!"

Oddly, and rather sadly, none of the newspaper accounts I read recounted a single incident during which he'd cut anybody, let alone butchered them. Still the reporters warned their readers, Leather Apron remained a genuine threat to the unfortunates of Whitechapel. His attitude toward respectable women was not addressed.

All the printed stories, and all the street gossip, regarding Leather Apron seemed, in my humble opinion, pieced together from the tittle-tattle of whores, lodging house proprietors, and low-class tradesmen with too much time on their hands; and without reliable substantiation. Beside, I already knew any suggestion of his having had a hand in the recent murders was bollocks, didn't I?

The fun of it for me, I would discover, was that like all murdering phantoms, once the public was aware of Leather Apron's existence, the monster was suddenly seen everywhere. His whispered name became a terrified scream every time a thug took a wrong step before the right person. All the villains in the world were suddenly 'Leather Apron, the Whitechapel killer!'

On the other side of the scale, and at the same time, several papers tried to calm their readers by assuring them Leather Apron was already in police custody. That version of the story had the villain nicked as early as Sunday, 2 September, at a fourpenny lodging house off Brick Lane (impossible to prove or disprove without police comment; there were dozens of houses, housing thousands of men fitting that description). When one house was traced, in which Leather Apron had reportedly slept on occasion, the manager denied him utterly. The reporter opined the fellow was shielding the villain. But the police joined in the denial; they had not arrested Leather Apron.

A second eyewitness claimed to have seen the villain within the week in Leather Lane, Holborn.

A third informant reported seeing him crossing London Bridge into Southwark, looking in a desperate hurry, yet (somehow) as stealthy as an animal; head bent, skimpy coat turned up about his ears, with his horrid apron showing from beneath.

A pair of witnesses, two potty old women in Philpot Street, told reporters Leather Apron would most likely be found in Commercial Street, opposite the Princess Alice Tavern. "Just look into the shadows," one of them said. "Whether you see him there or not, look into the shadows as if he is there. For he will surely be out of sight."

A sixth witness even claimed to have seen Leather Apron walking in Baker's Row with Polly Nichols the morning of her murder. That was sensible reporting! No thought whatever! The slag lived in Thrawl Street, but went to Baker's Row (a stone's throw off Buck's Row) for a nice walk with Leather Apron. After, she went home without her doss, was refused a bed, then returned to Buck's Row to earn her doss – where, that time, Leather Apron murdered her. A lovely story, that!

With those witnesses, what thinking person could doubt the mad Leather Apron and the Whitechapel killer were one and the same? But fear not, the papers insisted, the police were on his trail.

Owing to this, and other juicy tales of street insanity, the papers were selling... like mad.

With the murder of the Queen of Tarts in Buck's Row, public interest, even among the disinterested and disengaged rabble, greatly increased. The papers (including the conservative press) rose to the occasion. Mind, the police were no more generous with information gleaned in their investigations, but the coroners' inquests were; those were public meetings. The press collected every gory detail and ran with it; to the delight (and horror) of their customers.

Monday, 3 September marked the second day of the Nichols Inquest. As with the others, my good landlady and her Dress Reformists unknowingly kept me abreast of the details.

Inspector Abberline, Mrs Griggs recited to her gathered, and Detective Sergeants Enright and Godley again observed for the CID. The witnesses for the day; two Inspector plods, the peeler who'd been patrolling Baker's Row when informed of the murder; Charles Cross, the carman who'd done the telling after discovering Nichols dead; William Nichols, the slag's grieving husband, and others.

Emily Holland, a friend and fellow unfortunate, testified she'd met Polly (wearing her new bonnet) in Osborn Street at 2:30 am. Despite raising the money (4p for her bed), three separate times that day, Nichols had spent it on drink and remained broke and unwelcome at her Thrawl Street lodging house.

I'd come down and was passing the sitting room as Mrs Griggs read aloud, "The inquest was adjourned again until Monday, 17 September."

"My heavens," one of the ladies declared, "the poor unfortunate thing will be buried before anyone knows what killed her."

Unable to help myself, I asked, "Wasn't her head nearly severed? That should provide a clue as to what killed her."

The woman (whose name escapes me; all Dress Reformists are created equal) reddened. But she raised her chin righteously and rephrased. "I meant, of course, *who* killed her."

I nodded understanding. "I doubt they shall ever know that."

There, however, even the open-minded Mrs Griggs drew the line. Rising, she came to her friend's defense and admonished my cynicism in the same sentence. "Mr __, the Yard never fails!"

The Dress Reformists were back at it several nights later, gossiping over the just of an article in the evening edition of the *Daily News*. That reporter had spent the previous day mingling with the crowds loitering around the murder site in Buck's Row. He told of groups of women gossiping nervously in a circle around what they took to be bloodstained paving stones. While, hear this, 'their sullen and taciturn men, hands thrust in their pockets, puffed at their pipes and looked on'. (British reporters never used ten words, when forty would suffice.) All up and down the street, shouted gossip and whispered rumor, bubbled in a cauldron of emotions; wasted compassion for the victim, undeserved anger for me, and understandable fear for themselves.

"Don't see what everyone is bawling about," one fellow growled, going against the current. "Weren't nothing but a harlot were she? No shortage of them."

"No matter what she was, poor thing," another spit back, "taint for the likes of us to judge her now."

"No, that's right enough, whatever she was it was an awful cruel thing to do to her."

"Mornin' paper says the murder was done by a gang of robbers," a young fellow chimed in.

"That's a got up yarn," an old boy shouted back, coming up on his toes. "I rather wish it was true. If there was a gang like that, it'd all come out." He shook his head ruefully. "Bet your money t' ain't been done that way."

The women moved from tears to gritted teeth, getting up a shrill discussion on what they'd like to see done to killer. The men chimed in, "He deserves to be turned over to the women of Whitechapel."

"That'd serve 'im right!"

Of course, not all the ladies agreed. One old thing, so the reporter declared, shivering in place, was heard to pray out loud, "Thank God I needn't be out after dark!"

"No more needn't I," said another, with terror in her grey eyes. "But my two girls have got to come home latish and I'm all of a fidget till they comes."

Still another said, "Life ain't no great thing with many on us, but we don't all want to be murdered. If things go on like this it won't be safe for nobody to put their 'eads out o' doors."

So it continued, day after day, the excitement growing.

From Aldgate to Mile End Old Town, the details of the tragedies were discussed on every street corner in the East End. Morbid sightseers were still coming, a week after Polly Nichols' demise, in clusters of twos or threes to stare at the faded green gates of the workhouse mortuary. (No doubt to imagine the colourful workings inside.) While crowds numbering in the twenties and thirties at a time continued to gather along the byways, and in the streets, in Buck's Row, George Yard, and Osborn Street to ogle the murder sites.

It was, all of it, deliciously exciting and infinitely enjoyable. Yet, as I sat alone in my room, I felt neither excitement nor joy. I had a great deal on my mind. With one troubling thought returning again and again. It was this: Buck's Row was a mistake.

No, not the event, not the murder. That was beautiful and delicious and well-carried through. The world was well-rid of Mary, or Polly, or whatever-the-hell her name was, Nichols, and the damage she did and would do, and the diseases she might otherwise have spread. No, don't think for a moment I regretted the event at all. When I say Buck's Row was a mistake, I merely refer to the location.

Buck's Row was only a few minutes' walk south across the Whitechapel Road to London Hospital, my place of employment. That was the mistake. I should not have risked my employment.

That night, as I stared out hospital window, the dock fire showed me the way. I could not, need not have resisted the urge.

But I ought to have been more wise in selecting a location to carry out the work. I should have taken the whore elsewhere for cleaning. Realizing this, I resolved then and there to fight erratic urges in the future. To avoid carrying out my job anywhere near my employment. Even a dog knows better than to relieve himself in his food.

Later that Thursday, by accident, I read of the Queen of Tarts' afternoon funeral. Make no mistake, once I'd put her in her place, I couldn't have cared less what they did with the remains. But I did read it and something about that article caught my keen eye. She was buried, it said, in a polished elm casket paid for by her son, husband, and father. Polished elm! With a shiny metal plate screwed into the lid, reading: 'Mary Ann Nichols, aged 42; died August 31, 1888.' All well and good.

Then came the horrid part. It further said she was transported to the City of London Cemetery via cortege consisting of a hearse and two mourning coaches, supplied free of charge by Mr Smith, a Hanbury Street undertaker. The bastard!

I have no complaint concerning the hard working men of her family, let them have their coach and their ride into the City on a fine Saturday morning. But why a horse drawn hearse for the likes of her? She ought to have been in a barrow, pushed by the blokes she'd debauched.

But she had a horse drawn hearse. How lovely was that? A kind and compassionate undertaker in Hanbury Street. I couldn't help but know that Hanbury Street, in Spitalfields, was west of Buck's Row, running west to Commercial Street. Plenty far away from the hospital to meet my new criteria and nowhere near my 'dog's dish'. Now I'd read the paper, I couldn't help but wonder if the undertaker didn't deserve more business for the generous trouble he'd taken with the last? I laughed, to myself at first, and then, unable to help it, out loud. How could I not?

That was it. I would take my work west. Where there were fancy funerals with all the trimmings, including free hearses for every whore in Hanbury Street!

Seventeen
Stockings

It was early morning, 8 September, a week and a day since that little job in Buck's Row, and Yours Truly was on the hunt.

It was almost dawn, meaning very late for me. In my last two efforts, by then, I was safely back home and in bed. But there it was, nearly dawn and I was still looking for a prospect; the right kind of whore (one disgusting with drink). And running out of time. I considered the notion with my previous outings I had delivered such a strong message the besotted prostitutes had all gone into hiding, but knew that couldn't be true. Those people didn't learn that quickly. No, my work was not done.

I had to admit I'd made my chore more difficult by insisting the night's effort had to be conducted in Hanbury Street. Why I took that risk, locking myself in, I couldn't quite say. Other than I owed it to the generous morticians plying their trade there. One of the local undertakers had sprung for a portion of the Queen of Tarts' funeral. That would never do and they might as well learn that. I'd been given the power to name the price of these slags' drunken debauches and to make them pay full measure. Who were the undertakers, once I'd spoken, to give them gifts, thereby lessening the expense of their sins? I was resolved. To set things right, a drunken Hanbury Street whore it would be.

I confess, that resolve had begun to ebb to mere hopefulness a subject for my work would soon put in an appearance. Time was passing. The employed locals, few and far between as they might be, would soon be crawling out and going about.

Speaking of out and about... One bloody peeler was out and about.

More than one obviously, there were police constables everywhere, like weeds; but one officer in particular kept popping in and out of Hanbury Street. Apparently that was his patch, as I'd seen him three times now making his round. He'd had the opportunity to see me on his first pass, but hadn't bothered to notice. (I've mentioned my talent in remaining unseen.) He'd forced me to employ them twice more, slipping into the deep shadows. Now there he came again – in the distance.

I knew better than to press my luck. To ensure he did not see me, I made myself scarce. I got off Hanbury Street; took Brick Lane to Pelham and waited in the shadows there, giving him time to come and go. Go! That's what my mind began to cry. When even my jumbled thoughts warned me time had come and gone, that I had better forget the job and get away from there... But I ignored it.

I slipped back south a block to Hanbury again, intent upon one last peek. The copper was gone. Brilliant. Better still, as if divinely delivered, there stood the object of my search!

I had no more than reached the corner of Brick Lane and Hanbury, and looked to the west, when I spotted an unprepossessing woman of obvious low character. She stood gazing with, I imagined, bleary eyes through a storefront window at vases of flowers surrounded by red curtains. That was a mistake on her part; not for the danger she was in (though there was that) but for the esthetics. The background made her appear all that much more colourless and bland. She matched the three-story building before her (grey, weathered, filthy), and the building beyond (same description) and, in a different way, the building this side of her, a laundry mangling house in dingy peeling yellow. The flowers and curtains before her occupied the only window without closed shutters in what looked a closed shop on the ground floor. She seemed to be merely loitering. But was she drunk?

91

I started her way, intent on discovering exactly that.

Hanbury Street curved southeast from Commercial Street on its west end to the junction of Baker's Row and Old Montague Street on its eastern end. No 29 Hanbury, the building before which the woman stood, sat well-toward Commercial, on the north side of the street in the dead centre of the block between Wilkes Street and Brick Lane; one of those old factories, built originally for immigrant weavers, whose hand-looms died a sudden death with the advent of steam machines. The place had become a multi-dwelling house for the labouring poor with many apartments above and to the rear.

As I approached, I saw the woman was on the high end of forty and plump, made to look more so as she was only five foot tall. She wore a black figured coat to her knees, with a black skirt showing below and lace up boots. She wore a white cotton kerchief (with a broad red border, folded three-corner ways) round her neck as a scarf with a single knot in the front. She showed no sign of fear, made no effort to move away, at my approach. Instead, she smiled gratefully.

Outside of my work, I'm no artist. But, in my humble opinion, nothing of her looks went together. Her fair complexion and blue eyes were spoiled by a too-thick nose. The whole of her aging face was framed by incongruously young wavy brown hair. When she turned in the glow of the one lamp nearby, and spoke, she gave away the treatment she'd met on the streets; she was missing several teeth in her lower jaw and wearing an old bruise on her right temple. Then, glad I'd found her, she slurred, "Hello, love." Her boozy breath assaulted my nostrils.

Oh, delightful. Hanbury Street and a drunken whore! How would mother have said it, breathing beer all over me? You have everything a boy could need! I wasted no time propositioning the teetering slut. She giggled and tapped my chest but didn't answer.

"Will you?" I demanded.

"Yes," she said.

That was the moment I noticed a thin middle-aged woman walking past, carrying an empty basket, headed west. She hadn't made any sound and I'd no idea where she'd come from, or that she was even there, until I saw her at my side. She eyed us both without stopping or speaking. Let her stare.

The women reached Wilkes Street, and continued west, without looking back. She appeared headed for Commercial Street and, at that hour, probably for the Spitalfields Market. Good riddance.

I had ridding of my own to do. "Shall we..." I started to ask the whore.

She was already on the move, headed into the building before which I'd found her loitering.

There were two latched doors into No 29 Hanbury Street, beside each other on the west end front of the building. A signboard above the door on the left proclaimed, in painted white letters, that *'Mrs A Richardson, rough packing-case maker'* waited inside to serve me. An off-kilter piece of paper near the door on the right suggested, in hurried ink, *'cat's meat'* might also be found within if I cared to look. Little businesses run by insignificant people. The whore entered through the door on the left.

It opened to a fairly common design for low-class housing, an enclosed space with a set of stairs heading up to the residences and another door. She took that second door into a dark passageway that led straight through the building. The passageway, I would learn much later, was well known to the vagrants in the area and often utilized as a place to escape the weather (or take naps) at unusual hours. On the far end of the passageway hung a creaky door on a loose spring that opened out onto a backyard frequently used by prostitutes.

The whore started through the back door. Behind her, I slipped a hand into my pocket and took hold of my shoemaker's blade.

The whore led the way from the tiny square porch, down three stone steps to a small (14 foot deep by 12 foot wide) enclosed backyard that was part dirt and part paving stone. To the left, about three foot away behind the door, running the depth of the yard was a roughly six foot fence, separating the back yard of No 29 from that of No 27 beyond. To the right of the door, in the yard, looking like an open grave, was a dark stairwell leading down to the door of a cellar workshop. Along the back fence at the end of the yard, a tiny storage shed stood in the far left corner and a smaller privy stood in the far right corner. Outside of these *markers* I had no opportunity to look the yard over further. The black night had almost gone, replaced by blue, as the sun began to rise. If I intended to see the job through, there was no more time to lose. Thankfully the whore was as eager to begin as I.

Then came the conundrum. I needed to hurry; couldn't afford to wait. Yet her willingness, combined with her age, her profession, her drunken face, infuriated me. As the others had, this one transitioned before me. She wasn't woman, nor was she merely a whore; she was worse even than the last disease-ridden bitch I'd taken care of. Suddenly, in my mind's eye, this one literally turned into an animal. She was a pig in need of slaughter.

At the bottom of the steps, she unbuttoned her long black coat and turned to me, revealing a brown bodice beneath, over a second bodice (whores dressed for the weather), and the full length of her black skirt. She smiled the same smile (missing teeth) she'd given me in the street when she'd agreed to our lewd coupling. I ran a hand lightly across her chin, fingers and thumb twinning her fat neck.

"You've brought men here before?" I asked her in a whisper.

"No."

"Don't lie. Tell me. You've gotten drunk and brought men right here to this spot?"

She giggled nervously, looking oddly uncomfortable. "I never."

That was as far as I let her get. I snatched the whore's throat. The sudden pressure prevented her crying out. Even in the gloom, her eyes indicated my success, she could neither squeal nor get air. I held her just so, for several minutes, shaking her to keep the pressure on. Trust me, strangling someone, even an out of shape and drunken slag, takes effort.

Suddenly she lost consciousness and dropped as if she were a Tyburn convict whose horse cart had been whipped away. It took me by surprise. I nearly toppled with her. Falling, I caught the fence with my shoulder and got my feet under me. Balanced again, I lowered the whore to the yard on her back.

She lay below and to the left of the steps, parallel with the fence. Her head boxed in by the steps, the house wall, and the fence. Her feet pointed the way to the shed at the end of the yard. Her right arm lay down her right side. Her left arm rested on her breast.

I knelt beside her, to the right of her head, with my back to the house. I cut her throat, twice, deeply, from left to right, severing the artery with the first stroke. Blood hit the fence and her left arm, a healthy gush if not a spurt. With the second stroke, for the fun of it, I tried to cut her head off. That would say something to the crowds!

But the muscles and plumbing (especially the discs and bones) gave me hell and caught my knife. It was no good. I did, however, produce a jagged rip that reached right round from one ear to the other. That was a good one. But time was wasting and I couldn't fool with it further. The sun was nearly up; folks would soon be about. I had more to do. As she seemed to want it so bad, I decided the whore could keep her head.

I needed, I'd decided the previous night, several items necessary for new games I'd been considering. To that end, I pulled a small towel, borrowed for the occasion from Mr Griggs' shop, from my pocket and unrolled it on the ground. Inside the towel was a washed and clean ginger beer bottle. I removed the bottle and set that aside (the first step in what would be quite a lark when the time was right). I turned back to the whore and threw up her skirt and both petticoats, ready to get down to business. But I had to pause – to admire the whore's bright red and white striped woolen stockings, jutting from the tops of her laced boots like a pair of clowns escaping the circus. That was a sight!

I also discovered a large pocket, hidden under the skirt, tied with strings about her waist. It was amazing, the surprises waiting round every corner in my line of work. I promised myself I'd return to the pocket when I had the time. Until then, I had work to do.

Saucy Jacky

My last job, the Queen in Buck's Row, had been an amateur effort, lacking in the confidence needed to deliver the proper message to the world. I could do better. That meant I had to get my hands dirty, in a way of speaking. I had to show the people of London that I loved by job. So I bent to it.

With my trusty knife, I deftly laid open her trunk and – determined to have fun – began the work of eviscerating her. I cut off a flap of the abdomen and laid it, near me, on the stone floor of the yard above her right shoulder. I hacked out the small intestines and laid them with it. A cord, still attached, stretched from the flesh pile down across her and back inside the body with the rest of the intestines. I left it that way; it looked good. I clipped off two flaps of skin from the lower part of the gut and, with a reach, laid them on the ground above her left shoulder. I cut out a goodly portion of the stomach and, along with a surprising quantity of warm dripping blood, added that to the new pile.

I moved between the whore's legs, drew them up to what was no doubt their natural position, knees bent (*Oh, those stockings!*) with the feet resting on the ground, legs spread wide; the better to entrap weak men and spread disease. I reached in and moved her insides around, found the bits I wanted, and struck a blow for decency. I cut out her uterus, her bladder and, with more effort than I expected it would take, a representative portion of her filthy vagina. These I carefully held above the open pit of her corpse to drain. Steam rose from her insides into the cool morning air as I watched the red rain drip down inside her. I couldn't help it, the sight was giddily inspiring. I sang under my breath.

Oh, the bloomin', bloody spider went up the spider web,
The bloomin', bloody rain came down atop the spider's head.

I wrapped my lovely drip-dried trophies in the towel and slipped that bundle into my coat pocket.

The bloomin', bloody sun came out and dried up all the rain,
And the bloomin', bloody spider went up the web again.

I didn't want any of that nasty blood to give me away, did I? I confess, I did not know what I'd do with the bits I'd collected. But a fellow should be prepared. In future, should a sample of my work come in handy, I'd have them. If not, I could always dispose of them later.

I grabbed the pig's skirts to wipe the blood from my hands – and returned my attention to the hidden cloth pocket around her waist that I'd discovered earlier. As I promised I would, I tore into it. What treasures had the nasty pig secreted away? They were these: a piece of coarse muslin, a small tooth comb, and a pocket comb in a paper case. There was also a corner piece, torn from a mailing envelope, being used to carry two pills. In other words, her secret pocket held nothing at all of value to anyone. But I didn't let that spoil my mood.

In fact, I looked at it all again, reconsidered, and decided I could get some value from her junk. I could have a bit of fun at the coppers' expense. And, simple as it would be, I would not let the shortness of time stop me. I took the whore's nothings, the muslin scrap, the small tooth comb, and the comb in the case, and carefully arranged them in a line on the ground at her feet.

Whatever for? Well for the mystery, of course!

I took the tiny makeshift envelope pocket, with the pills inside, and laid that on the ground beside the fancy pile of pig innards near her head. The mystery grows!

What did either display mean? Not a damned thing! But wouldn't the police, when they discovered it, be standing on flat feet in a great thoughtful circle scratching their collective heads wondering at the obvious significance of it all? ha ha.

At about that time, for the first time, I noticed the whore wore three brass rings on the middle finger of her left hand. More fun! These I wrenched off and tucked into my pocket. I wasn't a thief, don't get that ridiculous idea. I no more wanted the pig's swag than I wanted to be Prime Minister. It was merely another lark, another opportunity to cloud the issue and raise questions in the minds of, what I had no doubt would be, the confused coppers. What was the killer's motive?

Saucy Jacky

I took another moment for my other prank. I lifted the ginger beer bottle. I removed the cork and dipped the empty vessel into the hollow I'd created in the slag's guts. As best I could, I collected a portion – several healthy swigs worth, at least – of her tainted red blood in the bottle. I corked it. I wiped the outside dry on her skirt and slipped the bottle back into my pocket.

But time really was getting on. I moved to the steps before taking one last look at the pig. Daylight burned full upon the yard now and I could clearly see my work for the first time. She lay in profile with her swollen and greying face turned to the right and the tip of her bulging blue tongue protruding from between her front teeth like a choked goose. Below, her mid-section was a wide-open window to her new world and, even in those ridiculous striped stockings, she was an absolute work of art.

It was past time. I needed to be gone.

Eighteen
Flower and Dean Street Riot

Having fun at the expense of the whores and the police, I'd pressed my luck further than I ought have done. I'd overstayed my welcome in the backyard of Hanbury Street. I had pockets full of gifts; stolen jewelry, and stolen flesh and blood; I had blood on my hands. All of which would be more than a little difficult to explain should some peeler tap me on the shoulder between Spitalfields and home. I was nearly a mile away from my lodgings.

I returned up the passageway and saw the sun full up as I stepped back out onto Hanbury Street. The road and byways were quickly filling up. Unless I had extraordinary luck, the coppers were soon going to be up in arms.

Not having prepared an escape plan, and knowing suddenly I needed one, I created one on the fly. Instead of heading for my own lodgings, I hurried four short-blocks south on the less-traveled Osborn Street (as opposed to busy Commercial), then dove into a common lodging house on Flower and Dean Street. There I knew, morning, noon, or night, four pence bought the use of a common washing place and a coffin-like bed on the floor, with no questions asked.

The blood on my hands? Thankfully that was only a small problem.

Bloody hands might draw the attention of, or elicit a few half-hearted questions from, a patrolling constable who's had his tea and was full of piss and vinegar. The bobbie's question would be, "Where did you get bloody?" The test would be to answer without nervous hesitation. In the East End. blood, by itself, was really not a clue indicating anything worth getting excited about. Nothing at all for doss house managers to question. Between the butchers, the slaughtermen, the cat's meat vendors, and the meat warehouse labourers, there were hundreds of men walking the streets in bloody aprons, blood-stained coats, or with drying muck on their hands.

To avoid uncomfortable questions meant merely avoiding attention. To that end, I laid down my doss money. The house deputy jotted a bed number in his book, without asking my name, and pointed; first to the passage leading to the washing place, then to the stairs to my rented fourth floor accoutrement.

There were two other fellows washing when I entered the common room. One ignored me, the other gave a nod. I returned as I got. I grabbed a rag from atop a pile of what, no doubt with a straight face, the management called towels. I pumped a pan of water. I found a spot and set about scrubbing the dried blood from my hands, without the help of soap. The doss house provided none and, as my presence was spur of the moment, I'd come unprepared.

From somewhere outside, distantly, I heard the tones of a shrill, excitedly blown, police whistle. The other gents heard it as well. They traded exclamations I didn't bother to hear, finished their ablutions, and vacated the wash room; whether to investigate the cause or to put distance between themselves and the noise makers, I didn't know or care. My interest lay in my situation.

I took full advantage of my having been left alone.

I rinsed the blades of my knives, rubbing hard with my thumb as the blood had started to dry. As the coast remained clear, I rinsed the whore's borrowed parts; first the one, then the other, then the other as well. The clots looked like old cherries in the deep pink wash water. The specimens themselves were fine, each a prize. I noted this quickly, without taking the time to unduly admire them. I was aware that someone might well have walked in at any moment.

I tucked the knives and flesh trophies back into my pockets, out of sight. I dumped my bloody wash water down the sink drain. I was just whistling my way to the door when some bloke stuck in his head from the hall, gasping and looking like a fish out of water. "It's happened again," he said breathlessly. "They've found another. Another woman's been killed!"

"Oh?" I managed. "Where?"

"Hanbury Street. In a house on Hanbury Street!"

Thankfully, no caring or intelligent response was required. The fellow, having delivered his news to all the lodgers present, meaning me, was gone as quickly as he'd arrived. I made my exit as well. I by-passed the stairs leading to the fourth floor and the lice-ridden bed I'd rented and, instead, took the central ground floor passageway through the building. I kept on walking right out the back door.

I crossed the yard and hopped the fence to the north. I crossed the neighbouring yard, acting for all the world as if I absolutely belonged there, then hopped their north fence, coming out into Fashion Street. I headed casually back to the west, to the major artery, where a spick-and-span fellow like me had every right to walk in peace. But there wasn't any peace.

The wide Commercial Street curved right there, so I couldn't see the blocks to the near north. But if the thundering horse teams, whipped up by frantic coach drivers, one steering an ambulance; the heavy and excited foot traffic; and the scattering of panicked coppers. all rushing north was any indication... something interesting had happened on Hanbury Street. Whatever might it have been? ha ha.

But wait a moment! Something... else... was just then taking place. More than even I knew.

Suddenly there came a great cacophony; a new round of police whistles, followed by a roar of shouts, a rush of wild cries, and a riot of motion. The coaches, coppers, and residents I'd been watching on their way north were met, and overwhelmed, first by a trickle, then a stream, then a breaking wave of people running onto Commercial Street, from the direction of Hanbury Street, all headed south.

What in the name of...?

In the lead was a short odd-looking man, muscled like a prize bull, covered from head to toe in tattoos, and sprinting down Commercial Street toward Aldgate like a hare in fear of its life. Behind the man ran a handful of plain-clothes coppers, chasing him for all they were worth. How did I know they were the police? Since the murder in Buck's Row, the procedures had been amended and the police had been permitted to carry – normally outlawed – truncheons. The fellows chasing the tattooed fugitive, were waving theirs, with menace.

But there was more, much more, for behind the club waving coppers came a mob of running citizens, all screaming for the fugitive's blood.

I didn't know what the fellow had done to get the police after him. But, unless I missed my guess, the sight of a man fleeing the neighbourhood of that morning's murder, with the men of the Met on his heels, had whipped the crowd into a paroxysm of blood-thirsty excitement.

In sussing the situation, I'd momentarily lost track of the chase itself. The tattooed fugitive had reached me, on the far side of Commercial Street, and was still running. Then he turned hard left, crossed the busy street, dove between the legs of a horse pulling a furrier's cart, and slid to the curb before me. He jumped to his feet, looked at me with his tattooed face and eyes shocked with deathly fear, and bolted around me, headed down Flower and Dean Street.

The police arrived, paid enough attention to me to get around without wiping themselves out or knocking me to the ground, and left me standing there following in hot pursuit of their man.

Then came the crowd, running, roaring, "The Whitechapel killer! The Whitechapel killer! Lynch him!"

Bless me! ha ha. Bless me! I didn't know the tattooed man but, bless me, wasn't he in a fix!

At the same time, I couldn't help but wonder at the thoughts tumbling through the minds of the men of the Met. They had a villain, the Whitechapel killer (if the crowd was right), hotfooting it in front of them. They had the equally hot, perhaps hotter, feet of hundreds of angry citizens tramping the brick street immediately behind them. What an amazing sound that must have been!

What an amazing once in a lifetime sight for me! *Oh! Bless me!*

The crowd roared past in a storm, following the coppers and their villain. What could I do? I followed them. Though, truly, I saw no reason to run. By that time, the miscreant had ducked like a scared rabbit into a common lodging house down the street. And wasn't it a wonderful world of odd coincidences! It was the same house where I'd recently rented accommodation, bathed myself, washed my trophies, and left by the back door. The very same.

The hard-breathing detectives were scurrying to cover the entrances, and exits, front and back, surrounding the house, with their man trapped inside. They had the hare cornered.

A stand-off began. It took the lot of them a moment of serious planning, and several more of quiet contemplation, before they worked up the bollocks to head in after him. But, finally, the detectives entered the lodging house.

The coppers outside said nothing. Not that one would have heard them if they had, as the crowd continued to shout for blood. The screaming mob outside was like nothing I, or the police I imagined, had ever seen before; worse even than the howling socialist foreigners they'd dealt with on Bloody Sunday. They'd surrounded the coppers who were surrounding the lodging house and it was the crowd now who held the building in a state of siege. "Lynch him!" They continued to carry on. "Fetch him out! It's the Whitechapel killer!"

One could only guess what transpired inside.

Oh, how I would have loved to have been a fly on the wall inside that house! What fun it would have been to see a lynching. That little tattooed maggot strung up for pretending to be me, taking undeserved credit for all my hard work. He deserved it; a lynching would have been too good for him. But all good things must come to an end. And so, too, the siege of the Whitechapel proxy.

To make a long story short, the coppers set up a cordon, brought a four-wheeled cab into the street, and ushered their terrified-looking little tattooed fugitive out of the house.

The crowd roared, seeming to go mad all at once, and rushed the cordon together. But the coppers held fast. The villain was gotten aboard. The police (and their prisoner no doubt) thought themselves home free. But the insane crowd had other ideas. They rushed the cab, demanding the man's cold blood. The police attempted to move the rig down Flower and Dead Street. The crowd nearly turned it over. Before they reached the Commercial Street intersection, the cab had to be abandoned.

The coppers got their prisoner out of one of the worst streets in the slum on foot and, struggling against the enraged mob, all the way to the Commercial Street nick. Even then, the riot wasn't over. Again and again, the station house was assaulted. Beefy constables manned the doors, while plod inspectors poked their heads from upper floor windows shouting to the crowd that their prisoner had been wanted for another charge entirely; had nothing whatever to do with the murder.

ha ha.

By then, I'd had more than enough excitement. As curious as could be but, not being a great fan of crowds, and more than willing to wait and read about it in the paper later, I left the riot behind and turned in the opposite direction, headed south.

It had been a delightful morning. The Hanbury Street undertakers had been given something to ponder. The streets were most definitely cleaner today than they had been yesterday. Both thanks to me. I anticipated a lovely walk home.

Nineteen
Morning in Hanbury Street

I awoke in afternoon to find Mrs Griggs in an uproar. That was not surprising. I expected, eventually, to find the entire City of London in uproar. That was my goal. The surprise came when I discovered my charming landlady's alarm was not at news of the new murder. There was that, of course, and it had upset her. But her true alarm had been initiated by what she called the 'prophecies of murder'!

I would never have thought my iron-willed landlady superstitious. To suggest as much, would most certainly have drawn her ire. But a separate article in each of the two newspapers she carried in with my tea, she claimed, had predicted that morning's murder. They had been written the night before. The papers had gone to press in the early hours, probably as the horrible deed was being done, and hit the streets as the murderer ran back to ground.

"You must hear these," poor reddened Mrs Griggs insisted as she lifted the first, the *East London Observer*, and read:

'The two murders which have so startled London within the last month are singular for the reason that the victims have been of the poorest of the poor, and no adequate motive in the shape of plunder can be traced. The excess of effort that has been apparent in each murder suggests the idea that both crimes are the work of a

demented being, as the extraordinary violence used is the peculiar feature in each instance.'

I offered the woman my most serious face, ripe with mirror-practiced solemnity (while stifling the raucous laughter inside). "I'm sorry, dear Mrs Griggs, I don't perceive the..."

"The prophesy of which I spoke?" she asked. "That was the lead up, Mr __, outing the characters of the victims and the criminal. Now..." she refolded the Observer and lifted the other, the *East London Advertiser*, "tune your ears to this."

'The murderer must creep out from somewhere. He must patrol the streets in search of his victims. Doubtless he is out night by night. Three successful murders will have the effect of whetting his appetite still further.'

Three, I wondered? Before the... Yes, of course, this writer was also giving me credit for Emma Smith. But Mrs Griggs was still reading.

'Unless a watch of the strictest be kept the murder of Thursday will certainly be followed by a fourth.'

She lowered the paper and glared at me over her glasses. "He wrote that last night, for publication this morning," she declared. "Before this newest victim was found. That, Mr __, is a prophesy of murder!"

Later that evening, the Dress Reformists piled into the house again and, I confess, the old crones were causing me to lose touch with place and time. Their normal weekly (then bi-weekly) meeting nights were gone entirely. They seemed now, in fluctuating numbers, to be constantly in session. Their reason for existing had, at least temporarily, gone out the window as well. They met now to gather clues in the mystery of the Whitechapel murders.

I stood in the doorway to the sitting room, having greeted the ladies with the expected superficial courtesies, when Mrs Griggs started the party with a blood-curdling excerpt from the *Star* in regards to the newest outrage, reading:

'The killer had cut the victim's throat so fearfully that, thinking he had severed the head, he had tied a handkerchief around the neck to stop it rolling away.'

I turned away, rudely I admit; I had no choice! I gave the gathered women my back and threw my hand to my mouth. I bit my knuckle. I couldn't help myself. Had I not acted so, I would have burst out in uncontrolled laughter. The notion I would have gone to the trouble and made a special effort to keep the beery whore's foolish noggin in place nearly brought me to tears. ha ha.

The kerchief had been hers. And, no doubt, she'd tied it ever-so carefully in place, ogling her own reflection in some filthy storefront window, before she'd headed out to her own murder.

I tied her head on. That was a corker!

But I needed to recover, as much for my benefit as for the startled ladies. I pulled my own handkerchief, covered my eyes, turned backed to the staring half-circle of Dress Reformists, and apologized for the outburst. "Surely," I said, blowing my nose, "there is something hideous in the air."

"It's all right, Mr _," my landlady assured me. "But you should see a doctor."

"Thank you. I shall."

With that, London's most dedicated contingent of amateur outrage sleuths returned to their detecting. The papers had already begun to reconstruct the morning's event in Hanbury Street and the girls dove into the details with relish.

A carman and resident of 29 Hanbury, John Davis, had been the lucky fellow to discover my work in his backyard. He'd ventured downstairs to start his day at 5:55 am. He noticed the passageway door to the street open (nothing unusual in that) but headed the other way, down passage to the rear (probably for the WC). He opened the door to the backyard and got himself an eyeful.

His first vision of the stocking-wearing corpse had to have been stunning!

Stockings, that's it! There she lay, Stockings (a woman he likely didn't know, though I couldn't be sure), flat on her back on the ground to the left of the steps. Her throat had been deeply cut across, her head (carefully tied on by her killer, ha ha) lay in a pool of her own blood. Dead as romance, she laid by the fence on her left with her skirts up above her middle. Her legs were bent at the knees, her awful stockings bared to the world (ha!), with the toes of her flat boots pointing to the shed at the back of the yard. Her left arm on her breast, her right at her side. Her abdomen...

There Davis had to gulp air. The whore had been mutilated, her bits tossed about like the makings of a posh salad. The carman turned on his heels, hurried back up the passage, and out the front door. He saw two fellows, later identified as James Kent and James Green, standing outside their workshop at 23A Hanbury Street, waiting on co-workers. "Men! Come here!" Davis cried. "Here's a sight. A woman must have been murdered!"

Kent and Green crossed over and entered the house with Davis. A fourth fellow, a passer-by called Henry Holland, heard the commotion and followed the trio inside. Holland, a pushy bastard, overtook the three in the passageway and wound up as first out the back door.

Holland stared from the yard. The others ogled the scene from the doorway. The four of them were working stiffs (not a scientist, doctor, or alienist in the lot), still I'm sure my efforts left no doubts in any of their minds; good ol' Stockings was stone dead – by violence.

All turned and raced like frightened women back up the passage. They split up as they poured out through the front door. Davis ran for the Commercial Street Police Station. Holland ran with him, but with the Spitalfields Market in mind and, in particular, the constable (he knew) stood a fixed watch there. Kent and Green returned to their shop. Green, a practical fellow with no eye for art, went back to work. Kent, he claimed, went in search of a canvas with which to cover the poor woman's body. He found a bottle of brandy instead.

Another resident, a Mrs Hardyman, the cat's meat seller, woke to the sounds of the four men running in the passageway. She sent her 16 year-old son to investigate. "Don't upset yourself, mother," he told her upon his return. "It's a woman been killed in the yard."

Amelia Richardson, a widow, was the building's entrepreneur. She rented a good many rooms of the house and sublet most of those to others. She also operated the packing case business (ballyhooed by the sign out front) out of the cellar. At 6:10 am, upon hearing news of the murder from her grandson, Widow Richardson took her own peak into the yard and saw the lonely mutilated corpse. It was the calm before the storm.

Inspector Joseph Chandler was at the corner of Hanbury and Commercial Streets when he saw Davis and Holland, separate but equally terrified, running his way. "Murder!" one shouted, while the other offered a more detailed, "Another woman has been murdered!"

A crowd had already begun to gather in the passageway when Chandler arrived at the scene at 6:13. Still, the inspector found, none had had the nerve to venture all the way out back. James Kent, fortified by brandy and carrying an arm-load of sacking (he couldn't find a canvas), returned to No 29. He pushed his way through the crowd at the rear door to find Chandler in charge of the backyard. A handful of peelers began to appear and, on the inspector's orders, cleared the passageway.

With the scene in hand, and the tourists banished to the street, Chandler set his men to running. He sent a bobbie for the Divisional Surgeon, Dr Phillips, at his residence in Spital Square. He sent another for an ambulance and reinforcements from the Commercial Street Police Station (with a message to be sent to headquarters in Scotland Yard). Then, utilizing the sacking neighbour Kent had been thoughtful enough to provide, the inspector covered up my lovely knife-work.

Dr Phillips arrived at 6:30, removed sacking, and got a look at what I'd left him. Even as its author, I can only imagine Stockings' condition by then: blue swollen face with its bluer, more swollen tongue protruding between the teeth, the bright red rip in her pale throat from ear to ear, rigor mortis setting in. Deceived by the heat so quickly escaping her gutted carcass, Phillips mistakenly estimated the whore's *Time of death* as being at or about 4:30 in the morning. Oh, if only we'd had that much time together!

Outside of Phillips, none of the gathered representatives of law, order, and the monarchy had an overwhelming urge to draw too near the body. That being the case, it wasn't until the ambulance arrived at 6:40 and the doctor ordered the slag's body removed, the clever clogs of the Met began to find the clues I'd left them. Taking hold of her feet to lift her to a stretcher, the constables spotted the lined-up goodies from her hidden pocket, the muslin, the combs, and the comb case. Phillips, an obvious genius, told the Inspector he thought the items had been arranged on purpose.

Chandler agreed they had. But why?

Then the doctor and inspector, together, found the torn envelope corner near the well-cooled innards I'd placed beside her head. Seeing it for the vital piece of evidence it was, they examined it closely. It bore the seal of the *Royal Sussex Regiment* (soldiers again! murdering soldiers everywhere!), the postmark 'London, 23 August, 1888', and part of an address, the letter 'M' (in a man's hand) in the title line and, beneath, the number 2 and the letters *Sp* in the street address line; both torn through. The pair widened their search around the body, while the peelers went over the yard again.

Outside of blood spots, ranging in size from a pin point to that of a sixpence, on the stones, fence, and wall of the house near where the tart's head had lain, the doctor and the inspector found nothing else of note. The constables, meanwhile, found an empty nail box and a piece of flat steel. Then, I learned later, they found something else...

It was only 7:00 am, when Sergeant Edward Badham learned first-hand that news of the outrage had spread beyond the scene of crime. Ordered to convey Stockings' remains to Old Montague Street, the peeler was met by several hundred outraged citizens already waiting outside the Workhouse Infirmary Mortuary to get a look at the body of the newest victim.

At the same time, starting his day off right, heroic Inspector Abberline reached his office. Before he'd tasted his tea, before he'd removed his coat, he was handed the telegram reporting the new murder.

Twenty
Drunk with Blood

In the days following Stockings' untimely demise, I began to feel restless.

And decidedly curious. All I knew about what was happening in Hanbury Street, in the streets of the East End, throughout ol' London-town, or behind the scene with the investigating plods, I gleaned from Mrs Griggs and her papers at home, or Miss Adler and her party of nurses at work, complete with the facts, fictions, guesses, and opinions mixed into the writing or attached in the telling.

The papers on their own were little help. The stories were all over the place. The radical press had the coppers stumped, a-sea without a clue. The liberal press was hopeful the unfortunates would find help in these troubled times. The conservative writers had the heroic coppers hot on the miscreant's trail. I had no idea what was happening.

It should come as no surprise I wanted to know. With each event I found my indifference falling further behind and my curiosity growing. If for no other reason than self-preservation. A lot of people were, if rumors were true, making up their minds to come after me.

So it was I made up my mind to go out. To walk the streets of Whitechapel and Spitalfields, to listen and to see for myself what was and was not taking place. No, believe me, my concerns regarding the possibility of being nicked had not dissipated. There was always the possibility the coppers had a description of the perpetrator from a witness they were keeping to themselves. I knew that. (Suddenly the old bitch with the shopping basket was a concern.) I also believed there might be a way around that eventuality. I gave the endeavor considerable thought and developed what I believed would be a workable plan. If the peelers, and their plod bosses, were looking for me, all I really needed to do in my sorties away from my lodging house was... not be me.

If I didn't match their imagined description, I had nothing to fear. I would disguise myself.

With that in mind, on my way out of hospital at the close of my next working shift, I quietly and unobtrusively pocketed a bottle of Nitrocellulose (evil of me, petty theft) and hurried home.

Nitrocellulose? Just over forty years ago, a couple of Frenchmen discovered that cellulose nitrate, dissolved in ether, created a sticky clear gelatinous liquid that, when mixed with a number of acids, worked wonders as a wart remover. All well and good; and the hospital did use it for that purpose, but that was of no importance to me. What I cared about was the sticky aspect!

I should have described Nitrocellulose as a *very* sticky clear gelatinous liquid. So sticky in fact that, within a year of its discovery, a Boston physician began using the concoction as a medical dressing to hold wounds closed. Liquid bandages were born. An American doctor dubbed the solution 'collodion' (from the Greek *kollodis*, meaning *gluey*).

What had any of this to do with the price of Her Majesty's tea in the Orient?

As an interesting side note, and the object of my interest, was the fact Nitrocellulose, when applied to the face, tightened as it dried and pulled and pinched the skin. Carefully applied, the substance created realistic-looking (because they were real) wrinkles. Often used in the legitimate theatre as a makeup application for actors, I was certain it could be used for roughly the same purpose by a jolly East End street cleaner like myself, determined to fool the yobs with a facial scar or, perhaps, by appearing older than, in truth, I was.

The application was temporary. Once the fun was had a cotton swab, bathed in ethanol and rubbed over the made-up area, removed the scar or wrinkles with only the slightest wear and tear of the underlying flesh. The wearer was instantly young again.

So I made myself decidedly older. I dressed the part with some of Mr Griggs' clothes from the closet in the rear of his shop. I headed out for a leisurely walk (I was an aged gent, after all) to the north and the west, through Whitechapel and into Spitalfields; my first walk through the murder district since the well-earned death of my gal, Stockings.

My god, the streets were barking mad!

Thousands of absolutely hysterical East Enders stomping about or wandering lost; swearing or crying. And, to show it was not my imagination, I quote a reporter from the Observer:

'... *East London became panic-stricken – for there is no other term to describe the aimless, frightened way in which the people paraded the crowded thoroughfares. The first three days after the murder witnessed extraordinary scenes in the vicinity of the crimes. Crowds gathered in Buck's Row and Hanbury Street outside both entrances to the mortuary, and about the police stations in Commercial Street, Leman Street and Bethnal Green.*'

Men fought each other on the sidewalks. Angry passions exploded everywhere. Blind fury was unleashed upon anyone who acted suspiciously or spoke stupidly regarding the crimes or the victims. I saw several such scuffles in my walking search for knowledge. I saw blood. (Not mine and not spilled by me. With no desire to have my name jotted down as a witness, I kept walking.) Anyone, the people suddenly realized, might be the killer! Therefore everyone might be subject to attack! Foreigners and foreign-looking individuals, of which there was no shortage in Whitechapel and Spitalfields, appeared especially guilty.

Tourists walked in it. Horse-drawn coaches, carts, and cabs fought through it. Women and children watched it from the upper windows of the lodging houses all up and down the streets.

Saucy Jacky

And the coppers ran hither and yon, blowing their whistles and shouting for order.

"Out!" came a gravelly female voice, shouting from inside *The Britannia*.

In an attempt to escape the insanity, I had turned the northwest corner at Commercial and Dorset Streets and was trying to get by the front doors of the public house. Trying without success!

Only tourists called it The Britannia, by the way. The locals called the pub *'Ringer's'* after the landlord (though Walter Wringer had been dead and gone seven years). Matilda, his widow (who'd taken to signing things *'Ringer'* as it was easier), served behind the bar and ruled over the criminals and whores that her husband, and life, had left her for customers. But I'm off topic again...

Back in Dorset Street... Entering this new herd of humanity, I had to stop outside Ringer's not to be trampled. Barging out through the pub doors, backwards into the crowd, with his hands above his head, came a well-dressed, but unkempt, fellow. He was five-eleven perhaps, thin and dark; with receding brown hair, a heavy moustache and a thick beard; sunken cheeks, piercing grey eyes, and a pointed nose. His defensive stance was owed to the grey-haired lady pub owner following in his wake with a wooden club over her shoulder.

"Out!" Matilda Ringer shouted again, though the frightened man had already obeyed.

"Please," he cried.

"Please, nothin'. I've had enough of you, y' creepy bastard! Every time I turn round yeer back again, staring the girls down w' yer searing eyes, demandin' drink, wantin' money, beggin' for a bed; and each time passin' y'self off as some un' different."

"That's ridiculous!"

"Is it?" she demanded, cocking the club, straining to swing. "Ya told the barman last night y' was Count Sobieski, son of a Polish king. Ya told the bar boy y' were Ostin, or some such, escapin' the consequences of a duel in Germany. Ya told one of my girls yer name was Max, a Russian of good family. Yeer a creep!"

114

"Told me he was Bertrand Ashley!" shouted a blousey tart from the doorway.

"And me," added a pub crawler beside the girl, "Said he were Nabokoff and wanted to borrow a guinea. A guinea!"

The pub owner curled her lip in disgust. "Yeer a student, yeer the gentry, yeer on the run from... name yer favorite country! Yeer the bleedin' killer for all I know." The crowd gasped. "Come back in again and y'll be fleeing a cracked skull!"

The vagabond owner of evil eyes, and many identities, moved on. Matilda Ringer and her customers returned to the pub and their places. Saddened (but educated) that life in the slums went on outside of my work, Yours Truly continued my tour into Dorset Street.

Dorset Street ran parallel with Brushfield Street (to the north) and White's Row (to the south), connecting Crispin Street (to the west) with Commercial Street (to the east). An alley called Little Paternoster Row connected Dorset Street with Brushfield. Laid out, as Datchet Street, two hundred years before, the name changed owing to an influx of immigrants with poor English skills. The residents of the crowded doss houses referred to it as 'Dosset' or 'Dossen' Street. A dead and rotting rose, by any name, stank as much.

Despite being short, only 400 feet long, and narrow, 24 feet wide, Dorset Street had a great reputation as the worst street in London. I'll touch that later but, this day, every street in the East End looked the same. It overflowed with alarmed peoples chattering murder gossip.

Amid that gossip, for the first time I heard two names; 'Annie Chapman' and 'Dark Annie'. Both, I came to understand, belonged to the same person. Apparently 'Dark Annie' Chapman was the true name of ol' Stockings. (It's interesting to hear, for the first time, the name of a person you recently murdered. Not particularly affecting, but interesting all the same.)

"What was she doing on the street at that ungodly hour?" someone asked.

"What would she 'ave been doin'" someone else asked with a derisive laugh.

"Got thrown out of her lodging house," another answered. "For stealing potatoes."

"Well, that wasn't called for. Still, she ought not have stole. Not if someone was watching."

By the middle of the block, the story had changed to Dark Annie being cruelly ordered to leave, on the night of her murder, in the middle of peeling potatoes. That made as much, or as little, sense. Both versions of the tale reached the far end of the block before I did.

I entered a bigger crowd in front of No 35, one of William Crossingham's lodging houses (one of the two biggest, most underhanded, landlords in the East End slums; the other was Jack McCarthy. Both will come up again). That was the gloomy doss house where, apparently, Stockings had been a resident. Though I wasn't sure of the charge, a fellow on the stoop stood loudly defending himself. Somebody in the throng identified him as the house deputy, another called him the nightwatchman. Whichever, if either, was true, the bloke was mad as a hornet.

"Eating potatoes!" he growled. "She was sitting at kitchen table, gone half-one Saturday morning, eating a baked potato and gabbing with other lodgers. Evans asked for her doss and she didn't have it. She poked her head in my office. I told her if she could find money for beer, she could find money for her bed. She didn't argue. Said, 'Never mind. I shall soon be back. Don't let the bed.' S'all was to it."

He pointed to the alley at the corner of the lodging house. "Evans seen her. She walked up Little Paternoster Road, turned right into Brushfield Street, headed towards Christ Church."

The crowd grumbled. Unfairly. I knew the fellow was right. She passed the church, headed for Hanbury Street; headed for a meeting with Yours Truly.

I returned to my lodgings with a light heart over all the frantic to-do in the streets. The entire East End was in near riot over my antics. I couldn't have been happier. I doffed my theatrical makeup and the borrowed clothes and returned, upstairs, to my other life. Then...

Pity me! Mrs Griggs delivered me some awful news.

I mentioned earlier the coppers did a search of the backyard of No 29 Hanbury Street, and started to tell all they'd found. I left one item out. This was the moment when I learned of it. Nosing in one of her papers, my landlady brought an article to my attention and ruined my good mood. That morning, in the backyard at Hanbury Street the peelers had found... a leather apron. An honest to god leather apron, washed, neatly folded and laying on the ground not ten feet from where I'd done my good work.

I'd apparently been too busy finishing up with Stockings. As the time had got away and the daylight overtook me, and the day time workers threatened to appear, I'd never seen it. Had no idea until, Mrs Griggs read the paper aloud, it had been there at all. A leather apron! Oh, pity me! If I'd only known! What tremendous sport I could have had at the expense of the coppers, and the neighbours, and the bloody Jews, if I'd only been aware!

I made myself a promise, silently of course as I didn't want to let my landlady in on it, to be more aware of my surroundings going forward. Such jolly opportunities would be rare indeed.

Reading further, Mrs Griggs informed me they found a basin of clean water resting beneath the yard's water tap, only a few feet from the body. Though I pretended that was news, it really was not. I had seen the hand pump and had ignored it.

Why didn't the killer wash his hands, the reporter wondered? Because the killer takes care to soil himself as little as possible, I thought, you feeble scribbler of old news. The killer enjoys the sport of walking home with his mitts buried in his pockets, casual-like as if he owned the street, and all the time *red-handed*. ha ha. Oh, the papers were suddenly a delight.

And the radicals, who'd been my friends in print since the morning after George Yard, were dripping blood from their fangs. On the day of the Hanbury Street event, the *Star* done up a four-column notice of the *tragedy* and prefaced it with this bit of poetry:

'London lies today under the spell of a great terror. A nameless reprobate – half beast, half man – is at large, who is daily gratifying his murderous instincts on the most miserable and defenceless classes of the community. There can be no shadow of a doubt now that our original theory was correct, and that the Whitechapel murderer, who has now four...'

From that point, I had difficulty maintaining my attention. My disgust was interfering. Again with the *four* victims. The stupid bastards had to make it four. I was to be saddled with the ape-like throttling of Emma Smith, regardless of my innocence, regardless of the care I'd shown in my work since. Every murder in London, it seemed, was to be laid at my doorstep!

The fools in the press would need a lesson. They would need to be shown my murders were singular, to be confused with no others. From that instant forward, I committed myself to making the difference clear. Thus determined...

I took control again of my attention and returned to the good Mrs Griggs and her reading:

'There can be no shadow of a doubt now that our original theory was correct, and that the Whitechapel murderer, who has now four victims to his knife, is one man, and that man a murderous maniac. Hideous malice, deadly cunning, insatiable thirst for blood – all these are the marks of the mad homicide. The ghoul-like creature who stalks through the streets of London, stalking down his victims like a Pawnee Indian. He is simply drunk with blood and he will have more.'

I was drunk! Drunk with blood. ha ha. The idiots were unable to see their own irony. I would be forced to show them.

Twenty-One
Leather Apron Farce

My Tory landlady was quickly becoming a raging radical! Or she was raging against the radicals! I was, frankly, losing track. Mrs Griggs waved a copy of the Monday morning *Star*, reading out loud, interrupting herself in exasperation to complain about the differences (and even the outright lies) in the details of the same stories printed only the night before regarding the Hanbury Street crime. It was, she insisted, an egregious admission.

"We were compelled in our later editions of yesterday to contradict many of the reports which found admittance to our columns and to those of all our contemporaries earlier in the day. For this the senseless, the endless prevarications of the police were to blame."

The *Star* blamed the police for their own prevarications! That was rich. The *Star* were the ones who said that, after nearly decapitating her, I tied the whores head back on with my handkerchief. The *Pall Mall Gazette*, if I'm not mistaken, claimed her rings had been torn from her dead fingers and laid at her feet. That was a load of tosh. Didn't I know? Her rings were downstairs in one of Mr Griggs' boxes! The *Daily Telegraph* reported the most idiotic story of all regarding Stockings' murder and the items found round her carcass, such a gross lie, I committed the offending sentence to memory.

'There were also found two farthings polished brightly, and, according to some, these coins had been passed off as half-sovereigns upon the deceased by her murderer.'

That's right! To suggest the whore had her own money was ridiculous. If she'd had money she'd either been somewhere drinking or would have paid her doss and been safely tucked away for the night. To suggest I gave those bitches money was even more outrageous; in that economy! But to state I brought two polished farthings with me, and left them with the dead whore (supposedly to pay the ferryman) but had cheated her as the proper fare was one pound sterling? That was insulting.

Other reports had farthings, or other coins, or rings (depending upon the paper) found strategically positioned – in different places – about the body. Some wondered why. Some went ahead and guessed, suggesting a sinister rite of some kind had been conducted. Rumors in the streets, owing to these reports, now suggested or stated outright *ritual murder*.

Oh. Bless me! The whore had a piece of muslin and two cheap combs; that was the bleeding lot!

The papers were, literally, making it up. Now, called out for their fictions by the police, the *Star's* editors claimed they'd been forced to make it up – because the coppers wouldn't take the time from their investigations to meet with the press! Meanwhile, on the front page of the same paper, the radicals were, yet again, having a go at Scotland Yard for a lack of progress with the killings.

Contradiction and farce. No, it was worse than that. The news reporting in the East End, the panic throughout London, the reactions amongst the poorest of the poor from drunken jubilation in the streets to silent shivering terror, could all suddenly be symbolized by the theatrical masks of *Comedy and Tragedy*; though it made more sense to think of the situation in terms of *Hilarity and Pathos*.

While residents of Hanbury Street, Buck's Row, and George Yard, screamed to the papers, hurled insults at the police, and cried about inadequate protection, rumor had it the same individuals opened their doors to the street crowds; let complete strangers into their homes to gaze from their windows down onto the murder sites. Those not in a panic were in the midst of an endless party.

That's it! I'd made every day Halloween! I'd brought all of the celebrations of the world home to Britain. Our own Bank Holiday with blood. The American Mardi Gras with murder. The Venice Carnival with carnage. Yi Peng with prostitutes. St Patrick's Day with intestines for snakes. Oktoberfest with the whores paying dearly for their beer! And Yours Truly running from the bulls. ha ha.

The coppers hated me and wanted my head. The papers resented the police and wanted their heads. Londoners blamed the government and wanted 'their' heads (though they weren't precisely sure whose heads those were). The unfortunates of Whitechapel lived outside of the lot and merely wanted bread and a place to lay their heads. But... they had sex in alleys and spent their pennies on beer instead.

So I wanted their blood.

What else? So much was happening. I get confused and am probably telling it badly.

I know! Have I re-addressed the leather apron? No, not the villain threatening prostitutes! The protective garment!

The apron found by police in the backyard of 29 Hanbury Street (a few feet from what I'd left of Dark Annie Chapman) the morning of the murder. I said I was disappointed in not finding it then, at the height of the Leather Apron scare! The sport I might have had. But with my other games that morning, and having started so late, I missed the opportunity.

Now the truth of its presence at the scene came out! The leather apron found near Stockings... belonged to one of the house residents. His mother had washed it the evening before and left it out to dry. How's that for a let down! ha ha.

The apron had been a washout as a clue; less substantial than London fog. But it was not the end. Leather Apron, the villain, remained a frightening character and a wanted man. On that score, the news reports of 10 September ended up rescuing my dear landlady from her disappointment. For, lifting another issue from her fresh stack of news print, Mrs Griggs gave forth with an exclamation that shook the windows. "They've got him! They've got the murderer!"

I must confess, I doubted her. And, safe and snug as I was in my own lodgings, it will come as no surprise I doubted the news reporter's claim. Still the good lady had my interest. "The police?" I asked. "Mrs Griggs, you say they've got the..."

She had her glasses in place and was reading: "At nine o'clock this morning, Monday, 10 September, Detective Sergeant Thicke of H Division..."

I remembered DS Thicke – and not merely owing to my association of his name with my general opinion of most coppers. I'd seen him at hospital; of course I'd seen a good many coppers at hospital, they infested the place at times. But I'd seen him in person, in action. (I'll tell that story in future.) But, for now, I'll say this, Sergeant Thicke had made big news early that summer. He'd caught some burglar with a bundle of stolen goods under his arm. He'd snatched the miscreant, by his neck tie, causing the fellow to drop his swag. Thicke then stood atop the bundle, holding the villain by his tie, and holding off a group of slum n'er-do-wells who'd run to the burglar's assistance. Threatening the lot with his truncheon, Thicke hustled the burglar into a nearby hairdresser's shop to complete his arrest. Like Abberline, Thicke was a hero. Unlike the beloved Inspector, Thick was also mean. He was a fellow you remembered, Sergeant Thicke, with his dark brown hair and heavy drooping moustache (at odds with his own erect posture).

But I'm wandering again. Mrs Griggs was reading.

The article concerned an event in Mulberry Street, a short block of residences and shops (east of St Mary's) occupied by foreign tailors and boot makers. They might say *artists*, and perhaps they'd have a point, as the vast majority of the shoes worn by the stage performers of London's West End and the Continent came from the slipper makers of Mulberry Street. But... the article.

Detective Sergeant Thicke of H Division, accompanied by three constables knocked, at No 22 Mulberry Street, Commercial Road East. The door was opened by a dark, short, thickset Polish Jew with thinning black hair and a well-trained black moustache. This was John (or as several papers had it, Jack) Pizer, a shoemaker. The sergeant and Pizer knew each other on sight. More, Sergeant Thicke had discovered that Pizer was known on the streets as Leather Apron.

What happened in the doorway cannot be known for certain. What the public believed happened depended entirely upon which paper one read.

In the radical versions, the *Star* and their ilk, the meeting was a congenial affair on the part of Pizer with the police acting the roughs. Thicke advised Pizer he was wanted. The shoemaker politely asked what for and Thicke replied, "You know what for. You will have to come with me."

"Very well, sir," the law-abiding Pizer reportedly answered, "I'll go down to the station with you with the greatest of pleasure." Pizer went along peacefully.

I preferred the more dramatic version as reported by the *Telegraph* and other conservative papers wherein, the minute the door of the residence was opened by the scofflaw rat, the heroic sergeant reached in and grabbed Pizer by the shoulder, declaring, "You are just the man I want."

In response, the startled and instantly pale Jew-coward cried out over the opposite shoulder, "Mother, he has got me!"

Then, with each of the four policeman grabbing hold, Pizer was jerked from the house and taken in charge to the Leman Street Police Station on suspicion of murder. To ensure the reader understood and approved of whatever abuse was heaped upon the villain, the Tory papers recounted the crimes of Leather Apron and Pizer's own history in the criminal courts.

Meanwhile rumor, meaning Mrs Griggs and her Dress Reformists, and later Miss Adler and Archie, fleshed out the story with many behind the scenes details, including the fact that, in the Metropolitan Police Stations and in their Scotland Yard Headquarters, nobody; not a peeler, a plod inspector, nor any of the chiefs or commissioners had the slightest evidence against the shoemaker.

Nothing mattered, particularly facts. The murdering Leather Apron was off the street and the drunken whores were safe once again. Or so they thought.

Finally, details emerged regarding the marvelous chase, near riot, and arrest I'd witnessed in front of the doss house in Flower and Dean Street on the morning Stockings died.

The tattooed fugitive, target of the chase, was a repeat offender known to the police as Squibby. He had a long history of arrests – and a reputation for never going quietly. Which, coupled with his hard physique, explains the coppers' hesitation in rushing the lodging house. Every arrest, it was said, became a battle requiring six bulls (minimum) to get the fellow into nick. By the time his cell door was slammed, charming Squibby was usually naked and the constables minus helmets and sleeves. Even Miss Adler's Archie had once suffered a black eye by Squibby's hand (or elbow).

Story was... several weeks earlier, Squibby had been hurling bricks at a constable. One, badly thrown, missed the copper and injured a child. As appeared to be his routine, the tattooed villain ran and hid; obviously in Hanbury Street. The morning of the Hanbury Street event, the wanted man (like everybody in the neighbourhood) heard of the murder and came out to gawk. Squibby mingled with the crowd in front of No 29 watching the coppers. Soon, at least one of the law men recognized him. The villain saw he'd been recognized and was off like a shot. The plods, without considering consequences, blew their whistles and took chase. The rest can be imagined.

The crowd, thinking the alarmed officers were onto the murderer, in one huge wave, took off after the police – all in pursuit of Squibby! Thus was born the chase for 'the Whitechapel killer' (right round me as if I were a bleeding Maypole) and the riot in Flower and Dean Street.

I'd been there to see the stand-off, and the hesitation before the police found their bollocks and headed in after him. Now I knew, thanks to Archie, the plod version of what transpired inside the lodging house. They found Squibby, inside, a changed man. Instead of the usual animal, foaming at the mouth and swearing, ready to fight to the death, he was a cringing coward with a ghastly white face, violently trembling as if he were a freezing mutt. The shrieking rabble outside of the house wanted his blood and Squibby knew it.

Terrified, poor Squibby begged the coppers to get him out alive. They promised as much and, as I've already said, delivered with the arrival of a large contingent of uniformed reinforcements. The police got Squibby to nick and, many hours later, finally managed to convince the screaming throng outside that the poor shivering bastard inside was not the Whitechapel killer. The disappointed crowd went home without having tasted the murderer's blood.

News wasn't merely being reported that Monday, it was also being made.

At 10:00 am, at the Working Lads' Institute, Coroner Wynn Baxter convened the first session of his inquest into the death of my girl, Stockings (Annie Chapman, to the rabble). Proceedings began with a field trip for the jury, down to the mortuary in Old Montague Street, to view the cold corpse and see my work first hand. I hoped they enjoyed it half as much as I enjoyed bringing it to them.

Four witnesses, John Davis, Amelia Palmer, Timothy Donovan, and John Evans, prattled on about their relationships with the whore before I got to her.

Donovan, manager (for owner Crossingham) of the doss house the whore called home, at 35 Dorset Street, told the jury that near 2:30 in the afternoon (of 7 September) Stockings arrived at lodging house and asked to be allowed to sit downstairs in the kitchen. He asked where she'd been all week and the whore replied, 'in the infirmary.'

At 5:15 pm Chapman was seen in the street by Palmer, a charwoman and friend, who asked her, "Aren't you going to Stratford today?"

Chapman replied, "I feel too ill to do anything." Ten minutes later, when Palmer found her standing in the same spot, the whore said, "It's no use giving way. I must pull myself together and get some money or I shall have no lodgings."

John Evans, the doss house nightwatchman, testified that, 'Soon after midnight she (Chapman) came in saying she had been to Vauxhall to see her sister, who gave her 5d. She immediately sent one of the lodgers for a pint of beer and then popped out again herself.'

Fascinating, stimulating testimony all. She was sick and needed money for her bed. When she got the money, she bought beer. To which I say:

'Farewell and adieu to you, Spanish ladies, Farewell and adieu to you, ladies of Spain...'

Coroner Baxter adjourned the inquest until Wednesday, 12 September, no doubt on account of being bored to bleeding tears.

Twenty-Two
Mile End Vigilance

The morning of 11 September Mrs Griggs was at her papers again carrying on about the press, and most particularly the radical press, illegitimately accelerating their written attacks on police and Home Office in regards to the recent murders. Certainly they (the crimes) were awful, she conceded, but as certainly the Metropolitan Police were doing everything in their power to track down the miscreant!

It will come as no surprise I agreed with the good lady.

No sooner was that issue resolved, then Mrs Griggs turned to another, resurrected in new articles over the last two days. In those, for want of something horrible to print – to keep the paying public agitated – the publishers had revisited ancient history; the ghost of an earlier murder, of an unknown woman in Osborn Street, at Christmas-time the previous year.

Unknown woman, my arse!

The damned editors were at it again! Another badly written, poorly informed article relating the incorrectly remembered story of poor Emma Smith! It was not Christmas, it was Easter Monday of the previous April. I was being forced to hear it again – and wrongly. I've mentioned, repeatedly, how the event affected, eventually inspired, and ultimately depressed me. As Mrs Griggs went on, I grew more and more sick and annoyed. I didn't want to hear about filthy Emma Smith, named or unnamed. I'd grown tired of thinking of Emma Smith at all. I made some excuse (I can't remember what), and left the house early, claiming I had something I needed to do before heading to hospital.

I went out.

I went for a walk in the filthy teeming streets. Mind, I made my best effort to stay within myself, but I needed fresh air and time to contemplate who I was and what I was about. I shut out the noises of the rabble in the Whitechapel Road. I crossed the street to avoid the newsstand of Mr Frogg and tuned out young Tad's shouted headlines. I breathed deep, floated like a phantom, and practiced at being unseen. Soon I was feeling better.

Then I saw the sign.

I wasn't looking for it. But there it was and I could not help but notice. It had only recently been hung, that day, as I was seeing it for the first time on what was for me a routine route; a large bright poster placarded in a tobacconist's shop window. Once I'd seen it, I could not look away.

It read, in part:

IMPORTANT NOTICE – To the Tradesmen, Ratepayers, and Inhabitants Generally, of Whitechapel and District. – Finding that in spite of Murders being committed in our midst, and that the Murderer or Murderers are still at large, we the undersigned have formed ourselves into a committee, and intend offering a substantial REWARD to anyone, Citizen, or otherwise, who shall give such information that will bring the Murderer or Murderers to Justice. A Committee of Gentlemen has already been formed to carry out the above object, and will meet every evening at nine o'clock, at Mr. J. Aarons'. The 'Crown', 74 Mile End Road, corner of Jubilee Street, and will be pleased to receive the assistance of the residents of the District...

There was more to it, just as wordy and dull, but that was the general appeal. At the bottom of the handbill; one, two, three, four... Sixteen men, altogether, had signed their names in pledge, as members and officers of what they called the 'Mile End Vigilance Committee'.

I could not know then, but would eventually discover (yes, I checked up), this group of tradesmen; including a tailor, a licensed victualler, a cigar manufacturer, a picture-frame maker, and even an actor, had met for the first time only the previous night at the Crown Tavern in Mile End Road, to discuss my so-called outrages and toss about ideas as to how they might help Whitechapel in its hour of need. Sixteen men too foolish to see, or understand, I was helping Whitechapel, the East End, and all of London by my activities.

According to the signatures, twelve of their number took their places as sheep to follow their four elected shepherds. George Lusk, a builder and contractor, a member of the Metropolitan Board of Works, and a vestryman of the parish of Mile End Old Town, was named their president. John Cohen was elected vice-president; Joseph Aarons, treasurer; and Mr B Harris was chosen as their honorary secretary. The stated purpose of the Mile End Vigilance Committee was 'to strengthen the hands of the police by action on the part of the citizens.'

How wonderful! Sixteen mean little Jews, out for my head, intent on raising reward monies to see me copped. Make me laugh!

Then... speak of the devil! As I finished perusing the threatening poster, a police constable happened by on his patrol. I couldn't help but bring the notice to his attention. "Officer, have you seen this?"

He came to a stop and followed my pointing finger to the tobacconist's window and to the affixed handbill. Was that doubt I saw creep into his eye? "Oh, aye," he replied. "They're placarded all over the East End this morning, up and down the High, from Mile End to Houndsditch."

"Good idea that?" I asked. "A reward?"

The officer shrugged. "S'pose it's a matter for debate. The Home Office is against it, as I understand. I can't speak for the police, sir. But I don't see what good it will do."

"Fear treasure hunters, do you?"

The officer shrugged again. "I support vigilance, sir, by everybody in the community. Vigilantes are another kettle of fish altogether." He tapped the brim of his round blue helmet and started away. "Good morning, sir."

Over the next few weeks, of course, questions and controversy did begin to brew regarding this group of vigilantes – and many other groups of vigilantes that soon began to form themselves through the districts of the East End. Everybody wanted a piece of the Whitechapel killer.

George Lusk, the Mile End committee's elected president, later told reporters from several papers he and his group of concerned citizens 'wished it to be directly understood that the Committee was in no way antagonistic to the police authorities, who were doing their best, as they believed they always did, to bring the culprits to justice.'

I watched the peeler amble away, then turned back to consider the posted bill once more. I read it again in its entirety. Well, well, well, I thought. Rewards! Reward money for the capture of the Whitechapel murderer!

Well, well, well, Mr Do-good Lusk. Welcome to the game!

Twenty-Three
Inquests, Inquests, Inquests

Art critics! That's what the authorities and representatives of law and order in London's East End had become. Rather, that was the role to which I had reduced them as, day in and day out, from one end of the district to another, they were forced to convene one Coroner's Inquest after another, to observe, question, and critique my brilliant work. I'd made them all art critics!

The newspapers, meanwhile, owing to the public's right to know, the reporter's mania to tell, and the publisher's desire to grow fat off the lucre, had been forced to devote massive blocks of column inch space to the findings and results of those same inquiries. What a lark! I was everyone's darling! Even the radical press had been forced to abandon their usual propaganda, their unceasing attacks on Her Majesty's government and the police for imagined failures, to the specific *real news* accounts of their failures in nicking Yours Truly.

Every traumatized witness trembled his or her way to the stand to champion my work. Every printed edition of every local, city, and national rag, carried their awe-filled mumblings to the streets. Every decent citizen of the East End took in the details and shook their heads in disgust at the awful things those whores had done. The filthy women they were. The skill I'd employed in cleaning them up.

Message indeed. I held sway over the entire country. It was a delight to be me!

The second day of the Chapman inquest was convened on Wednesday, 12 September. The Police Department was represented by Inspectors Abberline and Helson, both upright and stiff in the cause of justice. Nearly a dozen witnesses were called to give evidence, including residents of the house in Hanbury Street and a selection of neighbours who had stuck in their noses. Between them, Coroner Baxter hoped to further reconstruct events. Also testifying was the sergeant who had nicked Leather Apron. And a surprise witness that had the reporters panting.

John Richardson testified he'd come into house, from his home in John Street, at 4:45 am. He assisted his mother, Amelia the packer, and often stopped en route to his full-time work as a porter in the Spitalfields Market. He took the passageway to the back door, looked out and down into the stairs leading to their cellar workplace, and saw the lock was secure. Then, as his boot had been paining his toe, Richardson stepped out and sat upon the middle step to cut off a flapping piece of leather. His testimony narrowed the time of the crime. Richardson saw nothing unusual. If a body had been there then, not two feet from his left hip, he surely would have seen her.

I got a shock when I read the testimony of Albert Cadosh, a carpenter, who lived at No 27, the house on the far side of the backyard fence. Between 5:20 and 5:30 he visited his backyard privy twice. In his hunger for, even fleeting, fame, the poor bastard spoke openly of a bladder infection or some such rot. On Cadosh's first return trip to house, he testified, he heard whispers, inaudible save for the word 'No.' That was the whore denying she'd been there before.

It was the first I learned someone had overheard me and Stockings from only a few feet away; the first I knew how close I'd come to being found out.

Minutes later, heading back in after his second trip to loo, the carpenter heard something fall against the fence. That would have been me, catching the palings with my shoulder, when the whore chose that instant to leave her shell and head for hell.

Cadosh, on his way to work, didn't stop to wonder what he'd heard. Bless him. He left the house and was ogling the Christ Church clock in passing at 5:32. It was enlightening testimony.

Little else from that meeting of the inquest interested me, till the coroner called his surprise witness to testify; John Pizer. Yes, ol' Leather Apron himself! Once Whitechapel's most wanted suspect. Would he confess his crimes? Hardly. What few knew, what I didn't learn until later, was that Pizer had not even come to the coroner's court from a police cell. He'd been released from custody the previous night and had come from home. He sat, waiting to testify, whispering with the Met's Sergeant Thicke as if the pair were long separated companions.

Why not? When Thicke detained the man in Mulberry Street, neither he nor anyone else in the Metropolitan Police had the slightest evidence Leather Apron was connected to the Whitechapel murders. There were rumors he carried knives, but shoemaker's did. As to the reports he harassed and assaulted prostitutes; there had never been a complaint.

The only complaint ever lodged against Pizer (in reference to dead whores) came the day after his arrest. That Tuesday, at the Leman Street Police Station, Emanuel Violena (a foreign vagrant) claimed he'd seen Leather Apron quarreling with a woman the morning of Chapman's death. That afternoon, Violena viewed a line-up of twelve Jewish suspects. Without hesitation, he identified Pizer.

Unfortunately for Violena, the identity parade preceded three hours of questioning, during which he repeatedly contradicted himself. Ultimately, the coppers concluded Violena fabricated his story. The blighter wanted a look at the corpse of the murdered whore and thought he could by pointing a finger at Pizer. And the news editors say I'm twisted! Outside of Violena's complaint, the police had nothing on Pizer. The knives confiscated as possible murder weapons were tools of his trade, nothing more. And Pizer had alibis for the last two murders.

He denied leaving the Mulberry Street house between that Thursday and Monday. His stepmother, brother, and sister-in-law corroborated him. They may have lied, but how would anyone prove it?

Pizer's alibi for the night of the Queen's murder was unshakeable. He stayed in a Holloway Road lodging house, north of London City. The same night I'd taken inspiration from the east London dock fire, Pizer and the Holloway lodging house proprietor had stood together, watching the orange glow in the sky. Two passing bobbies stopped and watched with them.

The whole day gone, the police issued Emanuel Violenia a severe reprimand for wasting their time, threatened to arrest him, then threw him out of the station. An hour and a half later, with no evidence (or complaint) against him, John Pizer was released. So it was Leather Apron testified, as a witness, not a suspect, at the inquest of Dark Annie.

I can't say I was surprised. I knew the man was innocent. ha ha.

But don't, for a moment, believe his innocence had any bearing on the way the papers treated the fellow. When Pizer took the stand, the reporter for the *East London Observer* described him as if he were the villain in a stage melodrama.

'He was a man of about five feet four inches, with a dark-hued face, which was not altogether pleasant to look upon by reason of the grizzly black strips of hair, nearly an inch in length, which almost covered his face. The thin lips, too, had a cruel, sardonic kind of look, which was increased, if anything, by the drooping dark moustache and side whiskers. His hair was short, smooth, and dark, intermingled with grey, and his head was slightly bald on the top. The head was large, and was fixed to the body by a thick, heavy-looking neck. Pizer wore a dark overcoat, brown trousers, and a brown and very much battered hat, and appeared somewhat splay-footed – at all events, he stood with his feet meeting at the heels, and then diverging almost at right angles. His evidence was given quietly and distinctly were it not for the thick, guttural foreign accent.'

His toes pointed out, thus he had to be a murderer! By the by, allow me to quietly confess that I, myself, have always been markedly pigeon-toed.

In the end, Leather Apron was another cock-up. Having no evidence to connect him with the murder did not prevent his arrest. Setting him free did not absolve him. The entire affair merely added to an already lively feeling of Jew hatred aimed at the slums of Whitechapel. The people were out and angry. The police were out and wary. As much as possible I stayed in, giving all a bit of a respite.

The medics and the coppers took over on the third day of the Chapman inquest when Coroner Baxter reconvened on Thursday, 13 September. Inspectors Abberline and Helson looked on for the CID while Inspector Chandler and Police Sergeant Badham gave evidence regarding their heroic efforts.

When the Police Surgeon took the stand, the newspaper's coverage was a letdown. But I couldn't blame the crime reporters. Dr Philips gave a wanting description of my work. Having concluded it was all too gruesome, he omitted the best parts in the telling. What a load of tosh!

To further embarrass himself, Phillips put the time of the whore's death as 4:30 am or earlier. Not a good guess at all! Then, in my opinion, he added another guess and made a laughing stock of himself. Phillips stated he believed, in order for the murderer to perform the mutilations he had, he most likely had anatomical or medical knowledge. ha ha. The good doctor thought I was a doctor!

Baxter adjourned the inquiry until Wednesday, 19 September.

Well before, on Friday, 14 September, to be exact, I learned an interesting lesson regarding Spitalfields undertakers. My goodness, but they were a generous lot!

Rumors a Hanbury Street mortician, Henry Smith, had paid for Polly Nichols' fancy hearse had irritated me and inspired me to take my show to the do-gooder's backyard. Well, someone's backyard in Hanbury Street. Now, word was, another Spitalfields death-dealer, Harry Hawes, had sprung for the hearse to cart Dark Annie's remains away. Damn blast those morticians with hearts o' gold!

Stockings' send off was a *hush-hush* affair, to keep the gawkers and the newshounds away, and to give the family members privacy – and a feeling of respectability. But, people being hungry for news as they were, details eventually came out, once the bitch was planted.

The fancy borrowed rig, pulled by combed black nags, rolled up bright and early to the old shed that served as the Workhouse Infirmary Mortuary that morning. All that I'd left of the Chapman whore was poured into an elm box (too damned good for her) and draped in black cloth. She was carted out and driven north to Undertaker Hawes' digs at 19 Hunt Street.

Hawes marked time there until 9:00 am, when – quietly and without procession – the hearse and its cargo were whipped in the direction of Manor Park Cemetery, Forest Gate. There the whore would be buried without a grave marker. Her relatives, who had themselves managed the remaining funeral expenses (if the press version was accurate), met the hearse at the cemetery. The Anglican graveside voodoo rites were short and sweet, attended only by family, then Stockings was sent on alone. The whole thing was rather redundant, if you asked me; I'd already done that.

Since her tragic demise, those investigating the Chapman murder had been looking for a good many persons of interest whose names had arisen in canvas interviews. Chief among these was a character known by Tim Donovan as the *Pensioner*; a man purported to be the dead woman's most significant other. The same day they stuck Stockings in the ground, the Pensioner surfaced.

A bloke named Ted Stanley, a bricklayer's labourer and regular visitor to her room (and presumably her bed), appeared at the Commercial Street Police Station. He'd heard in the streets he was being sought. He fervently denied ever having used the nickname Pensioner or having known of its use. He had come to them, he said, before they came for him; and proceeded with a voluntary statement.

Have no fear, I wouldn't bore anyone with it, even if I had it (and I don't). The few details released by the coppers were of no importance (neither Miss Adler nor her Archie ever mentioned Stanley) and were contradicted by later statements he gave at the inquest. The just was: despite being known on sight by Donovan, despite rolling around on Chapman for two years, and despite frequently paying the 8d for their double bed, he barely knew the woman, knew nothing about her murder, and wanted nothing more to do with the matter.

So much for the sought after Pensioner. Still the witnesses kept coming.

The following day, 15 September, William Stevens, a painter who occasionally took lodgings in the same house as Chapman, poked his head in at Commercial Street Police Station to offer evidence. He'd seen Dark Annie at the house the morning of her murder, before she'd been turned out. She'd been to hospital, she groused, where she'd collected a bottle of lotion, a bottle of liquid medicine, and a small box containing two pills. But the box had come apart. In answer, she had wrapped the pills in a piece of paper she'd found (near the fireplace) on Crossingham's kitchen floor. That *paper* was the envelope corner, containing the pills and bearing the Royal Sussex Regiment stamp. The one Yours Truly found in her secret purse and, being a clever clogs, left as a clue beside her dead head.

With that short interview, another line of police inquiry vanished like smoke in a breeze, and another link in the fragile chain connecting dead whores with a randy and murderous soldier fell away. Oh, the poor plods. Where were they? Nearer to finding their killer or farther away?

Mrs Griggs read to me the details of the third meeting of the Nichols inquest, on Monday, 17 September, which hit the papers the following morning. Inspectors Abberline, Helson, Spratling, and Chandler were in their seats on behalf of CID. They heard nine witnesses, all going over well-trodden ground, and learned little new. But the optimistic coroner wouldn't give up. He adjourned the inquest until Saturday, 22 September, to allow the men of the Met to dig deeper.

Mrs Griggs feared the coroner, and the police, had an impossible task ahead of them. How, she asked (in what sounded more a declaration) could anyone account for these acts of blood? She went on to explain that one of her ladies, unnamed, said the murders must have been owing to occult activity.

"What did she mean by occult?"

"I don't know exactly. But she spoke of dark things, evils from dark times."

"Why evil?" I asked. "Who is this person getting rid of? The lowest of the low. The worst of the worst. What is more filthy than these disease-ridden prostitutes?"

"Well, I don't defend their life choices, you know that. But... Oh, Mr ___," she declared. "You're having me on! Go on. Pull the other one."

Wednesday, 19 September, the fourth cluster of the Chapman inquest was called to order. Mrs Elizabeth Long took the stand. She was the woman carrying the basket, who passed us (en route to market, as I suspected) in Hanbury Street. I didn't have a clue how the authorities found her but, then again, I had no idea where she'd come from that morning either. Perhaps their experience had been the same as mine, she just appeared. Long recalled her sighting of the pair of us. She identified the corpse as that of the woman she'd seen. She repeated for the jury the description of the man (me) she'd given the police. She said I was dark, taller than the deceased, about forty. Not flattering, that. She said I was dressed in brown and wore a low-crowned felt hat. She described me as shabby genteel; the bitch!

They again adjourned the inquiry, until Wednesday, 26 September, when the terms of the verdict would supposedly be decided.

Three days later, 22 September, the Inquest into the death of Polly Nichols convened again (for the fourth and last time). The jury, after a short consultation, returned a verdict of 'Wilful murder against some person or persons unknown'.

Following the verdict, the community-minded Coroner Baxter remarked, for the record, on the need of a real mortuary (as opposed to the old shed) in the Whitechapel parish. It was true the current facility was lacking and far from being up to the task, but modesty prevents my suggesting that was mostly on account of me stacking the bleeding whores up like chopped wood.

Twenty-Four
The Hospital Chat

Saturday evening, 22 September, I was busy in the surgical theatre cleaning up after a procedure when I was interrupted by the sound of a side door coming open. It is often I am given assignments, but rarely am I bothered while carrying them out. Thus my surprise when Mrs Price, the matron, put in her head and demanded of the room. "Mr __?"

"Yes, please?"

She saw me beneath the light of the surgery table and recognition dawned in her eyes. "Aw. Mr __, there you are."

The door came further open. Mrs Price entered fully and, even in the gloom around her, I could see she led the way in front of two blue uniformed, caped and helmeted, police constables. I don't mind telling you, in that instant, my heart felt as if it had ceased to beat.

She led the officers across the theatre into the glow of the lights above the table I'd been wiping down. Her silver chatelaine belt chains, and the coppers' silver collar pins, all *winked* at me; hers with an authority to which I was long accustomed, theirs with an authority, and threat, entirely new to me.

"Mr __," the charge nurse said again, this time by way of introduction, as she was speaking to the men behind her. She turned to me. "These officers wish a word with you."

"With me? Whatever for?"

"No worries, sir," the apparent leader of the two said with a smile. He was a tall fresh-complexioned man with a straw-coloured moustache and brown hair visible beneath his round brim. The initials PC glistened on one side of his tight collar and the identifying 97 J shown on the other. "My name is PC Neil," he said smartly.

I returned an expression made of wood, but it took effort. I recognized the name. This was one of the peelers that had discovered the remains of the Queen in Buck's Row, the Nichols whore.

He gave a half-turn, then a nod, to the man beside and a step behind him, wearing a like PC and 96 J. (Stamped out, one after the other?) "This is Constable Thain." Thain was clean-shaven, lighter in colour; hair, eyes, and pale skin, but giving off a dark feel. I'd heard his name too. Buck's Row again? I couldn't recall. But I didn't like the feeling... or him. Even at that distance, I sensed a meanness that would bare watching.

The leader was going on. "We have been asked to speak with all hospital workers whose jobs entail specific duties."

"Oh?" I asked, rather stupidly. (I needed to get my wits about me.) "Which duties?"

"That will become evident, sir."

"You will do your utmost to assist the officers," Mrs Price told me. It was not a request. Mrs Price did not, as a rule, make requests. Nor did she wait for my reply. She turned back to the one called Neil. "If you don't require me any longer, I am needed in emergency."

"Thank you, Mrs Price."

The matron left us. Without ceremony, the copper started in... with rather dull and obvious questions. "Name?" Didn't he already know it, I wondered? Regardless, I answered without hesitation. "Age? Address?" He seemed pleased to hear that, though I lived in the East End, it was in a respectable working-class neighbourhood.

"You live alone, sir?"

"I am a lodger." I mentioned my landlady by name. Owing to her politics, I assumed she was known.

"Are you right or left-handed, sir?"

"Right-handed. Why?"

"Just a routine question in this inquiry, sir."

"You've worked here how long, sir?"

I told him that as well. I offered a brief history to fill it out for him, several years as a volunteer on the various patient wards; then as a paid orderly, in emergency, patient transport, on the wards as required, attending to the surgical theatre."

"What do you do here?" The constable asked. He eyeballed the room, the student's gallery behind the glass above, and finally – the elephant in the room, the item always looked at last – the surgery table (still partially besmirched with blood) I had been in the middle of cleaning with carbolic acid.

"I *do* everything," I informed him, "with the exception of the surgery. I ready the patients, transport them into theatre, and remove them to their ward for recovery. When the doctor and staff have gone, I clean up." I pointed to the mess. "As you can see. When necessary," I pointed at a linen wrapped object on a nearby table, "I remove and dispose of patient waste."

The second constable (Thain, was it?), silent so far, took a peek under the wrapping, and exclaimed, "Is that a leg?"

"Carriage accident, early this evening. . ."

"In Cable Street?" Neil asked.

I nodded. "Traumatic injury requiring amputation."

Thain covered the body part again and looked up as if he'd smelled something horrid. It was an act on his part. The amputated leg had hardly had time to develop an odor. Still, the copper kept the look of disgust. "You. . . dispose. . . of this?"

"Certainly. Someone must. It will be taken below for cremation."

"Getting back to our inquiry, sir," Neil said. "The coroner's court raised a possibility the Whitechapel murderer had anatomical knowledge. What training have you in anatomy, Mr __?"

"Anatomy? None. It isn't necessary. That's a leg. But I needn't know it. All I need know is I'll be burning it up. The contaminated bandages and rags, and the wrapped refuse left on that table, whatever they might contain. . ." I looked pointedly at Thain.

"It isn't my job to open them." I returned my attention to Neil. "Whatever they contain are taken below and cremated. I don't do surgery."

"Of course not. But you have access to surgical equipment; knives and the like?"

"No. Not really. They are secured away. Brought out by the nurses and doctors before a procedure, then taken away by the same. I don't set up surgery. Merely ready patients and clear the mess."

"You watch the surgeries?"

"I am not present during the surgeries. I am not needed."

"What is the gallery for?"

"Surely you are aware this is a teaching hospital? That's the students' gallery. They attend class here and watch the surgeries."

"You never join them?"

"They wouldn't have me," I said, with a derisive laugh. Then wished I hadn't done (I didn't regret it, merely wished I hadn't). "They will be doctors; we are orderlies. We have other duties. I bring patients in. I return to my duties. I return for patients when summoned. I could, I suppose, on a quiet night, sit amongst the students and watch a procedure. But why would I? As I said, I don't know anatomy. I wouldn't know what I was looking at." Then I smiled and took both in, friendly-like. "Frankly, officers, I get sick of looking at what I do see."

Both nodded their understanding and, if I wasn't mistaken, their agreement.

"Are you married, sir?" Thain asked, out of the blue. "Or have you a steady companion, sir?"

"I say! That's a bit much, isn't it?"

"Forgive us, sir," Neil said. "But our investigation requires we ask a few impertinent questions. Such as... Are you familiar at all with the social... amenities available on the streets and in the pubs of Whitechapel and Spitalfields?"

My jaw dropped open. I know it did; I made certain it did. "Are you implying," I stammered, "that I rent the dubious pleasures of street women?"

"Implying? No, sir," Neil said. "We're asking."

"And," Thain added, "we're still asking."

"Will you be asking the doctors as well?" I demanded. "Or are these questions reserved merely for the working class?" I should not have gotten into a snit, I know. But they had finally managed to catch me off guard.

"I apologize for the questions, sir," Neil assured me. "Do you refuse to answer?"

"I do not. I have nothing to hide and will answer anything you like. But, I must say, your questions are appalling. No, I am not married. Still I do not frequent, nor have I ever frequented, the streets of Whitechapel or Spitalfields or tasted the wares of their street vendors, in any capacity." I grabbed my rag and returned to wiping the blood off the surgery table. "If you must know, I do not care for random female thought. I've chosen a life without it. I read and keep my own company. I attend services at St George-in-the-East and contribute to the community, here as I'm able, and outside of work in... ways that occur to me."

"Are you aware, sir, the coroner's inquest into the death of Polly Nichols concluded today?"

"I was not aware."

"The jury returned a verdict of 'Wilful murder against some person or persons unknown'." The officer paused. I paused as well, to see both Neil and Thain staring at me. They seemed to be searching for my reaction. What reaction was expected, I was not sure. I had none to give. I waited with them.

"Person or persons unknown," the constable repeated. "That's unknown to us, not necessarily unknown to the victim. Polly Nichols may have known her killer. Did you know Polly Nichols, sir?"

I shook my head. "I did not."

"What about Annie Chapman, sir?"

"Again, constable, you have me consorting with a low class of people."

"Merely asking, sir, routine. But we must ask."

"I did not know Annie Chapman, or Polly Nichols, or Martha Tabram."

"We didn't ask you about Martha Tabram."

I frowned at Thain; a poor substitute for what I really wished to do, which would have been to cut the idiotic grimace from his face leaving just his clicking skeletal jaw behind. Instead, I condescended to address his weak point. "I *do* know how to read, constable. Like everyone in Britain, I've read about all of the murders. And of the Met's heroic efforts to solve same and protect the citizenry. I can't wait to tell my friends and neighbours what a generous amount of time you're… consuming… questioning gainfully employed, native-born Englishmen here at hospital."

"We do thank you for your time and co-operation, sir."

"You are most welcome," I assured them both. "I wish you the best in your hunt."

Twenty-Five
Dear Boss

One might think the spicy interview with the police in my own place of employment jangled my nerves, alarmed me, or caused me concern. That wasn't the case in the least. Truth was, my little talk with the flatfooted peelers set me entirely at ease. It proved, beyond doubt, the Metropolitan Police were adrift in their investigation. I was merely a hospital employee, among all of the employees to whom they were directing their open-ended inquiries. They didn't know a thing.

How interesting I found it, then, to read an overly dramatic opinion piece in one of the papers of the day that 'the spirit of Dark Annie Chapman was wandering Whitechapel... unavenged by justice.'

Oh, the picture that painted! How would those poor slags ever find justice?

How could the coppers catch me? In a way, I felt sorry for them, the police, for they had no avenue down which to travel that led to little ol' me.

What weapons did they possess for finding, let alone stopping, Yours Truly? The CID had no experience at that which they claimed to do for a living. They collected evidence poorly, when they collected it at all. With an unknown quarry, like myself, they proved over and over again they were unable to even recognize what it was that constituted evidence.

Their primary tool in crime fighting was knowledge of the *modus operandi* of the local villains. They counted upon informants and repeat offenders. But I was not, am not, a common criminal. I have no record; have never been arrested. I do not consort with street people and am not known by them. What could the plods do with that? Where could they go from there? How could they detect?

The bodies I left were pawed over by medical doctors conscripted by the crown to aid the police. Their expertize, such as it was, was in the physiology of the living. What did they know of the dead? The inferences those doctors drew from their examinations of my work were a laugh!

They guessed at the blade I'd used. But I traded off. I'd used three so far, had many at my disposal, and was not adverse to experimentation. Yes, in future perhaps, an experiment?

They guessed as to whether or not I was right or left-handed. As I confessed long ago, the answer was right-handed. But where would that knowledge get them? To what end? To shrink the pool of suspects from millions to thousands? From thousands to hundreds? It was the Red Queen's race! It took all the running the coppers (and their surgeons) could do to keep in the same place. I could use my left hand when necessary. I could trade off if need be. As for it being a clue, *bosh!* Over eighty percent of the population was right-handed. So what? The doctors knew nothing about me. They would discover nothing.

And the poor police. Clueless.

They had the capacity to collect blood. But what could that tell them? I'd done my studying and knew determining whether or not a sample belonged to a mammal was as far as science had advanced. They couldn't even know for certain the sticky red with which I painted their streets was human blood. (I assure you, it was!)

They had photographic equipment available to them, but could not conceive of a practical use for it and, thus far, had not bothered to record my events. If they had, they'd kept it a secret. The papers were filled with badly sussed and amateurishly realized drawings of me and the recipients of my correction. They should have made photographs. It was a shame they hadn't and, I think, a mistake.

But police mistakes were legion.

They questioned notoriously unreliable men and women of the Whitechapel slums as witnesses. But outside of my hospital work (where I had no choice), I did not associate with the lower classes. When I did venture out among them, I walked unseen. What could their witnesses have told them?

I considered the foregoing... and decided to give the police a hand. Perhaps that wasn't true. Honestly, I wanted another laugh at their expense. But, to get it, I needed to risk exposure and would, simultaneously, give the plods a hand; clues, if they were clever enough to decipher them.

It might be remembered I'd prepared for this. I'd taken a pocketfull of items with me from the last event and stored them among my secrets in Mr Griggs' shop. I retrieved one item now (the ginger beer bottle I'd filled in Hanbury Street) and uncorked it – intent on sending a letter in blood!

Oh the disappointment!

To find Stockings' carefully collected red juices had congealed and could not be used. I knew that happened to blood in the open air. But I had hoped that, bottled up, it might keep. No matter. We all must deal with our little disappointments.

I had no choice but to postpone my lark for a short while, run to the local, and buy a bottle of red ink (as I had my heart set on *red* and needed a stand-in). That accomplished, proper ink in hand, I retired to the quiet back room of Mr Griggs' shop to start the new game.

I would write to the police offering them clues.

Of course, I couldn't write directly. That would have done no good at all. It was likely numerous mentally unstable persons had already written, to garner attention for themselves. I was wise enough to know writing directly to the plods would only get my communication ignored. I had no intention of being ignored. To circumvent that eventuality, I decided instead to write to one of

London's posh news editors. That fellow, having a working mind, would bring it to the attention of Scotland Yard with a demand for action attached.

The police would respond. They would have to.

I put on the gas, sat down at Mr Griggs' old desk, dipped my pen in my new bottle of red ink, and began to write. It was '*25 Sept. 1888*' and I said so in the first line at the top. Then I contemplated the salutation. I wasn't certain who at the news agency would get first look at my scribblings (and I didn't really care). Everyone in the place lived for news, didn't they?

I wrote:

'*Dear Boss.*'

Whoever opened it, I was certain, would pass it on to where it might do all of us the most good. Having made a start, I was off, writing in a feigned uneducated hand:

'*I keep on hearing the police have caught me but they wont fix me just yet. I have laughed when they look so clever and talk about being on the right track. That joke about Leather Apron gave me real fits.*'

I paused, enjoying myself. I went back up and underlined the word 'right'. Right track, indeed. But it was time to be serious. I went on:

'*I am down on whores and I shant quit ripping them till I do get buckled. Grand work the last job was. I gave the lady no time to squeal. How can they catch me now. I love my work and want to start again. You will soon hear of me with my funny little games. I saved some of the proper red stuff...*'

A little confession wouldn't hurt, would it? Might even help them to understand my moods. I underlined the word 'red' that the stupid sods might get it.

'*... in a ginger beer bottle over the last job to write with but it went thick like glue and I cant use it. Red ink is fit enough I hope. ha.ha.*'

Of course, I underlined the laugh. The better for the newspaper blokes, and eventually the coppers, who I was certain would see my little note somewhere down the line, to laugh with me. I went on:

'*The next job I do I shall clip the lady's ears off and send to the...*' (I turned the paper, continued on the back) '*...police officers just for jolly wouldnt you. Keep this letter back till I do a bit more work then give it out straight. My knife's so nice and sharp I want to get to work right away if I get a chance.*'

Not bad. In all, a tidy job. But I needed a smash ending, to introduce myself to all of London. They'd tried to stick me with the name Leather Apron. Bollocks! The name of a bleeding Jew. Others had stuck me with a name, whispered through frightened lips, I hadn't minded, 'the Whitechapel killer'. But, now I thought it through, I knew they'd done so for nasty reasons; to keep me in the slums, to make me a foreigner, to tell themselves I was not one of them. I'd already proved them wrong, hadn't I? The first two whores I killed in Whitechapel, but not the third. Her I'd done in Spitalfields. Wasn't I expanding my hunting grounds? Yes, I would expand, further yet, to show them.

I determined then and there to broaden my horizons. The next whore I killed would be in St George-in-the-East. Yes, I'd come home while, at the same time, ensuring the East End knew to fear me. Let all of London know I might strike anywhere; none of their filthy whores were safe. I liked my brilliant idea better and better. I'd give myself a new name; a name they could use to offer me the respect I deserved. I proudly signed the letter with that new name and held it up to the lamp.

'*Yours truly Jack the Ripper*'

Twenty-Six
Gone to Gateshead

I admit to a swelling of pride at coming up with the moniker Jack the Ripper. Shakespeare himself would have been pleased and delighted by the way it rolled 'trippingly on the tongue'. I couldn't wait to get it out there and intended to listen carefully in near future for the reactions.

Still, not wanting to sound as full of myself as even I admit I was, beneath the lark I wrote a bit more, adding an apology of sorts that might also serve as a directive.

'*Dont mind me giving the trade name*'

It needed to be understood that the punters ought to start using the name immediately.

I looked the letter over again, top to bottom, front to back. It was just right and I was well-pleased. But – DAMN! – I hadn't blotted it and the red ink had mucked it up; made it look like I'd smeared blood on it. On second thought, was good enough for the likes of them; was just right for them.

But I didn't want them thinking I was some poser. So, looking at page two, I cocked the letter on its side on the table and added a post script going the opposite direction:

'*wasnt good enough to post this before I got all the red ink off my hands curse it.*'

Anything else, I wondered. Did it need anything else? In answer to my own question, I added one bit of payback for that irritating hospital interview and a jab for the police surgeon. I wrote:

'*No luck yet. They say I'm a doctor now haha*'

Again I couldn't help but underline the laugh. Everybody needs to laugh.

I got a small envelope and addressed it:

'*The Boss,*
Central News Office
London City'

All in all, a job well done.

The following afternoon, Wednesday, 26 September, Coroner Baxter convened the Inquest into the Death of Annie Chapman for the final time. He and his jury had already digested all the meat I'd left on that whore's bones and their gathering was merely a formality; a quick and painless affair.

Aware of the answer, Baxter officially inquired of Detective Inspector Chandler if there was any further evidence to be adduced. The inspector replied, "No," as arranged and the coroner began his tedious summation of their findings. He then charged the jury. Like good little soldiers, they returned a verdict of 'Wilful murder against a person or persons unknown'. Baxter thanked the jurists for their service and closed the inquest.

Like most of those in attendance, I imagine, I slept through the meeting. The difference being I was smart enough to remain at home and do so in my bed. As had become my habit, I learned the details from the newspaper report. There were advantages to being *big news*.

But being the most newsworthy subject in London had not eased my mind.

I'd been too long without activity. I was edgy. I spent that evening walking the East End, quietly passing by the scenes of my glorious work. And growing, I confess, edgier still by what I was seeing in the streets about me. Life for the residents of those down-trodden streets, from what I could make out, was quickly returning to its usual order. If *order* it was. I took a long while to watch those around me, to contemplate what I saw, and to suss it for what it was. Finally it dawned. The residents of the streets had lost their fear.

They were out and about, acting their normal filthy selves, heedless of their danger. Oblivious to my presence, by design, but oblivious to the possibility of the presence of a murderer in their midst. The bastards were drinking, carousing, and laughing as if the Whitechapel killer – Jack the Ripper – had never been among them. It was not my paranoid imagination. I heard it with my own ears.

While passing through Hanbury Street and directly in front of the door through which the whore and I had ventured – to her doom, I overheard a bloke who identified as a reporter discussing that concern with an elderly gent by the curb. The end of their conversation was what struck little ol' me a blow.

"There seems to be little apprehension," the reporter stated, in what ended up a question, "of further mischief by this assassin at large?"

"No," the old boy replied. "People, most of them, think he's gone to Gateshead."

What? Unbelievable!

I'd read about Gateshead, of course. In recent weeks, between my landlady and her coterie of Dress Reformists (turned Whitechapel detectives), and Miss Adler (and Archie) and her coterie of gossiping nurses, and my walks in the streets, and my sudden interest in Mr Froggs' stock in trade, I'd become the number one consumer of news in the East End and the City of London.

Among the items I'd read in the national press were several sketchy, but nevertheless colourful, reports concerning a murder that had taken place either Saturday night (22 September) or early Sunday morning near Birtley Fell, a small mining village in County Durham, in the north of England.

By those accounts, a boilersmith called John Fish, walking to work at twenty to seven that Sunday morning, had come upon the body of a murdered young woman. He ran for the local peeler, PC Dodds, who identified the dead woman as Jane Beadmore (or Jane Savage, her step-father's name). She had been violently stabbed with a long knife.

As the newspapers did not spare the details, why should I?

'The body lay in a ditch beside the waggon-way, at a spot three-quarters of a mile or thereabouts distant from the unhappy creature's home. Life had apparently been extinct for some hours. The hands were held upwards towards the face, as if she had been endeavouring to protect herself. Her clothes were disarranged, and the lower part of the body was exposed.

'There was no sign of a struggle having taken place. There were no bloodstains near the spot where the discovery was made, but the clothes on the body were literally saturated with blood. The police-constable had the body removed to the house of the woman's parents and examined the murder scene. He determined it was not a robbery.

'The police-constable sent for Dr. Walter Galloway, in nearby Wrekenton, and his commanding officer, Sergeant Hutchinson, co-incidentally in conference at the time with the visiting senior officer of the Gateshead Division, Superintendent Harrison. All three men were soon on the scene.

'The medical examination which followed revealed wounds of a frightful nature, all inflicted by a long knife or other sharp instrument. On the right cheek was a wound extending to the neck. But the immediate cause of death appears to have been a deep incised wound in the opposite side of the face. The instrument used entered the left cheek just below the ear. The wound extended backward and down, through the left side of the neck. The spinal cord was completely severed. This would have in itself been more than sufficient to cause death. The injury to the lower portion of the abdomen had been terribly cruel. The knife, or whatever instrument was used, had evidently been forcibly thrust into the victim, then pulled upward, opening the body and extending the wound for sev-

eral inches. The half-severed bones showed the force that had been used.'

The killer, whoever he was, seemed to have gone to some trouble to make the woman appear to be one of my victims. And, in spite of being a hack, at the outset at least, had some success. Hearing of the murder, the Metropolitan Police sent an inspector from CID, and the Whitechapel police surgeon, Dr. Phillips (who'd done Stockings' post-mortem), by train to Durham to ascertain whether or not the injuries inflicted upon their woman resembled my work.

Before they arrived or started their inquiry, it seemed, many of those reveling in the street around me now already believed the Whitechapel murderer had moved out; had left London and taken his party elsewhere. They were fools, the lot of them. Why would I travel all that way to kill a woman who, by all accounts, was respectable? Why would I leave when there remained so many filthy whores around me needed cleaning up? It was out of the question. Preposterous!

Suddenly I understood my edginess. I could now identify the prodding I'd been feeling. It was the keen points of my too well-rested blades poking me – insisting I get back on the job.

The laughing fools, celebrating their release from the terror, could not have been more wrong. Their killer had not up and gone to Gateshead. He was still in Whitechapel. It was time they found that out.

Twenty-Seven
The Squealer

The evening of 29 September the rain came down.

Have no fear, I didn't allow that to deter me. I'd planned all day, eagerly anticipated, going out and touring the town. My town, the East End. I had a new task, owing to a wrinkle in my mission, after all. Those who were supposed to be taking a message from my work, the wretched residents of the slums, the booze-guzzling unfortunates, were again back-sliding. Somehow, it appeared, they'd gotten it into their heads that I had gone away. That I'd left London and taken my show on the road, like an aimless gypsy, like an unemployed vagabond, like one of them. A punter in the north had fecklessly killed a respectable woman then tried to cover his tracks by imitating my work afterward. The fools living hand to mouth in the Whitechapel gutters had believed him. They'd decided I had gone away to Gateshead. Then, without remorse or a second thought, they'd returned to their debauchery.

They needed another lesson. I'd made plans to deliver them one.

Having recently given myself a new name, so the world would understand I was more than merely the Whitechapel killer, I'd made plans to expand my horizons and strike to the south. Jack the Ripper would pay a visit to the filthy sluts degrading my parish, St George-in-the-East.

For my debut in this new territory I'd decided to dress up a bit, not fancy but respectable-like; in black trousers, waistcoat, and tie. I'd polished my black boots. I readied a short dark jacket. I carefully chose a black deerstalker cap with a peak in the centre and a bill front and back. Casual, yet darkly elegant. And helpfully difficult to see in either the vast oceans of darkness or the tiny pools of gaslight through which I would be passing. But, as I said, when seen by those that took the time, respectable.

Then I sat down to bide my time. I waited while the rains came down. Few drunken slags would have their wares on offer in the heavy rain. Few *clients* would be out and about looking to purchase.

I sat in my room, in the dark, waiting. I heard Mrs Griggs go to bed on the floor below and I waited. The night ticked on, the rains came down washing the streets of the East End, and I waited. The rains would stop, I knew. They always did. When the rains stopped, also as always, the filth would return to the streets.

The rains finally did abate and I sneaked quietly downstairs. I passed Mrs Griggs' rooms, where she was fast asleep (snoring like a boar), and down again and into the back of her late husband's old shop. I donned my carefully selected short coat and deerstalker cap, placed earlier in the night, collected my knives from their hiding spot, and silently went out.

The sidewalk shined wet in the light at the corner, the breeze was fresh. My mood soared as, for the first time since I'd taken up my mission, I started my walk headed east (away from Whitechapel) and north toward Mile End. Tonight, as I'd promised myself, I would solidify my new name and leave a mark on my parish. For the first time, Jack the Ripper was on the prowl... and in his own backyard.

I hadn't gone far (I won't specify the distance) from my lodgings, when I reached Fairclough and paused in the shadows on the unlit side of the intersection to look up Berner Street. Berner was some distance from either of the last two murders; nearly a mile south of Buck's Row, the same distance southeast of Hanbury Street; a half-mile southeast of my first job in George Yard. Nowhere near the stinking and loud tenements of the Whitechapel slums. Berner Street was quiet, usually.

But not just now. Now I could hear a tinny piano and the revolting guttural sounds of a foreigner singing along in Russian. I knew immediately from whence that awful musical tripe flowed.

The International Working Men's Club stood a half-block to the north, on the west side of the street; an old three-story building at No 40. Like every word that dribbled from their members' mouths, the club's name was a ridiculous lie. They were a group of socialist foreigners, nothing more or less. Russian and Polish Jews, most of them. They'd escaped Communist pogroms in their own countries, with their families assaulted, raped, and killed; their houses, barns, and businesses taken or burned; and their money and lands confiscated. They'd gone through great hardship to get to England. And, once they were safe, and free, had immediately established a club to teach their friends and neighbours the same fucking politics that had destroyed their lives in their homelands.

As it was Sunday morning (30 September), they would have only ended their Saturday meeting at midnight, a half-hour or more past, and most of their members must, by then, have left and headed back to their hovels. But some had obviously stayed behind to pound on the piano and sing the praises of a new socialist regime here.

More than noise, there was movement in the street. A young man carrying a shiny black bag walked quickly down Berner from the Commercial Road. As he approached the socialists' club, a cottage door opened behind him and a middle-aged woman peaked out to watch him pass. The young man looked up at the club, where the Russians were singing, but kept moving. The woman vanished back inside. The fellow rounded the corner of the board school, across the street from me (unaware of me in the dark). Bag in hand, he continued east up Fairclough, ignorant of his brush with immortality.

Back on the west side of Berner Street came more movement as one of the Bolsheviks stepped from the gateway of the passage leading from Dutfield's Yard, the stable area between the socialists' club and the closed fruit and vegetable shop to its south. He stepped into the street, looked south to the pub on the corner (without seeing me), then to the east across the street at a row of sagging residential houses. He looked to the sky and took in air. The air appeared to be his only goal.

Then I looked past him, a full block and a short one to the far north end, where Berner Street met Commercial Road and there, standing beneath the light at the corner, I saw my goal. The luckiest unfortunate in London!

Everybody in the district knew the wide Commercial Road (an east-west artery for the East End, in concert with Whitechapel Road) buzzed with whore traffic. I determined in that instant that, if she was among them, this would be her lucky night. There she was – begging for it – and Jack the Ripper would be more than willing to provide.

She could have been, I imagined, anywhere between twenty and fifty years of age. Who could have told from that distance? She wasn't much over five foot tall. She wore a long black jacket decorated with a bauble of red (a red what, I couldn't make out at that distance) over her breast. And, of course, she wore what looked to be a black bonnet that, by the way she pawed at it, must have been newish and a source of some pride. Didn't those bitches love their bonnets?

I had an urge to march straight up Berner Street and stab her where she stood. But that would have been potty and reckless. Even if she deserved it, that was no reason to walk past the Bolshie and give him a good look at me. I wasn't crazy, so I tamped the urge.

The night was young. There was no great hurry. As for the girl, I wanted a better approach.

I took Fairclough east to a little street called Batty. I hurried up Batty to busy Commercial Road. I looked to the right and saw a police constable standing patrol duty a block east at the corner of Commercial Road and Christian Street. I looked to my left and saw... The girl was gone. Damn!

I hurriedly returned a block west to Berner Street and stopped. I started to turn a slow circle, looking to see if I could see where the whore might have... There she was.

Having found no success in Commercial Road, the whore had started her strut southward on Berner Street. She was now the short block, plus a piece of the full block away, headed towards the place I'd been only a few minutes before, strolling in an aimless fashion. If I'd only waited, she would have come to me.

I wasn't waiting anymore. She was a block away but I started south on Berner Street behind her, intent on catching her up.

Another Bolshevik appeared off of Fairclough, headed for his club, down the block ahead of the whore. He paid no attention to her and appeared not to have seen me at all. He tried the club's front door, apparently found it locked, and disappeared around the south corner of the building into the dark of Dutfield's Yard.

It was 12:50 am when I approached the whore in front of the socialist's club. We were finally alone. From the open first-floor windows of the club, the pathetic Russians continued to warble to their piano accompaniment.

Now that I was there, on top of her as it were, I saw she was five-foot-two at most and had already waved good-bye to her fortieth year. Her jacket was trimmed with black fur. The black crepe bonnet went well with the dark brown curls twisting from beneath. The red decoration, up close, showed itself to be a single red rose backed by a small fern and tucked into the decotage of her dark-brown velvet bodice. Despite her love of flowers, I'm afraid Mrs Griggs would never have approved. ha ha. The whore's old black skirt bulged over her petticoats and formed a tent above an incongruous pair of side-spring boots. She had a pale complexion with light grey eyes.

"How about the business?" I asked her.

She laughed, showing her upper front teeth missing, and blew fumes in my face. *Oh my vicious mother*, a whore breathing beer all over me. Jacky had everything a boy could need!

"Wait, love." She drew a tissue-wrapped something from inside her sleeve and started to open the packet with the fingers of one hand. It contained a small handful of cachous. Seeing that, it was all I could do to keep from laughing. What, I wondered, would an alcoholic pig need with breath lozenges? What was the point?

"My mouth tastes a brewery," she said with another airy laugh.

"Of that I'm sure," I said, reaching for her.

The whore pulled away. That made me angry. I grabbed her arm, intent on yanking her into the street and into submission. She struggled away and turned her back on me, as if to run through the open gates into Dutfield's Yard. That wouldn't do.

I grabbed her by her check silk scarf, twisted it, pulled it tight and yanked her back. Then, still from behind, I grabbed her shoulders, sinking the fingers of both hands into the fabric of her coat and the soft flesh beneath. She squealed, again, again. Three short bleats like an animal in distress. How dare she! Enraged, I shoved her hard. She spun on her big boots and toppled backwards like a felled tree (this time without a squeal), off the footway and onto the pavement in the mouth of the gateway near the wall of the socialist's club.

As she hit the ground, I felt eyes on my back and turned to see a man staring at me from the middle of Berner Street. He was a miserable foreigner, a Jew by his look; thin, dressed in brown, with an equally thin brown moustache on his worried angular face. He'd obviously come down the block behind me and had seen me shove the whore. Thinking himself witness to a domestic quarrel, I think, and wanting to keep out of it, he'd been crossing the street to avoid us. Wise choice on his part. He was still on the move; hadn't stopped, but was giving the pair of us the fish eye.

If that wasn't bad enough, further south down Berner, a bloke stepped from the pub on my side of the street lighting a pipe. Christ, I'd been in less-crowded train stations. The smoker, drawing on his bowl, spied the worried-looking Jew in the street. He eyed me. Then he spotted the big boots, flapping skirt, and kicking legs of the girl fresh on her arse in the shadows inside the Yard gateway.

Damn blast it to hell! I needed to be rid of both of the spying bastards! I pointed an accusing finger at the man in the street, turned to the pipe smoker, and shouted, "Lipski!"

It was common knowledge a Jew named Israel Lipski had been hanged for a poisoning murder the previous year. (This was the story, and the time, I alluded to earlier, my first meeting with Detective Sergeant Thicke of the Metropolitan Police.)

Back then, when I still spent most of my working hours on the hospital's upper floors, a yet-to-be-convicted Lipski had been admitted as a patient. There, he was the subject of an identity parade held by DS Thicke and a plod, with an even more unlikely surname, Inspector Final. Who could forget that farce? Charles Moore, the chemist who sold the murderer a dose of nitric acid, was escorted to hospital by the pair and told he would likely find his customer. They brought him onto the ward; featuring a bank of regular patient beds and one bed, Lipski's, with a plain clothes policeman standing guard at the foot. Here's the shocker: Lipski was identified as the purchaser of poison! What were the odds? He was, soon after, convicted of murder and hung by his neck until dead.

In the year since, throughout the East End, the name Lipski had become a routine insult to Jews, synonymous with miscreants, and indicative of a murderous presence. As I hoped, in that tense moment the name stood in well as an off-the-cuff accusation of assault and attempted murder. The girl's bleats only helped my cause. The fellow with the pipe looked sharply from the girl, to me, then hard at Lipski. He stepped off the byway onto the street.

Alarm exploded on the Jew's face. That look turned to horror as he realized he'd been incriminated. Forgetting the girl entirely, he darted frightened looks back and forth between me and the bloke with the pipe. Then, choosing his neck over the girl's, turned and scarpered off down Berner Street. The smoker, probably without knowing why, took off running after him.

I would have loved to follow; to see who won the race, and learn what happened to the Jew who had dared to assault that poor girl in the street. But I couldn't. I was busy. I turned to glare through the gate into the mouth of Dutfield's gloomy Yard. I took three long strides to where the drunk whore had landed after I'd shoved her. I pulled my knife from my pocket. I bent to where she lay on the ground. In a rage owing to who and what she was, and her squeals, and the interruptions, I reached out and slashed her fucking throat.

Twenty-Eight
Escape From Berner Street

It was just gone 12:55 am when, without ceremony, I slashed the Squealer's throat as she lay on the pavement outside the socialist's club. Can't blame me for the haste. Who needed her squealing again?

The whore grabbed at her throat with her right hand. The spurt from the severed artery hit her hand, the brick wall beyond, and the pavement and gutter to her left. Her bloody hand fell away; dropped back open upon her chest. But, have no fear, I was safe and dry. Lying on her left side as she was with her feet near the street, facing the outside wall of the club, I had completely avoided a dousing.

Then came the awful and sad realization, the bad news as it were; the delicious act of strangulation had, until this wretched time, been my routine. That should have been followed by the slitting of the throat as a start to the games. But this night had already been maddeningly different, and looked to continue in that vein. The socialist rats with their late meeting and pathetic singing into the night, the wandering Jew, the pipe-smoking pub crawler, the intrusions had ruined the game and destroyed the message I'd meant to send!

The time and the place were both suddenly and obviously wrong. There would be no time to finish my business. There was no time to start my business and, surely, there was no time to play. It was likely the socialists above had heard the commotion and were already on their way down to investigate. I needed to be gone.

I gave the drunken Squealer a last hate-filled look.

Her legs were drawn up, her feet close against the wall. A carriage-wheel rut in the dirt beneath her neck grew easier to make out as it filled with blood. Her open right hand lay on her chest, smeared with blood. Her left arm lay extended, her hand on the ground, her fingers still cupping her tissue-wrapped breath fresheners. *Aww,* too bad. She'd missed the opportunity to pop one and was headed for hell with her breath still stinking of beer.

The face was quite pallid, the mouth slightly open. The silk scarf round her neck, which I'd used to advantage, now had its bow twisted to the left and was pulled ever so tight. The new smile I'd cut into her throat ran nicely beneath it. (Sorry to say, I'd frayed the scarf's lower edge with my knife.) There was a great deal of standing blood to the left of her head with an impressive stream running down the gutter and back toward the drain near the foot of the club's back door steps.

The situation was all so regrettable. She lay slaughtered and ready to be dressed. But I had no time. With no other choice, I left the pig bleeding in the Yard.

In a necessary hurry, I cut round the corner of the gate and headed north. I passed the locked front door of the socialist's club, then a door in the residential cottages to the north about twenty-five feet up Berner Street. I didn't go ten feet further when I heard that second door come open behind me. (The same nosy bitch, I imagined, who'd looked out after the lad with the shiny bag.) I paid her no mind. Head down, collar up, I kept walking.

A few steps further, I cut left off of Berner into a thin dark and maze-like side alley that zigged and zagged its way west to Backchurch Lane. Behind me, I heard the distinct *clip-clop, clip-clop* of a one-horse cart passing the alley, headed south on Berner. I paid it no mind either. Head still down, collar still up, I walked on.

Saucy Jacky

A church bell tolled 1:00 am somewhere nearby. As before, I was hazy as to which clock, from which church. St George-in-the-East? St Mary's? It might have been either or both. Random thoughts were banging about inside my head. It wasn't fear, I wasn't afraid; merely thoughts dashing round.

I didn't know if I'd been seen by whoever had opened their door behind me. I didn't know if I'd been spotted by the cart driver who had passed in my wake. I didn't know a thing or bloody-well care. I didn't look up. I didn't breathe again. Just headed blindly, hurriedly through the alley in the direction of Backchurch Lane. When I reached it and came out, I turned again and hotfooted it north, wanting to put as much distance – as quickly as I was able – between me and what I'd left behind me in Berner Street.

In an effort to keep the night sorted, I'll mention now events unfolding behind me of which I was completely unaware, and of which I did not learn until days, even weeks, later. How I eventually came to know of them should, by now, be obvious; through the newspaper round tables held by Mrs Griggs in her sitting room of corset-loathing lady detectives, through the gossip sessions in hospital between Miss Adler (and constable Archie) and her coterie, through my newsstand gossips, and through my ever-more-interesting sight-seeing walks through the murder districts.

Remember, I was headed north. Not in a panic, surely. But with shifting levels of exhilaration. On an emotional high from a job done. Fighting the emotional lows of a job unfinished. Low from knowing I'd been seen by, not one but two, people. High from having turned that dangerous moment into a nose-twisting for the Jews (and the socialists as well). I was eager to be safe, and anxious to be successful and fulfill my mission to society. I was a lot of... things. Mostly I was merely headed north.

Whilst the excitement I had initiated in Berner Street had only begun.

I mentioned, no more had I cut the bitch's throat and walked away, headed north, I heard a cottage door come open behind me.

That was Fanny Mortimer, a resident, who'd heard footsteps out her door. Thinking they belonged to a copper, she opened up. And saw nobody. She looked out to the south, towards the gates to Dutfield's Yard. And saw nothing. Had she been able to see around corners, she'd have seen the whore with the cut throat lying in the Yard gutter only a few feet away. But she couldn't. Had she turned round and looked north, she'd have seen my backside as I moved up the street and turned into the little alley I mentioned. But she didn't. She merely stood in her doorway a moment, enjoying the cool air after the night's rain, seeing nothing. Then she went back in and closed her door.

A moment later, she heard the *clip-clop* of a pony and cart wheels grinding on cobblestone. Those were sounds ordinary in the extreme and she paid them no mind. So much for Fanny Mortimer's brush with immortality.

She'd heard the same pony and cart I'd heard. Remember? As I'd turned into the alley in hopes of a shortcut to Backchurch Lane.

The cart, I would eventually discover, belonged to Louie Diemschutz, the Bolshevik steward of the club. Diemschutz and his wife managed the place and lived on premises. But like most foreigners, and all Jews, he had his spoon in a dozen pots and his hands in a dozen pockets; aside from running the club, on Saturday nights he sold cheap jewelry in the market at Westow Hill, Crystal Palace. It was from there he was returning home. He maneuvered his two-wheeled barrow and pony slowly past Mrs Mortimer's and past the club's Berner Street entrance, seeing nothing out of the ordinary.

But, as he turned into the Yard gateway, his horse sensed something awry. The animal shied left and pulled up with a frightened snort, refusing to go further. Diemschutz steadied the animal. He looked to the right and saw something on the ground. What, he didn't know. The alley was too dark.

Prodding the lump with the handle of his whip helped not at all. With no option, the old man jumped down from his cart, came round, and struck a match. The wind had picked up some, after the rain, but the corner of the building gave the area inside the gateway a respite, allowing his feeble match to flicker. He made out a prone figure, in a woman's skirt, on the ground.

Diemschutz, no doubt, thought first of his wife (a woman of weak constitution) and knew he needed help. He led his pony, against its will, along the entrance wall furthest from the body, into the Yard. He left the cart and ran up the short stairs and in through the club's kitchen door. To his relief, he found his wife with her comrades in the ground floor dining room. "There's a woman lying in the yard," he exclaimed, "but I cannot say whether she's drunk or dead."

Without knowing it, the old Bolshie had hit the nail on the head. She was both; the first having led to the second.

Diemschutz grabbed a candle and, joined by a young tailor machinist named Isaac Kozebrodski, returned to the kitchen, to the back door and, stealthily, back out into the Yard. With Diemschutz's flickering light, before they even reached the body, the pair saw blood.

Both were startled by a gasp and turned to see Mrs Diemschutz had followed them as far as the door. There she stood peering from the kitchen, her mouth hanging open, her face losing colour, at sight of the heap on the ground. It was a woman, as Louie had said, with a ghastly white face, in a crimson pool. Mrs Diemschutz's eyes grew wide as she saw the blood had reached the gutter and was streaming down the Yard toward her (and the drain below her feet). Pent up horror reached her throat. The lady Bolshevik screamed.

Diemschutz groaned. He and young Kozebrodski gave up on his wife and returned their attention to the woman on the ground.

"What do we do?" the tailor machinist asked.

"We do nothing," Diemschutz replied. "Nothing to disturb the body."

A sudden panic of voices, from beyond the kitchen, then from the kitchen, then from behind Mrs Diemschutz, filled the air as the members from the first floor responded to her scream. They gathered around her in the door. Finding her all right, and realizing the reason for the scream, several of the bravest moved past her, down the stairs, and out into the Yard.

"We will touch nothing," Diemschutz repeated. "Isaac, you and I will go now and find a policeman." He turned to the others. "Touch nothing!" He and young Kozebrodski were on their way.

They turned right at the gates out of the Yard, ran down the block, and left into Fairclough Street. They raced east with pounding hearts, hallooing "Police!" and calling "Murder!" as loudly as they were able between gasps for breath. They passed a man and a woman standing outside the Beehive Tavern, at the corner of Christian and Fairclough, but kept going.

At Grove Street, a block further on, the pair stopped. Not a police constable to be seen. Huffing and defeated, they turned and headed back.

On their return, the fellow they'd bypassed at the Beehive accosted them. He was a horse-keeper name Edward Spooner who, curious to know what the hysterical Jews were up to, demanded, "What's all the fuss about?"

Diemschutz and Kozebrodski breathlessly told him. Alarmed by their tale of murder most foul, the horse-keeper sent his woman on her way, saying he would return with the men to Dutfield's Yard.

Twenty-Nine
Coppers Converge

Following their Bolshie meeting a handful of socialists had remained upstairs at the International Working Men's Club, singing, when club steward Louis Diemschutz brought word he'd discovered the whore's body. Thus ended the singing. A moment later, Mrs Diemschutz's scream brought an end to the gathering altogether. The excited Russian and Polish Jews all raced (or tumbled pell-mell) down the stairs and gathered round the terrified woman in the kitchen at the club's back door. Several squeezed past her, out the door, and into the Yard. One of those had been Morris Eagle.

Eagle, the club chairman, was the bloke I'd seen returning (at about 12:40) after escorting a lady friend home. He tried the front door, found it locked and went round through the Yard instead, just before I introduced myself to the drunken Squealer.

The chairman stood trying to get a look at Diemschutz's discovery. He couldn't see much, by light of the steward's candle, standing as he was behind Diemschutz and Kozebrodski. Eagle lit a match of his own and came round the heap on the ground. It was a woman. Horrible! He jumped back – into the blood running for the drain. He jumped again tracking bloody boot marks. His match went out then, thankfully, saving him from having to see the sight (or the mess he was making).

Diemschutz warned all not to touch anything (for what good it did) and he and Kozebrodski headed out to find a copper. Upset by the blood, and unwilling to wait with the body, Eagle decided he too would go for the law. Besides, he needed air. He followed the pair but, when the steward and the young Kozebrodski headed south from the gateway, Morris Eagle ran north instead.

Eagle reached Commercial Road and, immediately, spotted two police constables to the east, past Batty but this side of Christian Street. Eagle shouted, "Murder!" and took off running for the coppers. At that instant, the chilled chairman heard an echo and looked over his shoulder to see another man from the club (a new fellow, whose name he couldn't remember) had followed him and was trying to break in on his glory. Determined to be the first informant, Eagle sped up...

...and won. Eagle reached the bobbies first and came to a sudden stop, gasping, "Murder!"

"Here now, what's this?" Henry Lamb (252 H), the constable posing the question, advanced to meet the excited men. Walking his beat in Commercial Road, Lamb had only paused for a word with the *fixed point* officer on duty. The panicked socialist never got the brother cop's name. (As he never testified, neither did I.) There were coppers all over the damned place; only seven minutes had elapsed since Lamb last passed that very spot.

"Come on," Eagle and his companion cried in unison, "there has been another murder!"

Of course the police wanted to see my work. They took off running, two coppers led by two socialists, back in the direction of Berner Street.

By that time, Diemschutz and Kozebrodski had returned to Dutfield's Yard with Spooner, the horse-keeper, in tow. The three made their way through the small crowd clustered in the passageway left of the body. The blood-spattered brick wall, obviously, kept all away from the right.

With his candle nowhere in evidence, Diemschutz struck a match to give Spooner an eyeful. The horseman crouched, reached for the woman's chin and, finding it still warm, lifted. For the first time all in attendance got themselves a look at my handiwork. A gasp went up as the group saw how fearfully cut the whore was and what a great gash I'd left in her throat. The last of her juices bubbled out and ran down to the pool by her head and, from there, to the gutter and the drain beyond.

The perfect end to a perfect whore.

"Step back! Please, everybody, step back!" came the commanding voice of PC Lamb.

Morris Eagle, and his comrade, had returned with their coppers from Commercial Road. Lamb and his companion parted the crowd, took charge, and pointed their lanterns at the centre of everyone's attention. A new round of gasps erupted, followed by '*Oohs*', '*Awws*', not a few '*Oh, dear's*' as the crowd pressed in for another, longer and better lit, look.

"Please," Lamb repeated, "Keep back! You don't want any blood on your clothes. You'll have questions to answer if you're caught here with blood on your clothes."

Morris Eagle, chairman o' the bloody boots, gulped and looked about nervously.

"Please, keep back!"

As the horse-keeper had done before, Lamb knelt, touched the woman's face, and found it still warm. He took her wrist in hand but felt no pulse. A man of action, Peeler Lamb, he looked up at his fellow constable and told him to fetch the nearest doctor. The PC disappeared from the Yard. Lamb turned back to the Bolshie who'd summoned him. "You, Mr Eagle, off to Leman Street Police Station with you, smartish-like. Tell them what has happened here and get me some assistance." The Eagle flew.

The constable returned his attention to the victim on the ground. Oddly, she looked to be resting, as if laid quietly down. Her clothes showed no sign of disturbance. Her voluminous skirts were in place (the soles of her big boots just visible from beneath). Nothing about her suggested a struggle to Lamb.

Course it didn't. I'd given her no chance to struggle.

Lamb would later testify at the Coroner's Inquest that, just then, he couldn't tell whether or not the blood still flowed from her throat. He saw that the stream draining away was still a fun red liquid. But the pool of juice on the ground near her head had already begun to congeal.

It was ten after one in the morning when Lamb's colleague, Bobbie Anonymous, rapped on the front door of 100 Commercial Road, the residence of Dr Frederick Blackwell. While the servants rolled the old boy from bed and stuffed him into his clothes, Blackwell's younger and fitter assistant, Edward Johnston, jumped into his togs and returned immediately with the man of the Met to Berner Street.

Johnston examined my work, while PC Lamb chased the growing crowd of on-lookers from the Yard. "Members back into the club, please. All others, into the street outside." He had the gates closed and posted a constable at the wicket to see nobody ventured back in.

Then Lamb entered the socialist's club. He made a quick, cursory search of the rooms, upstairs and down, then spoke with the corralled members. He took the names, addresses, and details of what little each knew. He turned his light on their hands and clothes, and found nothing suspicious. (Eagle had taken his bloody boots with him to Leman Street.) Afraid he was wasting his time, Lamb thanked the lot for their co-operation and asked them to remain until the CID arrived and had a word.

Then, leaving the club by the (now unlocked) front door, Lamb turned his attention to the cottages across the street. The tenants there had, to a person, retired for the night. But the uproar in the street – and Lamb rapping at their doors – raised all, alarmed and in various states of dress. "There's nothing much the matter," Lamb told them, each in their turn, not wanting to scare them further.

Having bothered the neighbours to no gain, Lamb recrossed the street. He checked the door of, and looked in on, the dark fruit and vegetable shop, then returned to Dutfield's Yard. He walked the depths of the Yard, checked a closed store, the office of the socialist paper, and the two waterclosets there. Nothing, nothing, and nothing times two.

Meanwhile, behind Lamb, at the cooling whore...

Johnston unfastened the Squealer's dress at the neck, reached in, and copped himself a feel. The body was still warm (they'll stay that way awhile if not properly opened up). Her hands, however, were quite cold. The wound in her throat had stopped bleeding for certain. All but a little of the blood by the neck had run away and the remaining juices in the gutter had clotted.

Dr Blackwell, his trousers finally in place, arrived in Berner Street at 1:16 am. He pushed his way through the now-crowded street, was admitted through the guarded gates to the Yard and, by the amber lights of the peelers' lanterns, got his first eyeful of my work.

Two days later, Blackwell would confess to the coroner's jury what a horrid sight greeted him. He also admitted, more humorously, it was he who removed the tissue-wrapped cachous still clutched in the whore's left hand. "The packet was lodged between the thumb and first finger, partially hidden from view," he told them. Then, clearing his throat in embarrassment, he added, "It was I who spilt them in removing them from the hand."

ha ha. Breath mints bouncing to land in her jellied blood.

Then the muckety-mucks began to arrive. Peeler Lamb returned from poking about to find that both a Chief Inspector and an Inspector (West and Pinhorn, respectively) had taken possession of the carcass in the name of the Queen and the CID. West noted bloody foot prints near the body. Pinhorn suggested they like-as-not belonged to innocent bystanders. Morris Eagle silently breathed a sigh of relief.

Dr Phillips, the divisional police surgeon (summoned first to the Leman Street station), was finally on scene. Again the dead whore got a going over. Phillips findings, which mostly corroborated those of Dr Blackwell, were dictated to a scribbling Pinhorn. The surgeon would appear at the 3 October inquest to read the notes off, including his erroneous guess there were signs of a struggle and the delightful tidbit that I'd nearly severed the head from the body. If only I'd had more time.

As the gates to Dutfield's Yard allowed the police to easily seal the area off, they did not need to hurry – as they had at earlier murder scenes – to rapidly remove the corpse to protect the public. The plods occupied the Yard for hours. Meanwhile, once they controlled the environment, the men of the Met also took control of onlookers. Everybody in the crowd was detained, identified, and searched by the police; then examined by Phillips for bloodstains. No weapons, no clues, no suspects were found among them.

The remains of the Squealer, my fourth kill (my first kill that night), was finally removed to St George's Mortuary in Cable Street at 5:30 in the morning. Then, on Inspector West's order, Constable Albert Collins took a bucket of water and washed the last of the whore's gore from the Yard gutter and into the drain. The Met was 'calling it a night'.

I, one the other hand, had not done the same.

What none of the exhausted boys in Dutfield's Yard knew was, by that time, three-quarters of a mile away, I'd killed again. My second victim of the night was already four hours cold.

Thirty
Singing Whore

Again the happenings in Berner Street, at the time, were completely outside of my knowledge. As the body was being discovered and investigation in the gateway of the socialist's club was getting started, I was on the run. I did not have a destination. I merely needed to be away from Dutfield's Yard.

I could have gone home, certainly. Fact was, at the moment I slit the Squealer's throat in Berner Street, I was only a few short blocks from my lodgings. I might be thought crazy not to have gone home. But I couldn't, could I? I just couldn't! I'd accomplished my work. I had rid the street of a dirty whore, that's true. But not cleanly. No, the events in Berner Street had gone pear-shaped. Hadn't they? The results had been unsatisfactory. The whore was dead but, owing to her squeals, to the nosy Jew, the smoker, and the bloody socialists, the result had been a cock-up. The game had not been played. The message had not been delivered. How could I go home?

I reached Commercial Road. I saw a couple of figures moving through the corner lamp light to the west; men or phantoms, made no difference to me. I saw a couple of figures several short blocks to the east, jawing beneath a street lamp, bobbies by their headgear (or firemen or Cromwell's Roundheads). Again, I didn't care as long as they had no interest in me. I started west, crossing at an angle between Gower's Walk and Adler Street. I did not think it wise to remain long, even at that deathwatch hour, on that thoroughfare; I expected it would soon become busier. I turned up White Church Lane headed to St Mary's. Short of the church, I got off the street. I ducked into a doorway for a breath of air and a think.

I examined my hands which, until that moment, had been tucked deep in my pockets.

Blood.

Not a lot, a few specks on the one hand. I'm careful. The whore had given up her juices in a spurt to the side and against the wall of the socialist's club. Good for me. And, I said, blood in Whitechapel was not a cause for extreme alarm, but – times being what they were – it could be a cause for questions, as it had been for those three innocent butchers in Buck's Row. Just then, I didn't want to be stopped and questioned with even a spot visible on me. I pulled a kerchief from my pocket and, in that doorway, sat down upon the step to scrub my hands.

Wouldn't you know it, right then, even on that tiny lonely street a bloke wandered by. *Cor!*

I stayed calm and went out of my way to pay him no mind. I lowered my head and finished my hands, making it plain I had business and belonged there (whether he did or not). I felt him give me a look. But felt as sure he hadn't stopped to give me two. Then he was gone.

Damn. This being seen in the streets by punters was starting to be a bad habit!

I heard the sound of distant yelling voices. Couldn't make them out, but had no need.

I abandoned my attempt to think my situation over. The only thought I could muster was, I'd been in White Church Lane long enough. On my feet again, I returned to Commercial Road. I examined the way up and down and found all quiet for the moment. The coppers on that far corner were gone, left for Berner Street, no doubt; surely the Squealer had been found. They would just be getting a look, starting their investigations, or (more likely) sating their curiosities ogling my work. Let them have it.

Moving casual (like I belonged), but sharpish nevertheless, I took a side street off the Lane and from there out to the Whitechapel High, headed south and further west... a fine upstanding working class citizen walking briskly, but not suspiciously fast, in the direction of Aldgate.

By the time I found my bearings, I'd considerably stretched what ought to have been a ten-minute walk and wound up about three-quarters of a mile from Berner Street. The night was not going well. It was 1:30 (I heard the bells of St Mary's and Christ Church both). I was a-sea. My mood would have been so much lighter if I'd only known how close I was to a radical change in my luck. For it was only a very few minutes later, I met a singing whore in Duke Street.

I was headed up from the High. She was crossing Duke Street having come down the short block from Houndsditch. It was her singing caught my attention; heard it before I saw her.

She was warbling an airy tune, arms out in flight, pirouetting in a circle, her skirts billowed out, half hopping, half dancing, toward the corner; floating like a dandelion floret on the breeze. She looked drunk, but seemed almost too well-balanced. Sobering? Maybe. She appeared childishly happy.

She was too damned old to be carrying on that way. Looked about forty, I think, five feet tall and thin. She had dark auburn hair and hazel eyes. Her clothes were old and dirty; a black straw bonnet trimmed with green and black velvet and black beads; a piece of red gauze silk worn round her neck, a black cloth jacket trimmed with fur around the collar and cuffs and around the pockets in black silk braid and fur; a dark green chintz skirt (patterned in Michaelmas daisies and golden lilies) with three flounces and brown buttons on the waistband; a man's white vest; a brown linsey dress bodice with a black velvet collar and brown metal buttons down the front; a pair of men's lace up boots (the right boot repaired with red thread); and an old white apron.

In point of fact, I had no immediate interest in her. None until, as I passed her in the street, she addressed me and blew her unmistakably beery breath into my face. The foul odor of stale booze made all the difference. It made me so angry it brightened my night. Her appearance was a *coup de grâce*. And, if I might stay with the French an instant longer, my failure in Berner Street suddenly showed itself for what it was, merely an opening act in what would be a *tour de force* performance; a glorious double event that would shake the foundations of Scotland Yard, Whitehall, and the silver flatware of the old bitch in Buck-place as well.

The drunk whore was babbling on, calling me 'deary' and insisting I call her 'Kate,' disgorging for me a laundry list of compelling reasons to slit her bloody throat. She'd only been released, "Just now, just this minute, swear to Gord," she said, from police custody. She slurred all the filthy details into my defenseless face. Those she skipped I eventually sussed through Mrs Griggs, Miss Adler, and Mr Frogg, so I may as well pause to sort them, wring out the alcohol, and relate them here.

Much earlier in the evening, around 8:30 pm, the whore had caused a drunken scene (by imitating the wail of a fire engine, or some such rot) in front of a small crowd outside of No 29 on the Aldgate High. Then, either following her ridiculous performance, or as part of it, she laid down on the pavement to take a nap. A Constable Robinson (931 City), on patrol, saw the crowd and investigated. He lifted the whore to her feet and attempted to stand her against the house, but she toppled. Another copper (name of Simmons) arrived to assist. With a concerted effort, the pair shuffled drunk tart off to Bishopsgate Police Station.

The uncooperative woman gave her name as 'Nothing' to James Byfield, the station sergeant. He entered same in his log book, followed by *Drunk and Disorderly* as the charge for her arrest, and she was placed in a cell till such time as she sobered up. Ten minutes later, the softhearted Robinson looked in to see the sodden whore had fallen fast asleep.

PC George Hutt (968 City) joined Sergeant Byfield at the front desk at 9:45 pm. He was up-dated on all the drunk fish currently occupying Bishopsgate's barrels, including prisoner Nothing.

The singing whore spent the next three hours, and then some, dreaming whatever drunk prozzies dreamed, in the Bishopsgate nick. At a quarter past midnight, Hutt checked the prisoners and found the woman awake in her cell and softly singing. At 12:30 she appeared, for the most part, aware of herself and her surroundings. Nothing asked Hutt when she could be released.

The constable answered, "When you are capable of taking care of yourself."

"I can do that now," she called out. But Hutt had already left the cell area.

Twenty-five minutes later, convinced she was in fact sober, Hutt released the woman from her cell and escorted her to front desk. Sergeant Byfield, however, had no intention of releasing her until she gave them her name. To show her willingness to comply, and her readiness to return to the streets as a law-abiding citizen, the whore gave them her name. "Mary Ann Kelly," she said. "6 Fashion Street."

To put the night into focus, it should be noted that while the singing whore (whose name was most definitely *not* Mary Ann Kelly) was playing the coppers for fools at Bishopsgate, at that same moment (1:00 am), I was parish-hopping red-handed from St George-in-the-East to Whitechapel while, behind me on the south end of Berner Street, Diemschutz (the startled socialist steward), was poking his whip at a dark heap in the gateway of Dutfield's Yard.

The semi-sober whore in the Bishopsgate nick had no watch. "What time is it?" she asked the officers at the front desk.

"Too late for you to get any more drink," PC Hutt replied.

She didn't disagree. "I'll get a damn fine hiding when I get home," she admitted, fixing and retying her white apron back in place over her skirts.

"Serve you right. You have no right to get drunk," Hutt told her. "This way, Missus."

The constable led the whore down the station house passage to the exit and warned her, "Close the doors behind you."

"All right," the whore replied, pushing her way out. "Good night, old cock."

She turned left on the walkway outside the nick, headed for Houndsditch – singing.

Which brings the tale up to date.

I'd met her, as I said, singing in the street coming down from Houndsditch. And, interrupted by a belch here and there, she related the foregoing sad and boring story. "Told the cop I should get a damned fine hiding from my old man when I get home." *belch* "And he said, You deserve it. That's what he said. You deserve it. Oh, maybe I do."

"Of course you don't," I assured her, offering solace and a grand pretense of compassion (though the emotion was beyond me).

But don't think all emotion was out of bounds. At the same time, secretly I admit, I couldn't have had a warmer feeling for the police than I did just then. They'd dried the sot out for me, enough so's I could hear airy singing and gay laughter instead of the usual disgusting gurgles and burps. They'd warned the woman (far too late, I feared) of the evils of alcohol. Then they'd opened their doors, setting her free again into the streets – still stinking of beer – into my waiting arms.

I was standing, facing 'Call me, Kate, deary' the whore, at the badly lighted entrance of Church Passage, a narrow alley leading into Mitre Square. She had her hand on my chest and was giggling, and singing, and slurring her words in her semi-sobriety.

Thirty-One
'Call me, Kate, deary'

You might wonder how one could hate a singing dancing girl who insisted, with glee, you call her by her first name while she called you, 'deary'. Let me make it clear. Of all those whores up until that moment, I hated this one most of all. My mother, I may have hinted, was a pathetic drunk. Always had her empty head inside a bottle, or a gin glass, or a beer tumbler. Always. The only exceptions were the times she was fornicating with strangers she'd picked up in pubs, the lodging houses between which we bounced, or the gutters that separated them.

If she wasn't drinking or fornicating (or contemplating an avenue to either or both), she was sobering up. That's when her attentions fell on me. That's when I caught hell for all she was and was not. When the beatings and the abuse fell like rain. When I hated her most of all; when she started to sober up. In those few desperate moments when my mother was not hitting me or screaming at me, when she was pretending to be a mother... she wouldn't use my name. The bitch called me 'deary'.

I was saved, if that was the word, by an Irish aunt who took me in when my mother finally drank and fucked herself into an early disease-ridden grave. Believe it or not, that only ended in a worse situation (but I shant go into that now). Point was... I can not put into words how much I hated this sobering singing whore who called me 'deary'.

Then, as if the night hadn't been hectic enough, came more damned annoyance!

In the distance behind the whore, I saw three men, foreigners by their looks, Jews by their taste in entertainment, leave the Imperial Club on Duke Street. They came our way and passed the pair of us at perhaps fifteen feet distance. Only the nearest of the three seemed to take notice of us. The other two mumbled twixt themselves. The three continued past, down Duke Street and into Aldgate. But I'd been seen again.

No matter, not then. I'd decided.

Once the men were gone, the singing whore asked me if I had a couple of pennies to spare. I assured her I did, but hoped she was willing to trade for them. She laughed and said she thought she could do that. Then she nodded down Church Passage.

We slipped down the shadowed pathway and into Mitre Square. I pointed to the south, the darkest, corner, straight ahead on the other side. She giggled. "Shy, deary?" I remained a step behind as she led the way.

Vicious whore mother, no longer drunk but breath still putrid with beer. I had everything a boy could need. She reached the south corner, stepped up onto the walkway, and turned to face me. I was already reaching to throttle her. Her eyes popped in terror like great eggs. But that was all. Not a sound escaped before I had her throat, choked her into unconsciousness and (after several minutes of useless struggle), laid her supine upon the stones.

I kneeled along her right side. I drew out my trusty shoemaker's blade and slashed the soft white throat of 'Call me, Kate, deary' from left to right. She was dead already, so there was no spurt. But there came the glorious red gush and it was brilliant. Brilliant! My breathing raced again. I had to control it. I had to get on. I had to make up for the earlier disaster.

I crawled down her body to my station of comfort to the right of her filthy hips and rose up on my knees again. I threw up her skirt...

...to see she wore a pair of brown ribbed stockings. To see Mrs Griggs would have been proud – for she wore no stays. What a good girl. Then again, she wasn't wearing any drawers either, the dirty bitch. Not to say she didn't have undergarments. She had plenty, more than her share. Beneath her skirt was a grey stuff petticoat, an ancient dark-green alpaca skirt, an old ragged blue skirt with red flounces and a light twill lining, and a white calico chemise. She wore her entire wardrobe at once.

Tied or sewn into her skirts beneath (as with good ol' Stockings, only more so) were, a blue stripe bed ticking pocket and two calico pockets with strings. I dug into both and found them brimming: white cotton kerchiefs, white rags, coarse linen, blue and white shirting, two more bed ticking bags, two short clay pipes, a tin of tea, another of sugar, flannel, six pieces of soap, a comb, a table knife, a teaspoon, a red leather cigarette case, a tin match box (empty), red flannel (pierced with pins and needles), a ball of hemp. Hell's teeth, she was her own junk shop!

She was more than a drunk street whore, she was a full-fledged vagrant. On top of her full wardrobe, she seemed to carry every personal bit she owned. Everything about her, from her trilling singing voice to her bottomless pockets of shite made me angry. I hated this whore. I hated her!

I intended to do her up right.

I set my shoemaker's tool on the pavement beside me and pulled out my long knife. I reached between the whore's legs, keenly sharp blade up, and stabbed her as far in and... to the rear... as I could manage. I cut forward from the back filth hole, up the right side of her front filth hole, and continued ripping, up and over, in a great jagged gash to the navel. I cut a circle around that *belly button*, leaving it to stand alone on an upright tongue of skin, then continued up, ripping vertically across the pale bare stomach and on up to the breastbone.

I saw immediately I had accidentally stabbed the liver opening her up. How remiss of me. Well, I couldn't take it back, so I thought I'd best move forward. I stabbed the liver again. A good one, a two inch whack. As three's the charm, I gave the ol' liver another stroke, slicing off the end of the left lobe. It disappeared inside her. I got silly thoughts sometimes when on the job and, for a moment, I thought I'd look for it.

To that end, I grabbed a goodly portion of her intestines and lifted them out. Weren't that a mess, smeared as they were with blood, fecal matter (I guessed), and whatever other evil juices the whore was ripe. I laid those gore snakes on the pavement over her right shoulder. As with Stockings, there was a stretched piece, about two feet long, running from the pile back into her guts. I'd left it go then, but not now. This time I attended to it. I hacked the piece of intestine free and, reaching across, laid it on the ground between the body and the left arm.

I checked the pavement and saw nothing in the way of blood; no spurt, no splash, no nothing. Still it gurgled from her throat wound. As the juices were not running away, they apparently were collecting underneath her. Wouldn't that play hell with her wardrobe? But enough about my workplace aesthetics.

Back to the interior. I moved what remained of her insides about to get a look at the sacks covering the kidneys. I'd stood in, in the shadows of the salivating students, at a hospital class on kidney surgery. (Yeah, I lied to the peelers. I often watched.) The first thing the instructor stressed was the impossibility of getting to the organs from the front. The patient had to be prone. Tosh!

I was about to disprove that. All you had to do was get the other organs out of the way and, *voila*, there sat a fat left kidney waiting to be scarpered off with. I cut through the membrane, grabbed hold of the kidney, and cut through the connected artery. It was firm, like a ripe tomato.

But with it out steaming in the chill night air, the question dawned, how to cleanly carry it home?

I took note of the whore's white linen apron, decided that would do, pulled it clear of her abundant skirts and sliced off a section of the bottom. I laid the prized kidney upon it on the ground. Then I took another look inside of her, wondering, what ought I take... for afters?

The light was poor, time short; I didn't have much more to waste. I decided to take her baby sack as well, her uterus as the posh doctors would say. I took hold, felt the bag of still-warm flesh in the palm of my hand, and slipped my knife inside her.

That was when a flash of bright light hit my eye. It came from straight ahead, down the south fence line of the square, down the narrow Church Passage footpath. There was no mistaking it. A police constable, on patrol from Duke Street, had entered the passage and was headed straight for me!

Thirty-Two
I am Invisible

Light blinding me, I froze in position!

Instant panic welled within me. I was kneeling over the whore, I held a bloody knife in my right hand and her filthy womb in my left. I couldn't move; didn't know if I should or if I was better off remaining perfectly still. The light held me. I was copped!

I waited for the whistle. Waited for the shout. Waited on my knees with blood, bits, and the murder weapon in trembling hand. I waited. . . until it dawned the light had ceased its advance. It wobbled and slid slightly to my left. I stared hard and, behind the beam, saw the silhouette of the cop holding lantern – looking the other way, over his shoulder, toward Duke Street. He'd laid the beam on me but hadn't bothered to follow it with his eyes.

With his attention elsewhere, I slashed with my knife, completing the amputation, and pulled the uterus out. But not all, damn blast it to hell! In my fearful hurry, I'd mucked it up. A portion of the organ remained behind! I had no time to fret further about that. I hurriedly laid the womb beside the kidney within the sliced slip of apron and wrapped both up. I slipped that package in my pocket.

I checked the lazy copper again. Still standing there! The glare of his light still visible down the passage! But still facing Duke Street. Thank god for that! For it was then I realized I had nowhere to go. I was blocked, behind me and to my right, by the brick walls of the surrounding houses and by the metal fence. If I broke to the left and ran for the Mitre Street cart entrance, or attempted to flee north across the square to the footpath to St. James' Place, either way, the movement might draw the copper's attention again. And with a focused lantern and alert eye.

My position seemed hopeless as the bastard was bound to turn back this way. I felt done for.

Then a miracle happened. A miracle so wonderful I can not express it. Yet, so simple, it seems anti-climactic to say. For no reason, the torchbearer, the patrolling copper, without a look back, turned on his heels, pointed his light back into Duke Street, and withdrew. Without venturing further down passage, entering the square, or seeing me at all, he walked away. It was true; I was invisible!

In celebration of the peeler sodding off, a clear sign I was meant to be on the job, and to pay her back for nearly getting me nicked, I decided that instant the whore would forfeit her face. Yes, why not. It was only fair payment for what she'd almost done for me.

As I offer details of the work, keep in mind the care I used, the artistry employed. I'd nearly severed the head from the body when I killed her. It took real skill to go back and butcher her looks without entirely decapitating her. Now then...

I stabbed her through her lower left eyelid dividing it neatly through. I drew the blade back and flicked it down again through the upper eyelid on the same side near the nose. I stabbed her, on an angle between the eyes, above the nose. I cut through the right eyelid. I smacked her hard with the knife, and cut her deeply, over the bridge of the nose, slashing from there across the right cheek to the jaw. That was a good one! It divided the meat to the bone with the exception of the final thin inner lining of the mouth. Because my intentions were just, and to save the poor tart from having to smell her own foul odor, I hacked off the end of her nose. The follow-through on that slash, incidentally, divided the upper lip and cut through the flesh over the gum. Her right upper incisor peeked out at me like the fang of a snarling dog through the hole in a fence. But that was silly, she wasn't a dog she was a pig. Using the tip of my blade, I cut in from the side of her mouth at a right angle and dragged that slit on a parallel line between her lower lip and her chin. I cut a triangle flap into her left cheek, and liked that a great deal. Knowing the police surgeons would have a field day examining it, and that the plods would suffer a brain bleed trying to determine exactly what the design indicated, I cut another like-triangle into her right cheek. Let 'em eat cake! While I was at that game, I noted a spot of mud on the whore's left cheek. Unable to ignore it, I scratched round the mud with the tip of my knife. That, I imagined, would be lovely when the sun rose. Hovering, trying to decide whether or not to take the left ear lobe for a souvenir, I scratched the skin below. That was careless. To make amends, I left that ear intact. I switched sides and, instead, cut the lobe off the right ear. That was nothing less than slipshod. The ear lobe took flight and disappeared in the dark somewhere in the folds of her layered clothing. I was so disgusted with myself, I didn't bother to look for it.

Too busy enjoying the overall effect to worry about trifles, I'd begun to botch things. I'd let that copper shake me, and shouldn't have. My work was beautiful. I could feel it. Sadly I couldn't see it clearly. The corner of the square was too dark. Black-looking blood covered everything above her slit throat. I caught my breath and knew it was time to be gone. I got moving.

As I stepped out into the gaslight of Mitre Street, I confess, it occurred to me I might have overdone the work. Don't get me wrong, I didn't care a toss that I'd left the pig in her own mess, she deserved it. But, heading out to the High street, I realized I was a bit of a mess myself.

Then, as if led by an angel, I saw my salvation there on the opposite corner. The Aldgate Pump! With the copper who usually loitered there nowhere in sight. Providence was kind! A well-earned drink and a wash at the ratepayers' expense. ha ha. I had to stop, didn't I? I simply could not sock a gift horse in the face. I hurried over.

A historic landmark, the Aldgate Pump had stood as a public well there since the reign of King John. (A metal wolf head on the spout signified the last wolf shot in London-town.) A gaslight at top, twelve feet in the air, was for the tourists. In the deep dark of the night, it put out a light that amounted to no more than a four foot circular nimbus; a soft and dimly glowing ball floating in air.

Originally, the pump was fed by one of the many streams running under the city. Residents and visitors alike praised the bright, sparkling, cool water for its agreeable taste. That was... until several hundred people died miserable and painful deaths during the 'Aldgate Pump Epidemic'. Turned out the fresh water derived its delicious taste from the calcium (and other decaying matter) leached from the rotting skeletons in the host of new cemeteries and old church graveyards north of London through which that subterranean stream ran from Hampstead.

How's that for a laugh? ha ha.

The city fathers couldn't remove their national landmark. They couldn't openly admit they'd helped to poison hundreds, perhaps thousands, of unsuspecting people. At epidemic's end (twelve years ago), with the explanation the City intended to widen the streets, the pump was taken down and moved a few unnoticeable feet to its current location, the junction of Aldgate, Fenchurch, and Leadenhall Streets. There, with its water supply quietly altered to city mains, the pump was re-erected as a drinking fountain and to continue its historic duty as symbolic west boundary of London's East End.

Damn! Damn blast it!

I arrived beside that historic symbol realizing for the first time I'd left the confines of the East End. I'd entered the City of London and done the bleeding pig inside the City limits. I was about to have an entire second department of coppers on my heels; the Men of the Met, who'd been after me, and now the City police! I needed to get back to Whitechapel where I belonged.

Let me pause to say, I didn't know City of London Police Constable Edward Watkins (881) from the man in the moon. Wouldn't have known him if he'd bit me. I did not know he'd made a routine patrol of Mitre Square at one thirty in the morning (when all had been peace and quiet) or that his patrol beat took him exactly fifteen minutes to circumnavigate. I did not know it was now 1:44 am.

What I knew was, I had just reached the Aldgate Pump when, *bang*, out of the gloom, coming round the corner from the opposite direction, stepped a bleeding copper.

But thank god for minor favors! I saw him but, as I was still on the blind side of the pump, and he was looking straight ahead, he didn't see me. I silently slipped back into the shadows of the little gable-roofed shack that housed the pump.

The constable went by without a hitch in the step of his ever-so-shiny shoes. He crossed before me and, whistling softly as he turned into Mitre Street, headed for his 1:45 visit with the square.

The last PC that had ventured that way, coming from the opposite Church Passage, had been a derelict tosser. He'd had me in his sights and hadn't bothered to see me. If this fellow was different, if he was one of the Queen's loyal and ardent young officers, who gave every inch of his patrol the keen eye... ha ha. He was about to get an eyeful. I knew I hadn't better wait.

I stepped quickly to the pump pool and doused my hands... *whooo, bless me, cold...* and scrubbed. I splashed my face and gave it a wipe on the off chance the pig had spattered on me.

I heard a shout and a bang. The shouting of whom? The banging of what? I had no idea, muted as the sounds were by the apartment buildings and businesses surrounding Mitre Square. But I had the distinct feeling an alarm had been raised. Good on him, nothing got past that young constable. I hurried the hell up, pulling out my tools and giving their blood-covered blades a quick cleaning. The juices I added to the pool, from my soiled hands and knives, were nothing new to the Aldgate Pump! I gave my knives a shake dry and slipped them back into my coat. I was respectable again, at least I hoped.

But I might have taken too long. I heard running, or something like, echoing up Mitre Street off to my left. With nowhere to go, I leaned back into the shadows again and became the night. I made myself unseen (though I remained there, drip-drying) while I listened and watched.

Now came a police whistle, full and shrill as it wasn't buried by the square. A figure, bent and hobbling with obvious arthritis, came running from Mitre Street. It was not the copper. It was an old bloke, whoever he was, in a panic, blowing a copper's whistle with all the wind he had.

I didn't know what was happening. All I knew was I wanted to be away from there. But I stayed myself from bolting. The whistle was going to bring more coppers, who might well come from any and every direction. Mistimed running might well put me in the middle of a blue pack. I held my shadowy ground, worked at slowing my breathing, and stayed watchful.

I'd sussed it right. Two more peelers arrived on the run, one around each corner from Leadenhall Street and the Aldgate High. Both passed without a look to the pump, the shadows behind it, or at anything hiding in those shadows. They met the old boy at the mouth to Mitre Street. Excited mumbles, then the three disappeared down the street (presumably, into the square).

A moment passed then, again, panicked whistling, either from the shaken old man or from the coppers who, by now, must have turned their lanterns full-on the gift I'd left. Yes, lads, yes! Take it in. Call for reinforcements. Blow your heads off! I really must confess I was enjoying it; silently laughing myself to death. Blow those whistles. Blow till your hearts explode. Wake the neighbourhood, wake the night. Tell the world the Whitechapel killer had struck again!

The makings of a crowd began to appear out of the dark. *Ahh. The nosy citizens...* on schedule. They came individually at first, the boozy losers already up and wandering the streets, responding to the whistles like trained animals; eager to escape their pathetic lives by watching someone more miserable yet get his due. They came in twos and threes, onlookers less awake but more cognizant, with less curiosity and more concern in their eyes. They came in groups, rough looking men, tradesmen and shopkeepers still in their nightcaps, and desperate and frightened looking women, who'd had too long a respite from the horrors around them and were, only now, beginning to wonder, beginning to fear the worst. Shoving between and through the growing crowd were spare coppers arriving fresh from blocks away. A couple of them, the lowest in rank no doubt, who'd yet to earn a gander (or were too green to stand a gander) at what I'd left for them, were ordered to stay back and to stop on-lookers from looking on. Yes, the streets had quickly grown full of people. But none were looking my way.

I stepped from beneath the shadow of the pump housing and edged into the excited throng. At the same time, I worked my way around the back of the crowd. No one paid me any mind. But soon they would. When the police took control over the situation, they would begin to examine, question and, in some instances, search the crowd. It will come as no surprise I wanted no part of that.

I turned and slowly headed away, up the Aldgate High; a man about his business.

Thirty-Three
Coppers in the Square

There were three ways in or out of Mitre Square; one carriageway, between the shop of a picture frame maker (a bloke named Taylor) on the right and the Walter Williams & Co. warehouses on the left, from Mitre Street, and two narrow foot passages; one called Church Passage at the east corner of the square, leading to and from Duke Street (the route I'd strolled with the singing whore), and one without designation, at the north point of the square, leading to St James' Place (the Orange Market).

As I said, it was 1:44 am (a mere three-quarters of an hour after the socialists had found the gift I'd left at the mouth of Dutfield's Yard), when that City copper walked round the corner at Leadenhall Street and the Aldgate High, headed for Mitre Street. He passed me drip-drying in the shadows behind the famous landmark; walked right by, he did, without any suspicion I was there.

I've said I had no notion on earth (then) who Constable Watkins was. But quietly let him go. I've already related what I did next. I could only guess what he did.

Over the weeks to come, owing to the labours of hard-working reporters, to the loose lips of Mr Frogg and his tot Tad, to coroners' jury witnesses, and to the excited tittering of the Dress Reformists in Mrs Griggs' sitting room, by rounds of eavesdropping on Miss Adler (and Archie) and her coterie at London Hospital, and by the tales that raced through the streets like the flames of the Great Fire, I eventually learned in detail what Watkins, his colleagues, their alarmed superiors, and the doctors they knocked up that night from their warm beds, did over the next few minutes (and hours) at the scene, in the neighbourhood of, and about the cooling corpse of the singing whore.

The constable I avoided... and let live... Yes, the notion of slitting Watkins' throat as he passed had visited my racing brain. After killing, it's really quite easy to kill again. But I'm wandering. It wouldn't have been fair to the peeler, would it? To off the poor sod when he was already being devoured by de Balzac's monster, routine.

As he rounded the pump, he'd have had himself one hell of a prize if he'd merely looked hard to his left! But, as if he were a train on its track, he blindly followed his designated route, past the pump, into Mitre Street, and into Mitre Square. The beat took him fifteen minutes to patrol. On his last round at 1:30 all had been quiet in the square. Now again, at first glance, all seemed quiet.

The neighbours in the surrounding apartments were sound asleep; George Clapp and his good lady wife had been abed since 11:00 and, of all people, another bleeding copper, Richard Pearce (922 City) and his brood, had been snoring in their hovel at No 3 (in the west corner of the square), between the Williams' warehouses and Kearley & Tonge's, since half-gone-midnight. The Kearley & Tonge's night watchman, George Morris, was awake and sweeping the offices.

Watkins heard nothing but the echo of his own footsteps. He paused and shined his lantern (fixed in his belt) from left to right across the square. He halted as the beam reached the southern corner and fell upon a dark heap on the pavement – which had not been there on his last walk through. The constable stepped past Taylor's shop toward the object. Then he stopped again, feeling a tingle of alarm. (I knew that tingle well, from the other side.) Watkins took several more – now hesitant – steps, staring as his lantern caused the shadows to fall away. The heap became a body, became a woman on her back... in a pool of blood, became the most gruesome sight Watkins had seen in seventeen years of copping.

Watkins gasped in appreciation of my craftsmanship, turned on his heels, and ran like a wee girl across the square to Kearley & Tonge's. He knew Morris, the night watchman, was a Met pensioner. (Right! I'd killed the whore under the noses of three coppers. Four, if you count the tosser. *Cor!*) Watkins hoped Morris might be... Yes, he was in luck! The office door was ajar.

Watkins pushed it open, saw Morris inside sweeping down the steps, and cried out, "For God's sake, mate, come to my assistance."

Morris dropped his broom, grabbed his lamp, and followed the PC. Outside, starting across the square, the old man finally asked, "What's the matter?"

"Oh, dear," Watkins replied, "there's another woman cut up to pieces!"

By that time they were there, over top of the heap. Watkins and Morris both threw their lights on my work. Then both took a series of deep breaths to keep their own guts from erupting. "I'll... stay with... the body," the copper stammered. "You bring help."

So it was the old cove, Watchman Morris, I saw hobble out from Mitre Street and into Aldgate, blowing his brain's out on his whistle. A PC on Duke Street, James Harvey (964 City), heard the alarm and came running. He met Morris, who excitedly told him of the body. By then PC James Holland (814 City) had arrived too. And Morris told it again! At 1:49, Harvey and Holland, led by the retired Morris (three blind mice) entered Mitre Square together.

As had occurred in Berner Street (an hour earlier), the hubs of hell now broke loose on the edge of the City of London proper. All owing to the actions of Yours Truly. This night's message regarding drunken street trollops had been delivered – in duplicate – and would not be forgotten. As evidence to that claim I report that, within minutes, Mitre Square joined Berner Street in being frantic with alarmed coppers (sporting City badges on their starched collars). Crowds of panicked Londoners mobbed Aldgate whining and whispering the plague had reached their shores. And Metropolitan Police (not involved in the Berner murder) lined up at the city limits with their tongues hanging out, wanting a piece of the horrendous action and, at the same time, thanking god it wasn't their problem this time.

Like a West End thriller, cue the pandemonium!

Out of my own curiosity then, for completists now, I took in the details from my excited sources and, over the next number of weeks, catalogued the frantic activities of the Queen's representatives for law and order through the capital of the realm. Forgive me if it's dull, or wrong, or both. As I said, I was curious, which isn't the same as giving a toss. As I made my way back east, the following – or something very like it – occurred in and around Mitre Square:

PCs, current and former, Harvey, Hollard, and Morris met Watkins over the *no-longer singing* whore's still warm corpse. One look and Holland, on his own, took off on a run for 34 Jewry Street, Aldgate, the home and surgery of Dr George Sequeira.

At 1:55 am, the Bishopsgate Police Station got word of the murder. Inspector Edward Collard, who had been taught as a child to play well with others, immediately notified the Metropolitan Police Headquarters at Scotland Yard, by telegraph, the Whitechapel killer had gone wandering and paid the City a visit. He sent a constable to wake Dr Frederick Brown, the City Police Surgeon (at 17 Finsbury Circus), and to hurry that distinguished fellow to the scene of crime. (It irritates me to use that word, but the plods insisted so *crime* it was.) With his ducks so neatly in a row, Collard set out for Mitre Square himself.

As an aside... I'd never worked within their jurisdiction before and hadn't given the City of London police any thought until that night. It turned out that, though I'd never left them a corpse to deal with, they'd been responding all along to my little reign of terror.

My permanent correction of the first two whores, in August, had sent the City into action. With Police Commissioner Sir James

Fraser on leave (and ready to retire), the Acting Commissioner, Major Henry Smith, had instructed his detective department to employ extra plain clothes officers on the eastern fringes of the City, to closely watch their drunken whores, and to question men and women seen in company after dark. That had been news to me.

I had no way of knowing but, at the moment the singing whore and I were conducting our business in Mitre Square, three City plods, Detective Sergeant Robert Outram, and Detective Constables Daniel Halse and Edward Marriott, were searching the public passages of houses only a few streets away. The trio were little more than a block away, at the bottom of Houndsditch near St Boloph's Church, when they heard Morris' frantic whistle and ran to the square. They arrived, huffing and puffing, at 2:00 am, the same moment PC Holland returned with Dr Sequeira.

Beneath a circle of constables' lanterns, Sequeria bent over the woman, took one look, and realized no on-scene examination was necessary. Inspector Collard arrived from Bishopsgate (at 2:03) as Dr Sequeira went out on a limb and pronounced the woman dead.

"You've examined her?" Collard asked.

"No. Nobody's touched her," the doctor said. Then, to ensure the inspector understood, he added, "It wasn't necessary. She hasn't been gone long, fifteen minutes, probably; but she's certainly gone."

The Inspector nodded. "The City Police Surgeon is on his way."

Dr Sequeira knew Dr Brown well. "Then I'll simply wait with you and do nothing further."

Wait, yes. But Collard was hardly a *do nothing* sort of plod. The inspector began issuing orders, organizing a search. He accepted the fact that things, jurisdictionally speaking, were about to get sticky. It was doubtful the murderer, in his escape, had run deeper into the city. In fact, it was damned unlikely. It was no secret the suspects in this horrid string of murders (surely this was another), all hailed from the eastern slums. He would cover the west, obviously, but what was less obvious was what he should do for the east. He'd already notified the Yard, but that did not relieve him of responsibility.

Sod it! He ordered a group of his men, including DS Outram, and DCs Halse and Marriott, to separate and start searching outside of their own jurisdiction; into the Metropolitan Police patch and into the near streets of the East End. Halse, I mention in passing, started north up Middlesex Street.

Dr Brown reached Mitre Square at 2:18. He greeted Inspector Collard and Dr Sequeira then turned to the remains of the singing whore. There he got a lesson in anatomy! I'd redone her face, cut her throat, ripped her abdomen, lifted out her innards and deposited those about the body. Yes, he agreed with Sequeira, the woman was quite dead. Then, aware much might later depend upon his observations, the doctor examined the corpse (as carefully as the light allowed), made note of the injuries, and drew a pencil sketch of the body. Flattering that, he felt the need to recreate my artistry.

A Detective Sergeant Jones, ever in search of clues, signs, and symbols (after the mysteries I'd left them to solve in Hanbury Street), carefully picked up three black boot buttons, a metal button, and a small mustard tin containing two pawn tickets, from the pool of clotted blood left of the neck; and a metal thimble lying near the right hand. What could it all mean?

Collard sent word to rouse Acting Commissioner Smith from his bed at Cloak Lane Police Station. Then he returned his attention to the scene, recording for posterity two details he considered of import: The dead woman had no money in her possession. There was no sign of a struggle.

At 2:20 in the morning, Richard Pearce, the police constable who lived there, and whose bedroom window looked out upon the stage where I'd recently performed, rolled from the sack and stormed (in trousers and undershirt) into the crowd of gathered colleagues to see what all the fuss was about. It was then he first heard of the murder. *Oh*, I can just imagine his thoughts, matching those of old boy Morris, and Watkins, and the lazy sod with the lantern (James Harvey, already mentioned, more on him later);

each having been 'this close' to laying hands on the Whitechapel killer, before the opportunity slipped away. Their near-fame becomes infamy; disappointment, jealousy, bitterness. In solace, I, Jack the Ripper, would have only been able offer a touch of Whittier, 'For of all sad words of tongue or pen, The saddest are these: It might have been!'

As Pearce received his awful news, a new wave of coppers washed into Mitre Square, a Detective Superintendent, another Inspector, and two more Sergeants joined the throng. Each of them bent on preserving public order by grabbing me by the heels. My goodness, 'Call me, Kate, deary' had been one popular whore. But I'm not complaining, the more the merrier!

DC Halse, who on Collard's orders had been nosing outside of his jurisdiction, up Middlesex and east on Wentworth Streets, returned to Mitre Square via a quick patrol south through the short residential Goulston Street. That means nothing... yet. But it will. ha ha.

Meanwhile, an ambulance cart arrived at the square. His examination concluded, Dr Brown instructed that the whore's body to be placed aboard and taken to the City Mortuary in Golden Lane.

While, blocks west, word reached DI James McWilliam, head of the City Detective Department. He went immediately to their office, at 26 Old Jewry. As Collard had done (outside of his knowledge) McWilliam courteously wired the news to Scotland Yard to make them aware their killer had ventured into his territory. He then headed for Bishopsgate Street Police Station and, from there, to Mitre Square.

McWilliam found Commissioner Smith, Superintendent Foster, Inspector Collard, and a pile of plods and peelers on scene when he finally joined the fun. Smith and McWilliam put their heads together to hear all that Collard had done. Then the pair took over directing the search... for little ol' me.

Thirty-Four
Goulston Street

Those were the *goings-on* in Mitre Square, behind me and outside of my knowledge at the time. My worries were yet ahead of me.

On the move, away from that scene, I crossed Duke Street and paused there to watch two Met cops coming on the run down Aldgate out of Whitechapel. They went by, paying me no mind. Why would they? I was merely one of many innocent citizens on the street as a result of police whistles (praying the cause was not another outrage. ha ha.) Besides, the tiny silver 'aitches on their collars made it clear to all the world that, where they were headed, they had no authority. They were at the far edge of their Division and were merely rubber-neckers themselves.

Once they'd passed, I turned north on Houndsditch where I had to detour around another group of excited residents headed south and west in the direction of the whistles and the fun. My goodness, but hadn't I opened the gates? Doing the deed in the city, I had the City Police, the Metropolitan lads, and the friends and foes of both crowding in. It was still shy of 2:30 in the morning and the streets crawled with people like fleas on a doss house whore. And Jack the Ripper, *oh I loved that name*, moved unseen in the midst of them all.

My pockets were filled with the goodies I'd taken away (wrapped in a piece of the ripped whore's apron, still warm in their own blood), and my knives (and the string, chalk, and matches I always carried), and my hands still damp from the quick wash and drip-dry (tucked away to avoid the chill night air). Again it occurred, wouldn't I have been a jolly catch for some bewildered PC?

I had the coppers on my mind (who wouldn't then?) and had to take care in my movements. I couldn't run, running would have been a dreadful give-away, particularly running in the opposite direction of the excited flow of humanity. I couldn't ignore my surroundings either. Only by stopping to watch the police, to follow their moves, to hear their whistles (wearing a stupid look of alarm); only by seeming a part of it, could I disappear and become unseen. It wasn't necessary to flit from shadow to shadow like a phantom; with the streets so poorly lit, it would not have been practical, as it was they were mostly shadow. Steady progress from lamp to lamp, showing interest at each spot of light, that was the best way to disappear. That and, when possible, to get off the main thoroughfares.

I finally found an opening to make a casual egress from Houndsditch. I turned up a little nothing of an unlit street called Gravel Lane. I saw nobody and picked up my pace. The air was filled with the Mitre Square carnival behind but I no longer needed concern myself with that. In fact, no more was I out of danger than I got cagey. Safe in the real shadows, I darted behind a low wall, approached a dark house, and slipped into an even darker doorway. I leaned there, quietly catching my breath, giving a new thought a going over.

More than merely a thought; it was a new lark. What fun it would be!

I peeked from my hiding place and found the block quiet. I reacquired the wall and checked again. The lane was dark and empty. I hurried north and east at once, followed the maze round the little open square there, and came to the corner of Middlesex Street. I paused.

It was a good thing I did. A copper, with something on his mind, stood on the corner one block up (Middlesex at the west end of Wentworth), lantern in hand, turning slowing in a circle like the business end of a lighthouse. Then, still carving the dark reaches of the street with his light and scanning slowly with his eyes, he moved up Wentworth, disappearing from my view behind the buildings.

Outside of that fellow, Middlesex appeared quiet and empty. But I wouldn't wait for anyone else. I cut straight across and, keeping a block south of Wentworth, continued on my line up a short block to Goulston Street (the short residential street I'd mentioned in passing earlier).

I ducked back into a recessed doorway there and waited.

Sure enough, the copper with the scanning lantern reappeared at Wentworth and Goulston. He turned and started south, slowing making his way down Goulston Street in my direction. I hugged the recess, making myself unseen. It took an eternity but he finally passed, without realizing (I triumphantly add) I was there and watching him.

Three-quarters of the way down the street, he met another copper headed north. Christ, was there no end to those bastards? Small wonder Inland Revenue was starkers! The pair had a short visit, discussed me and my work probably, wondered at my location, maybe cursed their lot in life, then moved on. The breathing lighthouse continued down to the Whitechapel High, while the new fellow (whose manner was far less intense) continued up Goulston, past a block-long residential building there on, what most likely was, his normal patrol beat. The peeler passed me by without pause, then I waited him out until his disappeared at the end of the block.

Good on them. Both officers could report peace and quiet on their patrols. Meanwhile, I'd spent a lifetime in that doorway!

But I hadn't wasted the time. I'd taken notice of my location and added that to the already churning plan for the lark I was considering. I was across the street and just up from a great stretch of building, the large residential complex recently passed by the north-going bobbie, wearing a weathered and tarnished wall placard that identified it as the Wentworth Model Dwellings. I didn't know it, but I knew of it. The place let rooms almost exclusively to Jewish immigrants. Brilliant!

Saucy Jacky

Checking again, noting the street still empty, I left my door and bolted across the way and to the building. I sidled quickly down wall and slipped into the entry leading to the staircase that accessed (according to the signs) room Nos 108 – 119. I paused there, though I could not spare the time and ought not to have risked it, and leaned on the wall to catch my breath. I hadn't exerted myself in that short hop, so it must have been excitement and nerves. But breathless I was. So I caught up.

My hands were yet in my pockets. The right hand felt the apron package, wet with cooling blood, and (dirtying my fingers again) I gave the wrapped meat a squeeze, ha ha. Some urges were too strong to resist. The left hand shunted my knives aside to feel for one of the items I always carried (a boy needed to be prepared) but never thought of; my piece of chalk.

Then the silly notion became a plan, an explosion in my brain (leaving a warm and glowing fire burning) as an impish question took shape. What mischief, I wondered, could a bright boy cause for two plodding departments of peelers with the clever use of a handy piece of chalk?

I recalled the events of earlier in the evening, the giggles I'd had from the fools I'd encountered. I thought again of the wandering Jew who had stuck his nose in on Berner Street, and how – with the simple shout of "Lipski!" – I'd sent him running for his worthless life, with the pipe smoker on his heels. Thinking on that, I turned round and stared at the fascia of black brick behind me, the jamb of the open archway leading to the stairs, leading to the hovels of countless more unsuspecting Jews. I saw, not a wall, but an opportunity for more sport of a like-kind. Another jolly. A chance to shout "Lipski!" to the whole East End; the chance come morning to set a hundred, a thousand, foreigners running with an angry crowd on their heels like that bastard in Flower and Dead Street! The brick wall would be my lovely open canvas.

Things had gone to hell earlier in Berner Street. The whore had gone down, that was all to the good, and the streets were a cleaner better place. But the situation, the intrusions, had forced me to send her to hell without cleaning her up; without making her right. I'd more than made up for it with the slut in Mitre Square, good on me, but I still felt bad about it.

I had got a lick in on the filthy Jews and twisted the stinking Socialists' noses all at once. And here I had a chance to kick both again, to set them at each others' throats, and kick the coppers in the bollocks as well. Just before sun up the socialists would be trudging by en route to their daily toils. At the same time, the place would be crawling with sleepy-eyed Jews rolling out to count their pennies and start their scams. Plods were blowing through the neighbourhood like loose rubbish. What a lovely time it would be for another riot.

I didn't have the time, but I took the time all the same.

I looked Goulston Street up and down once again, saw no one, and drew the chalk from my pocket. Then, crouching before the right-hand side of the open doorway, taking special care to purposefully piss up the spelling, I scrawled a cryptic message across the bricks:

The Juwes are The men That Will not be Blamed for nothing

Lovely, I thought as I stood again. Just lovely.

But more was needed for the full effect. It was fine by me if they failed to understand the meaning of the message (all the better to start a row), but it would never do if they failed to understand who it was that wrote it. Couldn't have them guessing about that, now could I? Had to make the author plain. I put the chalk away and, in its stead, drew out and carefully unwrapped my package of whore's goodies. I returned the pieces of precious meat to my pocket, but retained the portion of bloody apron. That would be ample; it would be perfect. The coppers had no clue. All right then, I'd give them one.

I dropped the slip of linen to the ground below my chalked message where even the peelers, I thought, couldn't help but find it. If they weren't able, the rat Jew residents no doubt soon would. Wouldn't that raise a shout! A sticky message to set the people at each others' throats *and* one nice gooey piece of physical evidence for the Met plods and the City lads to fight over.

I left, laughing to myself. I'd had such a good time in Flower and Dean Street following Stockings' joyous demise. Wouldn't a riot this morning in Goulston Street be a riot!

It was five minutes before three that morning (Sunday, 30 September), mere minutes after I'd vacated the area, when the upstanding Met officer I'd seen earlier on patrol returned once more to Goulston Street. Constable Alfred Long (254A) paused by a staircase arch at Wentworth Model Dwellings. His lantern beam fell on a piece of fabric lying, in an aspect of having been discarded, on the pavement to the side of the door opening. Whatever it was, it hadn't been there before. He reached for it but, just before taking hold, stayed his hand. The rag was soaked in blood!

Long reassessed his approach and, carefully, lifted the item with finger and thumb by a clean corner. He dangled it in his light. *Cor, yes!* The rag was doused with blood (and besmirched with brown smudges that appeared to be feces). The young constable's stomach turned over. He took a breath not to heave and dropped the rag again.

It was then he saw the graffiti, written in what looked to be chalk, on the brick wall directly above the rag. He read it (though I wasn't there to report in exactly what manner). Perhaps he read it silently, but with his lips moving as the stupid were wont to do. Perhaps he read it aloud with a question, or even a tremor, in his voice. "The Juwes are the men That Will not be Blamed for nothing."

His brain wheeled round as that sank home. Then, most likely, he exclaimed under his breath. (Just what, the world would never know for he'd never confess it.) He most certainly betrayed his fear. Perhaps he swore or, if he was a good little boy, maybe he called out to his god or his mother. Either way the startled Long, realizing his duty, quickly shook off the shock.

He searched the staircases of the Model Dwellings, up to the first floor apartments and down to the basement, and a small portion of the surrounding area. But he didn't search long. He knew he was now a part of something special and eagerly wanted to share his glory with his mates.

That's mostly a guess on my part but, as I later learned, I was right as rain.

Only a few minutes gone three, Constable Long spotted and hailed one of his fellows, a passing peeler from H Division. He left that man in charge of the beat, to stand guard over my carefully thumbed poetry. Then Long took it upon himself to lift the blood and shite stained apron piece (carefully, no doubt) and scurry off with it to the Commercial Street Police Station.

Thirty-Five
Busy Morning

It should come as no surprise that, by the time I made it back to my lodging house that Sunday morning, I was exhausted. It had been a busy night. Sadly I couldn't go to bed just then. No, there was more needed doing if the night was to be called a complete success.

I'd left a gift for the police to fight over. Their first clue in the case! But I knew the coppers, at least I knew the complaints lodged by the news reporters about the coppers. They hogged evidence. They kept secrets. They wouldn't share. For my messages to strike the right tone with the people, they needed to be heard. If the police would not shout about them, I would. And would keep shouting till the bastards paid attention!

So, tired as I was, without bothering to wash up again, I sat down at the old work desk in the back room of Mr Griggs' shop, put on the gas, pulled my bottle of red ink from its hiding place, drew out a blank postcard, and made ready to write to my new pen pal, the Dear Boss.

I'd yet to hear what he'd done with my first correspondence, but that wasn't his fault. I'd asked him to hold it until I worked again. I assumed he'd done so. Now, with the work completed, I'd given him the go ahead. I trusted him. I had no reason not to and would trust him again with a second contact; an update as it were.

I addressed the card to my ol' friends at the Central News Office and turned it over. But what to say exactly? And how? I would leave off punctuation, I'd already decided as much. I would ignore proper sentence structure. I would forget good diction entirely (the better to keep them guessing as to my station and education). I considered the message for a long moment....

... then thumbed:

I was not codding dear old Boss when I gave you the tip. you'll hear about Saucy Jacky's work tomorrow double event this time number one squealed a bit couldn't finish straight off. had not got time to get ears off for police thanks for keeping last letter back till I got to work again.
Jack the Ripper

It only seemed right that I sign it with the trade name I'd given myself. The world needed to know me. They needed something to remember. They needed to know Jacky was on the job.

Tired as I was to finish, and in a hurry to see it done, I accidentally got the whore's blood on the card, great smudges on both sides. It couldn't really be helped, as I said, I hadn't taken the time to wash. I considered doing another, then thought better of it. I'd send it bloody; sauce for the goose.

I washed up out back, aware now what a poor job I'd made of it at the Aldgate pump. Luck must have seen me home, or a guardian angel. I took the time now to fix myself.

Then, back inside, I quietly dug in the back of one of Mr Griggs' cupboards for materials that I'd gathered earlier (a selection of glass jars, a container of ethyl alcohol) and stored out of sight; I got on with my next chore. With great care not to soil myself again, or mess the shoe shop, I pulled the whore's borrowed bits from my coat pocket and tucked them into appropriately-sized jars. I poured wine spirits in after, to preserve them, then sealed the jars up. I slipped the lot (one jar each) into several of the old shoe boxes that lived on the shelves in the back room, replaced the lids and replaced the boxes again. My private collection was growing. Done with the gross work, I stored my knives out of sight in a like fashion (cleaned and boxed). Then, finished with that, I returned to the backyard pump and washed a final time.

One more duty to perform; to send my all-important message on its way. No, it couldn't wait. I listened at the stairs and satisfied myself the house was quiet; my landlady yet fast asleep. Good that. I put on a different coat (I needn't explain), slipped the card in the pocket, and stepped out on a leisurely mission to deposit same in one of Her Majesty's mail receptacles in hopes of making that morning's post. I headed for the Whitechapel High and then east.

To my genuine surprise, as early as it was, the streets were already alive with the events of the night; and to my annoyance, I soon discovered, with one event in particular. I first heard about it as I slowly approached, and more slowly made my way around, a log jamb of barrows and pushcarts blocking the footway and curb in the vicinity of Frogg's newsstand and beyond. To get by would have forced me to risk the street. But, just then, I was curious enough to not need to get by. The sidewalk blockage was a veritable costermongers' convention. A grocer, a fruiterer, a bread baker, a pie maker, and a flower seller (apparently on the outs, as she kept butting in), were having a lively meeting, to which Mr Frogg occasionally contributed and young Tad occasionally interrupted with his shouted headlines.

"Whitechapel murderer strikes again! Double murder! Whitechapel murderer!" cried Tad.

"The murderer left 'em a present in the city."

"A present? Here, what are you talking about?"

"Last night, after the second murder! All over town it is. The killer left a note written on a wall and under it, a piece what he took from the girl."

"Whitechapel murderer strikes again! Two murders in one night! Whitechapel murderer!"

"A piece... of what?"

"What do you fink? A piece of the girl!"

"*Cor!* What piece?"

"Don't know for sure; heart, liver, sumpin' like that."

"Whitechapel murderer strikes again! Double murder! Whitechapel murderer strikes again!"

"What a load of tosh!"

"On me mother's! Got it from me brother-in-law what lives in the lodgings nearby and had to pass at sunrise."

"He saw the... piece?"

"He saw the blood, red as the Home Secretary's face, he said."

"Whitechapel murderer! Two murders in one night! Whitechapel murderer strikes again!"

"And what was the writing?"

"He didn't know for sure. But it must have been bad; with the market so near, and soon to open, the coppers had it covered up so's nobody could read it."

"But what did it say?"

"Don't know. Some in crowd claimed it said it was a Jew what done the murders. Someone else pipes up and says it said, in particular, it was not a Jew what done 'em. Someone else says, and here my brother-in-law was most emphatic, the message was writ by Leather Apron himself, who everybody knows is a Jew what's takin' credit for the killings."

"But which were it?"

"Can't be Leather Apron," Mr Frogg put in. "Leather Apron didn't do it."

"How you know?"

"Been cleared," the news vendor insisted, not bothering to hide his disgust. "Don't you read the bloomin' papers? Coppers cleared Leather Apron. Said he didn't do it."

"So which were it?"

"Don't know. My brother-in-law was right there and didn't know. Said they were arguing about it."

"The crowd?"

"*Oooww!*" Tad had stopped his selling to listen to the gossip and Mr Frogg had set him right with a whack. The boy got back to work. "Whitechapel murderer strikes again! Double murder! Whitechapel murderer strikes again!"

"The crowd was arguing?" someone asked again.

"No, not the crowd. The coppers! My brother-in-law says the coppers were arguing with each other there in Goulston Street.

Constables from the Met must have thought the Whitechapel murderer done it to crow, or that it said the Jews done it, as they wanted the message scrubbed off wall 'fore the market opened."

"Can't blame 'em," the flower girl chimed in. "Nothing but Jews and foreigners living over there."

"That's as may be, but the coppers from the City were shouting they had one of them fancy cameras on the way and wanted to photograph the writing, to have it as evidence."

"What about the bloody piece?"

"Whitechapel murderer! Two murders! Whitechapel murderer strikes again!"

"My brother-in-law didn't know about the bloody piece. I already said."

"So what happened?"

"No more did the sun come up than Sir Charles Warren, himself, showed up, right there in the street."

"No!"

"My brother-in-law don't lie!"

"*Cor!*"

"You say. Well, Sir Charles must have feared a riot as he ordered writing scrubbed off the wall, sharpish-like. Stood right there and watched while a constable got a bucket and washed it down, message, blood and all."

"There was blood?"

"It was writ by the Whitechapel murderer, wasn't it? Course there was blood!"

The excitement was lovely. The sounds of terror, of panic, in their voices. I was delighted. I was far less delighted with Sir Charles *bloody* Warren stepping in and marring my game with his cowardly sponge and water bucket.

The details came out later – proving the rumors basically true. Proving the rumors tame. Goulston Street, shortly after PC Long's discovery of my work, had become the third ring of that night's circus with the coppers acting as dancing dogs. They immediately set to yipping at one another.

Having delivered his trophy, and accepted full glory for his find, Long returned to his patch at five in the morning. He was surprised to find DC Halse, of the City Police, on the scene out of his jurisdiction. Halse had ogled my message and sent for one of his department's cameras to photograph the wall. Ten minutes debate of the issue... ended instantly. Halse stared wide-eyed, while Long and everybody else wearing a Met badge on the scene, jumped to attention. A coach rolled up and delivered Metropolitan Police Commissioner, Sir Charles Warren himself, on Goulston Street.

Sir Charles was shown the message I'd left and, it was fair to say, was not a happy soldier. Afraid of a riot, was he? Afraid of the Jews? Afraid of what might happen to the Jews? Who knew? But there could be little doubt he was terrified that, when the sun rose, he'd have another Bloody Sunday on his hands. As the bread bakers brother-in-law had reported, on Sir Charles' orders a constable was sent for bucket and sponge. Despite Halse's protests, my message was rubbed out before the people got a look.

That was a bleeding shame! But there could be no argument, I'd wanted a rise out of the coppers and had gotten one.

Already by sunrise that Sunday morning, Inspector Collard's house-to-house interviews were well underway. Mostly with negative results. Nobody in the residences, offices, or warehouses anywhere around the square had heard a sound or seen a thing to disturb them. The fireman at the St James' Place night station had slept soundly as usual.

But there was a thin ray of hope. Three Jews (Lawende, Levy, and Harris by name), headed home from the Imperial Club in Duke Street together, had seen a couple... Well, one of the three, Joseph Lawende, had bothered to *see* the couple outside of the square moments before the outrage. Maybe, just maybe, they might have been the whore and her killer.

Meanwhile, in and around Berner Street and Mitre Square, the searching and questioning went on.

The horrible news of the double killings swept through the city that morning. Thankfully by 11:00, I was in my bed and out of it as, it seemed, all nine hundred thousand residents of the East End were in the streets, either shouting in vicious anger or screaming in panic. The fools had awakened to the news, and the realization, the killer had not gone to Gateshead. The monster still walked among them.

Monster! To hear the shrieks, there were monsters everywhere. The killer was a monster, hidden among them, destroying them, ripping them apart from the inside. The coppers and the Crown were monsters for not finding the perpetrator, stopping him, killing him in retribution. Of course, the nagging thought had been renewed, was heavy on their hearts and sharply on their brains; the inescapable fear that any man (or woman) on the street beside them could well be the monster. That morning not one single soul in the East End of London trusted another.

Leading the Metropolitan Tabernacle in prayer that morning, it came to be told, Mr. Spurgeon, on behalf of his frightened flock, cried out to the Most High, "We hear startling news of abounding sin in this great city. Oh God, put an end to this, and grant that we may hear no more of such deeds. Let Thy gospel permeate the city, and let not monsters in human shape escape Thee."

An empty plea, from an ignorant man with no real grasp of sin or the methods by which sin could, or should, be eradicated. As I took it all in, the panic and chaos amid the filth as the morally sick fought against swallowing the medicine I'd given them, for the first time I truly understood the full measure of my calling. I was meant to come out from among them and be separate. I saw my future and grasped my own importance. But the price, for me, would be high. Outside of the excitement, and there was that, my infinitely vital existence was destined to be desperately lonely.

I bravely accepted my burden.

Thirty-Six
Who Saw Yours Truly?

Old Wynne Baxter, I imagine, was wishing himself back on holiday. That, or wishing I'd take one. But it was not to be, so Monday, 1 October, the Coroner for Southeast Middlesex found himself back at work with the first meeting of his Inquest into the death of the Squealer in St George-in-the-East. I'd had a laugh at these gatherings in the past but, all joking aside, I resolved to follow this particular inquiry closely and to read the newspapers with discerning interest.

The reason should be obvious and, trust me, ran deeper than ego.

By the time I'd finished on the night of the double event, I confess, I returned home concerned about my situation. Specifically about the witnesses. I'd done a grand job on the drunken whores. But I'd been slack in letting myself be seen by so many; two men for sure in Berner Street, one on little White Church Lane, and three men, at least, in Duke Street. That's not counting the daft copper had me dead-to-rights in his lantern beam in Mitre Square. It was careless. Thrilling, I admit, but careless. I feared being identified or traced and nervously watched for signs the police were on to me.

I wanted to know what the authorities knew. Oddly, I had one up on the law as the inquest opened. By giving her the festive (and sadly accurate) nickname of Squealer, I at least had something to call the whore into whose death they were inquiring. The authorities, having yet to identify her, were still forced to refer to her as the 'Berner Street victim' or simply as 'Unknown Female'.

As with previous inquests, after being empaneled, Baxter hustled his jury off to St George Mortuary to get a gander at what I'd left of the drunk whore. What's-her-name lay on a slab, still dressed but covered to her shoulders with a sheet, awaiting preparation for her post-mortem. In her case, that was all was necessary. I'd been hurried and hadn't had time to do any artistic work; just slashed her throat and took my leave. All the pertinent evidence was plainly visible to any of the twenty-four jurors with the nerve, or stomach, to look. Thus stimulated, the lot of them returned to the Vestry Hall in Cable Street to dive into the gossip.

Inspector Reid ogled the show, on behalf of the police, while Baxter called his first witness, William West. A member of the socialists' club, West made a meager living printing Bolshevik rags that passed for papers at an office in Dutfield's Yard. He testified he neither heard anything, nor saw anything, then went home with his brother. Fine witness him.

Next came the Bolshie club chairman, Eagle, who'd danced in the blood then went for a copper in Commercial Road. Followed by the steward, old Diemschutz, who'd found the body in the Yard. That was it for the day's witnesses.

Without calling either of the men who'd seen me in Berner Street, the inquest was adjourned until Tuesday, 2 October. I was left to wonder.

It wasn't until 3:00 pm, that day, as the attendants stripped the corpse of Unknown Female and gave it a good washing, that Drs Phillips and Blackwell arrived at the mortuary to conduct post-mortem. The bath gave all a chance to see the living hell the streets and booze had played on her. She was covered in partially healed sores, evidence of a disease-ridden slag's life. She had an old healed injury; a torn left ear lobe (nothing to do with me). Probably, she'd rowed with another drunk whore and, in the melee, had an earring ripped out. She was missing all the teeth in her left lower jaw. She had a crooked right leg; but I never got that far.

With their ogling over, the pair of medical experts dug in. Blackwell did the cutting, Phillips took notes. Two other doctors, Johnston and Reigate, looked on (for the fun?). There followed the heavy-handed jargon I was well-used to (and bored by) at hospital. They measured, weighed, and considered. They found she ate too much starch; a stomach full of partly digested cheese, potato, and farinaceous powder. They talked, they jotted; rigor mortis, hemorrhage, incisions, discolorations, *blah, blah,* and *blah.* She died of a slit throat; exit one worthless whore.

But I'm too harsh. Turns out everybody, even a whore, has friends.

Through my various means of gathering information I learned that, late that evening, after the Government-sponsored cutting was done, PC Walter Stride dropped by the morgue – not as a copper, but as a grieving nephew. He identified the corpse (from photographs) as that of Elizabeth Stride, a Swedish immigrant, who married his uncle.

The same day, a drunk and staggering Michael Kidney barged into the Leman Street Police Station. Kidney had been one of Stride's more committed bed partners, a faux husband, over the years. He shouted to the desk sergeant that, if he had been the policeman on whose beat 'Liz' was murdered, he would have shot himself! Then he demanded to see a detective.

Kidney told the police all he knew. Not surprisingly, in his condition, that wasn't much at all.

Oh, the papers were a laugh! The reporters needed copy on the greatest story in their experience. But the police would tell them nothing. What could the newshounds do? They wrote gossip, superfluous nonsense, fiction, and stories that amounted to nothing.

Thus eager readers learned the first victim of the double event, Elizabeth Stride ('Long Liz' to her slag friends), a 43 year-old unfortunate, was seen drinking in the Queen's Head pub that evening. Vital information. Who would have guessed? A prostitute! Drinking! Why, but for her being a drunk whore, would I have introduced myself?

Readers learned that at 6:00 pm Stride returned to her lodging house, from her boozy adventure, to smarten herself up and get ready for whoring. She attempted to borrow a brush from someone named Charlie. Fascinating, that.

In a separate article, the same paper reported that, as Charlie broke the devastating news to Liz that he'd misplaced his brush and could not loan it out, the night's second victim, Catherine ('Call me, Kate, deary') Eddowes, 46, was drunk on her arse in Aldgate High Street. That was nothing in the way of news, but reminded me of why I'd done her as I had.

Tidbits, unending, meaningless tidbits:

One paper reported that, at 12:40, when Morris Eagle went through the gate into Dutfield's Yard, he saw nothing unusual. *Bless me!* Stop the bleeding press! There's a headline, 'Witness Sees Nothing at All'. There was nothing for the tosser to see. But I saw him try the front door, find it locked, and go round through the Yard – as I approached the Squealer.

Five minutes earlier, apparently while I was leaving Batty Street for Commercial Road, PC William Smith saw Stride 'with a young man opposite the socialists' club. (A fellow I didn't see? Must have been, cause I never saw this copper!) He was five feet seven, dark overcoat, felt hat, carrying a newspaper parcel. Anybody having seen...'

What a laugh! Nearly 900,000 people lived in London's East End, a quarter-million of those in Whitechapel alone. Seventy-eight thousand lived in abject poverty. Nearly 15,000 of the dirty bastards were homeless and unemployed. Interview them all. Interview every damned one of them. None of them saw anything unusual. I am unseen!

But I knew that I had been seen. It was weighing on my mind.

None of the witnesses, the people I knew *had* seen me that night, testified on the first day of inquest. If the coppers were wise to me, they'd given no hint. I took extra effort over the next days to hear what Mrs Griggs, Miss Adler, Mr Frogg, and the street had to say about them. I was more than a little disappointed to find that they said nothing at all.

That wasn't the only thing that plagued me.

I may as well confess, too, to being annoyed by a *Times* editorial that got one hell of a snowball rolling, fast downhill, right at Yours Truly. In it, the editor reminded his readers of a case from twelve years earlier. The case first, then the trouble it started for me:

In March of 1876 a seven-year-old girl, Emily Holland, told friends at St Alban's School, Blackburn, she was 'going to fetch half an ounce of tobacco for a man in the street'. Two days later, the child's naked torso was found, by a labourer, in a field off Whalley Road, wrapped in two old bloodstained copies of the Preston Herald. The head, arms, and legs were missing. The same afternoon a child's legs, also wrapped in two dated copies of the Herald, were found in a drain in nearby Lower Curtliffe.

The post-mortem revealed the child had been sexually interfered with, and had her throat cut (from which she bled to death), before being dismembered. The police surgeon found hair clippings from several different people on the torso. Two local barbers fell under suspicion. One, William Fish (a father of three), was a collector of old newspapers.

Fish co-operated with the police, allowing three searches of his home. The third revealed four issues missing from his chronological collection of the Preston Herald. The missing issues corresponded with the papers used to wrap the torso and legs. Fish claimed the papers had been used to light his fireplace. Afraid their evidence was lacking, the police left without charging the barber.

Then Blackburn's Chief Constable, Potts, received a doubtful offer. A painter called Peter Taylor, owner of a Springer spaniel and a half-breed bloodhound, claimed the dogs could sniff out the child's missing remains. Potts gambled. On Easter Sunday, 16 April, the dogs searched Bastwell Field and Lower Curtliffe. They found nothing. Potts gambled further. The dogs were then taken to Fish's home, where the bloodhound (Morgan by name) began excitedly barking in front of the bedroom fireplace. The coppers went to work and, in a recess in the chimney, found a parcel containing a child's hands and arms wrapped in a bloodstained copy of the Manchester Courier. Fish denied responsibility, but later confessed. The case of Emily Holland was the first in England's history wherein the police used dogs to find a murderer, and William Fish the first killer hung owing to an animal's amazing sense of smell.

Why this lengthy tale? Because of a letter to the editor, written by Percy Lindley, a breeder of bloodhounds at York Hill, Loughton, in Essex (published Tuesday, 2 October) reading in part:

'As a breeder of bloodhounds, and knowing their power, I have little doubt that, had a hound been put upon the scent of the murderer while fresh, it might have done what the police have failed in.' Lindley suggested trained dogs be kept at a police station in Whitechapel, ready for immediate use should another murder occur.

I suggested a rolling snowball. That might have been a bit much. But it certainly started a flurry... of letters flying.

A dog breeder, in Surrey, claiming the largest kennel of bloodhounds in existence, wrote a response that upped the boast: 'ten well trained bloodhounds would be of more use than a hundred constables in ferreting out criminals who have left no trace beyond the fact of their presence behind them.'

The Home Secretary saw these and queried the Police Commissioner. Sir Charles, in turn, wrote Lindley asking how a dog might track a killer, without any of his clothing or blood, 'on a London pavement where people have been walking all the evening (and where) there may be scores of scents as keen as those of the murderer.'

Bloodhounds. The newspapers wanted to police to set bloodhounds on me!

The idea was ridiculous. But by dredging up that ancient one-off case, the *Times* editor might have given the plods ideas. What, for me, was worse than a policeman with an idea?

Finally, on the subject of ridiculous news stories...

Mrs Griggs read from a paper reporting, believe it or not, an interview with 'The Man Who Spoke to the Murderer'. This man, Matthew Packer, an old fool who ran a fruit shop by Dutfield's Yard (a shop I clearly saw closed), made the oddest claim yet concerning the outrages; so idiotic, I found it amusing.

The fruiterer and greengrocer claimed, at 11:00 pm on the night of the double event, he sold a half-pound of black grapes to a man and woman in Berner Street. Packer insisted the woman matched the police description of the victim and the man must have been her eventual murderer.

Packer was selling from his barrow on Saturday, 29 September, when the night came on wet. Not doing much business, Packer went home to relieve his wife serving in the shop. Between 11:30 and midnight, a man and woman walking up Berner from Ellen Street, stopped outside his shop, but did not come in. Packer usually conducted business through a half-window in front. The man was 30-35 years old, medium height, with a dark complexion. He wore a black coat and a black soft felt hat. "He looked like a clerk or something of that sort," Packer said. "I am certain he wasn't what I should call a working man or anything like us folks that live around here." (I was only a few blocks from home.) The woman was middle-aged, wore dark clothes, and carried a white flower.

After a minute, the man stepped up and said, "I say, old man, how do you sell your grapes?"

"Sixpence a pound the black 'uns, sir, and fourpence a pound the white 'uns," Packer replied.

Turning, the man asked the woman, "Which will you have, my dear, black or white? You shall have whichever you like best." Packer thought the man educated, with a sharp voice and a commanding way about him. The woman choose the black. "Give us half a pound of the black ones, then."

The fruiterer placed the grapes in a bag and passed them out the window. The couple briefly stood near the entrance to Dutfield's Yard. Then they crossed the road and, for more than half an hour, stood across from the shop. "Why, them people must be a couple o' fools," Packer told his wife, "to stand out there in the rain eating grapes they bought here, when they might just as well have had shelter!" The couple was still there when, a little past midnight (the public houses had shut), the Packers went to bed.

Mrs Griggs barely got to that point in the article when I burst out laughing.

Amusing, I explained, but not at all believable. Mrs Griggs (without suspicion) agreed. The true level of my amusement, I kept to myself. The idea I'd met a drunken whore in the street, bought her grapes, then stood eating them with her in a downpour, before getting down to the job of sending her where she belonged. The thought! *Mercy!* Were I to spend hard earned coins on one of those animals, it certainly would not be to buy her grapes; an apple would have been more likely. A nice fat juicy apple, to jam in her wide-open squealing pig mouth, before serving her up.

Thirty-Seven
Kidney and Onions

Speaking of serving her up...

Shall I talk of bliss? I didn't know but maybe, just maybe, the next hour would be bliss. I'd gotten the idea then and there, in Mitre Square, after the prying copper had nearly nicked me, while still kneeling over the slut's fresh steaming innards. I'd come home and preserved the pieces of meat I'd collected, hoping beyond hope for such an opportunity.

The late Mr Griggs was, by all accounts, a fine shoemaker, whose passing had created a tear in the fabric of the local society. It also created a wonderful place for me to play, owing to Mrs Griggs' refusal to get rid of anything her husband once owned or used. His shoe shop, long closed but otherwise untouched, was loaded with all a boy could need for all sort of sport.

With the hand pump in the small back yard, of course, for fast clean up.

Now to that wonderful night...

Mrs Griggs had to go out and was horribly upset not to have my meal ready. But she had purchased a fat onion and had a nice piece of liver for me. If I thought I could prepare it? Absolutely! I was grateful to her, and would have no trouble at all. The calf's liver looked delicious. I insisted she not worry as, surely, I could fend for myself for one night. I could soldier on. I nearly laughed at that, thinking of the early reports of the Whitechapel terror being a soldier, and had to control myself. I reassured the good woman and ushered her out of the house.

Once Mrs Griggs was on her way, I slipped into the back room of her late husband's shop. I pulled down a box from among the many shoe and boot boxes on the shelves. I opened it and withdrew a glass jar – one of several I had hidden away in the small jungle – filled to the top with wine spirits. And floating in the wine... the kidney I'd taken from the singing whore.

Mrs Griggs' fresh onion would get its due. But her liver could be damned. I had kidney on my mind, in my heart and, most decidedly, on the menu; whore's kidney and onions.

I cut the kidney in twain; half for my long-dreamed of supper and half to go back in the jar of wine spirits. I didn't know but that I'd have another use for it. I returned the jar to its box and the box to its shelf. I carried my prized kidney upstairs and set it to frying in a pan with a gob of butter and half of the onion. Didn't that make the kitchen smell all sorts of lovely!

While it cooked, I clipped a sliver off Mrs Griggs' shop bought liver. She expected me to eat, at least, some of it and there was no sense in raising the good lady's suspicions. But, not wanting to spoil the singular taste of the treat I'd procured for myself, I threw the piece of uncooked liver from the kitchen window to the cats roaming the backyard. They appreciated it and my landlady would have no reason to doubt I'd enjoyed the meal she'd generously provided. All was well.

The meal was indescribably delicious!

I grabbed a pile of Mrs Griggs' papers and, while I savored my whore's kidney and onions, read with delight about the police department's inability to do anything about me. ha ha.

In all seriousness, I had become a news devotee, any and all I could get my hands on, early and late editions, with a renewed – if not a manic – interest. I gobbled the newest accounts of the terror in the neighbourhoods of the East End like I gobbled... whore's kidney. The real joy came in finding the tasty crumbs of fact buried in the smorgasbord of fiction and crap posing as news.

The papers were full of nonsense, collected *clues* to the murders that were absolutely nothing of the kind. Two laborers, entering the Bricklayers Arms public house at 11:00 on the night of the double event, who claimed they passed Liz Stride coming out (in the company of a man). The whore and her escort were reportedly headed for the Commercial Road, at exactly the same moment I was supposedly buying her grapes in Berner Street.

She was seen forty-five minutes later, according to another paper, still in Berner Street, with a different man. Imagine that! A dirty whore with more than one man in one night. Hard to believe, yes? None of it meant anything. But every unfortunate on every corner was suddenly Liz Stride. Everybody was a witness to the infamous murder. Each held the clue the coppers needed.

Stride wasn't the only whore being covered. The bottom half of my double event made for a couple of lovely slices of entertaining tittle-tattle…

This was brilliant! When her corpse was stripped down at the mortuary, a hacked-off piece of Kate Eddowes' ear, that had fallen into her clothing during her well-deserved murder, had dropped out and plopped on the morgue floor. *Oh!* How I would have loved to have seen the attendant's face.

Later, a fellow named John Kelly, the poor fool who'd been bedding the singing whore on a semi-regular basis, had been brought to the morgue to identify his faux wife's body. Despite having known her for years, he could not do it for the grand artistry I'd worked on her facial features. Nothing that I'd left above her slit throat appeared familiar to him. Kelly managed to name her, finally, when he spied a pawn ticket among her personal effects given her, in his presence, by a mutual friend.

But, humor aside, I was serious in my reading up on that night's events. The nosy neighbours who'd gawped at me at the various scenes, and might identify me, were still on my mind.

The papers I had at table with me covered the second (Tuesday, 2 October), and third (Wednesday, 3 October) meetings of the Coroner's Inquest into Stride's death. Twelve witnesses testified over the two days; covering every subject from her childhood to her post-mortem. No! Of course, I didn't care about the details of the whore's passing; good riddance to bad rubbish. What I cared about, aside from the obvious entertainment value, was an answer to the question: What, if anything, had the authorities sussed about me? What had the eye witnesses said of me?

Something new did come to light; and weren't the authorities perplexed? ha ha. When the second meeting of the murder inquest met, the identity of the Squealer's corpse was back in question. Was it, in fact, Liz Stride? It appeared all they'd identified was the beginning of a new farce!

Out of nowhere pops a Mrs Mary Malcolm insisting the body was that of her sister, Mrs Elizabeth Watts. Malcolm claimed her sister was a destitute woman, existing hand-to-mouth in East End lodging houses, whom she had supported for years. That she'd met her every Saturday in Chancery Lane to bestow upon her a generous two shillings for her lodging; and had done for three years. Until the week of the murder, when Mrs Watts failed to appear.

Hearing of the murder, and fearing the worst, Malcolm claimed to have visited the St George mortuary at 9:30 that Sunday night to view the body. Owing to the poor gaslight, she claimed, she left unsure. Monday next, the day of the first inquest, Malcolm returned to the mortuary – twice – and did make an identification. There was no Stride about it, Mrs Malcolm insisted. The dead woman was her sister, Elizabeth Watts.

The police told Coroner Baxter they were not confident of the identification. Mrs Malcolm had been unsure to say the least. PC Stride had been absolute; Liz Stride had married his uncle. (The constable had never considered her his *aunt*; who could blame him?) Baxter asked the coppers to investigate the matter with all haste. Meantime, rather than return the inquest to square one, he would proceed under the assumption the dead woman was Liz Stride.

From there on, the only new evidence brought to light was the fact that aside from being a slag, and a drunk, Long Liz (wasn't I a friend; who had been as intimate with her as Yours Truly?), was also a filthy liar. One witness after another testified the whore often claimed to be a victim of the Princess Alice disaster.

For those with short memories, Princess Alice was a large saloon paddle steamer that, in September 1878, collided with the freshly painted collier, Bywell Castle, off Tripcock Point on the River Thames. Though empty of cargo, the coal carrier still displaced over 900 tons and dwarfed the steamer. The Bywell Castle struck the Princess Alice to starboard and split her in two. The steamer sank in four minutes. Hundreds were trapped and drowned.

To make matters more interesting, London's second release (of two daily) of seventy-five million gallons of raw sewage (from outfalls at Barking and Crossness) had occurred only an hour before the collision. The Thames, a muck of a mess at its best times, was foul from bank to bank. The Princess Alice cruise, that day billed as a '*Moonlight Trip*' to Gravesend and back, ended up quite the excursion for two shillings. Though they were on the return, the passengers ironically found *graves end* to be their final destination all the same.

The Board of Trade blamed the captain of the Princess Alice; the locals and press blamed the captain of the Bywell Castle. The over 650 passengers and crew who drowned in water thick with shite, in the greatest loss of life in the history of Thames shipping, didn't give a toss whose fault it was.

Why this delicious history lesson?

Because the Inquest revealed the dead whore made a habit of claiming she and her husband, John Stride, were employed (as a stewardess, and as a seaman) aboard the Princess Alice. That their children were with them on the steamer that day; and that John Stride and their children had drowned. Thinking that lie alone lacked weight, she frequently added that her hard palate had been broken by the heel of a passenger escaping up the companionway. Apparently, Stride wanted to make damned sure people understood how truly unfortunate she was.

The Inquest was adjourned again, until Friday, 5 October, with no assurance as to the identity of the corpse and without having heard any testimony from the men who had seen me. Why?

I'd been seen, seconds before slashing the filthy trollop's throat! Bloody hell! I shouted at the little Jew as he stared at me! And at the pipe smoker who'd appeared from the corner pub. It only made sense I wanted to know what they'd reported to authorities. I hadn't been wearing anything in the way of a disguise. How had they described me? What did the plods know? Who were they looking for? Why hadn't they testified?

I confess my concern was only heightened by the fact the police had boldly announced they would commence house to house searches throughout the City and East End that morning! What new information supported that intrusive step? What did they know?

I was left on pins and needles. What the witnesses told the coppers, the papers did not know and I could not learn. If the Jew had been called at the inquest, the papers did not say so. What the police would be looking for in their searches come morning, I could only guess at; and hope over the following days they would be as disappointed, and come up as empty, as I had.

Ultimately the newspapers, and their so-called news, were a disappointment. Thankfully, I could not say the same of the meal. The whore's kidney was delicious and no onion – in all the world's history of onions – had ever had it so good.

Thirty-Eight
Jack the Ripper!

Despite their best efforts in apprehending me, the police had so far failed miserably. I didn't blame them. I was a force to be reckoned with. But their efficiency was beginning to be questioned by large swaths of the population. What could not be questioned was the efficiency of Her Majesty's Mail.

Outside of my specific knowledge, my little love note, the blood-stained postcard *update* of my activities I wrote at home Monday morning (after the double event), and immediately mailed to the Boss editor at the Central News Agency, had been received at his office that same morning.

I didn't know a thing until Wednesday, 3 October, when, while walking past the Leman Street Police Station, I was forced to bring myself to a stop. A small (but quickly growing) crowd was gathering round a peeler who was tacking a placard on the public news board, beneath the blue lamp, outside the front entrance. The crowd, fighting for a look over his shoulder, were in an uproar. It took some time, and some effort, to make my way near enough to see what had engendered all the excitement.

I had to say, once I did, I felt a great deal of excitement myself.

The Boss had gotten his mail! He'd held it as I had asked. And, now that I'd done a bit more work, he had – as expected – turned my letters over to the police.

Obviously convinced, probably flummoxed, in a public confession that I had them by the bollocks, the coppers were asking again for assistance from the rabble and in so doing were showing their cards. The Metropolitan Police had both my *Dear Boss* letter and my *Saucy Jacky* postcard. They'd printed both together on a single poster, along with their pathetic plea, asking anyone who recognized the handwriting or had information regarding the author to contact them. This was the poster the constable had put on display. To a question from someone in the crowd, he answered, "Yes, they're being placarded outside of every police station throughout the city."

For the first time, I heard the name; not reverberating in my own head, but from the lips of strangers in the streets, as they read; whispered, then spoken, then shouted as a wave of terror moved through the crowd...

"Jack the Ripper?"

"Jack the Ripper."

"Jack the Ripper!"

The following day, Thursday, 4 October, the newspapers published facsimiles sent them by the Metropolitan Police. A reproduction of their poster, the tandem pictures of my letter and postcard along with their plea for help. It was a sensation.

My instincts had been perfect. The blood-like signature of *Jack the Ripper* had sent, was sending, a shock of horror throughout Whitechapel and all of London. That night the murders of the East End whores became international news. Jack the Ripper became a legend.

That wasn't, however, the end of Jack the Ripper's worries.

Thursday, 4 October, marked the first day of the Catherine 'Call me, Kate, deary' Eddowes Inquest, conducted by Coroner Samuel Langham at the Golden Lane Mortuary. Henry Crawford, solicitor for the City of London, was in attendance on behalf of the City Police force. I was in attendance in spirit and via the news. I wanted to know what they knew. Seven witnesses took the stand and the usual circus commenced.

John Kelly, the whore's almost husband, recounted his identification of the corpse. PC Watkins, the peeler who'd discovered her, told everybody how sick it made his little tummy. Inspector Collard, the lead investigator, explained the heroic procedures he'd carried out to set the City dog's loose. And Dr Brown gave a blow by blow description of the skilled knife work I employed in making 'Call me, Kate, deary' dead.

But again, as with the Stride inquest, no witness appeared to describe seeing the killer. What the hell?

It was round that time, 3 October, give or take, when a nervous (nearly frantic) Leon Goldstein shoved into Leman Street Police Station and begged for somebody in charge of the prostitute murders case. Asked why, he insisted he was innocent and had to clear his name of suspicion. The coppers in attendance shared a look – as none of them had ever heard his name before.

Eventually they got the story from the poor trembling Goldstein, who lived at 22 Christian Street and was, himself, a member of the International Working Men's Club in Berner Street.

Days earlier, he'd read an interview of Fanny Mortimer, one of the so-called Stride murder witnesses, in the *Daily News*. The article was, Goldstein recalled, much ado about nothing. She'd heard footsteps outside her door sometime around the time of the killing. (They were my footsteps.) She opened the door and, looking to the right, saw nothing. She heard nothing from the club or the Yard. She saw nobody enter the gates. The only person she'd seen pass through the street all night (before 1:00 o'clock) was a young man carrying a shiny black bag. He walked quickly down the street from the Commercial Road, looked up at the club (the Russians were singing), then continued south and around the corner of the board school.

The coppers stared, not seeing the problem.

"That article was misconstrued. The streets are full of rumors the killer is a doctor! That this murdering doctor carries a shiny black bag!" Goldstein's voice rose as he worked himself into a lather. "The man with the bag," he admitted, "was me. I left a coffee house in Spectacle Alley, came down Berner Street, past the club and Dutfield's Yard, not long before one o'clock. I was going home. My bag was full of empty cigarette boxes."

Ah! A powerful frightening combination; fear and fantasy. I, myself, had seen Goldstein, pass through Berner. I'd even seen Mortimer peeking out her door to see him. ha ha. Poor blighter hadn't done a thing. He was right, too, about the rumors. I'd heard them myself that morning.

The peelers patted Goldstein on the head, assured him he was not a suspect, and shoved him out the door. Whether or not that eased his mind, I don't know or care. But it didn't stop the rumors. Police Surgeon Phillips had suggested a man with medical knowledge. Mortimer had seen a shiny black bag. From that moment on, the *fact* that Jack the Ripper carried his knives in a black doctor's bag was cemented in the imagination of the ignorant populace.

The reproduction of my communications with Dear Boss was not an end to the police begging for help, it was only a beginning. The coppers had made up their minds to conduct house-to-house searches throughout the East End, and would take over two weeks to complete them. With many of the common lodging houses in the slums accommodating, whether they were able or not, two to four hundred bodies a night, the men of the Met had their work cut out for them. What, exactly, they intended to look for, they never did say.

The coppers ginned up a handbill and distributed same (over 100,000 in all) at each residence before they bulled their way in for their search. It read:

Police Notice.
To the Occupier.
On the mornings of Friday, 31st August, Saturday 8th, and Sunday, 30th September, 1888. Women were murdered in or near Whitechapel, supposed by some one residing in the immediate neighbourhood. Should you know of any person to whom suspicion is attached, you are earnestly requested to communicate at once with the nearest police station.

So the searches were begun.

Suddenly the number of police constables walking the beats of Whitechapel exploded. How many more men were there? Nobody outside of Scotland Yard or the Home Office knew for sure. Certainly there were dozens, probably hundreds; country coppers brought to the Big Smoke and mucked into the East End from sleepy hamlets all over England. A good many of them, I imagine, were shite-scared of their own shadows, and bleeding terrified at thought of mine. Armed with truncheons, the bobbies now patrolled in pairs and, rumor had it, a good many had taken to nailing strips of rubber (cut up bicycle tires) to the bottoms of their boots to move about the city streets more quietly.

Perhaps they should have placed an order with good ol' John Pizer. ha ha. What a lovely irony that would have been. Whitehall sending a few bob to Leather Apron in hopes he'd make a couple hundred pair of his famous *quiet slippers* for all the boys in blue. The better to sneak up on Jack the Ripper.

While on the subject of the police, this seems a good time to confess... My interest in chatty Nurse Adler intensified sharply on the evening of Thursday, 4 October. Not only did I find her break room *sca* unusually informative but, I began to see, it might well be a key to my freedom and welfare.

Miss Adler had a nasty habit, identical to a habit of dear Mrs Griggs, of reading her newspaper out loud while, simultaneously, peppering her monologue with comment (without delineating between the two). It was exasperating trying to decipher the news... from their opinions of the news.

But, before I head off on a tangent, back to Miss Adler.

She and her coterie were in their usual places, eating and having a gossip, when I took my break. In preface of spilling her recent Archie tidbits, Miss Adler was serenading all within earshot with the meat of an article she'd found in the *Times*. More interested in my sausage roll than her blather, I barely listened. Then she started on about the subject of 'bloody thumb prints' and 'microscopes.'

A bite of sausage stuck in my throat. The odd overheard phrases took hold in my brain. I coughed the obstruction free, apologized to the table of nurses (staring at me with varying degrees of concern), and asked Miss Adler if she would mind reading the piece again. Always grateful for attention, she obliged.

The article concerned Jack the Ripper, of course. (What article didn't since he'd named himself?) Specifically, it spoke to a discovery by the writer, Frederick Jago, that the Saucy Jacky postcard received by the editor of the Central News Agency featured on its surface a 'thumbprint in blood' as accidentally transferred in handling by the Whitechapel killer himself.

"So?" I couldn't help but interject. "What of it?"

"I'm not exactly sure," Miss Adler replied, quizzically twisting her lips and nose in opposing directions at once (another filthy habit). "Says here there is a theory the surface markings of no two thumbs are alike. The writer suggests police examine the thumbs of their Ripper suspects through the lens of a microscope and compare their findings with the print on the card. If the theory were true, they would then have their murderer."

I'd already dropped my sausage and, twisting my hands in the poor light, stared intently at the surfaces of both thumbs. Mind, the action had nothing to do with guilt; I didn't feel in the least guilty. Was merely instinctive curiosity. Perhaps I should have governed those instincts to avoid outing myself. But it seemed not to matter. The nurses were all staring at their thumbs as well.

"You date a constable, don't you?" I asked, Miss Adler. To ensure she understood her personal life was of no interest to me, I moved immediately to the point. "Is that real, do you know? Identifying people by the marks on their fingers and thumbs?"

"I don't know," Miss Adler replied, twisting her lips again. "I don't know at all. First I've ever heard of it. If I think of it, I'll have to ask."

"Do." She stared, forcing me to explain. "It sounds incredible. I'm curious."

She hummed her agreement, then returned to her friends, her food, and her paper.

For my part, I couldn't help it. Casually, covertly even, with my hands below the edge of the table, I took another peek at the lines, swirls, and loops on the surface of my thumb.

I scoured the evening editions of the Friday, 5 October, papers somewhat frantically. The fourth day of Stride inquest had come and gone that afternoon. The details are of no importance. What matters is the inquest again adjourned, until Tuesday, 23 October, and still none of the real witnesses in Berner Street, the men who had actually seen me, had been called to testify.

I had a lot on my mind. Witness sightings. Thumbprints. And, let's not forget, bloodhounds.

I did not know then, and would not learn for some time (I mention it here only to maintain order) on that same Friday, Sir Charles reached a decision regarding the lunatic notion of putting bloodhounds, four-legged mutts, on the streets of Whitechapel to run Yours Truly to ground. In a letter to the Home Secretary, the Commissioner requested authority to expend £50 in the present financial year, and £100 per annum thereafter, to keep trained bloodhounds in London.

Had I known, had I had access to the Commissioner's ear, I would have reminded him of *the rest* of the historic Emily Holland murder case. Yes, it was the first time in England's history the police used dogs to capture and hang a murderer, William Fish. And, yes, Chief Constable Potts had been right in employing the tactic in 1876. Still, in spite of its success, Potts nevertheless was ridiculed for his decision for the remainder of his career. A popular riddle of the day asked, 'When was Mr Potts like the beggar Lazarus?' And offered the answer, 'When he was licked by dogs.'

The mutts had compassion on the copper, not the people. If only I had known, I would have liked to have warned Sir Charles that, success or failure, he would be making a fool of himself if he set the dogs on poor misunderstood Jack the Ripper.

Thirty-Nine
The Search

Nervously, I admit, but without hesitation, I closed the door of Mr Griggs' old shoe shop behind me, then turned to open the front door of Mrs Griggs' home, my lodging house. Outside, one a step in front of the other, stoically staring from the stoop, stood two strapping young police constables.

I did not comically gulp, as might be imagined, but my throat did *go dry* as it were. What were they doing there? How, I couldn't help but wonder, had they found me? What had led these representatives of the Metropolitan Police to my doorstep?

"Good afternoon," I said, trying to sound as if I meant it.

"Good afternoon, sir," said the one in front.

I'd seen him before. Come to think, I'd seen them both before. Officers 97 and 96 from J Division. Yes, the pair that had interviewed me at my work in the surgical theatre of London Hospital. The speaker was the friendly bobbie, the quiet one behind was the light-coloured copper with the dark feel. I remembered. Still why were they there? Was it owing to that interview?

"I am Police Constable Neil," the leader said smartly, as on that earlier occasion. Also as before, he nodded to the man behind. "This is Constable Thain."

"Yes," I said. "We've spoken before."

The two shared a questioning look.

"At London Hospital, where I work. We spoke in the surgery theatre."

"Oh, yes," Neil said. "Yes, of course. You'll forgive us, sir? We've interviewed a good many people recently."

"I can't even imagine," I said.

Neil and Thain, looking exactly as before; Neil congenial, Thain... sinister. As before, Thain would bare watching. He jarred me. Something else about him drew the eye; a bundle of white paper bills clutched in his hands. He handed a single sheet forward to Neil, who mechanically passed it on to me. "Have you seen this, sir?"

I examined the paper and realized I had indeed seen it. It was a duplicate of the Police Notice posted in the streets nearly a week prior; reminding the reader of the recent murders and asking for witnesses to 'characters of a suspicious nature' to inform the men of the Met. "I have, constable. Regrettably, I don't believe I have any information that might help the police."

"Do you work here also?" he asked, chucking a thumb at the door sign. "Rather early in the day, isn't it, for the shop to be closed?"

I cocked my head, the better to examine his face. Was he putting me on? Testing my veracity? Or merely off his beat? Surely an officer from that district would be aware... Then it dawned, J Division. These yobs were down from Bethnal Green. Not enough flat feet to cover all the places Saucy Jack the Ripper had visited in his wanderings. They didn't know the neighbourhood.

"It is not my shop," I informed him. "It isn't anyone's shop; and it's always closed. Mr Griggs, the shoemaker, passed on over a year ago."

Neil drew a small note book from his uniform jacket and jotted a note. "I see, sir. Forgive me, but could you give me your name again?"

I did. Why shouldn't I? He wrote it down. His book now featured my name twice, and still he hadn't a clue. "I'm a lodger here," I offered.

"For how long, Mr __?"

"Years. Mr. Griggs was my landlord. Now I rent from his widow."

"By yourself?" asked the dark blonde, reminding me of the low opinion I already held of the brooding fellow. I didn't like his questions any more than I liked him. "Yes. As I told you before, I am unmarried."

"Odd that? Single man living with... a respectable woman?"

Was the hesitation his? Or had I added it? I couldn't say. But, again, I didn't like it. "I assure you, my landlady is the zenith of respectability. Mr Griggs and I got on famously. His widow and I do the same. I long ago made a home here. And, as her family and friends are aware of my presence and well-acquainted with me, we saw nothing improper in my continuing to board here."

"Of course not, sir," Neil put in, taking over again. (Fair cop, foul cop?) "Is Mrs Griggs at home?"

"She is not. She is a well-known political activist and is about her business."

"Yes, sir. And we need to be about ours."

"What may I ask, constable, is your business here?"

"In light of the recent murders, you may have heard, sir, we are conducting house-to-house searches throughout the East End. The Metropolitan Police ask your co-operation."

"You want to search this house?"

Both stared, one smiling, the other not. The smiling one said, "We do, sir. If you don't mind?"

"As I said, I am a lodger. I don't know that I have the authority to give you access to Mrs Griggs' property."

"As a well-known activist, sir," the blonde said. "I'm sure Mrs Griggs would want to assist the law in any way she could. Yes?"

"I'm sure she would."

"We can't insist," Neil said. "If you refuse."

"I do not refuse. I don't know if I have the authority to refuse. I merely state it is not my property. But, I agree with your colleague, Mrs Griggs would want to assist you any way she could. Please, come ahead."

With that, and with a sincere hope the churning in the pit of my stomach was inaudible to the men of the Yard, the impromptu search of Mrs Griggs' residence, and my rooms, was begun.

I led them upstairs, to the top of the house and pointed to the access to the attic. One or the other asked what they might find there. I assured them I did not know as I had never ventured in. Storage, I imagined out loud. I suppressed the urge to add that I knew nothing about it and cared even less. My mind was on... other areas of the residence.

The pair made entrance to the attic. They found the storage space we had all imagined, crammed to the rafters (Mrs Griggs was a pack rat, I've said). The peelers poked about long enough to convince themselves Jack the Ripper was not hidden amongst the piles. (While I kept it quietly to myself he was standing beside them.) Satisfied, they abandoned the room.

We moved below, to the second floor, to my sitting and bed rooms, and to two other spare rooms (ready for guests, but never used). I gave them full access and little attention, merely answered their rudimentary questions, as they searched. Outside of my clothing and my myriad collection of books, there was absolutely nothing secreted away and nothing of import to find. That was what they found – nothing. "I work. I read," I explained. "It's embarrassing, but I'm really rather dull."

As was their inspection.

I led them down to the first floor and showed them Mrs Griggs' living space, though I waited in the hall while they searched. I used the kitchen rarely, I explained, and I stepped into her sitting room on occasion to pass a polite greeting when her Dress Reformists gathered. The dark blonde asked what a Dress Reformist was. But, before I could explain, his fellow officer did. He seemed unimpressed. I put myself outside of the debate by assuring them that, respectable as the ladies of that political society all were, they were not my cup of tea. The relationship between Mrs Griggs and myself, I assured them, had always been business-like. I did not *visit* with her.

The constables could not help but notice my landlady's ever-growing, nearly mountainous, stack of collected newspapers, some fifteen separate titles in all; national, City of London, and local; morning and evening editions; daily, weekly, and Sunday papers; from the Tory, the Liberal, and radical press; the *Times*, the *Globe*, the *Pall-Mall Gazette*, the *Star*, the *Morning Post*, the *East London Observer*, the *East London Advertiser*, *Lloyd's Weekly*, *Reynold's*, and on and on; all neatly stacked, all accumulated since the advent of the brutal Whitechapel murders.

"Mrs Griggs," I explained. "She and her group, having taken up the mantle of armchair detectives, are carefully following the events in the East End. I imagine many people are?"

"I hear newspaper sales are up dramatically," Constable Neil conceded. Then he gave Mrs Griggs' voluminous pile another look and, smiling, added, "I didn't realize to what extent your landlady might personally be responsible."

The dark blonde did not smile. He continued to not smile as he asked, "What about you, sir?"

"I'm sorry?"

"If you don't mind, sir," Thain said, "what about you? You credit your landlady with the papers, her group of followers with the curiosity. I've noticed you haven't asked a single question about the murders, the investigation, or our search. Have you no interest?"

I studied him for a moment, then asked, "Would you have answered any?"

The constables shared a knowing look. "No, sir," Thain admitted.

Neil added, "That rarely stops anyone from asking."

"You'll remember," I told the pair. "I work at London Hospital. As horrible as these murders might be, I see all of the trauma, absorb all of the drama I care to, while on the job. Perhaps you understand?"

"Indeed, sir," Neil said, letting me off the hook. He turned and led his pardner toward the descending stairs. "We've many more of your neighbours to visit before we're done, Mr __."

"Yes, of course." I was about to breathe a sigh of relief...

When Neil added, "Shall we take a quick look at your ground floor?"

I gritted my teeth, hopefully not noticeably, and followed the officers. At the foot of the stairs I took the lead again and showed them into the shop, through the show room, through the back room, and out the door into the small enclosed backyard.

They took in the hand pump, a rubbish bin, a tiny wood shed, and the watercloset. The dark blonde took a look in the shed, saw nothing alarming in its meager contents, and closed it up again. An obvious completist, he examined the WC as well. We returned inside.

They turned slow circles inspecting the shop's back room; the seemingly endless rows of hanging foot apparel, the overstuffed shelves, the unmoved inventory (a museum collection), the deep closet of clothes (and Mrs Griggs' accumulated junk), the worktables, the tools – and the shoemaker's knives. These last got special keen-eyes attention. But there was no touching, no terrier-like digging, and no apparent suspicion-fueled hesitations.

"No dust," the serious one said. "All well cared for, well kept up."

"Yes." I explained that Mrs Griggs was a fastidious and tidy woman. "You saw her rooms. She is adamant her husbands things, his memory, be maintained. I see that wish is carried out."

The convivial Neil seemed to understand as he walked me into the front room. The dark blonde Thain. . . I didn't know. He stayed behind.

Neil rattled on, pleasantly, asking whatever occurred to him. I answered, though I don't recall what he asked. I was preoccupied trying to see Thain through the doorway. Trying to decipher what he was on about. He had returned his attention to the shelves along the wall, giving them another longer look. Something appeared to be niggling at him.

I stepped into the back room, asking, "Can I help, constable?" Though I felt Neil behind me, I did not turn. I kept my eyes trained on Thain.

I followed his gaze to a specific group of boxes on the shelves. A group I knew, above all the boxes in the shop. I'd claimed them as my own. But what about them attracted his stare? I'd gone out of my way to ensure there was nothing to see. Still Thain stared as if a light shined upon them.

I tried to maintain my calm, my outward decorum. But my heart had begun to race. My lips had gone dry. I could feel the sweat as it burst from my forehead. I tried to think of something to do, something to say, to divert the dark blonde's attention. It was not to be.

Without a word, Thain stepped forward, grabbed a box, and snatched it down. The officer tore the lid off and tossed it to the floor. He gawped inside and exclaimed, "Good lord!" He reached in and drew out my long blade – dripping with blood.

How? How was it possible? How could he have known the instrument was there? And why... As I'd gone to great lengths to care for my precious knives, why was the blade dripping with fresh blood!

He turned to his partner and raised the knife in triumph. He turned to me and thrust the weapon in my face. "You've got some explaining to do, mate!"

From behind, I felt the firm grip of the once-convivial officer's hand on my shoulder. "I arrest you in the name of the law," Neil said. "You will yield. You will come along quietly."

It was in that instant I lurched up in my bed sweating profusely and gasping for breath.

For weeks now it was always then, at that point, when I lurched up in my bed. That was as far as the dream, the nightmare, ever went.

It wasn't always the same coppers. Sometimes the heroic Inspector Abberline conducted the search and found the goods. Sometimes the fierce Sergeant Thicke would grab my shoulder and inform me that, 'In the name of the law', I was had. It wasn't always the same knife. Sometimes it was the long blade, sometimes the shoemaker's tool and, once, the penknife I'd used on the soldier's whore in George Yard. It wasn't always a knife. Once Constable Neil opened a box to uncover a dripping uterus. Once Thain nicked me for possession of Stockings' stolen rings. They even found items I didn't have, things I'd never took; the Queen's new bonnet, the scarf that held Stocking's head in place, a freshly washed leather apron, the Squealer's red flower. Point being, in the nightmare, I was repeatedly nicked with evidence and headed for the gallows. Then I'd wake, sweating and trying to breathe.

I believed in dreams, believed they held meaning. I took this warning to heart and visited my collection often to ensure nothing about its outer appearance gave it away. But the dreams did not end. There had to be a meaning yet unrealized. Then it dawned!

The searches! It was the bloody house searches themselves!

For weeks I lived in mortal fear of the house-to-house police searches. I don't suppose that makes sense. The coppers had no idea what Jack the Ripper looked like. They had no clues to his (or her) whereabouts. They'd already spoken to me at hospital and walked away without a suspicious thought in their heads. Even had they come, and gone over the place diligently, they would have needed to be clever (more so than they'd yet proved themselves) to discover my hidden tools, toys, and trinkets.

But now, more than a week into their searches, it finally dawned! The dream was a twisted lark; my mind having fun at my expense! I wasn't being warned about the searches, I was being teased. There wasn't going to be a search of our lodging house. The coppers weren't coming at all. The police, even with the men they'd brought in from other districts, didn't have near the manpower necessary to search every house in London. Now it dawned, they weren't going to try.

The Home Secretary's Office, or the police (Sir Charles, Abberline, or whomever), had had to select the search areas. When that time arrived, their prejudices took over. They knew, the killer could not be a British subject. No man of means, breeding, or learning, would stoop so low. No Englishman would do such a thing. They weren't looking for me or anybody like me.

They knew, or thought they did, the criminal class was comprised of the poor and the stupid. Thus only the areas of concentrated foreign (likely Jewish) residents needed to be searched; only the slums, where the lowest classes dwelt. To look in decent neighbourhoods would surely have been a waste of time. The murderous criminal, in their minds, had arisen from filth and degradation, ventured out into the night to commit its outrage, then slithered back like some evil snake into the depths of the slums. The authorities would have proceeded from that set of *facts*.

So it was, I eventually learned, the house-to-house searches were conducted only in the worst of the slums of Whitechapel and Spitalfields, with the eastern boundary of London as the west boundary of the search area. The Great Eastern Railway as boundary to the north; Albert, Dunk, Chicksand, and Great Garden Streets the eastern most edge; and Whitechapel Road as the southern boundary. Only the slums! They weren't searching anywhere near my lodgings!

The nightmare was a game my mind played to amuse itself. They hadn't searched my house, nor were they about to. (Not that it would matter a jot. The precautions I'd taken to secret my evidences away, without cause or need of fear, were more than adequate. They caught me in my dream because *I* knew where the items were.) I had nothing to fear and knew, from that moment on, I would never dread the dream again. It was only a dream, the dream every copper was having in his bed, that – owing to their prejudices – would never come true.

Forty
Murder Is Good Business

The fourth meeting of the Stride Inquest, on Friday, 5 October, held nothing new and nothing of interest. No word from any of the witnesses from whom I wanted to hear. I had to know something, anything, about where I stood.

By Saturday, I could take it no more. I couldn't breathe in the house. So I went out – into the carnival.

The streets of the East End were filled to overflowing with tourists begging for an eyeful of, at least, their fantasy of what the murder scenes looked like. Everywhere, local entrepreneurs did all they could to exploit those morbid curiosities.

Cabs and omnibus carriages shunted tourists hither and yon about the murder districts; from George Yard to Buck's Row in the east of Whitechapel; down to Dutfield's Yard in Berner Street in the parish of St George-in-the-East; back up to Osborn and Wentworth (they were still blaming me for that bitch Emma Smith); up to Hanbury Street in Spitalfields; then into the City for a quick trip through, a now constantly congested, Mitre Square. Paying customers could take the full ride, hanging their noses out the windows in passing or, if the fever took them, could alight at any time along the way to join the throngs at the scene of a particular outrage.

I passed on the notion of a guided riding tour and chose instead to walk the streets among the rabble, the horse drawn conveyances, the bicycles, enjoying all of the rabid fear and raucous festivities on a personal level. I visited each scene in their turn, in the order I'd done the work. (That seemed the right way to appreciate them.) It wasn't as if I had a long walk ahead of me. The East End had nearly a million residents, but they were packed in like crated Cornish pilchards. All of the 'job sites' together wherein I'd done the whores were within a single mile of each other.

At every location, and on nearly every street corner in between, young news boys and old news men shouted the most recent headlines as they hawked their papers. Yes, I passed them and, yes, Frogg and Tad, were hard at it. Tory, to Liberal, to dangerously radical, all of the Fleet Street rags enjoyed massive sales thanks to me.

And the broadsheets. How I loved (and in a few cases, hated) the broadsheets!

Many were written in verse. Some were read out loud and many were sung, to already popular tunes, by their authors or their sellers in the streets. Some were lame, and a good many were turgid as hell, but some were genuinely clever. One of my favorites, I stood for a long while committing to memory and offer in part:

'as anyone seen him, can you tell us where he is,
If you meet him you must take away his knife,
Then give him to the women, they'll spoil his pretty fiz,
And I wouldn't give him twopence for his life.

Now at night when you're undressed and about to go to rest
Just see that he ain't underneath the bed
If he is you mustn't shout but politely drag him out
And with your poker tap him on the head.

Words, I fear, cannot accurately describe the swarms of people, the sounds of their cries and their crying, and the boisterous sounds of trade being conducted. Yes, trade! There was no doubt about it, the residents of each of the affected neighbourhoods had found nearly uncountable ways to turn the terror that I alone had created into thriving businesses for themselves.

Two gangs of miscreants had blocked off the entrances to George Yard, one at Wentworth Street on the north, another at the Whitechapel High on the south (whether or not they were working in concert, I did not know). At each end they charged tourists two pennies apiece to enter and wander up, or down, the Yard past the fateful staircase and murder site of the soldier's whore. A resident, or witness, or either, or neither (who knew) stood on the stairs endlessly repeating a short speech regarding the event and his own personal brush with the legendary killer – whoever the hell he was. Mind, I sussed most of that from a distance, outside the Whitechapel entrance. I saved myself the fee by not going in.

The normally pleasant stroll up Whitechapel, past the white chapel, toward the hospital on the right, and beyond to the left-hand turn into Piss Alley on the way to Buck's Row, was anything but pleasant that morning; it was hectic to say the least. The streets teemed with excited, and frightened, residents, tourists, coppers, and loiterers of unknown origin. I'm talking people in the thousands!

A pavement artist was attracting immense and lingering crowds with his, it would not be unfair to say *graphic*, chalk depictions of the murder victims as they'd been found, drawn by hand on the sidewalks of the Whitechapel Road. The gobsmacked mobs swamped the artist and his drawings. The fruiterers, bakers, and fish mongers pushed their barrows of eatables into the street and around those throbbing huddles. The cabs, cart traffic, and pedestrians wound their separate ways around it all. The police, foot patrol and fixed point men, were up to their eyeballs in people and pains in the arse. The coppers on horseback were, thankfully, only up to their knees. Amazing lunacy reigned.

In Buck's Row, every fifteen feet one fellow or another was claiming to have been *the one* to have carried out a bucket and washed the blood off the street and down the gutter at the behest of the police. Allow me to make it plain, the disease-ridden Queen of Tarts was stone dead from strangling before I cut her throat.

There simply wasn't that much blood. It will come as no surprise, however, that I kept that knowledge to myself.

In Hanbury Street, an old woman did excellent trade selling handmade swordsticks. "Here you are, now," she cried, waving a murderous cane in my face with one hand, while clutching an ill-balanced armful of like-weapons with the other. "Only sixpence. Sixpence only for a swordstick. That's the sort to do for 'em!"

While I had no intention of buying, I did pause for a long look, making a detailed mental note of the appearance of her merchandise and their mechanism of operation. If and when, some early morning, I met one of her customers in the streets, I wanted to be aware of it.

At the same time, inside No 29, Mrs Richardson (the entrepreneur), her son, and her grandson, were now raking in pennies *renting* looks out the window at Stockings' *death spot* in the backyard from their ground floor back room kitchen. "Just crane you head to the left. That's it!"

Two spinsters, the Misses Copsey, were as busy in their second floor back room apartment. Though their clients' visits were decidedly short, the sisters provided chairs at their window for comfort. If Mr Waker and his son, the occupants of the first floor back room, or Mrs Sarah Cox, with the vertigo-inducing view her attic back room would have provided, got in on the game, I never discovered. If not, they should have done.

Sadly for them, the other eleven residents of the house, all with rooms in the front (Hanbury Street) side of the house, had no access to a view of the murder site and no avenue to the sudden largess.

While I'm on the subject of punters making money off my labour...

When my walking tour of the district took me back to Berner Street and to the gateway of Dutfield's Yard, I must confess, I laughed my arse off. Oh the hypocrites! Even the organizing committee of Jews at the International Working Men's Club had turned to capitalism for the opportune time being. Yes, the socialists were charging tourists a fee for admission to their premises and a look out the kitchen door at the back side of the murder site – and a close-up gander at the yard drain down which the Squealer's blood had run.

The ancient fruiterer on the other side of the Yard entrance appeared to be doing a smash business and was grinning from ear to ear.

By that time in my tour I was, frankly, exhausted. The crowds, the cries, the coppers; it had been its own special joy but, at once, all too much. I felt guilty, not hiking all the way back down Whitechapel Road, with its explosion of people, into the city to visit the corner in Mitre Square upon which I had graciously immortalized the beer sodden singing whore. But I knew she would forgive me.

In Berner Street I was only a few short blocks from my lodgings; that was where I decided to go.

One more story from work... I mean my work at London Hospital.

In his final summation before verdict, at the 26 September Chapman Inquest, Coroner Baxter had alluded to the possibility of a foreigner being responsible for the crimes. In particular, he addressed the reports (or were they rumors?) of an American doctor or scientist who'd purportedly come to England in the market for various body parts for experimentation; specifically for uteruses. While he had no evidence this medical man was the murderer, the suggestion had arisen – if only in devious minds – he may have paid someone to procure the female organs without any questions.

It sounded like nonsense to me but any theory that led authorities away from instead of toward Yours Truly was fine by me. It was not a fine theory to a group of London doctors, who heard it and were rankled. So annoyed, in fact, they rebutted the theory in the October issue of the *British Medical Journal*. (No, I'm not a reader, but nurses are not the only gossipers in hospital.) Wrote the aggravated medical men:

'It is true that enquiries were made at one or two medical schools early last year by a foreign physician, who was "spending some time in London, as to the possibility of securing certain parts of the

body for the purpose of scientific investigation." No large sum, however, was offered. The person in question was a physician of the highest reputability and exceedingly well accredited to this country by the best authorities in his own, and he left London fully 18 months ago. There was never any real foundation for the hypothesis, and the information communicated, which was not at all of the nature the public has been led to believe, was due to the erroneous interpretation by a minor official of a question which he had overheard and to which a negative reply was given. This theory may be dismissed, and is, we believe, no longer entertained by its author.'

Meanwhile, life was again comedy and tragedy for me.

Ever since my Dear Boss letter and Saucy Jacky postcard had found their mark (forcing the Met to take heed), I'd had reason to rejoice. Not only had I frightened them into taking me seriously, and given myself a nickname that had caught like an orphanage afire, but I'd given myself endless joy. I was laughing my arse off again.

I quote Miss Adler. "It's all over town! Archie says, every mother's son ever picked up a pen is writing to the police now. Writing the most horrid things and claiming they are Jack the Ripper. What can the police do? They have no choice but to run ragged trying to trace each one down – to ensure they are hoaxes. It is an awful waste of time and men!" Amusing, yes?

What was not amusing, what was in fact a tragedy, was the Monday, 8 October, funeral of Catherine 'Call me, Kate, deary' Eddowes. Just what in hell is it with those London morticians and their obvious weaknesses for dead drunken slags?

At the expense of Mr Hawkes, the undertaker, Eddowes was shunted through the streets, lined with ogling punters, all the way to the City of London Cemetery, in an elm coffin carried by an open-glass hearse. Hard working decent people were going to pauper's graves in pine boxes, and the likes of her. . .

It was a tragedy.

Forty-One
Bloodhounds and Vigilantes

Wednesday, 10 October, Mrs Griggs was in her sitting room, buried in one of her newspapers (this time the *Daily News*) going on again about the possibility of the police employing bloodhounds in their search for the Whitechapel murderer. Again? Bloodhounds! I had hoped that subject had disappeared from consideration.

The thought, sniffing dogs in place of detectives!

At that point, I mentioned, the populace (including Yours Truly) had yet to learn of Sir Charles' request of the Home Office for bloodhound funds, let alone the response of Secretary Matthews. The country would eventually learn, the secretary declined a commitment until it could be demonstrated bloodhounds could be usefully employed without danger to the public. But he sanctioned one payment of £50 to be spent on the use of dogs in the Ripper emergency. Meaning, in the hunt for me!

I knew none of that. Outside of rumors and my own fears, all I would ever know of bloodhounds, I had already heard from Miss Adler or would learn from Mrs Griggs. My landlady, I must confess, had my attention. The idea of bloodhounds, it might be remembered, had arisen from a suggestion by an Essex dog breeder in a letter-to-the-editor of the *Times*. Unlike many cock-eyed notions that saw print over the last month, this idea concerned me.

For, Mrs Griggs' article now made it clear, the notion had advanced beyond remote possibility to having been put into practice! As Mrs Griggs read the account, I listened with bated breath.

Edwin Brough, a bloodhound breeder from Wyndyate near Scarborough, had arrived in London on Saturday, 6 October, with Barnaby and Burgho, two of his finest animals. Brough had been quoted, in a competing paper, complimenting the bloodhound as being able to follow 'a lighter scent than any other hound.' He'd added a properly trained dog 'will stick to the line of the hunted man, though it may have been crossed by others.'

I didn't care for the sound of that. Of course I kept that thought, and my concerns, quiet as Mrs Griggs read on.

Brought to London at the expense of the Metropolitan Police, it was agreed among the authorities, the dogs needed to be tested before being utilized (neither Whitehall nor the Home Office were convinced of the plan's merits). Tests in Whitechapel were out of the question; public safety being of the highest concern. With no idea how the animals might react to the rush of the city, the parks were chosen as a proving ground. So it was that, on Monday, 8 October, at 7:00 am, trials of the sniffing dogs' abilities commenced in Regent's Park and had, since, been quietly underway for two days.

In Regent's Park, a volunteer constable, acting the part of... Well, acting my part... was given a fifteen-minute start for nearly a mile, before Barnaby and Burgho were set upon his trail. Despite the grounds being coated in hoar frost, the paper reported, the hounds successfully tracked their quarry. A second test took place that night in Hyde Park. This time with the animals on a leash and in the dark. The bloodhounds again succeeded in finding their faux killer.

I found myself clenching my teeth. It required supreme effort, and a deep intake of air, to relax my jaw. Meanwhile, my widowed landlady went on. The *News* reported the following morning the coppers were back for additional tests; this time with the police Commissioner in attendance.

Mrs Griggs tittered, in a rare display of amusement, and fluttered a hand before her mouth. "It says here," she said, ruffling the paper, "a half-dozen trials were conducted in all and that, on two of those occasions, Sir Charles Warren himself acted the part of the hunted man. Can you imagine?"

"Yes," I replied, taking care not to reveal the sneer I most definitely felt. "I very well can imagine hounds nipping at the commissioner's well-polished heels."

Mrs Griggs hadn't heard the animosity in my voice. I'd agreed, that was enough. She went on.

In each test the bloodhounds were made to hunt a complete stranger. Brough worked the dogs or instructed the officers at the reigns; he did not act the part of the murderer. On a number of occasions the trail of the faux killer was deliberately crossed by others in an attempt to deceive the animals. Each time, the hounds were momentarily checked. But, the paper reported, the confusion was short-lived. One or the other of the animals, casting around with noses hard to the ground, invariably reacquired the scent and were off again.

I didn't like that either!

In summation, the paper reported, the hounds worked slowly (in consequence of the cold scents) but demonstrated they could successfully follow the trail of a stranger on the run. Sir Charles, without openly stating an opinion, seemed pleased by the results of the trials.

The coppers were not playing fair! It wasn't enough they'd brought in reinforcements from districts all over England and had, literally, flooded the streets of Whitechapel and Spitalfields with flatfooted peelers and posh-suited plods. Now, to add insult to injury, they'd brought in bloodhounds!

And too, if sniffing hounds weren't enough, the streets were overflowing with sniffing do-gooders as well. What did I mean? As of midnight on Wednesday, 3 October, an all-new nemesis was after me in the streets. President George Lusk, and the mean little Jews that comprised his Mile End Vigilance Committee, the group that had worked so hard collecting subscriptions for reward monies for my capture and conviction, had reared their tiny heads anew. Dissatisfied with the efforts of the police in tracking the killer down (and removing me from society), their committee had now put their own foot patrols onto the streets of the East End.

These amateur soldiers (gangs?) were hired from among the unemployed residents of the slums and paid a wage, by the committee. They patrolled the dark streets and alleys from 'just before midnight to just before five the next morning'. Each gang member was equipped with a police whistle, a heavy stick, and a pair of galoshes. He was then assigned his own beat to walk.

By this time, it was common knowledge, the Mile End Vigilance Committee was meeting nightly at nine in an upstairs room of the Crown public house, Mile End Road. When the house closed at 12:30, the mean little Jews themselves took to the streets to supplement their patrols. Their intent was not to replace or undermine the police, but to aide their activities. The Mile End committee plan was to pass information regarding suspicious characters on to the police. To advise them in the organization and supervision of all this amateur police work, to make sure they got it right and didn't break any laws themselves, the committee hired the services of Grand & Batchelor, a private detective agency in the Strand. And, bleeding hell, if there wasn't more still!

The union labourers got in on the action. That's correct, the patrols of the Mile End Vigilance Committee were soon being reinforced by volunteers from a group calling themselves the 'Working Men's Vigilance Committee'. Neither the papers nor the street talk helped much in defining these men. Outside of the fact they were born of the waterfront trade unions and held their meetings at the Three Nuns in Aldgate, little was known about them. It was said however that, by 9 October, they'd established fifty-seven separate street patrols.

I couldn't help but wonder, in the end, how these amateur patrols might pan out for the cause of public safety. Clearly their presence in the streets could, probably would, make things unpalatable for me. But, it occurred, the vigilance committee patrols might well make life harder for the police as well. The constable on patrol would now be confronted with more strangers moving in and out of the shadows than ever before. How much time would be wasted checking up on their new help-meets?

It might be remembered that, in August, I stayed in my rooms because I didn't know what was happening in the streets. Now, in October, I was staying in because I did.

In the days to come, that was exactly what happened – and the newspapers made hay of it. I got a massive chuckle from an 8 October article in The *Daily News*, which read in part: 'in several instances some of the plain clothes men who were strange to the neighbourhood were watched by members of the Vigilance Committee, while they in their turn came under the scrutiny of the detectives.'

The blind leading the blind... in search of the unseen. Despite the humorous aspects of it all, there was no getting around it. The streets were a dangerous place for a fine fellow like me.

Forty-Two
A Fitting Verdict

On Thursday, 11 October, the coroner's inquest into the death of Catherine Eddowes met at the City Mortuary in Golden Lane for the second and, shockingly, last time. It had originally convened during the previous week, Thursday 4 October to be exact, with a single adjournment. Fifteen so-called witnesses testified, including two doctors, three plod detectives of varied ranks, and five peelers. It was a dull affair, of course, and the newspaper accounts did nothing to liven it up. There were, however, several points of interest.

First, I finally discovered, the fellow that had stared me full in the gob on Duke Street, the attentive one of the three Jews that left the Imperial Club and ogled me and the singing whore, Joseph Lawende by name, was in attendance – behind the scenes. But, it turned out, the City Police did not want him to testify. Detective Superintendent Foster feared letting the reporters in on the killer's description would somehow interfere with their investigation and subvert the cause of justice. Lawende was sequestered and Coroner Langham agreed. The description of Yours Truly, which I had so long feared getting out, remained a secret unspoken to press and public. What the police heard... I still did not know.

Meanwhile, a bold lie was set loose.

PC (peeler clown) James Harvey claimed he walked down the Church Passage and gazed into Mitre Square at 1:41 am. "I saw no one," he stated. "I heard no cry or noise." To anyone paying attention – and believe me, I was – that raised a bit of a question.

Constable Watkins (remember him?), same department, different route, testified on the first day of the inquest his patrol brought him through the Square every fifteen minutes. He'd been there at 1:30 and all was quiet. He returned for another walk-through at 1:45, three minutes after Harvey's supposed patrol, and found the mutilated body.

Put together, that should have told the coroner's jury what I knew all along. Harvey was a damned liar, interested in protecting himself. He'd scared the hell out of me. Had me red-handed, with his light blinding me. But he hadn't come down Church Passage. He'd thrown his beam from the street, without bothering to look after it. Had he done, he would have seen me and become the most famous constable in the history of the City Police.

Don't misunderstand. I wasn't angry. I was having difficulty stifling my delight. Had the copper not shirked his duty, I'd have been nicked. Had he not lied to the coroner, the lot of them might have been closer to the truth. In the end, everything worked out wonderfully.

As Mrs Griggs came to article's end, and the official finding of the Eddowes Inquest, I had to admit to a sneaking appreciation – if not outright admiration – for Langham, the City Coroner. He showed the good sense not to adjourn his court repeatedly in hopes of new evidences to make him a hero. He thought prolonging the proceedings, as the other inquests had, to be a waste of time. He believed the function of his jury was finding *Cause of death*, period. He left solving case to the cops. Good on him.

He reminded all present of the magnificent reward offered for my capture, and suggested that as the means of setting the *right people* (the law? vigilantes? the rabble?) on the track and bringing to speedy justice the creature responsible for that atrocious crime. That brought tears to my eyes!

In summation, Langham thought it unnecessary to repeat the witness testimony. If the jury wanted their memories refreshed, he said, he would refer to the evidence on that point. That the crime was a most fiendish one could not for a moment be doubted,' he said, 'for the miscreant, not satisfied with taking a defenceless woman's life, endeavoured so to mutilate the body as to render it unrecognisable.'

If only I'd been there. "Not in evidence!" I would have cried. ha ha.

I got a better laugh when he suggested the police abandon their search for a maniacal doctor in favor of someone more likely; a resident of the slums (certainly not a Londoner) who, though without true medical training, yet had an understanding of basic anatomy. He suggested a butcher, a slaughterman, or someone in a like-trade. What fun!

But all good things must come to an end; so too the Eddowes Inquest. Out of summation and out of steam, Langham finally, and most importantly, gave me my due. As the other coroners had done, the City authority at first presumed his jurors would return the standard verdict of 'Wilful murder by Person or Persons Unknown.' Giving credit for the deed to no one and everyone. What rot!

Langham, however, had been wise enough to see the little signatures I'd left. Reflecting upon that, he'd altered the wording of his official jury charge. 'Inasmuch as the medical evidence conclusively demonstrated only one person (meaning, I'm sure, only one brilliant perpetrator) could be implicated.' The jury willingly obliged, giving me the full credit I deserved, with the verdict:

'Wilful murder against some Person Unknown'

That verdict buoyed me up, I must admit. Suddenly, like never before, I felt the full extent of my power. Owing to that power, I knew it was time for another bold move on my part, time for more shocking good fun.

Sending correspondence to the Central News Agency had been a lark and had certainly added to the game. It had given the Whitechapel murderer a name! But I wanted more out of it, a greater return for my effort. I wanted to send something more, something alarming, to someone who would become alarmed.

Something to let the world know Saucy Jacky remained a man to be reckoned with.

What ought that something be? Well, allow me to say I was not without ideas. ha ha.

But to whom ought that something go? That would take some serious thought.

Not the police, surely. Writing to the coppers, or sending them anything fun, would have been a waste of time. The men of the Yard wouldn't have recognized a clue had it been hung from the tip of Sir Charles Warren's nose. If they did see it, they'd keep it to themselves. Hadn't the news editors griped of that right along?

Then an idea came. I would send my little gift, whatever I decided it would be, to the leader of one of the volunteer groups of do-gooders prowling the streets; the vigilante gangs making such a show of themselves for Queen, country, and pitiful neighbourhood. They, all of them (and there were by now a good many) wanted desperately to be a part of the game. All right then, let them. But which group was most deserving? And which group leader?

Confession time. Before leaving work early on Monday, 15 October, I made sure to complete one important task. I made sure to *bump into* Miss Adler when I knew the nurse had a free moment to talk. That accomplished, our talk was short, to the point, and went something like:

"*Blah* and *blah* and *blah.*"

Once the superficial banalities were covered... "Oh, by the by, Miss Adler, did you ever get the chance to ask your Metropolitan friend about the practicality of chasing after Jack the Ripper's bloody thumbprint?"

"I did, now you mention it." She shook her head, then did that revolting lip thing. "He says the paper's full of it. Scotland Yard has no confidence whatever in finger or thumb printing. Says the journalists were dreaming. There are too many people in the world for fingerprints to even make sense. Says it's a myth, like snowflakes. Even if it were true, how would you ever prove it?"

I nodded my agreement, well-satisfied.

I took that satisfaction back to my lodgings and relished it while, again, pulling out my trusted bottle of collodion. It had worked a treat to tighten the skin and make me appear older. But, I knew, the theatrical artists had found other uses as well. Sticky as it was, it was used (with care) to hold false facial hair, beards and moustaches, in place.

I'd been thinking over my new lark, and the problems it posed, for days. Those thoughts had led to the realization I would need a disguise. With that in mind, I had busied myself with some advance procuring. For what? In point of fact, I needed a beard! Yes. The stereotypically popular Victorian male, stern, masculine, and courageous; someone to be reckoned with; clothed in black, would be best conveyed, I thought, with the added gravitas of a black beard. Who questions a man with a beard?

Buying a false beard at a dandy shop catering to theatrical types was out of the question. Shopping for a disguise whilst looking like myself would have been pointless. I needed either to find or to make a beard. That meant a search. All searches, for me, began among the plethora of long-stored and mostly forgotten boxes and bags, shelves and cupboards, nooks and crannies, in the back of Mr Griggs' shoe shop. Not only had he been an avid collector of all that was collectible, but his devoted widow (I've mentioned), since his passing, stores everything. What better place to start?

As usual, I soon met with success. At the bottom of a pile, in the bottom of a dusty trunk, I found a long forgotten grey woman's coat with a luxurious wide white fur collar. Perfect. Clearly, she would never miss it. I carefully cut the collar away and restored the coat to its resting place.

I lay the amputated collar on Mr Griggs' desk, maneuvered a floor length mirror into place, gathered the necessary accoutrement about me, and set to, using the morning to prepare my beard.

I held the furry white collar over my chin and examined the reflection in the glass. It looked daft then, but I had confidence in myself. So the question, what beard ought I wear? An elegant chinstrap? A wise Van Dyke? An American Shenandoah? (Heavens no, hadn't Mr Lincoln been shot for wearing his?) Sense finally put in its hand; I was in search of disguise, not style. Let it be a full beard and nothing less, all the better to befuddle Scotland Yard.

I again measured the collar against my chin and cut. Measured and trimmed. Until I had a grand approximation of a heavy-looking beard. I applied the collodion to my tender face, pressed my artificial beard on, and held it in place. The collodion heated up as it set, an uncomfortable feeling to be sure, edging toward burning, but an artist had to suffer for his art. (And annoying the police required risk.) It took time but, eventually, I found myself wearing an excellent beard. But it was stark white and that would never do.

Once the beard had set, I darkened the thick white fur with a lead Tinto-Comb (from The Parisian Comb Company) bought for 6 shillings at a thrift store in Thrawl Street; a store I had never visited before and would not patronize again. With each stroke, the beard grew blacker and blacker. I fluffed and darkened my own moustache to match.

To make the incognito complete, I added to the disguise with a costume; a soft felt black hat drawn down over my forehead, a clerical collar turned up, a long black single-breasted overcoat, and a special pair of shoes from Mr Griggs' collection – with lifts in them.

Taller, thinner, darker, and heavily bearded, I stared in wonder at the image in the mirror.

Janey Mack, as my Limerick auntie would have said, I was pure class! Utterly brilliant! Just that sudden I realized the sinister article staring back at me, my character for this new lark, was an Irish immigrant. I'd get what I needed with no fuss and return home safely for. . . wearing me new look, the eejits would stay dog wide of me.

I was a new bleedin' man indeed. ha ha.

Forty-Three

From Hell
Mr Lusk

Shortly after 1:00 pm, fully disguised, I left home headed north to Commercial Road, then east to Jubilee Street, walking tall in my *lifting* shoes, altering my pace (with varied swings of the arms, and carrying myself in different ways) until I found the combination to fit my Irish man. Settled on a brisk stride and feeling the savage craic, I strutted north with my character firmly in place.

Lowering my head (and keeping it down as was my wont in public recently), I entered a shop that traded in leather at 218 Jubilee Street. Why pick on them? Simple enough; they had a bill posted in shop's window offering a reward, from Mile End Vigilance Committee, for my capture. At poster bottom was printed the name of my chosen do-gooder; the man I decided had earned my special gift.

Who deserved it more? This fellow, though dedicated to my destruction, had nevertheless been in my corner from the beginning. As president of his committee, he'd made repeated pleas to Henry Matthews of the Home Office to organize a government reward for information leading to my capture. Though the Secretary had repeatedly refused, George Lusk, had persevered. In his latest request, he'd called not only for a substantial reward but also for the offer of a pardon to any accomplice of mine willing to rat me out to the authorities. The idea was bollocks, of course, but it was the thought counted. I liked the fellow's sincerity. I liked that his pleas for money came with compliments aimed at me.

It's true!

Lusk was quoted as having written: 'that the present series of murders is absolutely unique in the annals of crime, that the cunning, astuteness, and determination of the murderer has hitherto been, and may possibly still continue to be, more than a match for Scotland Yard and the Old Jewry (financial centre of London) combined, and that all ordinary means of detection have failed.'

I was touched and confess to a fleeting emotional wave that, before it faded, I took for pride. Yes, George Lusk had earned a larger spotlight and a bit of personal attention from Yours Truly. I would send him a special gift.

Marsh Leather Goods, obviously a Lusk supporter, seemed the place to get the last item needed to put my new lark into motion. The young woman minding the shop asked if she could help me.

"Aye," I said, in my best accent. "C'mere to me." I indicated the poster in her window and asked for the home address of George Lusk, the president of the committee which had printed it.

She showed an awful puss and seemed wary. "Mr Aarons, the Committee Treasurer," she said, "lives at the corner of Jubilee Street and Mile End Road, thirty yards away. You might see him."

"I won't see him," I told her, not being rude, merely Irish. "I don't want to go there."

She nodded. To please a difficult customer, she reached under her shop counter and produced a newspaper. She dug in, found a specific article, then reached out offering the paper to me.

"I won't take it." I took a note book and pen from my pocket instead. "Read it out."

By then, she may have thought me away with the fairies, still she did as instructed. She read out Lusk's address, Alderney Road, Globe Road, but stopped short of giving me his house number. I made no argument, I didn't need it. The Royal Mail would see to the rest. I wrote what she said in my book.

That done, I thanked her for information, and left the shop, passing an old man coming in as I went out. He might have been the girl's father. From the look he give me, I didn't doubt it a bit.

Safely back home, I put on the gas in the back room of Mr Griggs' shop. I took a specific box down from a shelf (one I'd had down before), opened it, and extracted the jar from inside. I've mentioned it before, on the day I filled it and stored it away and, again, on the night I'd had a delicious meal with onion. Inside, swimming in wine spirits, bobbed the preserved remains of the singing whore's kidney. I held it up and examined it in the light.

Yes, it was time to send somebody a bit of a gift.

I dug in the old drawer for a small cardboard box, roughly three and a half inches square, that I had seen ages ago and knew to still be there. I removed the kidney from the jar, let the excess wine spirits drip away, noted that in spite of my preservation efforts the organ had begun to smell slightly, and slipped it inside the tiny gift box.

But half a kidney, by its lonesome, wouldn't be enough. Would only confuse. It needed a greeting to go with it that the recipient, and whomever he passed it on to (as well he might), would appreciate from where the gift had originated. But such a greeting would need be cunningly conceived.

To continue the game properly, any accompanying message would have to convince the recipient while, simultaneously, confounding any coppers who put their noses in. Horror and confusion, those were the goals of this game. To that end, I decided, the rotting meat would serve as proof of sender, while the enclosed communication ought not look to have been written by Jack the Ripper.

Lusk would shudder. The coppers would once again scratch their aching heads!

Though in the end it amounted to only a short note, I took greater care with this communication than I had either of the previous documents. The writer should appear to be only semi-literate. To that end, I gave myself – and studiously followed –

these rules. The style needed cramping, the letters crowding together. The had to be tightly spaced. Vertical lines had to be ignorantly retraced. I held my arm stiff, shoulder and forearm, writing with thumb and fingers only. Bunging up the movement lent a stupidity to the script (the literate wrote with freedom and ease). I spattered ink blots randomly as proof that clarity and legibility were of no concern. I left out punctuation, capitalization, grammar, and forgot sentence structure entirely. I misspelled a goodly portion of the content, and pressed heavily as I wrote to show the author an oafish lout.

Writing like an idiot, I found, takes time and effort.

When I had made an end to the project, I gave it a read:

From hell
Mr. Lusk
Sor
I send you half the Kidne I took from one women prasarved it for you toher piece I fried and ate it was very nise I may send you the bloody knif that took it out if you only wate a whil longer
signed
Catch me when you can
Mishter Lusk

Brilliant. It was brilliant! And message, and rotting kidney, would only improve with age. ha ha.

I folded the letter and slipped it into the box lid. I closed box over the stinking meat and wrapped the lot up tight. I penned the address I had been so clever, and gone to such great pains, to secure, onto the wrapping.

When all was ready, I walked my little gift to a postal box in Mile End. I'd already checked, see, and found that none of the boxes in my immediate district featured a mail slot wide enough to swallow the package. And I didn't want to walk it into a Royal Mail office, now did I?

With the box safely in the bin, I chuckled at a job well done. How could I not?

Forty-Four
Waiting... Waiting

No matter how much one admires or despises the Royal Mail, one cannot expect miracles. I am a reasonable fellow and, therefore, do not. I mailed George Lusk his present on Monday morning, 15 October. Being reasonable, I did not fret (or even give the package a second thought) until second post on Tuesday. From then on began the interminable wait to hear what effect, if any, the receipt of a boxed and rotting partial kidney of a murdered whore would have on the president of the Mile End Vigilance Committee. Or what, if any, answer my gift might receive.

I waited. I heard nothing. I waited some more. Days went by. I saw nothing in the newspapers. I heard nothing in the streets. I waited some more.

I confess, I was disappointed – more than I can say – to think that my gift had made no impact, had no affect. I waited some more.

Friday, 19 October, turned out to be my Day of Delivery.

Word came, through Press Association reports compiled, they said, through 'inquiries made at Mile End'. The Royal Mail had not failed me. George Lusk had gotten his gamey little gift. He'd suffered embarrassment and disgust. Then shared his revulsion with a group of the mean little Jews who made up his 'Get Jack the Ripper' Committee.

That night, further word came – as most details involving the police did – through the loose lips of Miss Adler, and her talkative

Archie, in the hospital break room. That was a break worth taking!

I must say, as arduous as the wait had been, it was worth waiting for; had produced joyous results, delicious fruit! And, I learned, I need never have worried at all.

Lusk received his small brown paper-wrapped box that Tuesday evening. He was gobsmacked, as well he should have been considering the effort I'd gone to in order to procure it for him. The item left him stunned. The personal letter left him wobbling. He had to sit, to take it in. He looked again into the box, saw and smelled the slowly browning, ever-more foul kidney, then covered it over – for good. He sat in silence, wondering; what ought he to do?

He read the enclosed note again.

'*From hell Mr. Lusk*'
To him. It had been written directly to him... by the killer. By the killer? By the killer!

'*I send you half the Kidne I took from one women prasarved it for you*'
Preserved for me! Why me? George Lusk couldn't have helped but wonder. Why am I in the killer's sights?

'*toher piece I fried and ate it was very nise*'
My god! He no doubt whined, imagining that tasty meal.

'*I may send you the bloody knif that took it out if you only wate a whil longer*'
How did he take that, I wondered? As a friendly promise. As a fearful threat? Didn't that keep the mean little bastard up all night?

'*Catch me when you can, Mishter Lusk*'

It looked real. By then it sure in hell smelled real. Most frightening of all, I had to believe, the entire package felt real. Did he think it a bizarre hoax? Or did he believe it? What was he to do? I cannot say with any accuracy what Lusk really thought or did that night. But if the newspapers had it right, the next evening, at the Crown public house in Mile End Road, before the scheduled meeting of their vigilance committee was called to order, President Lusk pulled Aarons, their treasurer, aside in a state of extreme agitation. "What is the matter?" Aarons asked.

"I suppose you will laugh at what I am going to tell you," Lusk said, trying to keep his voice down, "but you must know... I had a little parcel come to me on Tuesday evening." He licked his lips, or I imagined he did, for surely they'd gone dry. "To my surprise, it contains half a kidney... and a letter from Jack the Ripper."

Aaron did laugh, if the news got it right. He laughed and replied, "Someone is trying to frighten you."

"If so, he's done a fine job of it," Lusk said, visibly shaken. "It is no laughing matter to me."

Aarons could see it was not. He wiped the stupid grin from his own face and addressed the subject with the seriousness it damn-well deserved. "Look here," he told Lusk. "We're already late starting and we'll be late by meeting's end. Let us let the matter rest until morning. I'll speak with some of the other members quietly and we'll call round to your place and have a look at this package."

So it was that, at 9:30 on Thursday morning, Treasurer Aarons, accompanied by committee secretary Harris, and two other members of their gang, Reeves and Lawton, called upon President Lusk at his home in Alderney Road. Skipping the superficial courtesies (no tea, lads), Lusk hurried them to his study, opened a desk drawer, and withdrew the cardboard box; the *objet d'art.*

He hadn't seen it since the night it arrived. He'd tucked it, and the letter, into the drawer... and had not gone near it. The thought of it sickened him. "Throw it away," he said, handing the box to Aarons. "I hate the sight of it!"

With the others grouped around him, the treasurer opened the box. Four sets of beady eyes suddenly grew wide, four mouths fell open, and four nosy noses jerked away in outrage. Inside, two and a half weeks out of body, more than three days out of preserving spirits, dried, brown, and stinking, lay what remained of 'Call me, Kate, deary's' left kidney.

I'm certain they could hear the clock ticking on the far side of the room for the total silence within their stunned gang. Lusk finally broke it, saying, "This came with it," as he pushed my carefully crafted note into Secretary Harris' hand. (I'd like to think there was a tear in Lusk's eye.)

Oh glory! But getting on...

They debated. Hoax or not? Human or not? Sheep's kidney? Swine's kidney? Slag's kidney? Finally, forced to admit their ignorance, Aarons proposed they take the horror to the surgery of Dr Wiles, a friend and physician, down Mile End Road. Wiles wasn't in, but his assistant, Mr Reed, had a look. Reed, who knew his business, said the kidney was human and had been preserved in spirits of wine.

Reed wanted to be certain. He tucked the Jew merchants into a waiting room, told them he'd return shortly and, package in hand, hurried down the road to London Hospital. There, he showed the prize to Dr Thomas Openshaw, Curator of the Pathological Museum, a fellow I'd seen many times. Openshaw gave the kidney a look under his microscope.

When the papers hit old Frogg's newsstand, they quoted Openshaw as declaring the organ to be 'a portion of a human kidney, a ginny kidney, meaning it belonged to a person who had drunk heavily. That it was from a woman of about forty-five years of age, and had been removed from the body within the last three weeks.'

Another Openshaw interview, conducted the same day with a different paper repudiated much of the foregoing. The doctor told the *Star* 'he was of the opinion it was half of a left human kidney. He couldn't say, however, whether it was that of a woman, nor how long ago it had been removed from the body, as it had been preserved in spirits.'

Either way, Aarons' gang were convinced the plods had to be told. They took the parcel to Leman Street and handed it over to the heroic Inspector Abberline.

The routine regarding the evidence of the parcel was begun. The wrapping bore two penny stamps, available anywhere (including Mrs Griggs' sitting room desk) and untraceable. With the exception of a few letters of the London postmark, nothing else was legible. Their best guess was the box had been mailed in the East or East Central district.

As to the *From hell* note, Abberline and his mates in Scotland Yard (I can only imagine, and do truly hope) were flummoxed. It looked to have been written by an eejit labourer, surely not by the same hand or mind that composed the Dear Boss letter. It had to be a hoax; would have been written off as such but for the item that came with it. The kidney was a harsh reality.

With no good avenue down which to venture, and out of experts, Abberline (with the consent of his superiors) sent Lusk's gift to their colleagues in the City Police. Acting Commissioner Smith turned the organ over to their surgeon, Dr Gordon Brown (who'd examined the singing whore in Mitre Square). Brown returned to London Hospital to consult a senior surgeon named Sutton (yes, I'd hauled rubbish for him as well). Sutton, the papers say, pledged his reputation the kidney had been submerged in spirits within hours of being disembodied. It looked to be genuine, said the doctor.

It was indeed.

Others read the news accounts of Lusk's surprise package. One of those was Emily Marsh.

I met her the afternoon of the previous Monday, when I'd entered her father's leather goods shop in search of George Lusk's mailing address. Like an upstanding citizen, Miss Marsh made contact with the police and did her duty by recounting that short, but memorable, meeting for them. She described me: slim build, sallow face with a dark beard and moustache; wore a clerical outfit; stood near six feet tall, was probably 45 years old, and spoke with an Irish accent.

Savage! ha ha.

Tuesday, 23 October, marked the last day (and end) of the Coroner's Inquest into the death of... Well, wasn't that the second greatest question needed answering. Who the hell's murder were they inquiring into? The jury had met for the first time three weeks earlier, at the Vestry Hall in Cable Street, St George-in-the-East, Coroner Wynne Baxter had gone about his duties in utter sincerity. He'd questioned witnesses exhaustively. He'd adjourned the proceedings four times to allow the police to discover new evidence. But he still wasn't certain of the victim's identity.

They believed the murdered woman was Elizabeth Stride. But one witness, Mrs Malcolm, had raised doubts by insisting the corpse was that of her sister, Elizabeth Watts.

The question was finally resolved when Mrs Elizabeth Stokes (not Watts), the sister in question (the reported victim) showed up alive and well – to unload. Stokes stated for the record that Malcolm's evidence was infamy and lies. She was not dead, obviously. She was not indigent and living in doss houses. She was married to a brick maker and living in Tottenham. She had not seen her lunatic sister, Mary Malcolm, in five years. "And I am sorry," Stokes concluded, "that I have a sister who can tell such dreadful falsehoods."

It was official, I'd killed Elizabeth Stride in Berner Street. That unburdened my mind. ha ha.

Baxter summed up the proceedings with a heartfelt speech acknowledging his sorrow that, when all was done and dusted, they had not succeeded in unmasking the killer. After deliberating, came the same old thoughtless verdict, without any consideration (as had been shown by the Eddowes' jury), without any respect for my singular artistry. 'Wilful murder by some person or persons unknown.' Could have been any bleedin' body done the killing!

That took my mood back to where it had been, forced me to run the gamut; irritation, injured pride, depression, paranoia. Didn't they understand who I was nor understand the importance of my mission? I had two police forces, comprised of the greatest detectives in London, on my trail. Who was I, any bleeding person or persons! Obviously, there remained lessons to be taught – and learned.

Forty-Five
Grapes of Wrath

October of 1888, at first glance, would look to be a *nothing* month in my career, as I went on hiatus and the East End experienced thirty-plus days without a whore's murder. To the uninformed observer, it may have seemed as if good ol' Jack the Ripper had lost his anger or his nerve. Nothing was further from the truth. I was waiting... patiently.

Don't imagine I was happy or bored. Activity abounded; plenty to make Jacky saucy.

The irritations had mounted. The police, out searching in force, with extra patrolmen transferred into the East End from districts all over England. The vigilante mobs, galoshes in place against the rain, toting clubs from street to alley. Bloodhounds at the ready. Newspapers demanding a microscopic search of the doorknobs, bricks, and windows of every home in Whitechapel for the so-called *prints* of my thumbs and finger tips. The weather growing cold and, in the last half of the month, with the appearance of the famous (but miserable) all-consuming London fog. The drunk whores now carrying knives of their own. Yes. The seemingly quiet murder-free days of October were, for me, a month of pent up rage; thirty days of suppressing hatred. Still I waited... ever so patiently.

But I confess to one area where I lost my patience. To one niggling complaint, one irritant that drove me to the brink. That which – above all other considerations – kept me on a literal murderous edge that October... That fucking fruiterer!

I mentioned him, fleetingly, once; a greengrocer called Matthew Packer whom I first learned of through Mrs Griggs' newspapers. Packer was the fool who claimed, in an article in *The Evening News*, that on the night of the double murders, from his insignificant shop in Berner Street, to have sold a half-pound of black grapes to the Whitechapel killer and his victim. He further claimed they, meaning me and the whore, then stood around in the down-pouring rain, eating his grapes for more than half an hour before I did her in.

I vividly remember my amusement as my landlady read the preposterous story aloud. The notion I was out there to feed those pigs. I was working, not spending money on expensive fruit. The old boy may have sold a score of grapes that night but he sold none to me. It was a complete fiction. But I'd read and heard many a fiction regarding me and my work since August, so I laughed and let it go. I gave the story no more thought... until Matthew Packer intruded in my life again.

Mind I knew, from my reading and from what I'd overheard from Miss Adler, the police – as a matter of policy – refused to give the newspapers all but the most elementary facts regarding a crime. To do more, they believed, injured the cause of justice. Reporters had column inches to fill. Without *official* facts with which to work, they were forced to be creative; rumors or outright fictions could, and often did, serve instead. That October, Packer would prove himself a godsend to Fleet Street and the fact-starved reporters unleashed throughout the murder districts.

As the month progressed, Saucy Jacky hungered but dared not work, owing to the threats to my life and liberty. Meanwhile, through my various avenues of communication, I heard constant infuriating updates regarding Packer's ever-expanding tale. To begin with, I learned the 4 October article detailing his infamous sale of grapes was not the fruiterer's first brush with the affair (nor even his second). That had come two days earlier.

The heroic Inspector Abberline, heading the investigation of my work, sent two officers to Berner Street the Sunday morning following the dual murders, to conduct routine house-to-house inquiries. At 9:00 am, one of the two, Sergeant Stephen White (H Division), became the first detective to talk to Matthew Packer – long before the reporters got to him.

In his notes, White (according to Miss Adler's Archie) described Packer as a 'fruiterer in a small way of business'. The sergeant asked what time he closed his shop the previous night. Packer replied, "Half past twelve, in consequence of the rain. It was no good for me to keep open."

White asked if he saw anything of a man or woman going into Dutfield's Yard, or anyone on the street about closing time? The fruiterer replied, "No. I saw no one standing about; neither did I see anyone go up the yard. I never saw anything suspicious or heard the slightest noise; knew nothing about the murder until I heard of it this morning." That was Packer's whole story Sunday morning. He saw nothing, heard nothing, knew nothing.

With that, Sergeant White considered the fruiterer out of it and moved on to the next apartment and the next interview. It did not end there. That was only the beginning.

Two days later, two private detectives (Batchelor and Grand) hired by the mean little Jews of the Mile End Vigilance Committee were poking about Dutfield's Yard and asking round Berner Street, in search of clues the coppers had missed. They found two delusional sisters living at No 14 (Mrs Rosenfield and Miss Harstein) who claimed that in the Yard, where the body had been, they saw scattered flower petals and a blood-stained grape stalk. (The police mentioned no such find.)

Batchelor and Grand returned to Dutfield's Yard to look again. They saw neither petals nor the refuse of grapes. Concerned the police, in their hurry to prevent the crowd seeing Stride's red juices, might have washed both away with the blood, the sleuths dropped to all-fours and checked the yard drain. They failed to find petals but, if their story was true, did find a grape stalk. (To my misery!)

The private detectives took news of their discovery to the local fruit seller. Yes, Matthew Packer (who knew nothing and saw nothing). Suddenly he recalled selling grapes to a mystery couple round-about 11:45 the night of the murder. The pair then stood across the street eating his grapes in the rain, he said. He described both, quite generically.

When word of Packer's interview with Batchelor and Grand, coupled with the detectives' rumored grape-stalk discovery, reached a reporter for *The Evening News*, he sought out the fruiterer. *That* interview, Packer's third, became the amusing article trumpeting 'the man who spoke to the murderer'.

Having learned he originally saw and heard nothing, I was no longer amused.

When I first mentioned Mrs Griggs' recital, I neglected to say how the article had ended. I'll tell it now. *The Evening News*' reporter concluded his story by taking a shot at the police. "Well, Mr Packer," he asked, "I suppose the police came at once to ask you and your wife what you knew about the affair, as soon as ever the body was discovered?"

"The police?" Packer reportedly replied (in all capital letters for effect). "No. They haven't asked me a word about it yet!!!"

The fruiterer admitted a plain-clothes officer (no doubt Sergeant White) had visited the shop a day after the murder to look over the backyard, but the reporter added, 'No policeman had yet questioned him about what he might know of the tragedy.' Packer made no mention of his prior ignorance.

The police, fully aware of the sergeant's interview, were bewildered by the article. The CID sent a puzzled White back to re-interview the fruiterer and, if he was found to be credible, to escort him to mortuary to see if he recognized Stride's body. At the shop, Mrs Packer told White two detectives had been there, collected her husband, and taken him to St George's Mortuary. They were still there.

White headed for the mortuary on foot. On his way, he met the fruiterer, accompanied by a gent in a suit (private detective Batchelor), coming back.

"Where have you been?" White asked.

"This detective asked me to go see if I could identify the woman," Packer replied.

"Well?" White asked. "Have you done so?"

"Yes, I believe she bought some grapes at my shop about 12 o'clock on Saturday."

Then another gent (Grand) caught up with them. Sergeant White asked both what they were doing with Packer? Grand said they were detectives. When DS White asked to see their authority, Grand rephrased, saying they were 'private' detectives. He produced an identity card, showed it to White, but pulled it back when the sergeant tried to touch it. Then Batchelor and Grand, according to White, *induced* Packer to leave with them.

His duty yet to do, White returned to Packer's shop later that day. Whilst talking with Packer, damned if Batchelor and Grand didn't appear again, in a hansom cab. They told White they were taking the fruiterer to Scotland Yard to see Police Commissioner Sir Charles Warren. They delivered Packer to the Yard. While it is unlikely the fruiterer met Sir Charles, he did meet Senior Assistant Commissioner Alexander Bruce, for Bruce wrote a report on their interview. In it Packer repeated – and embellished – his account of doing business with the Whitechapel killer.

That's how it went. Every time a new detail (true or not) appeared in the press, or when gossip changed the accepted narrative, Packer altered his story. Among the ever-growing discrepancies. . .

The fruiterer told the private detectives the killer wore a *wideawake* hat. He then spoke with the *Evening News* and said the hat was *black, soft, felt*. In the course of that meeting – trying to make news – the reporter asked, "Did he (the killer) speak like an Englishman or more of this style?" then imitated what he called 'the Yankee twang'.

Packer instantly replied, "Yes, now that you mention it, there was a sound of that sort about it."

The fruiterer then, no doubt, read two other news items that appeared at the same time; the first, covering a discussion before the Coroner for South-east Middlesex, Wynne Baxter, regarding a theory that an American doctor (in search of uterus specimens) may have been the culprit and; the second, an opinion piece suggesting a close examination of the Dear Boss letter showed the writing to be filled with *Americanisms*. True to form, in his next two interviews Packer spoke of his murderous customer wearing *a Yankee hat* and then *an American hat* respectively.

Packer first recalled the woman carrying a white flower. Later, no doubt after reading the erroneous testimony of Spooner the horse-keeper (who saw a red and white flower pinned to the dead woman's coat), in his interview with Bruce, Packer's flower became a white and red geranium. PC Smith and Inspector Reid were correct, trust me, the whore had a red rose (with petals intact). Packer was making it up as he went along.

As to the grapes… A *Daily News* report on Monday, 1 October, alleged Diemschutz, Kozebrodski, and Fanny Mortimer saw the dead woman clutching sweetmeats in one hand and a bunch of grapes in the other. The breath lozenges are right, I said as much. The grapes were bollocks. At inquest, Police Surgeon Phillips testified, 'Neither in the hands nor about the body of the deceased did I find any grapes or connection with them. I am convinced the deceased had not swallowed either the skin or seed of a grape within many hours of her death.' Dr Blackwell, not having perceived any grapes near the body in Dutfield's Yard or having heard any person say they had seen grapes, corroborated him. And despite the News report, Diemschutz (the only one of the three to testify) denied noticing Stride's hands at all, let alone seeing grapes in them.

Still, the potty old sisters read about grapes, believed in them, and told Batchelor and Grand they saw them. The detectives told Packer and, *voilà*, he sold grapes to the killer.

On Saturday, 6 October, the same day the Stride whore was buried at East London Cemetery, the *Daily Telegraph* (in an article by a bloke called Richardson) published a new Packer account. This time the fruit seller changed the killer's description. He darkened me up, perhaps to fashion a dirty sinister foreigner. With their new description, adding insult to injury, the Telegraph had a number of woodcut sketches prepared showing men of different nationalities and ages of the working and lower classes. (Not an English gentleman in the lot.) Packer, according to Richardson, '*unhesitatingly*' picked one of those, a clean-shaven man wearing an American felt hat, as his grape-eating villain. Packer's selection, along with a sketch picked by Richardson, was published with the caption: 'SKETCH PORTRAITS OF THE SUPPOSED MURDERER.'

The average reader may have ignored the details; I did not. To dissect Packer's various versions is to find him all over the map. He told Bruce he sold the grapes at 11 o'clock. Other accounts placed the episode up to an hour later. He told Richardson it was 11:30, gave the time as 11:45 to Batchelor and Grand (and *The Evening News*), and told Sergeant White, in their second interview, he made the sale at midnight. He told Bruce he closed his shutters and left the whore and me in the rain at 11:30, with Batchelor and Grand (and The News) he made it 12:15, and he stretched his closing time to 12:30 for Sergeant White.

In each version, I grew younger. He told the detectives I was middle-aged. He told *The Evening News* I was thirty to thirty-five. He told Richardson I was 'a young clerk; not more than thirty' and, in Bruce's version, he had me as 'a young man, between twenty-five and thirty.' Those last, most likely, owing to PC Smith's sighting of a possible suspect he described as, "Aged twenty-eight."

I'm not the only one thought the greengrocer a liar. He was not summoned to give evidence at any meeting of the Stride Inquest, because his story was built of bollocks and gossip. But why did the fool go to the trouble to invent, and re-invent, our supposed meeting? To enhance his status amongst his neighbours? Perhaps. He was a nobody; an old man selling wilted vegetables and rotted fruit. Still, there may have been more to it.

I wonder if the escalation in the amount of reward money, for information leading to my capture and conviction, wasn't the impetus? On 30 September, Packer said he saw nothing. The two days following the double murder saw a fivefold increase in rewards being offered, including a generous £500 from the Corporation of London. Why wouldn't the old boy put his hand in? Amateur detectives filled the streets of the East End like red Indians, all hoping for a piece of my scalp.

The radicals thought it a possibility. On 2 October, the *Star* editorialized on the plethora of residents '*who turn in descriptions on the chance of coming near enough the mark to claim a portion of the reward if the man should be caught, just as one buys a ticket in a lottery.*'

Afraid Packer's lies, abetted by the papers, might mislead rather than inform the public, and damned upset by the purported 'portraits', the police printed a disclaimer in *The Police Gazette* warning that the Telegraph sketches were "not authorized." And, as a correction, printed three anonymous but reliable descriptions of 'men of interest' actually seen near the scenes of crime. Who could have guessed by any manner or means concerning the Whitechapel murders the police and I might be in league with one another? As far as that fruiterer was concerned, we most assuredly were. Packer was a bloody lying tosser giving all of us a royal pain in the arse.

Had my work in the streets not been my mission, during quiet October, I would have happily taken another stroll up Berner Street for the sole purpose of cutting that fruiterer's throat.

Forty-Six
London Fog

The fruiterer caused me a good deal of stress. I might have gone to the trouble to kill him had I not found relief elsewhere. But, with the end of the Stride and Eddowes Inquests, with the final reports that emerged, I got an incredible sense of relief concerning the question of eye witnesses from the night of the double event – and why they had never testified as to my description.

All that time I had been worrying myself sick... over nothing.

Through news and gossip I eventually discovered... The pipe smoker in Berner Street had no idea what I looked like. He'd spent his energy trying to remember the looks of the nosy Jew I'd put him onto. The Jew, meanwhile, who'd seen me shove the whore (and for whom I'd shouted "Lipski!" to the pipe smoker), had been too frightened to describe anything specific. His name was Israel Schwartz and, I was right, he was an immigrant who spoke no English. Through a translator, he admitted running, in fear of his life, as far as the railway arch. The pipe smoker did not pursue him that far. Schwartz told police and reporters alike he was unsure if the men (me and the pipe smoker) were together or not.

As to the others, the door opener, Fanny Mortimer, hadn't seen me; the cart driver, old Diemschutz, hadn't seen me. The fellow in White Church Lane had barely noticed and couldn't describe me.

The man in Duke Street, Lawende (whose testimony was kept from the public), one of three Jews who'd stumbled from the

Imperial Club and passed by, gave a description that matched nobody at all. He saw me as thirty-ish, five foot eight, medium build, with a fair complexion and a small moustache. My clothes in particular he got wrong. My short black jacket he described as 'loose' and of a 'pepper and salt colour'. He claimed I wore a red neckerchief tied in a knot. (The whore had a red scarf, my tie was black.) He credited me with a grey cloth cap with a peak fore and aft. I wore a deerstalker, to be sure, but black as the night. He called me *shabby*, the bastard. The two men in his company denied any memory of me at all.

And I got a laugh when my landlady brought her interpretation to the news! Mrs Griggs found an item I'd missed; a comment by Lawende. After giving his *erroneous* account of my wardrobe, he summed up for reporters that I had the 'appearance of a sailor'. That, Mrs Griggs informed me, was the word on the street. Jack the Ripper had been seen by a number of witnesses and, with his short dark coat and peaked cap, was evidently a sailor.

"With the docks so nearby," the good woman added, "I've always feared as much."

I agreed with her, of course. The women of the street ought really be mindful of sailors.

I needed the laugh. My life was about to turn dismal.

For nearly the whole of the third and fourth weeks of October, the fog – thick as creamed soup, grey as a shroud – settled in and covered a goodly portion of the City of London and all of the East End.

Long ago I mentioned the ridiculousness of a romantic foggy Victorian London. Anyone thinking these poorly gas-lighted streets of the dock area, the working class neighbourhoods, and the slums might be a great place for Jacky to return to his work had given the subject no thought at all.

Jack the Ripper stalking his victims in the London fog... *Bosh!*

You couldn't make out anything five feet in front of you; meaning you couldn't spot a whore in the night lest you were on top of her. And you can't kill if you can't find your victim. I had no interest in cleaning up respectable women. If you did spot a drunken slag, if you had her in your grip and stood ready to cut a gusher in her bare throat, you could not know if a copper (or six) were standing ten feet from you. You can't run away if you can't see the streets, or the alleyways, or the cold brick walls that separate them.

The Metropolitan Police constables, the City Police constables, the street gangs of the vigilante committees, the newshounds, and the bloodhounds, I imagined, were all out and about searching for me. But if they were, even in full force, not a one of them could have found his arse with his own two hands. Not in that fog.

Days later, the fog remained as thick as ever.

It was Halloween, a night of ghosts and ghouls, of communing with the dead, of making your peace or facing your destruction in that dark other world. Or, for those damned fools that continued to insist the fog held romance, for the fans of Robert Burns, a night for having your lover's future decided.

If only for a stroll, if only for the romance of it, Jack the Ripper had to venture out on Halloween.

Saucy Jacky knew his Burns and, as it was All Hallows Eve after all, I recited some under my breath, as I moved... through the heady fog.

> 'The auld guid-wife's weel-hoordit nits
> Are round an' round dividend,
> An' mony lads an' lasses' fates
> Are there that night decided:
> Some kindle couthie side by side,
> And burn thegither trimly;
> Some start awa wi' saucy pride,
> An' jump out owre the chimlie
> Fu' high that night.'

The nuts in the fire. ha ha. It was the matchmakers' and the seers' way to decide the fate of others. I had my own way.

As I walked alone in the fog in Cable Street, I tumbled that thought about in my head. I considered my career, the special ways employed by Yours Truly in helping to decide the fates of those around me. I was lost in thought, felt lost in time, when, I was startled by something moving out of the thick fog. I was caught off guard... by a toff who appeared suddenly, from nothing, as if he were a phantom in a penny dreadful or a Walpole Gothic. Robert Burns to Wilkie Collins in an instant!

We both jumped and "*Ooohhed!*" each other in alarm.

He was in his early twenties, of medium height, with dark hair and a formidable moustache turned up at the ends. He was dressed fastidiously from his patent boots, past his black coat, and to the top of his high hat, with a *la-di-da* umbrella over his arm. There was nothing frightening about him in particular. I can only say that the time and atmosphere accounted for my surprise. To my credit, for what it is worth, he was startled by my appearance as well.

He excused himself, in English but with a heavy foreign accent; perhaps it was Russian but, if I had to lay a wager, I'd have put my coin on Polish. He cursed the filthy London weather and turned to put key to door lock of the dark shop before which we stood, No 126. He disappeared inside and pushed the door closed behind him.

Even in the dark, I could read the elegantly painted sign, in red letters (black in the gloom) on a white background, beside the door. '*Chapman's*' it said and, beneath in a smaller yet equally elegant script, '*Tonsorial Parlour*'.

It was that sort of night, wasn't it, when even Jack the Ripper could go for a walk in the fog and be frightened by a lone foreigner (a hairdresser at that). Having had enough there, I diverted to the south down Cannon Street headed for the London docks. That's what I needed, a nice long look – if the fog would permit it – at the melancholy River Thames.

Speaking of melancholy, a pall of mind covered me as I passed St George-in-the-East, Mrs Griggs' parish church. Yes, I attended as well, but laid no claim (physical or spiritual) to the structure. The church's bell tower was invisible, and her distinctive '*pepperpot*' towers mere ghosts, in the grey.

I found the docks then wound my way along the river for some time. No, I wasn't thinking, certainly not about anything in particular or of consequence. I wasn't in a mood. I was merely walking. The sound of the river was my constant companion, but sight of the deep, dark, cold waters came and went with the whims of the thick fog. The street lamps, soft balls of amber atop each pole, no more than one visible at a time all along the embankment, did nothing to light the way. Each stood a silent and lonely witness to the futility of it all.

Still walking silently along, the fog suddenly parted and I saw the figure of a woman near the embankment, a phantom herself. I slipped my hands in my pockets and approached her. She turned and saw me... too late for her.

At least it would have been too late had she been drunk. But she was not. She was sober as a parish priest; more sober (by far) than the average parish priest. With wide eyes, but a surprisingly steady voice, she asked, "You goin' to hurt me?"

Hands still in my pockets, I took a slow deep breath and gripped my shoemaker's knife. Then I shook my head. I walked on, passing her by.

"Are you him?" she called to my back. "Are you him?"

I ignored her cries and her question and continued on until she was lost in the fog behind me. Or I was lost in the fog before me. It didn't matter which. We were, the both of us, mere phantoms in a Collins' novel... a penny dreadful... the London fog.

I returned to my lodgings late, quietly found something to eat in the kitchen and, quieter still, examined the newest newspapers in Mrs Griggs' sitting room. I was not at it long, a very few minutes when... Damn blast it to hell! There, in that evening's *Evening News*, another article about that bastard fruiterer. Matthew Packer was wagging his tongue again.

This time it wasn't a rehash of the same story. No, in this article, Packer was claiming to have seen Jack the Ripper again. An all new sighting!

Supposedly while selling his wilted marrows and rotted melons from his rickety barrow at the junction of Greenfield Street and

Commercial Road, I came upon him. Then, for an unspecified reason, perhaps because I recognized him and the great threat he posed to my freedom and welfare, I gave Packer '*a most vicious look*'. The grocer claimed he stood his ground and sent a bystander to find a policeman. Realizing my jeopardy, I escaped his clutches by jumping on a tram bound for the docks and Blackwall beyond.

Bastard!

I went to sleep that night dreaming of redecorating Matthew Packer's pathetic little greengrocer's shop. I would drape that fools intestines in and around the rows of vegetables, hide his lungs amongst the melons, and drop his liver, his kidneys, and his black little heart in among the apples.

Forty-Seven
Toff for a Tart

Another week, and then some, went by. On the outside I maintained my composure but, inwardly, I was raving. November had come – and the streets were filthy again. There was nothing for it.

Saucy Jacky would go back to work.

But what of everyone in the streets searching for shabby me? For some unknown reason, I thought of the foreign hairdresser who, on my walk earlier in the week, had stepped from the fog to give me such a scare. As the encounter had, obviously, been memorable I dedicated my dress for the evening – Jack the Ripper's return to the streets – to his inspiration. The shabby killer would take the night off. I would go out hunting again... and would do so dressed as a toff!

I remembered, particularly, the fellow's fabulous moustache and decided that night's drunken whore deserved to see a moustache every bit as elegant. So, again, I gathered my accoutrement and I made myself up. I brought out my trusty Tinto-comb. I darkened my hair. I darkened my eye lashes. I darkened my moustache; then I fluffed it outrageously and twisted in wax to curl up the ends as the hairdresser had done. I completed the look with powder to pale the complexion.

I dug into Mr Griggs' closet (and my own, of course) and dressed myself up; dark trousers, a dress shirt with a white linen collar, a black tie with a horseshoe pin, a light waistcoat under a dark jacket, button boots and dark gaiters with white buttons. Looking respectable... No.

Looking dapper... Yes!

Sometime before, hidden away among Mr Griggs' things, I'd found a thick gold watch chain, with a decorative round seal and a glinting red stone depending from it. I brought that out of hiding now and tucked it in and hung it from the pocket of my waistcoat. I folded a blood red kerchief for the breast pocket square. I examined the results in Mr Griggs' long mirror and, I must confess, I looked the swell.

I didn't have a top hat – and was glad for it. I wouldn't have worn one if I had; the one the hairdresser had worn that night had made him look a Nancy. I wasn't going to the opera; though I had every intention of putting on a show. ha ha. I found a dark and respectable, if slightly sinister, felt hat and placed that atop my dome. Again I consulted Mr Griggs' glass. Yes!

Not bad at all. I turned the hat down in the middle. I examined first one profile and then the other. Unable to help myself, I stroked the ends of the uplifted moustache. That would do nicely.

I parted the curtain covering the front window of the old shop, just enough, to give me a peek outside. The weather looked bleak, with a misty off-and-on drizzle that had neither the heart to stop nor the soul to work itself into a rainstorm of merit. Merely a drizzle. I was British and would forgo an umbrella in defiance of it. But, as it was November and the evening would be chill, I bowed in respect to the cold and donned a long black wool coat with shimmering black astracan at the collar and cuffs. My will was strong but I was not a fool.

Only two things remained...

First, in my coat I pocketed a small fold of fabric and a short length of lovely cloth ribbon. With peelers out in force as they'd been all month, with bloodhounds sniffing at my heels, with vigilantes bumping into one another, with plodders toting magnifying glasses in search of fingerprints, and whores toting their own knives for protection of their filthy treasures, with all the East End frantically looking for Jack the Ripper, I could not afford (and wanted no part of) prolonged lurking before I made my choice. The cloth and ribbon, I believed, might aid me in circumnavigating that difficulty.

Second, and most important, was the pocketing of items that would make my dress-up labours all worth while. I opened the drawer in Mr Griggs' old desk (having taken them down and hidden them earlier) and drew out my shoemaker's knife and my surgical blade. It had been too, too, long for both. They felt marvelous, at home, in my hands. I tucked my friend safely into my coat. Then I turned to the long mirror and laid the long cold blade of the scalpel against my cheek. Saucy Jacky was ready.

I couldn't help but smile in silent anticipation.

I slipped the long blade into hiding as well.

At that moment I decided, in honor of my return after having been away from the game so long, that Jack the Ripper would return to Whitechapel. NO! Better yet, I would stroll through Whitechapel as if I owned it (didn't I?), then march boldly up into Spitalfields. Yes! I'd traveled the East End and into the City, it was time I went home – to the filthiest whores of all. To the worst streets in London. I would find my prey among the doss houses, the pubs, the gas-lit but still ridiculously dark streets, Flower and Dean or Dorset Street, where even the coppers feared to go alone, amid the even more ridiculously dark-souled whores of the worst slum on earth.

Yes, after a month's long hiatus, Saucy Jacky would go home. I smiled again, silently wondering if home was ready for me? Only time would tell.

I closed the shoe shop door quietly not to disturb dear Mrs Griggs sleeping above, opened the outside door, and stepped from my lodging house. I walked briskly away headed west straight into the cold mist. I turned the corner, to the north, and started up Backchurch Lane for the Whitechapel High; a society gent in search of a sodden whore, a toff *en route* to a tart.

I had been right. The weather was abominable, the November air chill, the spritzing rain ice cold. But I pulled my coat around me with a light heart. It was a lovely night for a walk.

With a special hope for a very special morning, I'd made my way through Whitechapel, searching as I went and eventually finding an open 'Fish and Chips' shop. There I ordered a takeaway dinner of fish, dipped in a flour and water batter, and as advertised 'fried in the Jewish fashion'. It came with potato slices deep-fried in oil. The combination, honestly, was served in a wrapping of old newspapers. While I had never imbibed myself, to the best of my understanding the meal was a standard among the working classes and an absolute delicacy for those of the lower class.

Why the dull recital? For the game, of course. With the meal in-hand, I produced the fabric and ribbon I'd brought specifically for that purpose. I wrapped the meal in the cloth and tied it up in the ribbon. ha ha. Grapes indeed! Matthew *Bleeding* Packer!

With my Fish and Chips tied into a lovely gift for bait, I began to troll the gloomy narrow streets and pitch black alleys; to wade the waters of London's overcrowded slums. A fishing expedition like no other that eventually brought me to the corner of Thrawl and Commercial Streets, just two short blocks from George Yard. George Yard, where the soldier's whore and I had had such a memorable little meeting back in August; the meeting with which I originally started this tale.

I stood there, a few short minutes, looking the streets over in all directions. It was ten minutes to two in the morning, and I was starving. No not for the Fish and Chips under my arm; not for food of any kind. Jack the Ripper wanted blood.

It was at that moment, on the street north of me, I saw a light from heaven. A whore appeared... All right, I'm being over-dramatic. She stepped... out of the Queen's Head Public House on the corner of Fashion and Commercial Streets. But she was manna all the same.

And, I saw immediately, she was not like the others. This one was a lovely little trollop. But that, as I've made it clear in the past, was neither here nor there. The questions that night, as always, remained: What was her profession? What was her condition? The answers would decide her fate.

That's what I was doing, contemplating the fate of a complete stranger, a block away, when I was passed on my corner by a fellow, a labourer by the looks of him, tramping up Commercial Street into Spitalfields from the Whitechapel High. Beyond me, approaching Flower and Dean Street, he stopped to speak with the young woman who had caught me eye.

I didn't know yet if the girl was drunk. She had been drinking, no doubt. She was spreeish, speaking in a too-loud voice, and unsteady in her stance. Feelings of anger and excitement began to build within me in equal measure. As I've already stated my conviction... promiscuous alcoholic slags in a state of pseudo-sobriety, as far as I was concerned, were the worst drunk whores of all.

They were talking.

"Mr. Hutchinson," the girl said, addressing the labourer, too loudly and with too much affection, "can you lend me sixpence?"

"I cannot," he replied. "I have spent all my money going down to Romford."

Her eagerness disappeared like a wisp of smoke. "I must go and find some money."

With that and nothing more she left him and took to walking toward Thrawl Street, in my direction. Even at that distance, the sight of her (and her slightly drunken sway), the sound of her (and her slightly slurred Irish lilt) began absolutely to give me an idea.

Forty-Eight
The Irish Lass

I've never told it.

I am English. Born in London – in the East End; as English as tuppence. A proud, penniless subject of Her Majesty. My mother, the drunken whore, was an immigrant. Mind, coming from Ireland, she was as much a subject of the Queen as the stable muck at the Royal Mews in Buck-place. But she was a foreigner (to the English). Following her early (far too late for my tastes) demise...

No I shant go into the whole thing. I'll make it simple.

Orphaned, it doesn't matter how, I was several weeks in a workhouse hell, in London, before being sent to my auntie's in Limerick. I've already said my mother was a loose woman who imbibed to her detriment and to mine. My auntie was, believe it or not, worse; a much younger, prettier, twisted slag, who derided me and humiliated me because I would not (could not) join her in that twisted existence. Oh, yes, many times I was invited... ordered. None of it bears going into. Nor even thinking about. But a good deal of filth, degradation, embarrassment, and pain, brought me back to England and – to that moment in Commercial Street.

Each of the horrid whores with whom I'd dealt since August (from first to last) had brought it on, brought me on, by their own selfish actions. By drinking and selling their sins like my mother. The last had sobered slightly, called me 'deary', and gotten what was coming to her as a result, also like my mother. The young and pretty one, coming down the street, by virtue of her teetering step, her slurred speech, and her heritage... had already earned the worst of my wrath like my auntie. I'd been a month away; too, too long.

It was decided. That Irish lass, whoever she was, was already dead in an alley. Her red juices already running in the gutter. Her insides already exposed and cooling in November air. The flies already laying their eggs. The headlines already written. 'Jack the Ripper Strikes Again!'

She simply wasn't aware of it yet. It was time she see it. So I allowed her to see me.

The fellow she'd left behind stood pitiably watching us as we came together on the street. No, I didn't care that I was being seen. My toff disguise was impregnable. Hadn't the last two months proved it? I would not, could not, be found out. The fellow she'd left behind, her watcher, was no doubt straining to hear as I put my hand on the Irish lass' shoulder and spoke to her. Straining, the sad Nosy Parker no doubt tried but could not quite hear me.

The whore did... as I offered her a gift and made her a promise. She nodded. I burst out laughing. She joined in, singing, "All right!"

She looked at the wrapped parcel in my hand (decoratively tied with my makeshift strap), then looked a question at me. I nodded. Yes, that was it, as promised. She smiled brilliantly, gratefully, then eyed the package again.

"You will be all right for what I have told you," I said, and wrapped my arm round her shoulders.

We walked slowly in the direction of her watcher. Alarmed, but trying not to show it, he turned and walked ahead of us.

At the corner of Fashion Street, he paused, leaned against the lamp of the Queen's Head in an attempt at casual loitering, and continued to watch us from the corner of his eye. I tugged my hat down as we approached. Then – the nerve! As we passed, the blighter stooped to ogle my face. I returned a look of murderous intent and he stood back up. Nothing was said – and we were past him.

We crossed Fashion Street at the corner, with the watcher watching our backs, then cut across the wide Commercial Street and started past The Britannia (in future I would hear, with no surprise, the Irish lass under my arm had been one of Matilda Ringer's best customers). But she was not a customer just then. The whore *had* a customer. Yours Truly.

Beyond the Ringer's stretched Dorset Street. In the heart of the Spitalfield's rookery, as I already mentioned, it was reputed (and lived up to the reputation) to be the worst street in the city; filthy, foul, filled with criminals and the suffering and fear they engendered. They were not the geniuses, the masterminds, or gentlemen of crime. Counterfeiters, forgers, bankers, and politicians, did not abide there. Dorset Street was home and hive to nasty low-life criminals, pickpockets, petty thieves, violent robbers, razor-slashing hoodlums, lecherous deviants and, undoubtedly, a murderer or two yet to be found out. It was the breeding ground for tomorrow's criminals. The police, who entered the street only on business and only in teams of two (or better, four), despised it. And, at once, appreciated it as the holding pen it was. When need arose to drag in the usual suspects, the police didn't need to comb London. They knew where to find the scofflaws.

The street was taken up with lodging-houses and dilapidated rentals, controlled by the two slum landlords I've mentioned, Jack McCarthy and William Crossingham; suspected criminals themselves (illegal prize fights, racketeering, fencing stolen goods, procuring). Crossingham had been Stockings' landlord (when she paid her doss) at 35 Dorset at the corner of Little Paternoster Row.

I'd had a long month to read up on many subjects. To think about many subjects.

As we walked, I thought about my whore and about whores in general. It was important to often reassess your work. To that end... It occurred to me that women came in four classes; respectable, immoral, prostitutes, and whores. Respectable women guarded their bodies and their minds against evil influences. Immoral women used their bodies to meet their needs. Prostitutes were young and attractive and used their bodies to meet their wants. Whores were debauched, drunken old bags with no moral underpinnings, drowning the rest of society in a lake of beer and fire. Dorset Street saw neither of the first two types, and only an occasional prozzie who moved through, saw the danger, then disappeared to safer neighbourhoods. Dorset was a street of whores.

I let the girl lead me to a narrow archway, between Nos 26 and 27 on the north side of Dorset Street. A simple metal sign there assured us it was the entrance to Miller's Court. In mid-century it dawned on a fellow named John Miller he could pull in a few extra bob by renovating the back gardens of his properties at Nos 26 and 27. He built one room cottages around the garden, all facing a paved centre (where no one dared twirl anything larger than a small cat), creating Miller's Court. The Irish lass said she lived at No 13.

But even that wasn't what it seemed. No 13 was not one of Miller's cottages. It was, originally, the back room of 26 Dorset Street. The landlord, McCarthy (who liked money himself), blocked the back room of 26 off from the rest of the house (with a pasteboard *wall*), made the old back door of 26 the front door of this new single room looking out onto the court, and called it 13 Miller's Court.

Enough real estate. Back to the story.

I could sense his eyes upon us. Who? The watcher, of course. I turned and looked and, sure enough, from the corner of my eye saw the fellow, her jealous watcher, who'd followed us from Flower and Dean Street and into Dorset Street. He was standing outside of Ringer's, casually pretending not to watch us. Poor sad bastard.

The Irish whore sneezed. I turned back to see her searching the pockets of her apron. "Oh, I've lost my handkerchief!"

I produced the beautiful red kerchief from my pocket, shook out the fold, and handed it to her. She took it gratefully, used it practically (if not daintily), then offered it back. I waved it away. She smiled again as she tucked her new kerchief into her apron. Then she placed her hand on my shoulder and kissed my left cheek.

"Your dinner," I told the girl, "and your customer are both getting cold."

"All right, my dear," she said. "Come along. You will be comfortable."

She turned into the entrance to the Miller's Court passage. I tarried behind. No, I wasn't having a case of nerves; there were no doubts. It was merely, as we passed, I couldn't help but notice that, on the storefront a yard from the entrance, weathered and askew with one corner rolled and dangling, hung a bill posted by the publishers of the *Illustrated Police News* promising £100 reward for my capture. I thought to straighten it, to make the bill easier to read (in a den of semi-literates and foreigners), to recapture the dignity and sincerity with which it was first hung – over a month before.

I stopped myself. Perhaps I'd set the poster right on the way out. Meanwhile, the girl was on the move... and my job awaited me.

The passageway was twenty feet long but only a yard wide. She led me to the end, without entering the Court proper, and stopped before a door on the right. "Just here," she said.

Instead of opening the door of No 13 by knob or latch key, the Irish lass reached round the corner. "I lost the key," she explained with a smile devoid of embarrassment. "The broke window works a treat." Apparently, she reached into the room through the hole in the glass. The latch released with a *snick*. The door swung inwardly open then, halfway, *thumped* to a stop against something inside. The girl failed to react; all was routine. She merely smiled and stepped through and into the room.

I followed after her.

Forty-Nine
13 Mîller's Court

It made no difference whether or not the Irish lass' guardian was watching outside. We were inside 13 Miller's Court, the door closed and latched. A man's heavy coat, hung over the window in place of a curtain, prevented anybody seeing in. I doubted, too, whether any light from inside could escape. I nearly laughed at the thought as I eyed the girl. I knew for certain she would not escape.

But I'm hurrying the story again.

Even as I think of it now, the thrill returns. I found myself in a frightening paradise. I stood with a woman alone in her private room; outside of my auntie, I'd never been in that situation before. Never, since I'd taken on that sacred job, had I had solitude, warmth, and a seemingly endless amount of time in which to work. It was almost too much to look forward to.

The girl said something, I don't know what, and lit a stub of candle.

In answer, I presented her with her present. She squealed, grasped the package in both hands and, thanking me repeatedly, turned to her old *kitchen* table. She pushed several piles of folded clothes out of her way, mumbling, "My laundress," as if someone had to be blamed for the only clean thing in her life. She sat, excitedly untied the band, opened the fabric, and peeled back the newsprint wrap.

The greasy smell of fried fish and chips added to the room's stench. But the whore was euphoric. She '*oohed*' and '*cooed*' passing her face through the steam. She tore off a flaky white portion and pushed it into her mouth. She moaned and yummed. Then she dug in as if she were starving; a chip, more fish, a chip. She was in heaven, stuffing her gob with greased fingers, masticating cod and potatoes with open mouth and chomping teeth and, to my startled surprise, after the first few swallows, politely offering me a bite. I declined with a shake of the head and a soothing assurance that it was all for her.

What sort of man would eat part of her last meal? My feast would come later and, as the night progressed, I fully intended to glut myself. She smiled and dived back in.

I left her to it while I examined my surroundings.

The whore's room was far from prepossessing, perhaps twelve foot square, and cluttered. Sparsely furnished as it was the room offered little space in which to move. The bedside table, against which the door had thumped upon opening, was butted against the left side of an ancient wooden bedstead. The right-hand side of the bed sat close against the wooden partition that stood in for a wall and sealed the room off from the rear of the house (of which it had once been the ground floor back room). There was the chair upon which the whore sat, the rickety table at which she ate, a cupboard, a disused washstand and a second wood chair against the wall by the fireplace. A teapot hung above a small fire glowing hungrily in the grate. The bare floorboards were filthy; the pattern on the papered walls impossible to discern beneath the dirt.

The one decoration in the room was a cheap print of a painting hung over the fireplace. In it, a young woman in flowing white skirts and a bright yellow blouse sat upon the floor of her small home, her face (and obviously crying eyes) buried in the lap of some old bitch, a maid or midwife (a nosy mother? the village gossip?), who had even more obviously just brought her horrid, earth-shattering, life-altering news. A picture window, behind the women, looked out on a seascape, suggesting the news concerned a lost sailor or perhaps a drowned fisherman. Whichever, the grieving woman was now a widow. To drive home the less-than-subtle message, the grieving woman's table, in the painting's left background, featured a cutting board for a centrepiece with bread enough for two and untouched soup bowls, one at each end of the table, with their untasted contents now destined to go cold. Sad, I imagine.

But oh-so appropriate. Whether there by the seaside, or there in Miller's Court, the morning would bring with it mourning.

I again gave a fleeting thought to the whore's watcher, her guardian outside. What their relationship might have been, I didn't know or care. He may have been a jealous lover, unable to come to terms with the reality his woman was a filthy drunken whore. He may have been a jealous customer, unable to come to terms with his own empty pockets. He may have been a sexual deviant who followed whores for sport. Or merely a friend whose suspicions had been aroused by the sight of a well-dressed man in the worst slum in London. It didn't matter who he was.

What mattered was whether or not the bastard had taken up a vigil outside of the whore's apartment. Was he at that moment, at that dark and miserable hour, lurking outside, hands plunged deep into his pockets to ward off the cold morning air, huddled in the small court or against the wall of one of the nearby closed shops or doss houses of Dorset Street, watching and waiting?

Let him wait. As long as he didn't come knocking, let him wait. For the moment, I would give my time and full attention to the Irish lass and the job she represented. If need be, I would deal with the watcher afterward.

In the time it took to reach that decision, to remove my coat, to nervously open the buttons of my waistcoat, and to turn around, the well-fed, still-tipsy, little Irish whore had undressed and climbed upon the bed. In her frilly undergarment, with billowing white puffed sleeves, she reclined upon her soiled pillows, on the right-hand side of the bed nearest the wall, giggling and softly singing one of the songs that made up the repertoire of the pub crawlers of her ilk.

She interrupted herself to name her price, pointed to the top of the small bedside table, said, "Just put it there," then started singing again.

I took her in, in her slut's corner of the room, and silently considered the problem with which I then saw she'd presented me. I'd always worked from the whore's right before, using my strong right hand and doing her from left to right. The Irish lass had turned that around. She lay on the far side of the bed, against the wall with no avenue for me to her right. I would need to start the game with my left hand.

Ha ha! Wouldn't this give the plods fits come morning!

I turned and dug into my coat pocket. I found my shoemaker's knife, slipped the handle alongside my wrist and cupped the keen blade in my left palm. The feeling was admittedly odd, but what it lacked in comfort it more than made up for in challenge. I released the coat and turned back to her on an angle, my left hand concealed behind me, and stepped toward her.

It was in that instant I decided on another change. I'd snuffed the other slags first, before doing any cutting, to prevent their squeals. But there, in that secluded setting with doors, walls, and windows to protect our meeting. With the Irish lass suspecting nothing. I would not kill her first. I would slash her and see what came of it.

"Just there?" I asked.

She giggled and repeated herself, "Just there."

I reached for the small bedside table with the clenched fingers of my empty right hand, as if to pay her price. Then quick as you please I opened the hand, reached across the bed, and snatched the top of her head by a great handful of her luscious black hair.

"*Oh!*" she stupidly shouted, her bright blue eyes wide with surprise.

In the same instant I reached across with my left hand, let the handle of my trusty knife slip into my palm, saw stout blade glint in the glow of firelight.

"Murder!" the whore cried, in her charming Irish brogue, with a heavy dose of terror behind it.

She threw up her right hand, in an attempt to block me. I nicked her thumb with my blade in passing, easily brushed away her defense, and heard her knuckles rap the wall. I stabbed the blade into her throat, below the jaw, under her right ear, and slashed back toward me – severing her right artery and the plumbing beneath her chin.

Spurt... Spurt... Spurt... It was glorious!

She painted the filthy wall to her right with an arc of red... an arc of red... an arc of red. Then, in the same steady but notably slowing rhythm, on a falling line, an arc of red... an arc of red... an arc of red. I grabbed the whore by her left arm and left leg and jerked her from her place near the wall, two-thirds of the way across the little bed, toward me and onto the left-hand side that she'd intended for me. I like to be near my work.

The pillow, sheet, and mattress at the top right-hand corner of the bed, where she'd been laying, was saturated in blood. Blood ran down the partition wall and pooled under the bedstead. She'd stopped spurting, but was still running exceedingly red. And, outside of a barely perceptible gurgle, she was quiet as a church mouse.

Later, much later, I learned that several 'witnesses' in the houses surrounding the court had indeed heard the whore's faint, breathless, terrified, cry of "Oh, murder!" A failure on my part, I admit. But her shout had been one of pure instinct and had certainly not been powered by an informed decision. Make no mistake, the shock of my grabbing her, coupled with the speed of my blade, allowed me to sever the big vessel before she truly knew what was happening and to cut her windpipe before any opportunity to convey a message to would-be rescuers.

She didn't get out so much as another gasp. And, in that neighbourhood and throughout the slums of London for that matter, drunken cries of "Murder!" were an every night occurrence. The witnesses, as I knew they would, turned back over in their beds and returned to their dreams.

Speaking of dreams... With the Irish whore reclined, and within death's grasp, and at my mercy, the way I figured it, I had the whole night ahead of me and a number of dreams of mine were about to come true. But not in that miserably dark and cold setting. The fire in the hearth across the room was barely a glow. The single piece of candle on the table, by which the whore had gobbled her food, offered nothing in warmth and little in the way of light. That would never do! We needed a touch of warmth. And I wanted, and needed, more light.

So many of my good deeds had, through circumstance and necessity, been carried out in the dark shadows of the night. Now I had the opportunity, the rare, the once in a lifetime opportunity, to see all of my lovely work as I carried it out. To take my time, to communicate my message to the city and the world, in the full light of truth and reason. To see the results of my work before I presented them to the public. I needed a large fire and a wealth of light.

But I needed fuel. The whore had no kindling or coal lying about and I was in no position to go on a hunt. But problems, once determined and considered, are easy to solve. I grabbed the remnants of the whore's meal, wrapped it in the newspaper again, and tossed it on the grate.

I gathered the whores clothing. She wouldn't be needing them again. And began tossing those into the fireplace. A velvet skirt, a jacket, her felt hat. As if observing a conjuror's trick I watched the wirework frame appear as the substance of the hat was consumed.

I returned to the table and grabbed her clean piled laundry. I carried all to the hearth, unfolded them one item at a time that they might burn better, brighter, longer: two cotton men's shirts, a boy's shirt, a girl's white petticoat, a black crepe bonnet with black strings, and a pawn ticket for a shawl. Everything went into the flames. I went for the overcoat covering the window, then stopped myself. It seemed diplomatic to leave that in place.

It wasn't needed. The fire raged now in the fireplace. *Ah!* Enveloping warmth. Brilliant light!

I returned my attention to the whore.

She was dead now. Her eyes were wide and, I imagine, mine must have been too; hers with terror, mine with desire. I picked up my knife again. Now that her pump had quit and the juices had ceased to spurt. The chances of my soiling my clothes had fallen to little or none. I moved in to bring my desires to fruition. As if I were an orchestra conductor... No. Not a mere conductor, a respected and world famous maestro. Yes, leading the world's most prestigious orchestra, too modest to acknowledge I was on the verge of performing my masterpiece.

Fifty
Masterpiece of Horror

I began. I started on her left now and swung my keenly sharpened instrument back the opposite way across her pretty neck. Between the two slashes, I'd severed her throat three-quarters of the way around down to the bone. I had to pause, in fact, as I'd sunk the blade at an angle into two of the vertebrae. I took her by the hair again, to steady the lovely head, and keep it in place, as I worked the blade back and forth to prise it out. It came free with a jerk. It left a stark white notch amid all the lovely crimson. Not to worry, the glaring evidence of my zealous beginning soon vanished beneath the oozing flow.

What a beginning it was. What a big red grin she wore on her throat beneath the frightened white grimace of her mouth. I let go of her hair. Her head flopped back against the propped pillow, turned ever-so-slightly on the left cheek. That the weight did not completely detach the head and send it rolling onto the floor showed the breadth of my artistry.

Never before had I this opportunity. A brazen whore sprawled on her bed of iniquity; a private locked room with a fire, space to work, and all the time I needed. It was a gift to me for my month of patience; a prize for my good works. I would, in turn, give my own gift back to the world.

I'd already begun. With one stroke, I'd taken full advantage of the setting and situation. The pig lay in the middle of her wallow, spurting done but oozing and gurgling still noticeable from the great gash in her throat. Now came the symphony.

I started with her face. No one who was that filthy and disease-ridden had any business being that lovely. Like my auntie, her beauty was a lie. Her beauty was a sin. I had to get rid of it, immediately, that I could get on with the real work. I slashed and gashed her pretty face in all directions, hacking at and removing bits from the nose, cheeks, eyebrows, and ears. I slashed at her full lips, hacking incisions that ran at wild angles to her chin. I chopped everything from her chin to her hair line; removed all the evil features that had led so many men to their destruction. When nothing definable remained above her shoulders save for the hair and blue eyes, I called the job done and moved on.

In order to debauch herself, and in her effort to lead me to my doom, before climbing onto her bed the whore had removed all of her clothing save for a frilly white linen undergarment with feminine white puffs at the shoulders. Even as a faceless horror, she had all she needed to attract weak men and destroy them. This undergarment, already heavily besmirched with blood, had to be gotten out of the way that I could get on with my work. This I did with a quick slash down the front, and a rending of the fabric by hand, to expose all of that evil flesh.

She lay this side of the middle of the bed, the shoulders flat, the axis of her body inclined to the left. The left arm lay near the body, the forearm flexed at a right angle, lying across the abdomen. The right arm was slightly abducted from the body and rested on the mattress, the elbow bent, the forearm supine with the fingers clenched. A naked puppet without a face.

Where to begin, I wondered staring. Where to begin?

I stepped to the bed and lifted my knife. I cut her right breast off, squeezed it lovingly in my hand, relished the movement of the bubbles of fat inside; undulating dull yellow-white globules like tapioca gone bad. I considered my options and, finally, lifted her head and placed the glob of flesh behind; a delicate pillow. I cut the other breast free, squeezed it too to avoid complaints of favoritism, and laid it on the mattress beside her right foot. One for the top of the bed, one for the bottom. Good and bad. Right and wrong. The Irish lass had been so wrong.

It was now possible to look inside her through the two circular windows I'd created in her chest. Naked puppet filled with toys.

I swung my knife, back and forth, hither and yon, mutilating both of her arms with nasty jagged wounds. The legs were wide apart, the left thigh at right angles to the trunk and the right forming an obtuse angle with the pubes; the enticing nest of man's destruction. I started cutting, slicing away the surface of her abdomen, and laid the flaps off to the side. I would come back to those, when I found a place for them. In the mean time, I reached inside of the nasty whore and fondled the viscera while I considered my next action.

I cut out the sack of her stomach and the endlessly coiled snakes that made up her lower guts; slithering things. So happy was I, so delirious, I confess now I made less than a clean job of it. I hacked here and there in my enthusiasm. As I lifted the portions from their warm red basket, an alarming quantity of the recently gobbled fish and chips made a sudden and unexpected return appearance. Liquified to a semi-digested paste, and in quite unheard of colours, they dripped and dribbled into her abdominal cavity before I could think to catch them in... In what, I wondered?

I looked about, but already knew there was nothing at hand. There was a cupboard at the opposite end of the room, beside the roaring fireplace. I imagined it held a bowl or two, a couple of cracked plates with unmatched designs, bought for pennies (or more likely stolen) from a vendor in the Whitechapel High. Perhaps there was a tea set? I'd noted earlier, hadn't I, a kettle by the fire.

For an instant, I had an urge to set the table for tea. Images danced in my head of plates piled with bite-sized portions of the Irish lass, beside dainty cups topped with cooling and quickly gelling servings of her tainted blood. 'More tea, deary?' But, in the end, aware the fleeting giggle would hardly justify the effort, I abandoned the idea.

Where was I? Yes, I got back to the job.

I gingerly cut the bottom from the surrounding sack, carefully disconnected the plumbing works with my trusty knife, and removed the whore's heart. I held it aloft, watching it drip in the flickering firelight, aware I had found that night's prize. That being the case, I took the time then to cross the room and lay the heart on the table beside my coat. I would take it with me when the fun was done.

It was Christmas morning and I was Father Christmas. Presents to deliver.

The uterus and kidneys, soft and lovely, belonged with the breast under her head. Such a delightful girl deserved a bigger, softer pillow. The liver. Where, I wondered, ought the liver to go? Between the feet? I tried it there and it looked a treat. There I left it. The intestines, gory and gooey and amazingly sticky as the blood went thick, I laid at the pig's right side in one snaky pile. This I balanced out on the left side of the corpse with a small solid piece of meat that I thought, most probably, was the spleen.

Even as I laid it there, I hoped no one would hold me to that identification or judge me if I was mistaken. I was not, after all, a doctor. Just a poor orderly, bringing my little version of order to this sick world. But I thought it was the spleen. I returned to the flaps I'd created in opening the abdomen, picked them up again, and laid them on the bedside table.

I got between the whore's legs. What a lovely place to be when she could no longer spread disease. I cut the meat from her thighs, in thick chunks, both of them; shaved them down to the white bones, right hip to knee, left hip to knee. Both sides; round ass connected only by femur to the lower legs. Jolly! The two piles of fatty thigh meat joined the gut flaps on the bedside table.

It was a brilliant job of redecorating. The bed clothing at the right corner was saturated with blood; the floor beneath a deep red pool. The wall by the right side of the bed, at her height, was painted by splash after splash with lovely red juices.

I crossed to the fireplace, dripping, and shook my hands over the glowing hearth. The spatters landed with a series of charming *sizzles* and puffs of gamey smoke. The fire, by whose light I had carried out my night of ecstasy, had greatly died down. Yet evidence remained of its fierceness; the spout of the tea kettle had melted and drooped closed. No matter, the Irish lass would not be wanting tea that morning.

The freshly widowed fisherman's wife (in the painting above) was still on her knees, still bawling her brains out, but doing so now in ebbing light and growing darkness. Like the whore on the bed behind me, she had nothing to look forward to but a hopeless dawn.

I wiped what remained of the blood from my hands onto the last item of her laundered clothing, a skirt held back for that purpose. I tossed that onto the fire. It flared again, with a last gasp that was quite beyond its quiet and cooling mistress on the bed.

I stepped to the window, drew the coat curtain aside, and peered out. Miller's Court was deathly quiet, with no sign whatever of the watcher, no sign of life at all. ha ha. Inside 13 Miller's Court... roughly the same.

I donned my waistcoat and coat. I slipped the Irish lass' heart into my pocket. I took one more delicious look at my work, and was ready to retire after a job well done. I stepped from the warm room into the chill morning air. I looked the passageway up and down. There was nobody to be seen. The watcher had apparently got bored or, sulking, had moved on. Perhaps he would return in the morning and knock the Irish lass up. Or would try. Wouldn't that serve him right?

I pulled the door quietly closed behind me; heard the spring lock *snick* closed. I took a quick look about the small court yard. Again, nobody to be seen. Around the corner from the door, beyond the late whore's broken window and very nearby, stood a hand pump in the ground. I considered stopping for a moment, to finish off washing my hands and perhaps splash my face, but decided against it. Not out of fear of discovery, to be sure. I'd grown used to making my way home *red-handed*, besmirched, and smelling of the most recent dead slag. I had come to enjoy the thrill, the risk. I jammed my hands in my coat pockets and started out.

Just beyond the passage, on the Dorset Street byway, I stopped again and took the time to straighten the posted bill offering the reward for my capture. That was important. One should always leave the world in a better condition than one found it.

Fifty-One
It's Only Me... Saucy Jacky

I wasn't there to see it, of course, but the details of the following morning would quickly begin to come to light.

John McCarthy, one of my two favorite Whitechapel slum landlords, the landlord of the Irish lass, sat giving himself a hard time by going over his rent books. In time he worked his way down to an entry in his ledger, or more to the point, saw an annoying empty gap in his ledger had been ignored. McCarthy realized the renter – the squatter – in No 13 Miller's Court, the young Irish lass, had not paid again. It put her at... good god, 29s in arrears.

"Tom!" McCarthy called out. His assistant, Thomas Bowyer, entered McCarthy's office on the hop. "Get round the corner. Knock Miss High-and-Mighty up, and tell her I want my money. Don't take no excuse. And don't stare into them starry blue eyes of hers. She pays today or out she goes!"

That's how it would have been, I'm very much sure.

McCarthy's office was in No 27 Dorset Street. The whore's, remember, was at the back of No 26. It took Bowyer longer to find his coat and put it on than it took for him to go round to the girl's door.

So it was that, a moment later, at roughly 10:45 am, Bowyer rapped at No 13 Miller's Court. No reply. He rapped again. No reply still. That would not do. McCarthy had made it clear he wanted his rent. Bowyer stepped round the corner of the room. He looked about the court for fear of being caught window peeking, saw nobody was watching, then turned to peek.

A man's dark heavy coat hung over the window, acting as a curtain. But the window was broken, had been for almost three weeks. Bowyer slipped his hand through the hole (the same that, only a few hours before, the lass had used to gain access for the two of us). He pushed the coat curtain aside. And, you can damned well bet, he got himself a fat juicy eyeful.

I have no trouble believing Bowyer raced like a crazed man around the corner and back into No 27, shouting at McCarthy, "Governor, I knocked at the door! Could not make anyone answer! I looked through the window! I saw a lot of blood!"

I'm sure his statement would be much as that. At that, it would have been an understatement.

After the late summer and autumn seasons I'd given the peoples of London's East End, it should be easy to believe McCarthy and Bowyer both headed back to Miller's Court on pins and needles, with lumps in their individual throats. There, as Bowyer would want no more of it, McCarthy would be forced to reach through the broken window himself. To move the coat aside. To take his own look.

I wondered if the terror he felt, at first sight of what I'd left of the Irish lass, came anywhere close to the ecstasy I experienced at my last look at the same bloody visage? I left her a grinning, splayed, butchered horror with bits and pieces of body parts here, there, and everywhere.

I left her a bleeding work of art.

"Go... go... go... at once," McCarthy would stammer, no doubt licking his terror-dried lips to make them work. "Go at once to the p-p-police sta-station. Fetch... someone... here!"

Poor McCarthy. Never got his rent.

It was truly a shame I could not be there to witness it. To take it all in that morning.

A shame I couldn't be in Dorset Street as the coppers arrived and chased the residents out and away from Miller's Court. That

I couldn't hear the shouts over the building crowd, and the murmurs within, as the streets filled with first alarmed, then terrified and angry citizens of the East End as the god-awful rumors spread, were confirmed, and became news.

A shame that I couldn't be in the heart of the City of London...

That morning the Lord Mayor's procession swung into Fleet Street from Ludgate Circus. The streets were lined with celebrating crowds, thousands cheering His Honour. Then the news arrived, on the back sides of the crowded streets, and quickly spread forward.

"Jack the Ripper has struck again."

"Jack the Ripper has murdered again!"

"Another woman has been killed!"

The spectators immediately began to desert the Lord Mayor's show, in the tens, the hundreds, the thousands. They ran away from the celebration; raced from the city, headed east, to meet up again in the slums – a massive throng – growing at the edges of Dorset Street.

Nobody could get close.

The police had already established cordons at each end of the short street and at Little Paternoster Row. But the entrances to Bell Lane and Commercial Street were choked in minutes by crowds of terrified and angry people.

Blood. Blood. Blood.

I was sitting in the back room of Mr Griggs' old shoe shop. Had been sitting there for... I don't know how long. For a very long time. I'd come in... Had hurriedly removed the whore's amputated heart from my pocket. Had hidden my knives away in their boxes. Had sat down...

Long ago.

I was still sitting, my shaking hands out of my pockets and at my sides, still stained in the sticky-sweet blood of the dark Irish lass. Sitting and remembering... all that had transpired.

It had been a glorious, glorious return for Jack the Ripper!

Then I was out back, in the backyard, I mean. And, no, I don't remember ever having risen from my chair to get there. I was just there. I stood at the late Mr Griggs' hand pump behind his old shoe shop. My shirt was off, tossed into its own red-stained pile, and I was naked from the waist up. The water was running. I began to wash myself with handfuls of ice cold water; the blood from my hands and arms, the sweat from my face. I was, apparently, still reeling from the heady experience of the early morning. But I was slowly coming around, slowly becoming myself again.

I did not feel the presence in the back room of the shop. I did not hear the opening of the shop's back door. It was, I think, the movement of the door in my peripheral vision that first caught my attention.

Dripping water, as the last of the Irish lass' blood swirled down the yard drain at my feet, I turned to see the good and upright Mrs Griggs standing in the doorway.

"Oh, Mr __," she exclaimed. Then she stammered the start of a question. "What... are... you..."

Her voice failed her, as she seemed to freeze, in a moment locked forever in time. The only movement in the backyard was the water, still running at my feet, and the eyes of my landlady, growing wider and wider.

I wordlessly started towards Mrs Griggs. My good and dear landlady screamed.

Who am I? What am I? I take out the rubbish. I clean the streets. I am necessary. I am Death come among you. I am Jack the Ripper! I cannot be seen... only felt. I cannot be stopped. I am the footsteps behind you in the cold dark. I am the tingle of your nerves. I am the breeze upon your neck. In blind terror you scream the question, "Who's there?"

"Have no fear. It's only me... Saucy Jacky."

About the Author

Doug Lamoreux is a father of three, a grandfather, a writer, and actor. A former professional firefighter, he is the author of nine novels, a novella, and a contributor to anthologies and non-fiction works including the Rondo Award nominated Horror 101, and its companion, the Rondo Award winning Hidden Horror. He has been nominated for a Rondo, a Lord Ruthven Award, a Pushcart Prize, and is the first-ever recipient of The Horror Society's Igor Award for fiction. Lamoreux starred in the 2006 Peter O'Keefe film, Infidel, and appeared in the Mark Anthony Vadik horror films The Thirsting (aka Lilith) and Hag.

Other books by Doug Lamoreux:

- The Devil's Bed
- Dracula's Demeter
- The Melting Dead
- Corpses Say the Darndest Things: A Nod Blake Mystery
- Red Herrings Can't Swim: A Nod Blake Mystery
- Seven For The Slab
- When the Tik-Tik Sings

Other books by Doug Lamoreux and Daniel D. Lamoreux:

- Apparition Lake
- Obsidian Tears

Lightning Source UK Ltd.
Milton Keynes UK
UKHW011852301120
374378UK00012B/1421/J